# VIXEN

*by* Donovan Hoult

**Publishers:**
Inspiring Publishers
P.O. Box 159 Calwell ACT 2905, Australia.
Email: inspiringpublishers@gmail.com

National Library of Australia Cataloguing-in-Publication entry

Author: Hoult, Donovan

Title: **Vixen**/*Donovan Hoult.*

ISBN: 978-1-922618-89-4 (pbk)

# 1

'*What are you suggesting?*'

'I say we finish him off now.'

Alexander Stoyan's face broke into a cynical smirk of disbelief. 'So, someone just puts a gun to his head and pulls the trigger?'

'This person is terminally ill. My people can handle it with complete efficiency. There's no need for a gun or anything as crude and obvious. This is something we should have done years ago. We had the opportunity, but the person in my seat at the time probably considered it morally reprehensible.'

'My God, you are serious? I should not be listening to any of this,' Alexander Stoyan replied as he jerked upright in his chair realising the implications of what he was hearing. 'I invited you here as a friend and not in your official capacity as head of MI6.' He glared at his guest with an angry expression. 'As Prime Minister you have intentionally compromised me and I don't appreciate it. I must ask you to leave Linton.'

'Calm down Alex. I am here as a friend and you have my oath this discussion never happened.'

They had known each other since childhood and had never lost contact or trust. They had both been to Cambridge, Stoyan reading the classics and himself, law. But law was not his calling and he wandered aimlessly around Europe studying languages, for which he had a natural instinct. And then he got introduced to his current occupation through what he thought was a chance meeting, only to discover soon after he joined he had been watched and singled out for recruitment. They both socialised through mutual associations, that was until Stoyan became Prime Minister and the friendship took second place to the Affairs of State. They had met their wives at Cambridge - firm friends who met on a a regular basis.

'Believe me, I am here as a friend, a friendship I would never compromise.'

'But... but, you've set me up, haven't you? You knew you could not approach me at Downing Street, because the conversation could be overheard - there are always people coming in and out of my office demanding attention. I was delighted when you called and I invited you here so we could talk privately as friends do. But this was never intended as a social call, was it?'

Crowther shook his head slowly. 'No Alex, this is something I could not bring to your attention in your official capacity. This is a discussion between friends.'

'And now after three hours, two scotches, a bottle of fine Bordeaux, an excellent lunch and a snifter of the finest cognac, you think you have relaxed me enough to bring up your real purpose. It wasn't friendship, it was business and an extremely grubby business, I may add.'

Stoyan was annoyed his friend had trapped him. He should have been more aware. Rather than being a relaxed occupation where people played by the rules, politics was a dirty game, played with ruthless zeal and intent. Over the past ten years in parliament, before rising to his present position, he had played the game well with complete success, and now this? Here, he was being outplayed by an amateur. He should have known better – no MI6 director and certainly not Linton Crowther, was in the amateur class.

'I can see you are annoyed Alex. I did blindside you by steering the topic of conversation towards terrorism and then expanding on it as you became more interested in what I described as a potential crisis – a threat to our very existence.'

Crowther had laid the groundwork, gradually drawing Stoyan's interest when he casually mentioned terrorism. At first Stoyan did not react when he mentioned the IRA – it had been dormant and largely contained, but always a threat.

'Don't tell me they're about to stir trouble?

'I don't know about that. However, there could be a link, because the person we are targeting is Irish, an army deserter, a convicted thief and murderer.'

'Linton, you are out of your mind, ' Stoyan stiffened, the veil of friendship dissolving. He was being drawn into something he did not want to hear about, but realised it was already too late. 'What you are proposing is cold-blooded murder. Haven't you heard of due process. I can't be party to this.'

'Alex, there's no such thing as due process where terrorism is involved. When dealing with terrorists – we either kill them or they will kill us. I'm here because I want to alert you to a possible national disaster if we don't act and by that I mean, act now.'

'But, if he's dying as you've indicated, surely this whole business will die with him? Why the hurry? You're not over-reacting are you Linton?'

'We have been reading this man's occasional correspondence, listening to any phone calls and have attempted to alternate various cell-mates with him during the time he's been inside. However, he's a very violent character and the cell-mates never last long before suffering a severe injury. He knows we are using them to try and gain information. Up until a few months ago we had drawn a blank, but then we got a small glimmer of light. He sent a letter to his grandson care of Medicins Sans Frontieres, the humanitarian doctors who volunteer in the world trouble spots. The letter outlined the prisoner's terminal condition and was an appeal for the lad to visit him in the very little time he had left. The letter was returned unopened and stamped - *address unknown*. However, there are ways of opening a letter without it being obvious. We determined it had been opened before it came back into our hands. Apparently, the grandson resigned from the organisation twelve months ago and his whereabouts are unknown. However, we believe he is with the Kurdish rebels resisting the attempted takeover by the Turks of the ground the Kurds seized from the Syrians. There's no love lost between the Turks and Kurds - the Turks would like to see them totally subjugated, or more likely wiped out, as they did with the Armenians a century ago. Then the prisoner received a letter from his grandson, post- marked Istanbul. There was no return address, but the grandson said he would try and get away from his present commitments to visit him. He made no mention of when that would be, or where he was, or what he was doing. He had never met his grandfather and there was no record of any previous correspondence, so why the sudden familial affection? It came as a complete surprise as to how the old boy knew the lad was with Medicins, but then again all prisons have a communication underground. My concern is the grandfather will tell his grandson where he has hidden what an Australian journalist once described as Britain's *dirty deadly secret* about the after effects of certain secret Maralinga nuclear tests in South Australia through 1960-63. The tests have long been consigned to history, but it's what went missing following those tests, is why I'm here. The journalist was on the right track when he mentioned the deadly residue of those series of secret tests. However, he had no idea of the real threat – something we never divulged we had left behind when we pulled out. It has been blanketed in secrecy since that time, but I feel our dirty laundry is about to re-surface if we don't do something about it. And it's going to be aired right here in London. To ease your mind, it is not a bomb, but it is a diabolical threat to mankind.'

'And the prisoner holds the key?'

Linton Crowther, studied his superior without facial expression. 'Yes, he most certainly does and I can assure you it's real. We face a catastrophe on an unbelievable scale if it's unleashed. It would make the New York 9/11 terrorist attack or the nuclear melt-downs of Chernobyl and Fukashima look like minor incidents. London would cease to exist as a habitable community – it would remain in structural form, but be completely devoid of inhabitants.'

Stoyan looked aghast at Crowther. 'I demand you tell me what this threat entails. You just can't come in here and casually mention you are going to murder someone. That's outrageous and simply untenable. I thought you were joking, but now I can see you are deadly serious.'

'I simply can't tell you Alex. With all due respect, you would not be able to function and neither would the government if I was to divulge what I know.'

Alexander Stoyan leaned back in his chair with a scowl of disapproval. 'You are questioning my integrity?'

'No, but I have to make the message as blunt as possible. I'm doing you the courtesy of informing you it is my intention to have this man removed as a threat. It follows if he tells the grandson what he knows then he also becomes an immediate threat and must be dealt with accordingly. However, we cannot take action until he shows up. For all I know he may decide to reject what the old boy tells him and hand us back what we desperately wish to recover. On the other hand, he will quickly become aware of the destructive power he has in his hands and could revert to terrorism. At this point in time we believe he's in northern Syria, but we are completely in the dark in regard to his allegiances. In view of that, the grandfather has got to be terminated without the grandson knowing it was by other than natural causes. If the grandson does arrive in the country, we've put out an alert he's to be detained incommunicado and charged with suspected terrorism. It is an indictable offence to be fighting with any group in Syria. That should keep him locked up for six months while we establish the truth.'

'But, I still don't understand how this unnamed person poses a threat to the very existence of this city. Why is this person so dangerous? So he lets off a bomb or two and causes carnage and chaos. We've had numerous terrorist attacks in recent times and no doubt there will be more. What's so different about.......' He trailed off as he saw Crowther shaking his head.

'You haven't been listening. There's no hope of recovering from this one Alex. I reiterate, the structures of London will be left entirely intact, but it will have no living inhabitants. By that I mean anyone foolish enough to stay or contemplate returning will be signing their own death warrant.'

'Is it just us who are threatened? Are the American's likewise exposed?'

'New York could certainly be on the hit list.'

'Do they know of the threat?'

'They're aware, but certainly don't know what the actual threat consists of, otherwise they would have been all over us demanding an explanation. They have no idea we are the prime cause. Of course, they'd certainly be picking up the chatter in Syria something big is in the wind. We can only assume the prisoner has been communicating with his grandson or through a go-between we're not aware of, but the point is, he must have. Otherwise, the noise out of northern Syria, which the Kurds presently control, would not be sounding the increasing ring of alarm bells. His only visitor was his son who visited him from Australia twice in the time he has been incarcerated. They didn't see eye to eye and the son is absolutely clean – a law abiding citizen who runs a legitimate business. They correspond infrequently, but there's nothing suspicious contained. However, you never know, the son may be harbouring a grudge over his father being locked up for so long. It goes without saying, the American intelligence units operating in northern Syria and Turkey are tuned into all phone and wire chatter regarding terrorism threats. They get dozens a day and it's a full time job filtering out the more serious, then down through to the usual crackpots. It's odds-on they would be aware of this one because of its persistence, but they don't know its exact nature or the person posing it. And we're not going to tell them at this stage. It's our problem, we created it and we have to solve it. If we brief them fully I'm concerned the magnitude of the danger will leak and general panic will set in.'

'You say we created the problem? How, when and where are the obvious questions. God man, tell me what this is all about.' Stoyan leaned forward and pounded his fist on a side table. 'Have you gone out of your mind? I am the Prime Minister - I demand to know the facts.'

Crowther ignored the demand and remained impassive. 'All I can tell you is the problem originated more than fifty years ago, when a member of our armed forces became very negligent. He managed to cover up his negligence, or so it would appear. But the negligence compounded when someone discovered a cover-up and realised the magnitude. It went far beyond the officer in question. However, an example had to be made and a scapegoat identified, so a court martial was initiated. He was found guilty, demoted and reminded of the Official Secrets Act – ignore that and it would mean life imprisonment. The civilians involved, got away with it – they were too important to be named or implicated. They were the real criminals. The officer took the fall.'

'So, what's happened to him since? Is he another person you want to kill?'

'No, he's dead, murdered in Australia by the prisoner I'm referring to. We had our suspicions he had become associated with the IRA. It's a pity, as he came from a family with long military service. His grandfather died on the

Somme and his father rose to the rank of Lieutenant Colonel and landed in Normandy in operation Overlord in '44. We believe the officer in question turned rogue at some stage for what we can only assume was an act of revenge for how the military treated him and the fact he would not be upholding the family's proud military tradition. However, I have my suspicions he could have actually been working undercover for us. It's so long ago.'

'So, the person you want to kill is a British citizen and terminally ill. How can he be a threat? If you say he's close to death now, surely he's not capable of the magnitude of the disaster you're predicting? Where is this person now?'

'He's in Wakefield prison in Yorkshire. He's been in maximum security for more than twenty years for murder. He should have been out on parole years ago, but his file was marked *never to be released* on national security grounds.'

'My God, is he that dangerous? And you just want to rub him out? What is it? Give me something to go on. Is it some kind of germ warfare or nerve agent like that bloody novichok Putin is playing around with? You're not telling me we misplaced a nuclear bomb somewhere and this fellow has found it, are you?'

'None of those Alex. You can relax on that score. The Russians aren't involved and we've accounted for all our nuclear warheads.'

Stoyan gave a sigh of relief and relaxed into his chair. 'I'm pleased to hear that. Any hint of a nerve agent or a bunch of crazies with a truckload of ammonium nitrate would have the media all over me. We've had any number of the smaller terrorist acts. Those I can handle, but not something more serious on the scale you are suggesting. It would throw the country into absolute melt-down. This job is hard enough now without a major event such as you describe taking place.'

'It's worse. It's beyond anything you can imagine. In addition, the threat if carried out, will immediately cripple the world's currency system. The City of London financial centre handles in excess of $3.5 trillion per day in foreign currency transactions – that's trillions, not billions. It also trades more Euros than every other city in Europe combined. It trades more US dollars per day than New York. Not only the UK, but the whole world would grind to a halt within a couple of hours. You can forget about morality Alex – this man has got to die before it's too late.'

Stoyan was silent for a few moments as he drained the snifter of cognac. His face and expression hardened as he turned to Crowther. 'Forget the friendship Linton, it's just run its course. You either tell me now and I mean now, or I will have you removed from your position. I cannot possibly tolerate your attitude. You can tell me in the strictest confidence and it will not go outside these walls, or I will do as I threaten. I am serious, so don't test me.'

Crowther grinned inwardly – it was exactly what he wanted to hear from his friend Alexander Stoyanovich, the grandson of Balkan emigres – a prime minister who had the guts to act immediately, rather than resort to the common practice of calling in advisers who would also suffer the consequences if anything went wrong. A brilliant tactician and linguist who could discourse fluently in any European language. But to the establishment, he was foreign to the accepted mould of a British Prime Minister – he lacked restraint – he ignored his advisers – he had too much of the common touch. Linton Crowther was comfortable he had not misjudged his friend.

'Very well Prime Minister, sit back and pour yourself another cognac because you're going to need it. And I am relying on your assurance that this is for your ears only.'

Stoyan shook his head in disbelief half an hour later. 'Very well, but if you stuff it up, your head will be on a spike on Tower Bridge,' he laughed hollowly as he drained his snifter. 'But then again, I suppose mine will be right alongside. Don't tell me anymore – just get on with it.'

Stoyan got up, signifying the friendly lunch was over. 'You say this act of terrorism has a name? What is it, so I'm aware if it's brought up in parliament? Or more to the point, how do you know for certain the prisoner will carry it out?'

'The prisoner confirmed it when I visited him last week. The reason for the visit was a chance comment in a bi-weekly note I get from Wakefield regarding the prisoner's condition, both mental and physical and in particular, whether he's prepared to talk to MI6, now his days are numbered.'

'And the comment? What was so important that you rushed north to have tea and scones with him? Was it his birthday?' Stoyan could not keep the increasing tone of frustration and annoyance out of his voice.

'It was the name he called his cat Alex and that's the key to this whole problem. Although the man is close to death, the hatred and bitterness of what we've done to him has only increased. He's intent on revenge and he knows he has the means to carry it out. That's why he must die before the grandson arrives. If the grandson somehow slips through the net and meets with the prisoner, then we must ensure he doesn't leave the country. He must already know something about what granddad is threatening because as I've said, the Kurd telegraph has been humming with it for some months now. I believe the old boy will tell his grandson where he has hidden what we are looking for.'

Stoyan waved a hand at Crowther in dismissal. 'One last thing before you go, do SIS or SO15 know anything about this?' Stoyan was referring to the Secret Intelligence Service and Scotland Yard's anti-terrorism SOI5.

'As of today, no. If they did, I would have no doubt received a phone call. That is one of the purposes of this meeting – I want to confine this to MI6 and to your ears only. I want to test any leaks we may have in the system, because if either knocks on your door, you will know we have a problem with our intelligence systems and that includes MI6. If that happens, I would like to be immediately informed. In the meantime I know I can be sure of your complete discretion. I will report back to you regularly. And in the meantime, if the media gets hold of it, we'd both better start praying.'

Alexander Stoyan sank back in his chair and poured himself another cognac as Crowther let himself out of his study. Why the hell did he ever seek the top job and the crap that went with it? The answer was simple – he was enjoying himself. He was certain Crowther would come through, but if he didn't, that was for another day. He ran his hand through his hair as he sat back to contemplate what Crowther had told him.

Three nuclear scientists of the highest rank had conducted secret nuclear tests resulting in the deaths of thousands and lingering deaths of thousands more. One was made a Baron and the other two were made knights of the realm, honoured by the Queen for their contribution to science. The three had successfully hidden their crime from her government and the government of Australia – their victims, denied and forgotten. And yet their legacy would be evident and just as deadly until the end of civilisation. The three should have been charged with genocide and jailed. Stoyan drained the glass and ran his hand through his shaggy mane as he let out a sigh of resignation.

## Maralinga, South Australia 1963

The two *squaddies* snapped to attention, crushing the stubs of cigarettes under their boots as the British Army Lieutenant entered the warehouse casting his eye around the piles of equipment, supplies and machinery.

'At ease you two. Good news, we're packing up and going home. I want you to get rid of this lot.'

'How do we do that sir? Do we put an ad in the local paper?' The soldier drew an imaginary headline with his hands as he quoted the advertisement - *'your chance to glow in the dark with radio active fall-out - new and used army gear – closing down sale, everything must go – strictly no refunds.'*

The officer's smile vanished in an instant. 'Ever the clown, aren't you Connoly? What makes you think everything is contaminated?'

'It's plain bloody obvious sir, isn't it? I've been here since 1960 when they started blowing up material with TNT on those low platforms. No mushroom-cloud big bangs like the earlier ones, but a whole series of smaller explosions. I don't know what the hell they were testing, but the resulting dust and shit shot a thousand feet into the air. We were told not to worry as there was no danger, but what were all those guys doing running around with ear phones and black boxes after the blasts? They didn't look exactly happy with what the devices were telling them. I even caught one of them in here a couple of days ago. I could hear the bloody thing buzzing like crazy from where I was at the back of the building. He ignored me when I asked what he was doing as he had absolutely no authority to be in here. He said there was nothing to be concerned about. If there was nothing to be concerned about, why did he look so shit scared?'

The officer leaned into the squaddie's face. 'Private, nothing has happened to concern you and you keep your bloody trap shut about what you've seen or heard, or any observations you've made – you don't know anything. I would remind you the Official Secrets Act applies to you both. If I hear either of you is the possible source of a breach of that, I'll have you both charged. And you won't receive a slap over the knuckles, as you well know. It was only a few years ago treason automatically put you at the end of the hangman's noose. Nowadays, they're a little more lenient, but you'll still be staring in the face of life imprisonment without parole, or at the least twenty years behind bars. You don't seem to be smiling now Connoly?'

'No sir, b..b..but how do you want us to get rid of all this gear? Look at some of this lot, compressors, lighting plants, generators and diggers - they're almost brand new. Surely, they would be of use to someone.'

'My orders are that nothing in this shed is to leave this site. Too costly to ship home and likewise nothing is to be given away. It all stays right here and gets buried.'

The Lieutenant swept his arm wide. 'There are millions of acres of nothing but sand and scrub out there private. It doesn't belong to anyone, now the natives have been moved off. You are to dig some bloody big holes and bury the lot.'

'So I take it, there's nothing in this shed to be retained or shipped out? I can go ahead and dispose of everything?'

'Do all you Irish suffer from hearing loss private?' the officer snapped. 'I want this shed and its contents cleared right down to the last trace of rat droppings. The only remnants of its existence will be the concrete slab. And what's more I want it done within the week. I'm flying home in a couple of days and I don't want to ever set foot in this fly-invested shit-hole again. The natives are welcome to it.' The Lieutenant swung on his heel and started to walk out, the back of his shirt drenched with sweat and covered in flies.

'Sir, one last thing - there's a locked strongroom at the back of the building. It's where the boffins stored material which I assume they blew up on those platforms we helped construct. Is anything in there to be saved? Or do we dump everything?'

'Yes, I'm aware of its existence, but I don't know what it is. A security detail will be around in the next day or two to retrieve it. Whatever it is, is going to be shipped back home. I'm signing it off before I leave private, so you'd better make sure that happens. In the meantime, you're responsible for the contents. Just get rid of everything else,' the officer shouted over his shoulder as he strode off.

'The strongroom is locked sir. Do you have a key?' The question was ignored as he watched the retreating figure and then heard the vehicle fire up and drive away.

Connoly turned to the younger squaddie. 'You heard the man Casson, get on one of those machines and start digging pits and make them bloody big ones.'

'That bastard has certainly got it in for you. What have you ever done to him?'

'It's not only me, he just hates anyone not in his social class. A typical upper-crust arsehole who hates the Irish. He can't wait to get back on his horse and ponce around Hyde Park in the morning in his fancy uniform. He couldn't find his backside with both hands when he arrived out here six months ago. Ah, what the hell, let's get on with it. You know if we were closer to civilisation I would knock a bit of this gear off and make a few bob on the side.'

Casson snorted. 'Count me out on that one, it's not worth the risk. I just want to get out of here and head for home. Aren't you looking forward to it?'

'No, I could quite easily desert and just fade into the background in Sydney or Melbourne. I've never been to either, but I've got contacts in both and they're doing real well. I'm through taking orders from the fucking likes of Lieutenant Nicholas LeBrereton. He and the bloody English can stick their class system right up their fundamentals.'

Casson laughed as he walked towards the biggest digger. You've got a big chip on your shoulder Connoly. It will get you one day if you don't control it. I really can't understand why you signed up, you should have joined the IRA.'

Casson did not hear the subdued comment from his compatriot.

# 3

*e abandoned the Land Rover well off the main track in a thick patch of acacia scrub and stunted mallee bush. He had about two miles to walk to get past the guardhouse and road block without being seen and then it was a similar distance to the transcontinental highway, if it could be called a highway – a maze of diverging and reforming tracks hundreds of yards wide as heavily laden transports tried to find an easier path through the corrugations and endless choking bull-dust. The featureless terrain stretched a thousand miles to the west. He could flag down and hitch a ride with the occasional freight trucks, but it was too risky. He would be too easily remembered and it was an escape route the military police would check first. He was a wanted man, with at the most, an eight hour start.*

He crossed the highway and walked along the tracks of the parallel transcontinental railway to the small siding of Watson where all freight bound for Maralinga was offloaded. It consisted of a small shed which would keep the sun off four people and nothing else. He approached it warily and glanced inside. It was empty. He had about an hour to wait until the east-west freight train pulled into the siding to allow the east-bound passenger diesel to pass. One would be stationary while the other slowed to a crawl in case some authority from Maralinga wanted it to stop and pick up passengers. The top brass and scientists flew in and out of Maralinga, but military personnel were invariably transported by train or suffered a bone shaking ride in the back of a military truck. Connoly only had three weeks to go before he boarded either and was on his way to discharge from the army. He now faced a court martial, prison and dishonourable discharge at the least, if caught. Or it could be something far more serious if the truth came to light.

The hours ticked slowly by before he caught the sound of the labouring diesel engines and then the headlights of the converging trains. Also directly in front of him on the track leading to Maralinga he saw the approaching headlights of two vehicles. He was not alarmed as he quickly moved into the darkness behind the shed. They could not possibly have been alerted to the disappearance of two enlisted men. It had never happened before – the only way you got out of the place was under medical supervision for some undiagnosed neurological condition brought on by isolation and boredom, or your final discharge and repatriation. No one ever volunteered for a another tour of duty. And LeBrereton had already departed, so it would not be him who reported them missing. He watched as the two trains slowly approached before one of them diverted onto the inner siding, while the Indian-Pacific heading east, from ocean to ocean, pulled to a stop on the main line. He was on the inner loop track facing the freight train. All the activity was on the the main line and the passenger train. If they were looking for deserters the military police would soon become visible, but other than the sound of muffled voices against the noise of the idling diesels, there was nothing. The passenger train sounded a long blast of the horn as the driver increased the power and began to move. It was Connoly's only chance as he ducked under the couplings of two freight carriages and ran towards the rear of the Indian-Pacific as it began to slowly move. The lights were on in all the compartments as he waited for the last carriage, a flattop with its deck of cars belonging to those passengers rejecting the long brain-dead drive across the featureless Nullabor Plains.

He swung up easily and began to walk to the rear through two rows of cars until he found a large comfortable saloon. He had always fancied a Bentley with its reserved, but stylish flow of English coach-building tradition and here it was. He opened the back door and tossed his small bag in. He had enough water and some food for a long ride, but now he had found some comfort in which to endure the hours of boredom. The keys were in the ignition. He started the engine, turned on the radio and heater, and imagined himself driving as he laughed how easy it had been – he had music and heat for the cold nights ahead, plus there was a heavy travel rug folded on the passenger seat. Getting out, he opened the trunk and could not believe his run of luck. There was a case of wine and three bottles of Scotch – the owner believed in the trappings of success the car denoted. There was also a wicker picnic box containing cutlery, plates, cheeses, bread, assorted pickles and and a large fruit cake – a present for someone or from someone. Connoly laughed to himself as he cut off a large slice of cheese and uncorked a bottle of cabernet sauvignon – he could dispense with his own meagre rations. He pulled out a collapsible chair and poured a glass of wine, swirling and sniffing with the same contrived affectation he'd seen toffs do in a swanky Liverpool restaurant. He sampled the foods and finally finished the bottle an hour later, before tossing it over the side. A sudden thought struck him – what else did this passenger have in the two large suitcases stacked in the back? The first was hers, all neatly packed. He was about to shut it when he pushed his hand down the side and underneath and pulled out a large wallet and a small case – the wallet was stuffed with large denomination banknotes, the case contained jewellery. Connoly whistled to himself as he counted out the money – more than twice what he earned in a year. This lady did not travel light. He stuffed the jewellery into his jacket pocket and pushed the case back, before turning his attention to the second bag of the matching pair. He pulled out a jacket and tried it on and then held up a pair of trousers against his leg. The waist size matched and the shoes were a perfect fit along with the jacket. Within minutes he was a new person, his army kit following the wine bottle over the side. There was no need to search under the clothing – the money, passports and all personal details were contained in one of the pockets on the inside lid of the case and there were multiples of the money his wife had concealed. Mr and Mrs Zammit would be inconvenienced for a few days until they replaced the holiday funds. The ocean liner tickets said they were due to board the Mariposa in Sydney bound for San Francisco three days after their arrival in Sydney.

He began to wonder how many more had left valuables in their cars as he methodically searched through them all. The final two vehicles were a recent model Ford Fairlane parked beside the Bentley and a battered Land Rover immediately behind. The Ford yielded nothing, except for a couple of suitcases containing clothing far too big for him. He kicked the tire of the Land Rover as he was about to walk past in disgust – it was so battered, it wasn't worth searching. On a premonition he glanced inside to see a locked trunk in the back. He opened the driver's door and pulled out the ignition keys – all the vehicles had ignition keys – a requirement by the railways so the vehicles could be unloaded quickly by staff. He turned the bunch of keys over in his hand as he walked around to the rear door and opened it. There was only the wooden trunk, secured with a heavy lock at either end of the lid. He laughed as he found the right keys. The trunk contained nothing but a small shovel and pick, a couple of large tin dishes, mixed in with old clothing and screeds of loose maps of Western Australia. It was nothing other than an assortment of junk. Connoly slammed the lid shut, but hesitated as he started to back out of the vehicle. Why would a trunk full of worthless rubbish have two substantial padlocks? He opened the lid again and started to throw everything out until he reached a felt layer covering the base. He tapped it, but it was not the sound of solid wood - there appeared to be something underneath. He ripped up the felt and tried to pry up the close-fitting plywood floor. With the small pick he was able to smash away at one edge until he had enough leverage to lift the panel. Underneath were ten small bars wrapped in rags and old clothing. Connoly picked one up and tested the weight in his hand. It was heavy, but there was no mistaking the metal with the instantly recognisable colour and value. He went back to the Ford, retrieved a small leather suitcase and emptied its contents. Wrapped in the felt, the gold bars fitted in neatly. It was too heavy to simply jump off the train with at his final destination and disappear into the crowd. The Ford was the last to be loaded onto the flat-top, so it and the Bentley would be the first off. He repacked the trunk, locked it and replaced the keys in the ignition. He would be long gone before the owner discovered his loss. He put the heavy bag in the trunk of the Ford and went back to the comfort of the Bentley – his home for the next four days and his sole source of food and drink. He switched on the radio and scanned for new stations as the train lumbered across South Australia and into New South Wales. Most of the time he either sat bored staring out into the featureless terrain with its isolated clusters of small settlements, or sleeping. On one occasion he was standing outside stretching his legs when they rolled through a small station. He was in full view when he saw the figure in railway uniform step out of the terminus, his gaze and wave of his hand fixed on the engine driver. Connoly threw himself back inside and slammed the door just as the figure began to turn in his direction. It was close.

It was mid-morning when the train crawled through the suburbs and pulled to a stop. He had cleaned up the Bentley, swapped the registration plates and concealed himself as best he could, behind the driver's seat of the Ford. The train was hardly stationary before he could hear railway staff uncoupling chains to remove the cars. The front door of the Ford swung open, the car started and was being backed down a ramp. Within a minute it was parked, the engine turned off and the door slammed as the driver headed back to the flat-top for another.

Connoly looked up and around. There were people everywhere, but no one was paying any attention to the Ford as he climbed over the front seat and started the engine. He drove across the yard, through the main gate and out into the traffic. It had been all too easy. The Ford was now carrying the Bentley plates. His vehicle would be reported as stolen, but the owner of the Bentley would be in such excitement at the thought of the voyage he would hardly be looking at the registration of his car. It would probably be an hour before the Zammit's checked into their hotel to find clothes and money missing, not to mention the contents of the hamper and all the fine wine and Scotch – the thief had endured the endless trip in solitude and quiet inebriation. The confusion of reporting it to the police, while replacing the money and the pressure of their imminent departure would ensure their car, with its new registration, would remain dormant in some underground hotel car park until they returned in two months.

He was sitting reading the morning paper in the lounge of a small hotel when he flipped the broadsheet page and saw the photo of a Land Rover with police standing alongside. *"Gold Heist – Suspect Arrested"* was the headline across the top of the page. He read the article slowly and grinned to himself as it confirmed what he now had in his possession. It had been stolen from a gold mine in Western Australia by an employee who had now been arrested. However, the gold was not found in his vehicle, but the crime had been admitted to. It was the last couple of lines stating police were hunting for a stolen Ford sedan, cargo on the same train, which caught his real attention. He folded the paper and went up to his room to pack his few belongings. He had intended to go shopping and then look for somewhere quiet to rent – Sydney appealed to him. But that was out of the question now. Within half an hour he had checked out and was heading south to Melbourne.

Martin Bellamy suddenly saw the figure appear in the road signalling with a painted fluorescent sign. The heavy rain and oncoming headlights had momentarily blinded him as he tried to swerve to avoid the impact. There was a solid thump as the figure was thrown into the air and onto the bonnet of the Mercedes - he was looking at two very dead eyes through the sweeping wiper blades. He pulled over and placed his head on the steering wheel in shock and despair – his whole world was about to come crashing down.

'Out arsehole.' He felt the hand on his collar and then the violent action of being dragged out of the vehicle and thrown onto the road. The knee dropped onto the middle of his back as his hands were cuffed behind him. He could already feel the freezing water soaking his clothing as he made to roll over in an attempt to stand, but a boot crashed into the back of his neck. 'You just stay there fella,' was all he heard as he blacked out from the force. The glaring lights of an ambulance were blinding as he came to, propped against the side of his car, the cuffs biting into his wrists. He could see a covered form being loaded into the ambulance.

'Get a blood sample off this one doc. He's obviously been drinking and I want to make sure he goes down for what he's just done.' The cop pushed him forward to unlock the cuffs and roughly helped him remove his jacket to expose an arm.

'Jesus, take it easy man, you're breaking my arm,' Bellamy groaned.

'That's the least of your worries mate. You've just killed one of our officers. You're up on a murder charge if you've been drinking, or at the very least culpable homicide. Now give me your bloody driver's licence.'

'It's in my wallet,' he said indicating his jacket.

The cop retrieved and flicked it open, thumbing the exposed money. 'You carry a lot of cash fella – what's your line of business?'

'I thought you wanted my licence, or is it the cash you're really after?' He tried to restrain himself, but the sarcasm was automatic in the face of blatant authority.

The cop pulled out the licence and flipped it open, dropping the wallet on the ground. 'Don't get smart with me Bellamy or I'll add a charge of attempted bribery. That'll add a couple of years to the ten to twenty you're facing now. Why didn't you stop when the officer flagged you down?'

'I didn't see him until it was too late. I was dazzled by the oncoming lights and the rain didn't help. He just jumped out in front of me - I didn't stand a chance of avoiding him. Can I get up? I'm soaked and freezing.'

'Constable, chuck him in the back of the wagon. You can cool your arse in there Bellamy for the next hour until I get clear of here. And then it's down to the station to be formally charged. Don't expect to be granted any special privileges when you kill one of us.'

It was two hours later before he was charged, photographed, fingerprinted and had his belt and shoelaces removed. He signed for his watch and the total cash content of his wallet, before being put in a cell along with petty criminals, drunks, drug addicts and wife bashers – the usual detritus of the night. He was still visibly shaking from his sodden clothes when he asked for and received a threadbare rug to put around his shoulders. There was no thought of discussion, it was a freezing night. The drunk had passed out and the junkie just propped himself against the wall while gazing into space.

He attempted to stay awake, but must have dozed off in exhaustion, when he heard his name called.

'Okay Bellamy, you're in the most trouble, so you can call your lawyer if you have one. If you don't, we'll arrange for someone to represent you.'

He pushed himself to his feet trying to overcome the cramp in his legs and aching back and neck. 'I'll call my lawyer. What time is it?'

'Six on a very fine morning. You'll be in front of the magistrate at ten and then on remand I hope. You won't be seeing the outside for a long time yet.'

He followed the cop out and was shown a phone. He dialled the number and slumped into a chair. 'Tony, it's Martin, I hope it's not too early for you?'

There was a burst of laughter from the other end. 'You know very well my day starts when I wake, turn my meter on and think of someone to bill. It looks as though you've drawn the short straw. However, you never call before seven, so what's going on?'

'Tony, this is serious and I need your help. I've been arrested and up on a charge of I don't know what, but it's serious. I've been locked up all night.'

'What the hell did you do?' The hilarity had gone out of his voice. Bellamy was one of his closest friends and best client in his commercial legal practice.

'I ran into a cop and killed him.'

'Holy fuck, you weren't drunk were you? No, don't answer that. I know you wouldn't have been intoxicated behind the wheel. Look my good friend, I'm not the person you need. You need serious assistance from a specialist and I'm not a specialist in the field of criminal law. I'll call in a favour and contact someone I know well. He charges like a swamp buffalo and looks as though he permanently sucks lemons, but he's the best.'

Bellamy had been shown to a small interview room. He was still damp and miserable as he waited. Finally the door opened and Tony Basili was shown in, closely followed by a short rotund individual with swept-back greying hair matching the colour of his tailored suit. The black horn-rimmed glasses complimented the immaculate goatee beard.

'Hi Martin, this is Creighton Ashbury.'

Ashbury nodded, but there was no further acknowledgement extended as he sat down and took a pad and copy of the charge sheet out of his monogrammed satchel. 'My fee is five hundred to represent you at this morning's hearing Mr Bellamy. Any further appearances will incur the same charge. Should it go to trial, my fee is two thousand a day. Mr Basili has already given me an assurance he will cover my initial invoice in view of the fact in your present condition, you are unlikely to have that much cash on you. All my appearances and representations are payable in advance. If you fail to do so I will make immediate application to vacate your representation. Is that clear?'

Bellamy glanced at Basili who smiled and raised his eyebrows. 'I guess it is Creighton.'

'Well, you'd better stop guessing. Have I made myself clear? I don't want any misunderstandings.'

'Perfectly clear.'

'Good, now let's get on with it. The blood and breath tests were negative, so that's something in your favour. However, you are in deep trouble with every copper in this State after your scalp. You're undoubtedly going to serve time and the prosecutors will be after the maximum. You're going to be a marked man when you get out, if you ever get out. People convicted of killing police are inclined to meet with nasty accidents in prison. However, if you do emerge in one piece I would suggest you make immediate plans to leave the State or even the country.'

'Will I get bail today?'

'I don't like your chances, but it won't be for the lack of me trying. Now, give me a list of your assets, your bank balance, the background to your present employment, a list of any driving offences going back to when you got a licence. I want to know about any convictions for anything from your past and by that I mean every last detail – don't dare hide a thing as it will come back to bite you. Believe me, the police will already be dredging up every negative they can find about you. Are you married, how many kids, legitimate or otherwise? What are you hobbies or interests, what organisations do you belong to such as Lion's, Rotary or Toastmasters? I want the lot if I'm to represent you. I don't want to be confronted at a trial by some secret you maybe hiding.' The eyes were fixed and penetrating.

'What about that bloody sergeant who roughed me up last night. I would like to lay a complaint about his treatment.'

'Mr Bellamy, he's the least of your problems. He and his colleagues will deny any such thing occurred. Just shut your mouth and let me handle things. And make sure you maintain a humble expression and don't make any comment unless you are asked by the magistrate. This is only a hearing today with my main purpose being to convince him you are a fine upstanding member of the community and should be granted bail. The prosecutor will get really personal, but don't react. He's determined to ensure you're locked away in remand for a month or more until your next appearance.'

The clock on the wall said quarter to ten when the interview door opened. 'Ok, you're on Bellamy.' It was the sergeant who had arrested him.

The magistrate was looking down at the charge sheet as the prosecutor read it out before a disinterested audience of waiting offenders with their legal counsel milling around, feigning the appearance of concern for their clients. He looked up, giving Bellamy a brief dismissive look before turning to Ashbury who was already on his feet.

'Yes, Mr Ashbury, I gather you are seeking bail for your client. This is an extremely serious charge.' Without waiting for a reply he looked at the prosecutor, an overweight senior police sergeant who lumbered to his feet.

'Yes your honour, prosecution is strongly opposed to the granting of bail. This man is responsible for the death of a police constable, a married man with a wife and two young children, entirely dependent on his support. Mr Bellamy was driving dangerously at the time and not paying due care and attention.'

'What were the road conditions at the time this occurred?'

The prosecutor turned to the arresting sergeant for instructions before addressing the question. 'Light rain with poor visibility your honour.'

'What was his estimated speed when he struck the constable?'

Once more the prosecutor turned to the sergeant who shook his head with a quiet reply. 'That has not been determined as yet.'

'Sergeant, you have already stated Mr Bellamy was driving. Due to the conditions, that would suggest excessive speed to me and yet you are now telling me you are yet to determine that? I note he was breath tested at the scene of the accident and a blood sample was taken. The first test was negative, but what of the blood test. Was there any alcohol detected?'

'No your honour. I've just been handed the result and it is also negative.'

'Before I make a determination, do you have anything to say on behalf of your client Mr Ashbury?'

'Yes your honour.' Bellamy listened as his known life story was revealed. No wonder the man charged the fees he demanded. It was straight hard-hitting facts about an exemplary person with an impeccable record of probity and civil involvement - a man who was no risk to the public, with no possibility or intent of absconding.

The magistrate made some notes and then looked up at Ashbury. 'Bail is granted on the condition the defendant reports to the police twice a week. I'll set a hearing date for a month from today.'

The prosecutor rose to his feet. 'Your honour, we ask you to impose a substantial warranty. This is a serious offence.'

'From Mr Ashbury's pleadings I note Mr Bellamy has substantial assets, has a well established business and has an unblemished record. I don't consider him to be a flight risk.'

The prosecutor was about to object when the magistrate ignored him, turning to the bailiff and instructing tersely. 'Next case. I've got a long list this morning.'

Ashbury picked up his papers and slid them into his satchel, nodded to the magistrate and swept out of the court without a backward glance at Bellamy or Basili.

'I told you he was the best Martin. Without him you would have been escorted to a prison van for transport to remand by now.'

'So what happens between now and the trial?'

'It's not a trial – it's a hearing and then a trial date will be set. In the meantime, keep your head down and report to the police as directed. You are no doubt going to be subjected to some sort of harassment. Your phone will be tapped, despite the police having no power to do so. Make sure you strictly observe speed limits when driving. And don't drive at night as you're a marked man and anything can happen in the dark. Don't fart in public or walk on the grass. I'm sure you get the message?'

'Loud and clear Tony. Thank you. I'll transfer ten grand to your account to cover Ashbury's demands. That should take it up to the trial?'

'More than enough. Creighton will probably lay another couple of dozen fine wine into his cellar when I tell him he won't have to remind me to chase you for funds. It will also take a load off my mind.'

'What, didn't you think I was worth it?'

Basili was flustered. 'You know I didn't mean it that way. You are my most valued client. It....it's just that Ashbury is a barrister and if I retain him on your behalf, I'm in effect guaranteeing your debt if you fail to pay. Barrister's can't lose. If they stuff up your case you can't sue them for incompetence – they get paid win, lose or draw. That's the reason I only handle commercial law with client's I know well. I won't touch criminal law, but in your case I could not refuse.' They stood on the footpath together as Bellamy flagged down a cab. 'Don't forget to report to the police twice a week. You may as well skip town if you don't.'

'Are there any set days I should report?'

'No, but I would make it Monday and Tuesday to keep the rest of the week clear.'

'That should give me plenty of time,' Bellamy remarked as he stepped into the cab. Basili wrinkled his brow as he watched the departing taxi before turning back towards his office. What did he mean by that comment?

# 5

*M*artin Bellamy looked down from his penthouse apartment overlooking the Yarra River and the city. He swirled the scotch in the crystal glass as he contemplated his next move. He had no personal assets, everything was locked into offshore trusts. He had transferred the money to Basili and drained almost the entirety of his local bank accounts into various offshore tax havens. In seven years he had gone from Declan Connoly, an army deserter on the run, to become a wealthy property developer and investor. One of his trusts had constructed the exclusive block of six apartments he was now standing in. He cursed his luck, but he had always known one day the piper would come calling. Despite that, it had come as a shock when it happened. Fate had delivered him a wonderful hand when he hitched a ride on that train those years before. From a penniless squaddie on the run, he was now a multi millionaire and it had all started with the financial* *assistance of the Zammit's and a bullion thief. In another five he would have tripled the figure at the very least. He adored women, but the liaisons never lasted, he made sure of that. He could not afford to put his signature to any marriage certificate, nor could he prove his identity. He had to live with his forged passport and assumed identity. At first he lived under the cloud of discovery, where a knock at the door to be confronted by the police was a constant fear. It gradually dissolved over the years as he became more comfortable and successful. As in any city there were plenty of such examples, but they hid within their ethnic groups and faded from view, melding with the passage of time. He had the uneasy feeling his world of success and comfort was about to disintegrate.*

Monday had been easy. The duty constable had written his particulars in a daily log and spun it around for him to sign.

'Is that it?'

'Yes Bellamy. Twice a week at this station and I would warn you to comply.'

The following day he was confronted by the arresting sergeant. 'Aha, the driver who killed a police officer.' The clatter of typewriters and voices ceased as all police heads swung in his direction. None was smiling – he was a condemned man. Two elderly civilians also at the counter drew back in shock. The sergeant signed the book, noting the time and date before swinging it around for him to sign where indicated. 'By the way Bellamy, would you mind bringing your passport in next week.'

'That was not a requirement of the bail conditions. Why do I have to produce that?'

'You don't. Forget I asked for it. See you next week then.'

'That's okay, I'll bring it in.' Bellamy felt all eyes on him as he turned and walked out. He had made a mistake by challenging the request and played right into his inquisitor's hands. His offer of compliance sounded hollow and the sneer on Sergeant W.Wills face confirmed it.

The whole room watched him walk out. 'Why did you ask him that sarg, if he doesn't have to produce it?' a young constable enquired.

'Just let's say it's a hunch son. It's the Irish accent and the fact he's only held a driver's licence for less than six years. I'm checking with the other States to see if they've got any record of him. This city is full of illegals of every nationality who've jumped ship at some stage. Ten bucks he forgets to bring his passport next week.'

The constable laughed and turned back to the two elderly people. 'Nah, I can't afford that sergeant.'

Wills walked back to his desk and picked up the phone and dialled. 'Have you run those prints of Bellamy's yet?'

'Still getting around to it sergeant. We're really busy at the moment. We've got a major flap on regarding a group of local mafia crims.'

'Yeah, I know – overworked and underfunded. Keep on it please, it's urgent.' He swore under his breath as he replaced the phone and pushed himself back in his chair. Bloody stupid prosecutor should have asked for the surrender of Bellamy's passport, or at the very least a ban on approaching any international departure point, whether it be air or sea. He had a feeling about Mr Bellamy.

# 6

'*Hi Tony, anything new to tell me?*'

'Where the hell are you Martin? The police have been looking for you. I've had a couple of detectives call on me twice. Apparently they only just missed you when you signed in last Tuesday. They were banging on my door on Wednesday and then again on Friday. Apparently they've also been hammering on Caroline's door a couple of times. They barged right in to make sure you weren't hiding in a closet. She was really shaken up. And here you are phoning me on a Sunday evening trying to sound all casual.'

'I don't know what they're on about, I don't have to report in again until next week.'

'Martin, don't screw me around. You know bloody well why they want to get hold of you. Declan Connoly is a wanted man. It is Declan I'm talking to isn't it?'

'Yes it is, but this country is full of illegals like me. Okay, I changed my name, but with my record I should be able to get an attorney to make an application for permanent residency.'

'That's just the problem Martin – it's your record. You're wanted for questioning over the theft of gold bullion, jewellery and a quantity of cash in South Australia seven years ago. There's no way you will be granted residency if the charges are proven. You'll serve time and then be deported. And then there's the small matter of the present charge of culpable driving causing death.'

Tony Basili had just confirmed his worst fears, they had matched the fingerprints from the Land Rover with those taken after his recent accident. 'If I report in, what are my chances of remaining on bail?'

'Zilch. The police are seething the magistrate let you loose, but with robbery charges being levelled, there's no way you will remain a free man.' The line went quiet. 'Martin, are you still there?'

'Yeah Tony.' He sighed in resignation. He had been trying to resist the inevitable. 'I'm not coming back Tony. I will phone you from time to time if I may?'

'No Martin, you can't phone me. The only exception to that is if you turn yourself in, I can then hand you back to Ashbury. I am duty bound to tell the detectives you've been in touch if they ask, which they most certainly will. My advice is to hand yourself in immediately. I know we've been friends, but I must put that in the past tense now. There is nothing personal about this. I will face a conviction myself if I knowingly assist you, or contrive with you to pervert the course of justice.'

'I understand Tony. I've put you in plenty of funds so you won't be chasing me for unpaid bills. Give my apologies to Ashbury.'

'What about Caroline?'

'I don't want to see her homeless as I think she may have a bun in the oven, but I don't know whether it's mine. She was going strong with someone else before she fell for my charms and that was less than four months ago. Anyway, she can have the apartment until I determine otherwise. Draw up a lease for a peppercorn rental to make it legal. You have power of attorney and also when the kid's born, make sure Caroline's taken care of financially. I'll have funds transferred to your account every month.'

Basili laughed cynically. 'You're going soft Martin. Why let her have the apartment free? I could get a substantial rental return from someone with a real job and security. And you're going to give her a home and money and provide for a kid that's probably not even yours. You're not thinking straight. Leave it to me to handle the problem for you. I'll get rid of her when you're gone.'

Bellamy suddenly saw his lawyer in a different light. Was he the trustworthy friend and confidant he portrayed himself to be, or was he the hard-nosed individual always looking for the advantage? He sensed Basili's resentment at him giving something away for no return. It was obvious the fact he had not been included in such largesse, did not sit well with his lawyer.

'Tony, if you're not prepared to follow my instructions, I guess I will have to appoint someone else.'

Basili's voice went up an octave in desperation. 'No..no...I apologise for those comments. I was thinking as a lawyer giving advice in your best interests, rather than as a friend. I will follow your instructions.'

'Fine, that's settled. I'll be in contact from time to time. You won't be able to contact me.'

'They'll get you Martin, you can't keep running.'

'I'll take my chances. I've been lucky to date. Maybe my luck will hold. If they do catch up with me, tell Ashbury I want him to represent me.' The line went dead.

Tony Basili slowly replaced the receiver and broke into a wry smile of admiration and resignation. He had no doubt his client possessed several identities.

# 7

*D*eclan Connoly signed his release, picked up his small plastic bag of belongings and walked towards the perimeter gate of the prison. He had served nearly ten years for culpable driving resulting in the death of the policeman. The sentence was concurrent with convictions for theft of money and jewellery from the Zammit's and bullion – the property of Hannan's Hope Goldmines, from the Land Rover. His fingerprints clearly identified him as the thief. There were also the minor charges, including the use of a forged identity and passports – he had been found with another in his possession when he tried to board the liner bound for Vancouver. Normally, he would have been out in seven years depending on behaviour and attitude towards authority, but he could not stay out of trouble. He did not initiate the trouble – it just followed him in escalating degrees as the time passed.

It  happened within days of being sentenced. He was being escorted down a set of prison stairs when he received the firm push from behind. It was totally unexpected - he had no time to reach out for the handrail as he stumbled forward and down, crashing onto the platform a dozen steps below. He came to in the prison infirmary, six stitches in a shaved part of his scalp, with a broken arm and cracked ribs, the result of his *carelessness*.

'You should watch where you're walking Connoly. Those steps are slippery when wet,' was the remark of the screw standing by his bed. It was he who had initiated the injuries.

'Constable Paulus' mates have asked me to convey a get-well message.'

Paulus was the cop he had hit and killed. When he recovered enough he was sent back to a new cell, with his arm in a sling, an aching head and painful ribs. His cellmate was a benign looking character with no apparent trace of aggression, but that was only the surface. They were equally matched in physique and height and the same age. Neither divulged what they were in for and neither asked. Connoly had enough experience from his army days to know you did not enquire into someone's background, antecedents, crimes, or interests. If someone wanted to tell you, they would, but just mind your own business and follow orders in the meantime. In this case, it meant enquiring about your cell-mate's crime. It was accepted every inmate was completely innocent of the crime they had been charged with and banged-up for. Connoly had him picked the moment he was shown into the cell – this one spelt danger.

'You two will get along fine, I'm sure.' the screw said with a burst of laughter.

The iron door with the single eye-level hatch closed as he threw his blanket, sheet and pillow onto the single bed. The prisoner sitting on the bed opposite just watched, but said nothing. Connoly turned and nodded before laying back and swinging his legs up and closing his eyes. He thought he had put this existence behind him, but here he was, the confinement, restrictions and regimentation of the army, an all too obvious comparison with prison life.

8

*He was seventeen when he decided to escape the bigoted life of the wrong religion in Belfast, at least that's what the loyalist police told him when they beat him half to death for hurling rocks and abuse at their beloved Orange day marchers thumping on their accursed Lambeg drums – the loud resonating sound that had persisted for the past two hundred years since William of Orange crushed King James at the Battle of the Boyne. But the war had never finished. He took the advice and caught a ship to Liverpool and joined the King's Regiment. It was the wrong army and the wrong regiment - he should have kept moving, but he was out of Ireland and out of danger. All he had to do was keep his mouth closed and avoid conflict. He would have been in more danger if he had stayed. The girl's father and brothers would have certainly killed him when the problem became obvious. They were navvies on the docks with fists of iron and short-fuse attitudes with tolerances to match. He often wondered what happened to the girl and whether he was the father of a boy or girl. He thought he was safe in the army and lost in Liverpool, that was until he was in a pub when he spotted Emmett O'Brien walk in and start looking around the crowded bar. If Emmett was there, his sons would certainly be present somewhere. He put down his glass and shielded himself among the crowd as he made for the back door. It had been close – too close. He was looking back over his shoulder as he pushed the door open. It was only his quick reflexes from months of exposure to hard military exercise that enabled him to dodge the blow aimed at his head. With a savage upthrust of his right forearm he caught his attacker in the throat and as he went over backwards he thrust his fingers into his startled eyes. His heavy army boot caught him in the side of the head, the thin skull-bone crushing inwards under the force. He knew the man was already dead before he hit the concrete. It was Dion, one of her brothers. He disappeared as quickly as he could down the alley and back onto the high street. The next few weeks he lived in fear, waiting for a visit from the Military Police before being handed over to the civil authorities for questioning. Nothing happened until a letter arrived. It was signed Emmett O'Brien "Sorry we missed you at the pub. There will be a next time. You're a marked man Connoly, both in Ireland and Liverpool." Volunteering for a two year tour of duty in the Australian desert had been easy.*

# 9

*He kept moving in his bed trying to take the weight off his arm and ribs to alleviate the pain. He could not sleep and was aware his cellmate was watching him. His mind was wandering when he felt a hand on his genitals gently massaging them. He swore as he tried to sit up while swatting the hand away with his good arm. The hand pushed him firmly in the chest. He cried out in pain as he tried to turn away.*

'You just lie back there and let Constantine have a little fun. You're going to do as I say.'

He felt the zip on his prison trousers being torn open. Every time he tried to resist the pressure was applied to his chest. The tears welled up in his eyes and began to stream down his face as he stifled the spasms of pain shooting through his rib-cage. He realised it was pointless in shouting for help. He ceased any resistance to ease the torment.

'That's it Connoly. It's pointless to resist or call for help. The whole cell block is waiting for my orgasm of pleasure and we don't want to deny them that, do we? They'll all be lining up for your services.'

He spat at his attacker, the defiance resulting in two solid punches to the face. He felt the blood burst from his nose and lips and then his testicles being squeezed until he started to dry-retch. The fight had gone out of him as he waited for an opportunity. The abuse stopped and he felt the hand gently rubbing up and down his naked groin. Constantine Janson stood and straddled him, careful not to put any weight on his chest. His erection was touching Connoly's lips and rubbing on his face.

'Now you are going to suck me gently until I explode, then I will leave you alone. I will probably fuck you tomorrow night, so that's something to look forward to. Now you will be gentle won't you?'

Connoly nodded his head in submission as he felt the weight of the man begin to settle back on his chest.

'That's the boy. You do anything and I'll smash all your ribs and you'll drown from the blood in your lungs. I don't care. I'm in here for life and another ten years won't make any difference.'

He felt his mouth being squeezed open and the penis being slowly thrust between his lips. It was a tentative move to see whether the victim was going to retaliate. He began to suck slowly as he'd been taught to do by Father Corrigan in the not too distant past. The memories of that bastard priest running the orphanage would forever be imprinted in his psyche - he took whoever he wanted whenever he wanted.

Jonas relaxed, closed his eyes and threw his head back as he felt the neurons of sensation begin to explode in his cortex.

But this time there would be no climax and no rush of gagging fluid in his throat as Connoly clamped his jaws shut and began to grind his teeth. If only he'd had the courage to do that to Corrigan, but what ten-year-old has? The screams of piercing pain echoed through the cell, the fists thudded into each side of his head as the screams grew louder and longer. He began to drown in the flow of blood filling his mouth and entering his lungs. He opened his jaw as he heard the cell door being thrown open. Janson fell to the floor writhing in agony clutching his half severed member, the blood flowing through his fingers and pooling within his fetal position.

Connoly swung his feet off the bed and staggered to the small wash basin to cough up and spit out the blood. He was in agony from the blows to the head and from the effects of his attacker putting his full weight on his rib-cage. His face, hair and chest were covered in blood as he turned towards the two warders who had entered the cell. One knelt down to examine Janson while the other drew his baton and aimed a solid blow to the side of Connoly's head. He had raised his broken arm to frustrate the blow, but it was only a token defence as the baton smashed through. It was quite obvious the prisoner had gone mad. There was no other reason for his appearance and the evidence of blood sprayed over the bed and walls. Connoly felt himself falling.

It was the following day when he was approached in the prison hospital by the screw leering down at him with a look of satisfaction. 'You're going to serve a couple more years for this unprovoked attack you Irish git. Where did you learn that trick? They had to amputate the knob end of his dick. He'll never get a thrill by sticking what's left into anyone again.'

Conolly glared back and snorted. It was no trick. It was survival. It was the culmination of torment no one who had not experienced it, could understand. 'You knew bloody well he was going to attack me, arsehole. You knew I had no defence because of my arm and ribs and that's why you put me in there with him.'

The screw laughed as he turned to walk off. 'Yeah, you've now got an identity in this place. You're now known as the *gobbler*. Mind you, Janson was asking for trouble picking on someone with teeth instead of gums.' He was still laughing as he strode off down the corridor.

# 10

*And now here he was at the perimeter gate and he didn't like what he saw on the other side. It was a face he recognised. It was a face that never normally smiled, but now it had a broad grin. And it was wearing a British Army uniform with two other British uniforms flanking him. The gate was open and he was free for the three steps it took for the two uniforms to detach and take his arms.*

'Private Connoly you are under arrest for desertion from Her Majesty's Service. You will be escorted back to England to face charges.'

Connoly noted the shoulder pips – LeBrereton had not made it past Captain. By his reckoning he should have been a Major by now, or even a Colonel. Had LeBrereton slipped up somewhere? He tried to show no emotion as he was bundled into the middle seat of a waiting car, with a mute uniform on either side. LeBrereton nodded to the driver and turned as the car began to move.

'I've been waiting a long time for this day private. We've had an extradition application out on you since we first heard you'd been charged with killing a policeman. Our application was denied until you had served your term. Rather than being thrown out of the country by the local authorities, I just knew you would get a thrill out of seeing me and being personally escorted back. You can look forward to another stretch when we get you home. You haven't achieved much since I saw you last, have you?'

'Likewise, where did you fuck-up ? You should have been a Colonel or a General by now. Did you fall off your horse or faint on parade in front of her Majesty?'

LeBrereton could not control the look of anger. Connoly noticed one of the uniform's suppressing a grin. 'I hear they gave you an interesting name in there private. Didn't they give you enough meat, or do you like biting into something with additional protein and a spurt of mayonnaise? Did you swallow or just chew?'

The remark stung. He knew LeBrereton would ensure the sobriquet would follow him home.

'Well, we've got you so that only leaves the other deserter, Darrel Casson. You two must have bolted together. Have you any idea where he is?'

Connoly snorted. 'I may, but I certainly wouldn't be telling you his present address. There's no mileage in that for me.'

'You two cleaned out that shed in Maralinga and buried everything as I instructed, didn't you?'

Connoly nodded. 'We sure did, just as you instructed.'

'Do you remember mentioning a locked room? You wanted to know what to do with the contents of that room. It contained two small barrels which you were supposed to hand over and for which I'd already signed off on. What did you do with them?'

Connoly shrugged his shoulders. 'Buried them along with everything else. No one came to claim them so we just tossed them into one of the holes. I wasn't going to wait around for someone to pick them up as you had indicated. Casson and I were intent on deserting the moment you took off and we weren't interested in a couple of barrels. Our only thoughts were to get out of that place.'

'Are you sure of that private?'

'Are you just shooting the breeze LeBrereton, or are you leading somewhere with this? Your orders were carried out, end of story. We buried everything.'

'It's Captain LeBrereton to you private. You're still in the army. And by my estimation following your court-martial, you will remain in the army for the remainder of the term you failed to serve before jumping the fence. You may even get a year or two extra to demonstrate the army does not tolerate deserters.'

Connoly nodded. 'Yes, I'm resigned to that now. At least it won't be as tough as the prison I was just released from.'

'You are going to Colchester military detention centre in Essex. You'll be back in uniform with a nice little badge on your chest signifying the nature of your offence. Following that you'll be given a dishonourable discharge. That might not be the end of your problems though. I hear the Liverpool police want to talk to you about the death of some character in a bar you were seen at some years ago.'

'Don't know anything about that.'

'I didn't think you would. I'm just doing you the courtesy of telling you the police may be waiting for you at the prison gate on your discharge from Colchester. That's something to look forward to. Of course, they will be kept informed of your release date.'

'The army thinks of everything,' Connoly replied with a shrug of sarcastic dismissal.

The long flight back to England was tedious and boring. He was free to roam around the cabin, but during the short stop in Singapore he was accompanied as he walked around concourse, even to the urinal, by the two uniforms. They had not said a word to him since his arrest, but suddenly the senior one opened up as they were passing a bar. 'Do you feel like a beer?'

'You'll be paying. I don't have any money on me.'

LeBrereton had them within eyesight, but did not join them. Neither of the uniforms introduced themselves and he did not ask. It was on their second beers with the talk about English senior league football and general topics, when the questions started to be casually introduced.

'How did you and Casson get away from Maralinga? It's a thousand miles from anywhere in the middle of that desert?'

Connoly looked him in the eye. 'We caught a bus. They come along every hour.'

The uniform did not flinch. It was the standard *mind your own fucking business* answer of army personnel. 'You were there for the atomic tests. Did you see any of them go up?'

'No, I missed the dancing elephants in the big top. I only had enough money for a bag of popcorn and a couple of the sideshow events.'

'That must have been quite an experience. Something to tell your grand kids about, eh?'

'Yeah, it was hilarious if you like being stuck in the middle of nowhere for a couple of years sitting on your quoit, freezing your nuts off at night and being scorched by the sun during the day, not to mention the bloody flies, wind and clouds of dust and shit. It was real fun.'

'What did you do wrong to cop that tour?'

'Nothing. I volunteered because of the promise of sun and surf, but it was all sun and no surf.'

'Is that why you caught the bus with Casson?'

'Sure, we just couldn't bear the thought of being separated.'

'So where is he now? Have you kept in touch?'

'You were in the car when LeBrereton asked me that question and the answer hasn't changed.'

The uniform held up his hands. 'Look, settle down. I'm only trying to be friendly and make conversation.'

'Don't hand me that crap,' Connoly snapped. 'I've been AWOL for a few years, but I haven't forgotten how the army operates.'

'Okay, okay, forget I asked that question, but we've got to talk about something. Can we talk about Maralinga? Although you think it's boring, I'm totally fascinated by what happened. I heard there was a lot of fall-out from the explosions which could adversely affect those who were close. Have you ever thought about it causing cancer, because that's what the medical experts are now saying? Our army veterans have launched a class action for damages, as a result of being exposed to the tests.'

'I've also read about that, but so far I've felt no ill effects or been sick in anyway. The prison doctors weren't too concerned about my health.'

'Apparently, there's a major push by the Australian government for a proper clean-up to be commenced. They suspect they weren't told the truth when we finally pulled out.'

'There was nothing to really clean-up when I was told we were leaving. I don't know about anything at the explosion sites because I was assigned to looking after stores fifty miles away. I never actually stood on ground zero.'

'What did you do with all the stuff you were guarding?'

'LeBrereton ordered us to bury it, which we did. Nothing left the site.'

'Was everything contaminated?'

'Sure was. There were guys running around with gadgets ticking like crazy. Everything was contaminated so we buried the lot, including the buildings. All that was left were a few concrete pads.'

'And you know exactly where you buried it?' The uniform noticed Connoly screw up an eye and crease his brow with a look of *fuck you*. 'Don't take that the wrong way. It's just that I'm totally opposed to the nuclear industry. It will be the death of all mankind if anyone starts a nuclear war. Would anyone be able to find what you buried and retrieve some nuclear waste?'

'Way out of my line of expertise to answer that, but I suppose they could. I wouldn't be too concerned about it. Although it's way out in the desert I'll wager it's still a controlled out-of-bounds zone to unauthorised entry. And even if you could get in there with a digger you would be quickly discovered and hunted out of the place.'

'Was there anything of real value you buried? After all, armies are notorious for burying stuff that's worth a fortune at a later date.'

Connoly shook his head, but yes, there was something he wanted to dig up sometime in the future. He was now becoming acutely aware of its possible value.

# 11

*T*he court martial was over in ten minutes. He pleaded guilty to desertion and was sentenced to serve three years in Colchester.

'I see you served time in Australia for killing a policeman,' the presiding Colonel of the three-man panel observed.

'Yes sir, it was an accident. It was raining and I just didn't see the copper standing in the middle of the road.'

'Nevertheless, you killed him,' the Colonel remarked without looking up. 'What happened to private Casson? You deserted together, but he's still missing.'

'We went our separate ways very quickly. Our accents were too obvious so we thought it best we separate. I haven't spoken to or heard from him since.'

Compared with his time in Pentridge, Colchester was a relaxed atmosphere as long as the army regimen was adhered to – obeying the barked orders of sergeants immediately and smartly saluting officers. Connoly knew how to play the game to survive.

He was surprised when a month before his release from the years of utter boredom, he was called to the command centre and confronted by LeBrereton. He snapped to attention and saluted.

'I see your attitude has changed for the better private.'

'Yes sir, this is a surprise. How can I be of assistance. I have nothing further to say about Casson other than what I've already said.'

'You didn't murder him then?'

'I've already told you sir, I know nothing of Casson's whereabouts.'

'Your commanding officer is going to sit in on this interview and it will be recorded. Do you want legal representation?'

Connoly shook his head. 'No sir, I've nothing to hide.'

'Be seated private.' LeBrereton pulled a letter out of a folder. 'This letter indicates otherwise. It was brought to my attention by Casson's sister in New York. It is dated a day before you both deserted, although on the strength of this, it would appear Casson was not in your company when you went AWOL. In my opinion, that would suggest he was already dead.'

'I don't know what you're talking about sir.'

'His sister has not received any communication from him since he supposedly deserted with you, whereas he used to write every week. This was not the only letter she received concerning you. You had subjected him to intimidation and bullying and had threatened on numerous occasions to kill him - isn't that true?'

Connoly laughed. 'Yes, he was a lazy bugger who wouldn't pull his weight and I did threaten to knock his block off regularly, but I didn't kill him.'

'Well, tell me exactly where you parted company after you deserted.'

'We jumped an east-bound train at a little station in the desert called Watson. That's where all the heavy goods for Maralinga were unloaded and we knew it would be easy to hop aboard.'

'And no one on the train saw either of you?'

'There was an open freight wagon with cars going east. We lived in the cars until we got to Sydney. That's the last I saw of him.' He realised his mistake when he noticed the smirk of disbelief. He wasn't thinking straight. He had wiped the cars clean as best he could, but was it enough?

'That's very interesting private. You have just confirmed Casson was with you all the way to Sydney. However, it would appear you were implicated in the theft of some gold bullion, a considerable sum of money and the theft of a Ford car from a railway wagon. Your fingerprints were found in the rear of a Land Rover and on the steering wheel, glovebox and inside of the Ford subsequently found in Melbourne. What have you to say about that?'

'I've already admitted to that when I was tried for culpable driving along with the other charges in Melbourne sir.'

'But there was no mention of Casson's fingerprints being evident. I've checked again with both Sydney and Melbourne police and yours were the only prints they were able to lift. Casson wasn't on that train. He was already dead wasn't he? You had already murdered him and that's the real reason you deserted?'

'No sir, what I've stated is the truth.'

LeBrereton shook his head while drumming his fingers on the desk. 'Let's change the subject, but not the scenery private. You recall I gave you and Casson the order to clean out and bury everything in that storage shed days before I was assigned back to England?'

Connoly nodded. He realised this wasn't about Casson – the army had written him off. It was all about what they had buried those years ago. 'Yes sir, and your orders were carried out. We even got rid of the building.'

'Do you recall you asked me about the contents of a strongroom in the back of the shed?'

'Yes sir, you told me the contents would be picked up and consigned back here. No one turned up to claim them, so we buried them.'

'What was in the strongroom?'

'Two small stainless steel barrels with no markings. They were like small versions of those beer barrels I've seen in the staff mess here.'

'Did you by any chance open them?'

'No sir, that would have been impossible. The lids had been welded on and they were really heavy for their size. Whatever was inside wasn't liquid.'

'Where did you bury them?'

'We dumped them in a hole along with all the other gear sir.'

'Along with Casson I presume?'

The Colonel looked up startled. ' I must object. Are you charging or intending to charge this man with murder? I must insist he is represented by legal counsel before this goes any further.'

'No sir, he's not being charged at this stage. I'm taking him back to Australia to show me exactly where he buried everything. It could be a very interesting dig.'

Connoly looked stunned as he interjected. 'But...but sir, I'm due for release in a few weeks. I've served my time so I'm no longer in the army or under jurisdiction when I walk out these gates.'

LeBrereton gave a mocking shake of his head. 'No, that's just where you're wrong private. You may be due for release, but the army hasn't finished with you yet. Depending on the result of what we dig up, you could be a free man, but on the other hand you could be back here serving life. I'll be back next week to pick you up. You're dismissed for now.'

The Colonel turned to LeBrereton as Connoly walked out. 'Tell me Captain, what you are really after ? If Casson's remains are buried out there somewhere, wouldn't it be best to quietly forget looking for them? I'm well aware of what the Australian press is like when they smell a scandal. We're already in enough strife with them about detonating nuclear bombs in their backyard. Surely, we don't need any more publicity? And what's this about a couple of barrels Connoly maintains he buried? What's so special about them, or are they what you're really trying to find?'

'Sir, with all due respect, I'm not at liberty to discuss anything, or answer any questions. As for detonating nuclear devices, we had the Australian government's complete approval. It's only now the nuclear objectors are gaining voice and the press is stirring it up. I would put you on notice that anything you heard in this room is to remain here. You heard nothing. There is to be no speculation as to why Connoly is being removed.'

'None of my business. I hear what you say.'

'You're Irish, aren't you Colonel?'

'I don't know the purpose of the question, but yes I was born in Belfast. However, that's been on file for the past thirty five years since I joined the army. I'm sure the file hasn't been lost, although you appear to have lost something other than a missing trooper. You were Connoly's commanding officer at Maralinga. I gather you're being asked to answer questions coming from higher up?'

'I'll see you next week Colonel.' LeBrereton ignored the question as he got up and walked out.

The Colonel watched the departing figure and listened for the car to start up and drive off before picking up the phone. Connoly was out of their grasp, but would they believe it? A month at the most and he would have completed his side of the agreement.

The call was answered with the usual series of unintelligible grunts only someone with familiar contact would recognise. 'Hi, Emmett. I'm afraid I've got some news you won't be pleased at hearing.'

Emmett O'Brien listened to the explanation. 'Can't you give him an early release?'

'No chance of that. I've been put on notice he's being taken out next week.'

'Ah, not to worry. We'll get him when he comes back. He won't have any protection once he's discharged and out on the streets.'

# 12

'*Are you sure that's the last pit private?*'

'Yes it is Nick. Christ, I'm going to be the longest serving private in the British Army when I get out of here.'

'You may not get out of here unless we find what I'm looking for Connoly. And it's still Captain to you, private.'

'So, Command still hasn't recognised your talents eh, Nick? Are you sure you're still on the payroll? I reckon it's getting to the point where we're both eligible to join the Chelsea Pensioners and get around in that fancy red gear for old soldiers. We could sit out in the sun, entertain the tourists and swap yarns until they chuck us in a box. I reckon we'd never be bored with each others company.'

'Fat chance Connoly. They don't admit privates, or criminals who've served time.'

'True, but I don't like red anyway. You know I was due to be discharged a week after you collected me from Colchester. We've been here six weeks digging holes in this fucking place, so I reckon I can call you what I want sport. You look stuffed. Here, have a drink of water before you collapse.'

LeBrereton took the water bottle, took off his cloth hat and poured some of the contents over his head and face before taking a long swig.

'I think that's about it Nick. I reckon we can pack up and go home.' Connoly indicated the tons of stores, clothing, and machinery recovered and pushed into piles. It was almost in the same condition as when he and Casson buried it, the arid conditions preventing rust or noticeable decay. 'No sign of the barrels or Casson, so I reckon we're wasting our time.'

'I don't give a shit about Casson,' LeBrereton shouted in anger. 'I want the two barrels you buried.'

'Well, you'd better keep looking, because we buried them in one of the many pits you've dug up, but which one I wouldn't have a clue. What's so important about them anyway?'

LeBrereton ignored him as the excavator driver stopped and shaking his head, indicated the bucket had bottomed into solid ground. With a look of frustration, LeBrereton signalled with a sweep of his hand to rebury the pile of rubbish.

'It's something to do with those bloody nuclear tests, isn't it? You were in charge of stores and you stuffed up somehow? You lost two barrels of some unknown material and as we both know, the army gets very upset when things that can go bang, just disappear. They must be desperate to find whatever it is. You could be standing in front of a firing squad when we get home.'

'I'd hold the humour if I were you Connoly. You're the one who's in more danger if we don't turn up those barrels. You forget, I wasn't around when you buried them, but you and your mate Casson were. Have you ever thought, if we don't find them, it may be easier to bury you back in the hole and just dump everything back on top. Problem solved. If the army closed your mouth permanently, then the source of any rumours about missing barrels would be silenced.'

Connoly gave a sickly laugh. 'You can't put the frighteners on me with that bullshit Nick. There would be too many witnesses.'

'Accidents do happen private. It might not be here at Maralinga. It could be back in Colchester or Liverpool or London, or anywhere. It's not uncommon for people to meet a messy end when national security is involved.'

Connoly let out a grunt of satisfaction as he stubbed out the cigarette with the heel of his boot. 'So that's it Nick. Those two barrels are of strategic importance and you're desperate to find them. You fucked up big time didn't you by skiving off early and not sighting and signing them off personally? What's in those barrels the army is so desperate to recover?'

He checked himself as the truth dawned on him. He had received an unintended, but clear message - he had the feeling he was going to meet an untimely end whether or not the barrels were recovered. Could he hope for some reprieve by pointing to their location? He would have to be guaranteed total amnesty before he would agree to that - Casson was buried with them. He glanced over at the remains of the steel wireless tower some fifty metres away. It now carried a plaque outlining and dating some of the events at Maralinga. It carried a dire warning not to proceed past that point because of the danger of nuclear contamination. Casson would forever be guarded by that authority - the tower his tombstone. He watched LeBrereton walk over and study the sign soon after they first arrived. Little did he realise at the distance he was reading the sign, he was within a few steps of what he was searching for.

If it was only the barrels, Connoly would have divulged their location to save himself revisiting this cursed landscape, but no longer. Maybe he had a bargaining chip?    He cast his mind back. After burying everything from the contents of the building to the structure itself, all that remained was for the two barrels to be picked up. It never happened. But what had happened in those intervening years? Surely, the contents would have long since decayed and be of no value or importance? Knowing the army, an enquiry would have been launched at the time, when some storeman back in the U.K. could not tick off the receipt of a couple of missing items? There had obviously been a cover up, which had been exposed - the importance of the missing items suddenly being realised – they had to be found at any cost? He thought about it – could he now disclose their location and hope to do a deal? The answer was no, he would be arrested for murder – that would be the sum total of the army's gratitude.

The rum induced fight over nothing was the reason for his current predicament. They were both badly cut about the face when he caught Casson with a punch that sent him over backwards into the shallow pit where the barrels were now buried under a few feet of red earth. He heard the neck snap as it twisted to one side. He sank to his knees in exhaustion and passed out. Sometime later, when he started to recover from his drunken stupor, Casson's dead eyes were open and covered in flies – the image still haunted him. The case of rum had been a lucky find with which they had been celebrating the looming end of their tour of duty, then home and two more years before discharge. They had shared some of the bottles with a couple of army drivers passing by from another unit. It would soon come out what happened. He had a cut lip and swollen eye and the corpse was equally marked. He had one of two options – serve time for murder or make a run for it. He made a run for it and was still running.

Connoly shook his head with a cynical sneer as he watched LeBrereton walk aimlessly off towards the tower lost in thought. He suddenly stopped and idly started scraping at the ground with his boot, before stooping and picking up an object. Connoly could see him begin to vigorously rub it between his forefinger and thumb to dislodge the dirt. It was a small circular disc which he held closer to read the engraving before turning it over to read the reverse. He pocketed it with a glance in Connoly's direction. He shouted down to where the excavator was laying idle, the driver squatting on the ground in the shade of his machine, smoking.

'You can finish filling in that hole later, right now I want you up here.' LeBrereton swung on his heel as the driver climbed back into his excavator.

Connoly did not move. He knew what was about to happen. In futile desperation he resigned himself to the outcome. He watched the excavator start to dig and after minutes heard a shout as the machine closed down. He saw LeBrereton scramble down into the pit before suddenly reappearing.

'Get your arse up here Connoly, there's something you should see.'

He got to his feet and slowly walked towards the command. His mind was racing as he tried to maintain an attitude of boredom. Reaching the edge he looked down at the partial skull LeBrereton was pointing to.

'I think you know who that belongs to, don't you? That's the mate you said deserted with you, Private Darrel Casson.'

'Looks old to me. It could be one of the local natives. They've been wandering around here for thousands of years.'

'Have a look at the jaw Connoly. See those fillings and in particular the silver crown on one of the molars. That isn't a native, that's what remains of Casson after you murdered him. And here's further proof,' LeBrereton said taking the disc out of his pocket and holding it in front of Connoly's face. 'This is his dog tag with his name, blood group, service number and religion clearly visible.'

'He was with me when I deserted. I don't know what happened to him after we parted ways.'

'Don't hand me that crap Connoly. You swore an affidavit at your court martial he deserted with you. And, if forensics confirm this is Casson, he could not have been with you when you jumped that train. You murdered him and then took off. There's no other explanation. You know, I was about to call it a day here and pack up and leave. But the chance finding of his dog tag has turned your discharge from the army into another jail term, only this time it will be much longer than the time you served for desertion. Why don't you come clean and tell me where you buried those barrels? It may mitigate the sentence.'

# 13

*T*he army lawyer leaned across the table and lowered his voice in the crowded room. '*I've been appointed to represent you Connoly. As you know, you've been charged with murdering private Darrel Casson at Maralinga in 1963. The case against you is rather compelling in that you lied as having deserted together. You've served three years for desertion, on top of ten years you've already served in Australia for theft and the killing of a policeman. And now this. You can tell me what happened. I'm here to defend you.*'

'I didn't murder Casson. We got drunk on a case of rum we found and had a fight. Two drunks fighting are generally not a threat to one another, but obviously one of my punches connected and he fell backwards and smashed his head on rocks. I must have passed out, because when I came to I could see he was dead. I panicked and deserted.'

The lawyer nodded as he took notes. 'So, you're maintaining it was a drunken brawl, rather than a vicious fight that had been fomenting for some time? There was no real animosity between you before that day?'

'No, there wasn't. We got along okay although we did have our differences, but nothing so serious as to physically harm one another. Your brain goes to shit when you get stuck in a place like Maralinga, it's the arsehole of the earth.'

'The prosecution is intent on sending you down for murder. I have discussed the lesser charge of manslaughter, but they won't hear of it. They want you out of sight for a long time. In someways you are lucky capital punishment was abolished in 1964. If Casson's remains had been found in '63, it's highly likely you would have been executed for murder, it being an army trial with no right to appoint your own civilian defence. As you know Her Majesty's Service looks at things through black and white glasses, there are no shades of doubt once its officers have made up their minds. However, in this case and in more enlightened times you may appoint your own civilian defence, or you can accept me.'

Connoly shook his head. 'I can't afford a lawyer. And after all, the army is paying, so I'll accept you. What are you going to do for me?'

'I don't think they'll be successful with the murder charge. My advice is you accept manslaughter and we go with that. I would argue for ten years, which would see you out in five, if you behave. However, don't take my word for that. All I can say is they'll be trying to inflict the maximum pain. Were you aware the Australian authorities wanted to detain and charge you with murder?'

'No, I didn't know anything about that.'

'You're lucky the army got you out of the country on a military flight before they could get their paperwork together. The Australians are still pissed off with the legacy results of secret nuclear tests they were not aware of. It's still too radioactive to go anywhere near those sites. Luckily, they're so remote no one but the natives bother to go there. Our government of the time certainly took advantage of the naivety of our colonial cousins. I have no doubt you would have been made an example of for the sake of publicity and enraged backlash and sentenced to life in an Australian cell. You were indeed very lucky the army looks after its own in your case. Now back to the present. Will you allow me to argue manslaughter and accept a lesser sentence, or do you want me to plead not guilty and be assured of a long term behind bars. As your counsel I strongly urge you to accept the lesser charge, as I don't believe you've got a hope if you try to get an acquittal for murder.'

Connoly studied the face of the young lawyer wondering whether he was not part of the system intent on putting him away for life. He didn't trust anyone in authority and in particular, none in uniform. However, in this case he had no choice.

'Okay, I'll accept your advice and go with manslaughter. You never know, I might get lucky.'

It was the following day when he was suddenly approached by a guard who escorted him to the Commandant's office. Present were two men in civilian suits with the air of authority about them. Neither introduced himself and Connoly could see the Commandant was nervous.

'These two gentlemen would like to ask you some questions Connoly. I believe it would be in your interest to answer them.'

'Thank you Commander,' one of the suits interrupted. 'Would you be so kind as to excuse us, as we would like to question the prisoner in private?'

A fleeting look of annoyance flashed across the Commandant's face. He was not used to be ordered out of his own office. 'I cannot allow that. This man is in my custody and anything discussed within these four walls will be carried out in my presence.'

'Corporal would you escort the prisoner outside for a minute please.' It was a barked demand.

The corporal standing behind Connoly looked to his superior who gave an imperceptible nod. The corporal had barely closed the door before they could hear the muffled argument inside. Minutes later the Commandant emerged barely able to control his outrage. 'Escort the prisoner in corporal and then remove yourself from the building. I will call you when the prisoner is to be escorted back.'

The Commandant's expression grew even darker when he walked back in and saw his desk and chair occupied by the obvious senior of the suits.

'I've already told you this is a private meeting Commander. I will call for you when we're finished.'

The Commandant spun on his heel and walked out, his face crimson with humiliation. The other suit closed the door behind him and stood in front to block any entry or exit.

'Sit down Connoly. We would like to ask you some questions.'

'I gathered that much, but who the hell are you? I'm up on a murder charge and my lawyer instructed me not to talk to anyone unless he's present. I suggest you allow me to contact him before we go any further?'

'That won't be necessary, our enquiries have nothing to do with your current indictment.'

Connoly pulled a face and snorted. 'I don't care what you want to know, I won't be answering any questions without my legal representation. I believe that is my basic right. If you are going to deny me that, I'm out of here.' He made to stand, but the observing suit thrust him back into the chair with a powerful hand clamped around the back of his neck. The grip tightened and after a few seconds he could feel himself becoming light-headed as his brain was deprived of blood and oxygen.

The suit behind the desk nodded, but his expression did not change. The pressure was released and Connoly fell forward trying to shake off the effects of the iron-hard grip. 'We're not here to mess about. You can make it hard or easy, but you will tell us what we want to know. And you can forget about having your lawyer present.'

'Go screw yourself.' Connoly coughed as he wiped the tears of pain from his eyes. He felt the hand clamped back and the grip begin to tighten again. He tried to fight it off, but the sensation of impending unconsciousness returned.

'Connoly, you can answer my questions here, or I can have you removed to a place where this interrogation may become extremely unpleasant for you.'

'Who the hell are you?'

'I can assure you we are here with full authority, as the Commandant finally recognised. I don't have to tell you who we are, but I can tell you it's imperative you accept and recognise our authority. Let's see if we can't come to a compromise? You are charged with murder. I can guarantee you will get life without parole if you don't co-operate. On the other hand, if you co-operate, the charge will be down-graded to manslaughter and you will serve five years maximum. With good behaviour and taking into consideration the time you've already been banged-up in here, you'll be out in three.'

'And you can guarantee that?'

The suit nodded. 'I certainly can.'

'Well, you deliver your guarantee in writing and I'll then comply with your request.'

The suit's face flushed red at being outsmarted. 'Don't fuck with me Connoly. You know it doesn't work that way.'

'Where I was brought up, it does. Don't trust anyone. I'm from Belfast and it's a tough place if you don't watch your back.'

'So, you're not interested in my offer?'

'I certainly am, but not on your terms. I've obviously got something to trade and you want it, but are not prepared to pay?'

'You know exactly what we want then, don't you?'

Connoly rubbed his neck and smiled. 'Yes, you want to know the whereabouts of two missing barrels of material from Maralinga, if I'm not mistaken.'

'And you know where they are?'

'No, I don't. I've been questioned about this several times over the years and I've not got a clue where they are now. As you are aware, I was taken back to Maralinga recently to show where I buried a heap of old equipment in '63. The barrels were buried with a mountain of contaminated stores in multiple locations. However, the barrels were not found.'

'You know what is in those barrels, don't you?'

'No, I don't, but whatever it is, it's something you are desperate to recover. You don't have to be Einstein to figure out that if we were exploding nuclear devices, what's in those barrels had to be somehow connected. In my opinion, wherever they're buried, that's where they should stay.'

'You're a liar Connoly. You know exactly where they are and you will tell me. Under the Official Secrets Act, the life sentence I mentioned is not mere threat. It's a certainty.

You can forget any thought of parole.' He leaned forward lowering his voice to a mere whisper. 'In fact, I doubt whether you will stay healthy for long. You will most certainly meet with an accident and if it doesn't kill you it will certainly leave you with permanent brain damage. You will wind up a vegetable, being spoon fed and having someone wipe your arse.'

'You're the second person who's made a similar threat. You might get rid of me, but you take the risk I do know where those barrels are, but have taken the precaution of recording their exact location and lodged it with a trusted friend.'

'The contents of the barrels are valueless to you. You can't do anything with them. They have no value, don't you understand that?'

Connoly laughed again at his inquisitor's mistake. 'I don't know how you can say that. They must have value, otherwise you wouldn't be here offering me a deal.'

'So what do you want?'

'I want out of here with the slate wiped clean. Then we can talk. I don't have any knowledge of the whereabouts of what you're wanting to retrieve.' He attempted to keep the lie out of his determined expression. 'I did not murder Casson. It was an accident when he stepped backwards and fell into the pit.'

The suit smiled and shook his head. 'I don't give a rats about Casson. It's the barrels I'm after. You know very well I can't give you a written guarantee. You tell us what we want to know and then we'll talk about letting you loose.'

'And trust a couple of mysterious thugs, too scared to identify yourselves? You've got to be joking. You've already demonstrated you resort to violence and intimidation. You're offering me nothing.'

'So, you won't help us?'

'I believe the Commandant will be back any minute to toss you two off the premises. I have nothing more to say.'

The suit looked at his colleague and rose from behind the desk. 'Okay Connoly, you've had your chance. You're going down for murder, but you'll never be released because of what you're concealing. You'll be moved from these cosy surrounds to the roughest civilian prison we can find. You're in for years of solitary confinement and hardship. You Mick's think you're tough, but the system is going to destroy you mentally and physically. You'll break and when you feel like talking, our door will be open.'

# 14



*The trial before the army panel was brief. There were no witnesses for the defence and Connoly declined to take the stand and plead his innocence.*

'You're a bloody fool,' his lawyer whispered to him as the prosecution completed its case. 'Don't you realise you're on a hiding to nothing if you don't stand up and say something. Your silence will be taken as confirming your guilt.'

'It wouldn't matter what I said. I've already been told I'm going away for life and it's about to be confirmed.'

The courtroom was empty except for the three man tribunal, the prosecutor, the two suits and his defence lawyer. The older of the suits had smiled and shook his head when Connoly was escorted in and seated directly in front of the panel.

'You don't know that. I'm pleading with you....'

Connoly held up his hand to cut him off. 'The result has already been determined by those two goons sitting at the back,' he hissed at his lawyer. 'Those three in front have been given clear instructions as to what the sentence will be. Who the hell are those two behind us?'

The lawyer glanced over his shoulder. 'Never seen them before. When did you meet them?'

'A week or so back. They tried a little rough stuff, but didn't get what they wanted. They made it very clear I would get life imprisonment if I didn't co-operate.'

'What did they want?'

'They wanted to know if I knew where the army had lost something in South Australia during the atomic blasts down there.'

'And you refused?'

Connoly was wary about what he said. The lawyer was army and his allegiance was confirmed by an oath. He could not trust him. 'I couldn't help them, because I didn't know where the missing items were. They were not where I thought I'd buried them. It was so long ago.'

'Did they explain what exactly they were looking for? It must have been high-priority if they were prepared to take you back down there. Was it something dangerous left over from the nuclear tests?'

Connoly shrugged his shoulders. He was not going to be trapped into admitting he knew anything. 'Search me. I was just a squaddie who didn't ask questions and didn't volunteer opinions. I was only there to follow orders.'

'Stand up Private Connoly,' the Colonel conducting the trial snapped, breaking up the quiet exchange. Connoly heard the term of twenty five years and something about being a disgrace to the army, but he wasn't listening. The suits had delivered on their threat. He felt the cuff snapped onto one wrist and then the other onto the arm of the younger suit. 'You are no longer in the army Connoly. You're now a convicted felon. These two gentlemen will sign you out of my care and take responsibility for your transport to a more secure facility.'

His defence lawyer picked up his papers and cap and nodded. 'The best of luck Connoly. I really think you should have given them what they wanted. Wouldn't it have been easier than rotting in a cell?'

He was about to reply when he was shoved in the back by the younger suit. 'The next step is the beginning of a twenty five year journey. I see you can't wait to start the adventure.'

The cuff was released as he was bundled into the back of a car next to a heavy-set person in a grey uniform he had not seen before, but spelt danger. He felt the cuff snapped back on. They drove in silence until Connoly began to doze off. He was pushed violently away as his head lapsed onto the uniform's shoulder.

'Keep your distance prisoner.'

'Who the hell are you?' Connoly retaliated as he sat up trying to shake off his drowsiness.

'You will address me as *sir* in future. You have no privileges or rights and will never speak to me unless I speak to you. You are a non-person, a criminal and a murderer. You will be spending the next five years in solitary with one hour a day in your own personal yard. You will have absolutely no communication with any other inmate and you will have no visitors, nor will you be able to communicate by phone or any other means with anyone outside the prison. Mine will be the face that controls your every movement, except your bowels, for the next five years until my retirement. I've no doubt the following twenty years of your sentence will be just as enjoyable and pleasant as I intend to make the first five. Mind you, you may find my face unbearable and decide to check out of this life, which I intend to ensure you don't, or you may want to come to your senses and talk to these gentlemen again. In that case you may get time off for good behaviour.'

'Arsehole.'

Connoly felt the round-arm movement beside him as the fist thudded into his ribs, doubling him over in pain. The next savage jab caught him in his exposed midriff driving all air out of his lungs, trapping any escaping sound. He threw his head back, clenching his teeth in a rictus of agony. The leering image did not see it coming as Connoly twisted, ignoring the pain and using his full force to launch his head into the face of his tormentor. He heard the nose crack and saw blood begin to stream from the exploding capillaries. For the moment the immediate danger was immobilised as the recipient tried to stem the flow of blood and streaming tears from the already blackening eyes. Without the restraint of the cuffs he would have finished him off. One of the first rules of conflict – never let your opponent get back onto his feet. The bullies never expected it, nor saw it coming. He leaned sideways and lashed out with his leg at the head of the driver in front, The boot caught him with full force on the temple, knocking him senseless. The older suit in the passenger seat attempted to grab the wheel to control the violent swerving motion of the vehicle, but it was too late. The car hit the shoulder of the road and spun before going into a series of sickening rolls that ejected the driver and passenger out through sprung doors. Connoly was dragged sideways by the bulk of the jailer who was thrown out by the centrifugal force, his head momentarily resting on the door frame. He saw it in slow motion as the door began to swing down again, crushing the bull-like skull with the ease of a hand on an over-ripe tomato. The effect was the same, with blood and matter splattering the interior of the vehicle. The car rolled one last time and came to a stop on its wheels. He was dazed, but not unaware of surroundings. He quickly retrieved the cuff key from the pocket of the jailer, unlocked himself and scrambled out. He looked back up the road at the two suits, both a mangled mess of blood and splayed limbs. He could smell the fuel dripping onto the hot exhaust manifold. Suddenly there was a soft whoosh as it ignited and flames began to gather energy as they fed on the source of the leaking fuel. Within seconds the whole front of the car was ablaze. He heard a vehicle approaching and looked around hopelessly for some avenue of escape. He began to hobble away, panicking at his futile desperation. The twin-cab truck drove past, before suddenly braking in a cloud of blue smoke from the locked tyres as it turned back towards him. It did not swerve to avoid the two bodies on the road, as it drove over them before pulling up. A back door swung open.

'We nearly missed you. Are you going to stand there all day Connoly? Get in.' He put up his hand and was wrenched into the rear cab as the truck began to accelerate. He lay back against the door gasping in agony from the pain of the tortured ligaments of a dislocated shoulder, the result of his arm being torn from its socket as the tethered jailer was flung from the car. The face of Emmett O'Brien appeared as he drifted in and out of consciousness. He saw the barrels of two shotguns propped in between the front seats. The truck slowed as they diverted through country lanes and cut across motorways, sticking to arterial roads before pulling into the entrance of an isolated farm an hour later. The truck bounced over potholes as they drove up a corrugated driveway through a forest of overhanging oak trees. It suddenly opened out into a clearing and a large two-storey farmhouse with a huge barn to one side, into which they drove. There was darkness and silence for a moment as the driver switched off, the only sound the crackle from a cooling exhaust.

O'Brien turned to Connoly. 'We made it. We've got an hour head-start before they work out what happened and realise you're not one of the dead. It was plain bloody luck I recognised you as we drove past. Nesbitt, the Commandant phoned and told me you were being moved and were about to be picked up. He was supposed to give me plenty of warning, but things moved too fast. It didn't register when we saw the accident. I told Dinny to drive past, but he recognised you, so you're in luck, boyo.'

Connoly nodded slowly as he rolled his head back. 'It maybe your luck, but I've a feeling it isn't mine. You were looking for me, weren't you? How did you know where I was?'

O'Brien laughed. 'I've known for a long time you were in Colchester. I was going to have you sprung, but they took you back to Australia. And then you were charged with murder which got you a life sentence. Nesbitt tipped me off you would be convicted and moved to a civilian prison to serve out twenty years or more. He didn't know why you would be handed such a long sentence, but he gathered you wouldn't hand over something the authorities were desperate to get hold of. What he did tell me, was the two people taking you to prison were from MI6 and those guys don't muck around with squaddies. You were top priority for some reason. I knew the car you would be in, but what we saw was a burning wreck and it didn't register at first, that was until your unmistakable mug pinged a bell in Dinny's memory card.'

'And now you've found me, I expect you're going to kill me?'

O'Brien reached over and pushed open the door. 'We'll talk about that inside, but for now Dinny and Pat will help you into the house. I can then take a look at that shoulder.'

Connoly tried to support his arm by holding it to his chest as they helped him out of the cab. The torment of pain was excruciating with every movement. The sweat was running down his face as he was helped inside and thrust into an armchair. O'Brien reached into a cupboard and pulled out a bottle of rum and a tall glass, which he filled to the brim.

'Get that into you and I'll pour you another. We don't have any anaesthetics so I'll put that shoulder straight when you're more relaxed.' He watched as Connoly slowly drained the glass and fell back exhausted, the empty glass falling from his hand. Within minutes he was asleep. The room was warm from the large open fire. O'Brien gently lifted the affected arm, placing a hand under the elbow and the other at the back of the bicep. With a quick twist and thrust the shoulder slid back into place, but not before the sleeping figure woke with a piercing scream of pain.

'That's fixed. Go back to sleep.'

# 15

*I*t was early evening when he awoke, rubbed his eyes and pulled himself up in the chair. The movement was noticed by O'Brien who was watching television.

'Just in time to catch the news boyo,' he said pointing at the screen. Connoly looked at the picture of the burning car. The TV crews had got there fast, but were being held well back by the police. He could see the covered bodies on the road and another burnt beyond recognition hanging out of the side of the car as police tried to hold up a screen to conceal the horrific scene. A reporter was giving a running commentary, while hinting at a more sinister reason for the accident - heavy skid marks were evident, suggesting there was another vehicle involved, but police would not confirm if two of the victims had been been crushed by a vehicle police were now trying to locate. It was the usual speculation police fed to the media in return for assistance.

'It won't take them long to work out there is a body missing boyo and the hunt will be on for you. Your photo is going to be splashed across every TV channel and newspaper in the country by this time tomorrow – you're a convicted killer sentenced to life who's just left another three dead men in his wake. I don't know how many others you've killed, including Dion, the son of mine you murdered in Liverpool. The media is going to have a field day with you. The moment you show your face, you'll be dead meat.'

'I didn't murder Dion. It was self defence as you well know. You were all after me and I wasn't going to survive if you caught me.'

'Aren't you going to ask what happened to Nancy?'

Connoly had been waiting for the question. He had often wondered himself what had become of her and their child. He was seventeen and she had just turned fifteen when on a warm midsummer day their petting had resulted in the most forbidden result in catholic Ireland – a civil crime on his part and a heinous crime in the teachings of the faith.

'I....I would like to know, but I fear it's not good news and that's why you've tracked me down and brought me here. Why haven't you killed me already?'

'Nancy committed suicide soon after your son was born. She was still alive when we caught up with you in Liverpool. She had brought shame on the family, but I was not going to disown her for that. I wanted you to confront your responsibilities and arrange to have some of your army pay provided for maintenance of her and the child. When you disappeared to Australia it was more than she could accept. She hanged herself.'

Connoly put his head in his hands. 'Oh God, I was scared out of my wits you were going to kill me. That's why

I volunteered for the Australian tour of duty. I would have happily supported her and the child if I'd known. And the child?'

'She smothered your infant son before she topped herself.' The statement was clinical without compassion. 'That's life son. There's no accounting for what desperate people will do. Nancy was a poor lost soul when you deserted her – she lost her mind completely.'

'And we were taught there is a God?'

'That's religion for you lad. In the eyes of the church they were both damned, only Nancy more than Declan, your son.' O'Brien crossed himself. 'The poor mite wasn't old enough to be baptised, but I'm sure he's in the arms of the Lord.'

'Are you going to turn me in?'

'No lad, we'll stay here until the heat dies down and then we'll take you back to Ireland. We can hide you there.'

'What's the point of that? Aren't you just stalling the inevitable? Is this some kind of sick game where you lead me on and then finish me off, or hand me over to the authorities at your leisure?'

'Calm down, I'm not about to hand you over to serve a life sentence in some stinking jail, or kill you, although it was certainly on my mind when I found out about you and Nancy. No, I think you may have something to offer of real value to the cause.'

'You mean Sinn Fein or the IRA?'

O'Brien nodded. 'Practically the same organisation these days, but we're still intent on causing the English the maximum amount of grief in Northern Ireland. What is it you're hiding the English so desperately want?'

Connoly smiled. 'If my guess is correct, it's one of the deadliest threats known to man.'

O'Brien burst into laughter. 'Tell me about it? Is it a nuclear bomb the English mislaid, or you stole? Surely, there couldn't be anything more deadly than that?'

'No, it's not a bomb, but it's certainly more deadly. I did a lot of reading while in prison and in particular anything I could lay my hands on regarding the Maralinga tests. Those dumb Australians were totally deceived - they don't know what they signed up for.'

'No wonder the authorities are after you. So, if I read it correctly, they were going to toss you in some atrocious prison for the rest of your life unless you told them where you've hidden it? I am right, aren't I - you have hidden it?'

'Yes, I have. I told them before my trial if I was given a full pardon and granted an ex-gratia lump sum by way of compensation for all the shit they've put me through, I might be able to lead them to it, but I wasn't promising anything. I told them the pardon and payment had to be settled first - I was to be out on the street and the money in the bank before I would draw a map.'

'Jesus, you've got a cheek lad. They would never have agreed to that. They would never have trusted you to deliver.'

'I didn't trust them for a moment either. I was running the real risk I would meet with a bad accident if I gave in. You see, it was a classic Mexican standoff. Even if I gave them what they wanted and they agreed to my demands, I figured they could not let me live. At some point, I might be looking for revenge and leak to the press just what happened at Maralinga. It was a giant cover-up of unbelievable proportions now that I'm aware of the possible outcome.'

'But wasn't the Australian government fully aware and in agreement with the atomic tests?'

'They certainly were at the time, but they were not aware of the consequences of a series of top secret tests which finished in 1963. Neither our government nor the Australians new the truth. Our nuclear scientists were on a romp of their own and even to this day, if it became general knowledge, it would cause an uproar. Thousands of our military personnel exposed to the danger died and are still dying from cancers as a result. When the truth did finally surface and the enormity of the problem realised, it was hidden from the Australian public and likewise our government went into denial. It was just too hot a potato to reveal. The Australian press did latch onto the residual danger of those tests some years later, but they were unaware of a ticking time bomb still out there somewhere. The Australian government has so far managed to keep the magnitude of the initial threat covered up, believing time would solve the problem. What did it matter if a couple of tribes of aborigines were wiped out by being exposed to the danger? It was regrettable, but they were expendable in the interests of science and the threat of nuclear war at that ime. The Australian government was suckered. The public would go ballistic if it was leaked to the media we had left, or more precisely lost, certain material that had now fallen into the hands of a terrorist. You can imagine the reaction? And as you're probably aware, when the press doesn't get answers to questions they already know something about, their level of enquiry and interest hits the accelerator. And the Australian press is like a dog sniffing a bitch on heat. There is only one result – unrelenting publicity. I've had a first hand experience of that when I hit and killed a cop. I was hounded and labelled a murderer, a drunk, and a criminal who had orphaned two children and guilty of culpable homicide causing death. And that was blazoned headlines the morning after I killed him. I had not been drinking and at that stage had not been charged. That was only the beginning. When they found out my background and identity and the fact I had skipped bail, they had the hangman's noose already prepared. I didn't stand a chance. And now this. I have no illusions I would not last long as a prisoner, as evidenced by the attitude of the bastard I was manacled to when the car overturned. They would have probably waited a couple of years to let the dust settle and I had faded into obscurity before I was found hanging in my cell. You certainly came along at the right time, but can I trust you?'

'You can only judge that for yourself lad. I've already admitted I would have happily killed you when Nancy could not hide her condition any longer. I mellowed after young Declan was born, but when she killed him and suicided, I would have willingly torn you apart with my bare hands. The way I read it, you are a dead man if you hand over what they want or they catch up with you again. I can't imagine what you are hiding, but it must be something unimaginable. Will you ever use it?'

'I don't know,' Connoly replied as he pulled a face and winced in pain as he inadvertently shrugged. 'I've certainly had second thoughts about what I did. I thought I could use it to cash in - a sort of insurance policy. I thought it would be worth a great deal of money to me at some point, or it would keep me out of jail if I disclosed its whereabouts. You do certain things you live to regret. I had no idea I was holding a grenade with the pin already pulled and it was too late to shove it back in.'

'So, you're the only one who knows where it is?'

Connoly hesitated. 'Y.. yes, I could not trust anyone else.'

O'Brien shook his head, his look of doubt obvious. 'Don't bullshit me lad. Someone knows what you know and they run a very grave risk they'll be subject to some heavy pressure. I maybe wrong, but it is a woman and I'll bet you've got another family down under. You were on the run for seven years after you deserted. No healthy Irish lad can keep his trousers on and zipped up for that length of time. You have a family down there, don't you?'

Connoly nodded slowly. 'Yes I probably do, but we weren't married.'

'I'll bet she's already been put through the wringer, her house ransacked and her phone tapped. They'll never let her alone.'

'Yes, I've no doubt all that has happened. But she knows nothing and they can search all they like and the answer is, they'll come up with nothing. I would love to contact her, but I daren't. That would only increase the pressure on her and any kid.'

'So you don't know whether you have a family. If you like I can get a message to her that you're okay.'

Connoly looked up in surprise. 'How can you do that without involving yourself?'

'Easy. Melbourne is the city the Irish built, the Italians run and the Jews own. The Irish flooded to the Ballarat and Bendigo goldfields in the 19th century and anyone with an Irish name still has strong connections with their homeland. I can get a discreet message through without raising any red flags.'

'Yes, I think Caroline would appreciate that. I made sure she was not wanting for anything when I left. She gets adequate money from a trust I set up and she lives in my apartment rent free.'

'Pity you hadn't paid the same attention to our Nancy.'

'Holy Christ,' Connoly snapped. 'I was seventeen and panicked at the thought of you catching up with me. And it was out of the question you would have allowed her to go to England for an abortion. I was in fear of you – I was a dead man if you caught me.'

'Okay, okay, simmer down lad. I'll get a message to Caroline for you. In the meantime, I'll go and prepare something for supper.'

# 16

Connoly *mopped his plate with a piece of bread before pushing it aside. 'You're a good cook Emmett, that was an excellent stew.'*

O'Brien grinned. 'It's straight out of Ireland. One of my sainted mother's recipes, not that she had many, nor was she a saint.' He laughed as he reached over and filled Connoly's wine glass. 'C'mon and sit down. Dinny and Pat will clear up.'

Connoly rested his head on the back of the lounge chair and stared into the fireplace.

'Well, are you going to help the cause lad?'

'What cause are you talking about Emmett?'

'There is only one cause lad. It's giving those English a good kicking they'll never forget. You're a Mick - don't you support that?'

'I learned long ago Emmett, to just roll with the punches. We can never beat them in Northern Ireland, so what's the point of wasting time trying? And, as to appealing to my catholic faith, I'm afraid I fell by the wayside on that one when I buried my Pa. The priest wouldn't give him absolution because he was a drunk, a fornicator and never attended mass. It was that same bloody priest who had earlier put me in an orphanage when Ma died. And I can tell you orphanages aren't good places to be when there are priests around.'

O'Brien could see he should never have raised the question of faith. It may be harder than he thought to get through to his objective. 'With what you've got hidden lad, we could give the bloody English one hell of a blood nose. That's if you think it's as dangerous as you say. What's your price?'

'More money than you could put your hands on Emmett.' He was still trying to work out O'Brien's real motive in rescuing him, or who was higher up the chain pulling the levers?

'You might be surprised there lad. The Irish are widespread with deep roots in America. And that's where the real money is.'

Connoly nodded and shut his eyes, but his mind was fully alert. 'Tell me Emmett, what was the real reason you turned up as you did with Dinny and Pat and a cab full of guns. Who were you going to have a shootout with? How did you know I would be on that road and how did you know I had something of value to trade?'

'As I've already said, I got tipped off by Nesbitt as to why you were there and the exact time you would be leaving Colchester.'

'But if he didn't know exactly what those two goons in the car wanted me to tell them, how did you know?'

O'Brien handed Connoly a glass of Jameson's whisky. 'Here, get some of that into you. Nesbitt is a member of the cause. He despises the English. However he was smart enough to realise whatever you were concealing, would be something MI6 wanted desperately to recover. And yes, those two characters who died in that crash were MI6 agents. He didn't know much more than that, but it alerted me to fact, if it was something serious enough for MI6 to get involved, then it was something the cause should try to get hold of.'

Connoly opened a jaundiced eye, but said nothing. He was in no doubt O'Brien was a member of the cause – the IRA. As a child he had listened to Emmett O'Brien rant in front of his children or in the pub about his opposition to the English. Connoly had grown up with the O'Brien brothers. They played it hard on the street with no quarter given to the royalist kids and none expected. They were under the absolute control of their father who ruled them and his wife with physical abuse and fear.

He, on the other hand had been abandoned by his father after his mother died and was considered a vagrant to be tolerated. He had no doubt O'Brien would have killed him if he hadn't caught the ferry to Liverpool. Violating his daughter was unforgivable.

He dozed off and awoke to the sound of someone quietly walking across the darkened room, dimly lit by the light from the embers of the dying fire. He caught sight of the figure's broad shoulders as he disappeared down the hallway leading to the outside doorway. It was Emmett O'Brien. He heard the door open and close with the effort of someone trying to stifle the sound. Was the effort to ensure the sound did not awake the guest, or was it for another reason? He decided to follow – he needed some fresh air away from the warmth of the fire. It was pitch black outside until his eyes began to adjust to a faint tinge of monochrome, cast by the haze of the cloud-obscured moon. He was about to light a cigarette when he caught sight of O'Brien striding down the long driveway. It was not a casual stride, but the determined walk of someone running late for a rendezvous. A good fifty yards separated them when he began to follow, occasionally losing sight when the light was totally blanketed by cloud. He heard a vehicle approaching along the roadway towards the farm gate. The headlights caught O'Brien as he walked into view and waved down the slowing vehicle.

Connoly moved off the road and in among the oak trees lining each side of the driveway. Unless he stepped out onto the road again, he was completely concealed from view. The car had pulled up across the front of the two massive stone entrance pillars. He crept as close as he dared as the driver got out and approached O'Brien. There was no greeting – the two obviously knew each other - it was straight into a discussion. He caught snippets of a conversation, but none of it made sense until he heard his name mentioned and O'Brien turn and motion his hand back up the driveway towards the house. He could see their forms, but not their faces, the driver's smaller stature obscured by the bulk of O'Brien.

The conversation ended and the driver opened the door and got back into the vehicle. The glow from the internal light revealed his identity before the door partially closed and the engine started. Connoly turned and moved as quickly as he dared back towards the homestead. Glancing back he could see the driver talking to O'Brien through the open window. There was no doubt of his identity.

He broke into a jog keeping as close to the fringe under the almost total darkness of the overhanging trees. He was out of breath from the pain of his shoulder and the exertion as he reached the house and walked quickly around to the rear, the common entrance for any country farmhouse. Pausing to comprehend what he had just witnessed, he walked towards the barn where the truck was parked, leaned back against the tailgate and lit a cigarette. He could take the truck and make a run for it. It was worth a try as he could feel death closing in on him if he stayed here. He flicked his cigarette away and walked around to the driver's side, reaching for the door handle.

# 17

'*Where have you been Declan?*'

Startled, he recognised the voice of his one-time friend. 'Oh, hi there Dinny, I was just out for a walk.' He caught the quiet chuckle of disbelief.

'Must have been a brisk walk, more like a bloody sprint I would say. You're out of breath. You were running like hell when you came around that corner - you're only just going to beat the old man back.'

Connoly nodded in resignation. 'Yes, you're right Dinny. I followed him down to the gate.'

Emmett O'Brien swung around the corner and was about to enter the house when he noticed the sudden glow of a cigarette in the dark and looked across at them in surprise. 'What are you two doing?'

'Just out having a smoke and stretching our legs, Pa.'

'You two been out here together all the time?'

'Sure Pa. We've just been chatting about old times when we were kids. Where have you been?'

O'Brien hesitated as he opened the door. 'Like you, just taking in the fresh air. See you in the morning.'

'Why did you do that?'

'Do what?'

'Cover up for me. Tell me Dinny, we've known each other since we could crawl - what the hell's going on? I'm sorry I killed Dion in Liverpool those years ago, but it was self-defence - he was going to kill me. And your Pa was going to kill me if he'd caught me. Were you with them?'

'No, I refused to go and Pa and Pat have never forgiven me for it. I should have been there.'

'I'm sorry about Nancy. I was scared out of my mind when you tipped me off to make a run for it. I was under no illusions what Emmett intended to do.'

'It wouldn't have made any difference Declan, you were just the fall guy, the excuse and perfect villain. I'm surprised Nancy didn't top herself long before she did.'

Connoly shrugged and was about to change the subject when the message hit home. 'What are you telling me Dinny? You mean I wasn't the father? Is that what you're saying?'

'No, you weren't the father Declan. You had a roll in the grass with her – I followed you and witnessed it from a distance. I know she loved you and you thought you were the only one, but she was well experienced long before that. She was being shragged at least twice a week from the age of thirteen after Ma died.'

Connoly grabbed Dinny by the front of his shirt and pulled so their faces were only inches apart. 'You're a liar Dinny O'Brien. You know bloody well Nancy was mine. We grew up together, you and I and Nancy. Dion and Pat were older and it was ever only we three who were always in each other's company. I practically lived at your house. Nancy would never look at any other boy. The child was mine.'

'Declan,' Dinny replied quietly as he gently dislodged the hand from his shirt. 'The child was not yours, although he was named after you. That was only done to remove all doubt and tag you as the culprit. He was an O'Brien, not a Connoly. If he had lived, one look at him would have confirmed that.'

Connoly let his hand slide. 'I don't believe it. Which of your brother's was it, or are you telling me it was you?'

'It was none of my brothers and it wasn't me.'

Connoly looked at him thunderstruck with shock. 'So you're saying it was Emmett, her own father? If what you say is true, then it was bullshit Emmett and the boys were in Liverpool to force me to support the child? You weren't there, so your Pa, Dion and Pat were really out to kill me? Did Pat or Dion know the truth?'

Dinny slowly shook his head. 'I don't think they did, but I'm not sure. As you know, Pa ruled them with his fists, while Nancy and I escaped because we were years younger.'

'So, with my death he could bury the crime of incest, escape jail and positively identify the culprit who had defiled his daughter. Is that it?'

'Now you're catching on. And he wasn't crushed by Nancy's death. In fact, it was a relief the secret would never come out. It was buried with her.'

'But he must know that you know?'

'I'm sure he probably does, because he would hunt me out of house on some errand when my brothers went to pub and he was alone with her. I always tried to resist to protect her, but the backhanders across the face soon convinced me it was useless to argue. However, I think the enormity of the crime has been catching up with him lately. He's hitting the booze heavy and getting more and more aggressive. I'm not going to stick around much longer. I'd kill him if I thought I could get away with it.'

'What I can't understand Dinny, is where he ties in with all this. I haven't laid eyes on him for years and here he is rescuing me from a burning vehicle on my way to life in prison. And it was no chance meeting by the look of the firearms you were packing in the truck. Was I really the target?'

'You were the one and only target, but it was not to kill you. It was to drive your car off the road and wield the firepower to threaten the other occupants if they resisted. We knew none of them was armed, so we weren't worried about meeting with force. However, no one was supposed to get hurt. They would have rolled over with the shotguns being pointed at them and meekly released you. I think it was all staged - you wouldn't tell where you were hiding what they wanted. They thought they would use a different tack by giving you life in prison and then having Pa rescue you in the hope you would be prepared to do a deal. So that's why you're here, but I have no idea what the next move is.'

'I think I can guess, but I'll just have to play along with it. I'm stuck in the meantime. I would be quickly picked up if I did a runner, even if I had the means of doing so.'

Dinny broke into a mirthless laugh. 'No one is looking for you. Pa was laughing about it earlier when you were asleep and we were out in the kitchen. What you saw on tele was the scene of an accident in which three people died. It didn't mention your name or the fact the cops were looking for an escaped prisoner. No doubt they're looking for you, but they didn't want the publicity if rumour got out the accident was to be a staged incident that went badly wrong. You didn't pick up on that fact?'

'It never occurred to me, but now that you mention it, I feel like a first class klutz. I suppose my mind has just been scrambled since the accident.'

'How did that car run off the road? Did you have a hand in that?'

'More like a bloody foot with an army boot on the end. I was able to twist sideways and kick the driver in the head. You saw the result.'

Dinny crushed his cigarette butt with his shoe. 'I'd imagine someone somewhere has marked your card. You're not going to be allowed to get away with that – bumping off three guys who thought they were merely actors in a game.'

'You're right Dinny. I'm a dead man no matter which way I jump. I must say, you've woken me up about a few things and a certain person. I can only thank you.'

'I'll help you if I can Declan, but remember Pa would not hesitate to turn the gun on me if he suspects I'm informing on him. You really have to think this one through on your own.'

# 18

'*What the hell are you two talking about?*'

Dinny jumped and swung around towards the voice. Emmett O'Brien was moving towards them across the openness of the yard, he could not have heard what was being said in the low voices.

'Just coming in now Pa,' Dinny replied as started to walk across the yard. Connoly flicked his butt into the darkness as he followed.

'I want a word with you Declan,' O'Brien said as he held the door open. 'No, not you Dinny. I'll see you in the morning.'

He followed O'Brien into the snug and slumped in a chair as the door was closed. O'Brien turned around and stood in the centre of the room. He was a big man with an overpowering presence, but behind that facade Connoly could see a coward, a man who had set him up to take the blame for a sordid affair in which he had no part. He wondered if O'Brien had actually put the noose around his daughter's neck and then snuffed out the life of the child to hide the crime? He felt like screaming the truth at him, but that would expose Dinny as the source of the truth. He sat back waiting for the proposition – he was sure it was about to happen.

'What am I to do with you Declan? First Dion, then Nancy and your son, followed by Casson and now three more deaths on your head. You're a wanted man and I don't like your chances of surviving when they catch up with you.'

'I'm entirely in your hands Emmett. You could phone the cops now and I'd be back behind bars within the hour. I can't offer you anything, other my thanks for you rescuing me. However, I don't think my freedom will last that long.'

'Oh, I wouldn't be too worried about that. For instance, you could take up farming and live on this place the rest of your life.' O'Brien started to laugh at his own warped humour. 'But I get the impression you don't like the rural life and smell of cow shite.'

Connoly pulled a face and nodded. 'You'd be right on that score Emmett. I'd go out of my brain. How long are you going to hold me here?'

'I'm not holding you.'

'Yes you are. As you've already explained, that was no chance meeting on the road, but I'm still trying to come to grips with who is really behind this. You no doubt, have an idea of what's in those barrels the authorities are desperately trying to recover, but what are you intending to do with them in the event I'm able to pinpoint their location?'

'Yeah, I don't know exactly what they contain, but I do know it's enough to send the general population into blind panic.'

O'Brien had just confirmed he was somewhat aware of the lethal nature of the contents. However, Connoly recognised his own existence would end if he disclosed their location. He could not accept MI6 was involved in some elaborate scheme involving the likes of Emmett O'Brien. It was an impossible thought. Both he and O'Brien were dispensable, only O'Brien was too thick to realise.

'What's in it for me, if the barrels could be found?'

'A new identity, passport and say four million euros. That would see you through until you're called to meet your maker. However, I don't think you'll be handed a harp and wings on arrival – you'll be sent down below to shovel coal and keep the fires burning for eternity.'

Connoly snorted at O'Brien's attempt at jest. 'And how are you going to arrange that? Forged passports don't guarantee a new identity and where and when would the money be handed over?'

O'Brien smiled. 'All in good time. I just want to get a confirmation you can deliver and then I'll introduce you to someone who will handle the details. If you screw us around you won't be leaving this farm. You'll be under part of next season's wheat crop.'

Connoly's mind was racing. It was not an idle threat. O'Brien could not afford to let him go. It was too much of a risk. 'Okay, you'd better arrange a meeting with whoever is bankrolling you. But, I'm not going to just draw a mud-map of the location without first settling the terms.'

O'Brien could not hide is expression of triumph. 'Good, let me make a call to see if the person is available.' He walked into another room and closed the door. Connoly heard a muffled conversation, but was not really interested in the contents. He already guessed who he would be meeting. It was an hour later when they heard a car pull up in the yard and O'Brien go out to meet it.

They eyed each other and nodded when the visitor entered. 'We meet again Connoly. Always in trouble and still in trouble I see.'

'Hi there LeBrereton, you're out of uniform. Did the army finally wake up and boot you out for misplacing some strategic goods, or have you been transferred to the undercover geriatric reserves division?'

'You haven't changed much Connoly, still the smart arse. Only this time you're not dealing with the army, you're dealing with me. Unless we reach agreement you have no future. I'll make that very clear.'

'Who are you working for then?'

'None of your business,' he replied as he sat down opposite. 'Emmett tells me you are ready to talk, so let's get on with it.'

'Okay, apparently I'm being offered a new identity, a passport that will withstand any scrutiny and four million euro. What comes first, the cart or the horse?'

'You're the only person who knows where those barrels are buried. You almost pulled if off. If I hadn't found Casson's dog tag you would be in the clear and not sentenced to life for murder. Obviously, I have to take you back to Maralinga so you'll need a new identity to match the passport. That much you'll get in advance, but as for the money, you'll have to first deliver the goods.'

'Nothing doing Nick. If you're no longer with the army, I take it you're working freelance so I have to have guaranteed ground rules. Unless I see the goodwill upfront, I'm not moving. I want the money transferred into an offshore account, the details of which I won't be able to give you until I have a new identity. When that's established and the deposit confirmed, you can then book our flight back down under. However, what if the barrels are not where I buried them? How do you know the Australian government hasn't dug them up already and quietly disposed of them?'

LeBrereton shook his head. 'I can assure you they haven't found them. I won't go into detail, but we would have immediately been informed to come and get our rubbish and immediately ship it out on a charter flight. No, the material will be exactly where you buried it.'

'In that case, who is going to guarantee I get paid? Someone must be authorised to sign off on it? You, I don't trust LeBrereton. How do I know my passport won't be cancelled and my bank account blocked at some point?'

'Life is a risk Connoly. There are no guarantees you won't be struck by lightning or have a fatal heart attack tomorrow. The weather is very stormy out there and your heart must be under a lot of strain, now you're on the run. There are no guarantees and I can't give you any. You have no alternative but to accept my terms.'

Connoly lay back in the chair and looked into the fire which Emmett had been stoking while listening. 'You've got my terms LeBrereton. Take it or leave it.' It was a bluff he had to take. He knew he was not going to survive if he showed LeBrereton where the barrels were and likewise he was as good as dead if LeBrereton turned him in – a life sentence with no parole was a lingering death. He would have to take his chances and find an escape route. At least he had some time on his side. He knew he held the aces while he waited for a reply.

'Okay, but if you don't turn up what I want, you know the consequences?'

'So, how long before you set me up with a passport and we move?'

'Two weeks and you'll be on a plane back to the land of sunshine and perpetual flies. A couple of days there and then you can go and buy yourself a bar in a coastal resort of Spain, or just relax and enjoy life.'

*Mark Bonner handed his passport to the Customs officer who held it up to compare the photo with the person standing in front of him. It was then scanned under an ultra violet reader before being stamped and handed back.*

'Have a good holiday Mr Bonner. I would like to be going to Australia at this time of the year. I was there two years ago and was tempted to disappear and become a beach bum.'

'Why didn't you?'

The officer laughed. 'Two many commitments here. A wife and a couple of kids were the handicaps and after a week they wanted to get home.'

Bonner grinned, picked up the passport and walked off with an inaudible sigh of relief. The passport had stood the test. LeBrereton had delivered once again. The previous week he had given him a read-out of a bank account in Bermuda. It was in his name and showed a balance of four million euros. 'The password is presently *mara 1963. Change* and memorise it as the funds can only be drawn down by you. When your passport stands up to scrutiny at the airport next week I will have completed my side of the agreement. You have a new identity and money. It's up you to finalise your part and there better not be any failure.'

First Declan Connoly, then Martin Bellamy and now Mark Bonner. Bonner sat back as the plane accelerated and lifted off. LeBrereton and O'Brien were seated two rows ahead while he and Dinny were seated together.

'Your first time on plane, is it Dinny?'

'Yeah Declan. I am bloody ner......'

'It's Mark. Forget Declan ever existed,' Bonner hissed.

'That's going to be hard, but I'll try.'

'Am I to assume you are my minder on this trip?'

Dinny nodded and laughed. 'Yeah, I'm not to let you out of my sight. Those were my instructions from LeBrereton. I'm to use force if you try to bolt. Also, I'll be operating the digger or excavator to find those barrels. Are they deep?'

'No they're not. It will only take a few minutes. LeBrereton is going to get one hell of a shock.'

Dinny looked concerned. 'Why, are they empty?'

'No Dinny, they'll be intact. But just watch LeBrereton's reaction when I tell you where to dig. He isn't going to be happy if this trip is being underwritten by Her Majesty's government, but I suspect he's on a romp of his own. If he is on the latter he should pay me a bonus. However, something about it just doesn't add up. Tell me, has Emmett given any indication who's behind this? Is it the IRA? If it is, you have no idea of what you about to get involved in.'

'Pa has never told me what's in the barrels, although I've asked him many times. And LeBrereton just ignores me. All

Pa would say is the English are going to get one hell of a surprise.'

'Have you considered you and I and your Pa maybe on a one way trip? If LeBrereton is acting for someone else, and it could be a terror group, he won't leave any witnesses when you uncover the goods.'

Dinny shook his head. 'Never occurred to me, but I really don't believe it. Pa is a member of the IRA and LeBrereton has promised him a big payday. Pa said we aren't working for the government.'

'Then who's financing this trip?'

'I suppose it's the IRA.'

'Dinny I don't think you realise what you're getting involved in. I know what's in those barrels and believe me it's lethal. It has the potential to kill millions of people if it gets into the wrong hands.'

'Why did you bury it then? What did you hope to gain?'

'I didn't know what they contained at the time, but believe I do now. And I really don't know why I haven't revealed their location. But, I suppose now it's more an act of revenge. LeBrereton had me demoted from corporal to private and my pay docked several times for insubordination. I kept giving him lip. I hid the barrels because I reckoned he was going to be in serious trouble if he couldn't account for them. I knew they had to be really important as they were locked away in a secure bunker. And then I deserted, which was a bloody stupid thing to do in view of what's happened to me since? You've been assigned as my minder and you're to report back to your Pa for any signs I may not complete the deal. Is that it?'

'Pa is certain you have no alternative but to comply. I overheard LeBrereton tell him you would be going back to jail, no matter what happened. You say what's in those barrels is absolutely lethal? I don't know whether I can go along with that.'

'It's lethal alright. It should stay exactly where it is, buried well away from civilisation. It would never be discovered as the land is really barren desert, of no use to anyone. The local natives still roam around on the contaminated ground, but the authorities don't give a toss they'll all die of some form of cancer. However, I feel the same way about the English. I don't know what LeBrereton's game is, but I can't see your father or you, being included in his plans.' He closed his eyes and leaned back in the seat. Dinny was not ignorant, he would have digested the message.

Several minutes passed in silence except for the sound of jet engines. 'You're going to jump ship the first chance you get, aren't you?'

Connoly opened one eye and looked across at his accuser. 'Are you going to try and stop me?'

'Nah, but do it when I'm out of sight taking a piss.'

# 20

*L*eBrereton and Connoly were sitting in the crew-cab of the Nissan watching as Emmett and Dinny went into the machinery yard to hire a backhoe.

'What's the gun for Nick? Are you counting on using it?' Connoly had seen the exchange as they walked out of Adelaide airport – a swift movement where an apparent stranger had walked into LeBrereton, apologised and hurried on. It had been quick, but Connoly had caught sight of the pistol being thrust into the jacket pocket. He had seen it innumerable times in prison where drugs were handed over by bent screws to dealers within the system. Blink and you missed the transaction. He almost missed this one because he was not looking for anything and did not expect anyone to be aware of their presence.

'It's insurance Connoly, or should I say Bonner. If you find the barrels, you're a free man. But if you're screwing me around, it's the end of the line. And if you try to make a run for it, Maralinga will be your permanent address.'

'Who the hell are you really working for LeBrereton? This must be a fully sanctioned operation, but who is really picking up the tab? It can't be the IRA - O'Brien is as slippery as shampoo on a doorknob and they'd be crazy to trust him. And he doesn't have any money, but you've obviously promised him a big payday. You're conning him aren't you? You know what I think? I think when you catch sight of the first barrel, you're going to pull out that gun you're hiding and deliver the coupe de grace. Perhaps, I should tell Emmett you're carrying it?'

LeBrereton turned to face him. 'You've nothing to be worried about Connoly and neither have the other two. You turn up the goods and you're free to go. The passport you're carrying is the genuine article.'

Connoly nodded, but was not so sure. He was convinced LeBrereton was running his own race and neither he, nor the O'Brien's were part of it.

'You're not still in the army, are you? Who are you really working for?'

LeBrereton was silent for a few moments. 'What makes you think that?'

'Because there's no way on God's earth the army would have the authority to hand over a false passport and four million euros to a convicted deserter and escaped murderer. Your assignment is being funded by a higher authority and I can only assume you are in control because of your background – you go a long way back with me and you know the complete history. Whoever is financing this operation wants a quick and immediate result. O'Brien and any IRA involvement is a smokescreen should anything go wrong and the Australian authorities get involved. The whisper of IRA terrorists poking around at Maralinga would quickly be dealt with by a few highly trained police units – no witnesses and bodies buried in the wilderness without trace – terror threat permanently eliminated.'

LeBrereton shook his head and laughed. 'A rather fanciful assumption Connoly. The local authorities would want an explanation before they condoned such an action.'

He was about to continue when they heard the machine start up in the yard with Emmett at the wheel. With the confidence of someone who had been around machinery all his life, he drove it up the ramps onto the tray of the truck. Dinny got into the driver's seat as Emmett opened the passenger door and pulled himself up and in.

'You're in for a long drive Dinny. A good day before we turnoff the main highway and head directly north over some pretty rough tracks for another day,' Connoly said as he lay back against the door and closed his eyes. O'Brien and Dinny took it in turns as the boredom of the monotonous scenery slowly disappeared beneath the wheels. Several times they had to shake each other awake as first their eyes started to close and then the head nodded off, followed moments later by the sound of the truck running off the road.

'Jesus, that was close,' O'Brien cursed as he swung violently to avoid an emu. 'Did you see the size of that bloody chook Dinny? Frightened shite out of me, it did.'

'Just make sure you don't hit one, or a roo, otherwise we won't be going anywhere, Emmett. I think we should stop and start again at first light. It's just too dangerous. You won't see a roo until it comes through the windscreen and onto your lap tearing your guts out with it's hind legs.'

That night they camped out under the heavens ablaze with millions of tiny pin - points of light of distant galaxies and the brilliant display of the Milky Way. It was late the following afternoon when Connoly pointed to the steel tower. 'Park up beside that tower Dinny. That's exactly where you're going to dig.'

LeBrereton looked across at Connoly with a flash of surprise. 'You tosser, are you telling me those barrels are buried only a few feet from where we dug up Casson?'

Connoly laughed. 'I knew you would get angry. The barrels were directly below Casson. Another couple of feet and you would have found what you were looking for.'

LeBrereton spat on the ground as he got out. 'Well O'Brien, roll that machine off and get into it. There's still plenty of light.'

'No boyo, I've had enough for one day. My back's killing me and I want something to eat and then I want to sleep. Those barrels will still be there in the morning if Connoly here is telling the truth.'

'They're there alright Emmett. The ground hasn't been disturbed since I was last here.'

'That's not good enough Connoly. I want to see the evidence now. Your father might be too tired Dinny, but you can operate that digger. You don't have to dig them out, I just want them exposed.'

Within minutes they heard the metallic sound of the digger bucket striking metal as the bright outline of a small stainless steel barrel became visible.

LeBrereton smiled as he looked down and held up his hand to Dinny. 'Okay, that's enough for today. Let's have something to eat and continue in the morning.'

# 21

*Connoly woke with a start. It wasn't the cold creeping into his swag, but the premonition of danger. He moved quickly, making no sound as he rearranged his bedding. He looked around at ground level under the belly of the digger. Emmett was sleeping on the other side snoring loudly while Dinny was curled up under the tray of the truck as though it provided a blanket of security. LeBrereton had moved off some distance close to a cluster of bush which partially obscured his form. His swag appeared to be empty.*

Connoly rose and carefully walked over to the truck, leaned in and took the key out of the ignition. As a precaution, he did the same with the digger, before quietly picking his way into the low salt-bush towards a small rise where he could look back over the sleeping figures. He squatted and waited. Maybe LeBrereton had gone off to relieve himself, or just couldn't sleep and gone for a walk. He suddenly saw his face exposed by the glow of a cigarette being lit some fifty yards away and tensed, watching for any movement. He saw LeBrereton stand and slowly stamp out the butt. It was only a minute or so since he'd lit it. The man was obviously nervous, or preparing himself for something he was about to do. Connoly watched as he strode towards the digger, leaned over the form of Emmett O'Brien and shot him in the head at point blank range. The sound awakened Dinny who sat up confused, crashing his head into the chassis of the truck as he made to scramble from under. LeBrereton squatted down, calmly took aim and dispatched the fear-crazed figure.

His premonition had proved correct. He crouched lower as he watched LeBrereton run around the front of the digger and loose a shot at the head of the sleeping form. LeBrereton swore as he kicked the empty swag.

'You can't get away Connoly,' he screamed into the night in frustration. 'You're as good as dead.' He repeated his threat into the wilderness over and over as he walked around looking for a figure to rise out of the scrub. Connoly remained crouched, just observing. LeBrereton had made the mistake of not killing him first – he was dealing with someone who had not forgotten his military training - the constant vigilance for danger. The O'Brien's were soft targets who could be dealt with at leisure. But he still had the upper hand in that he had the vehicles, the weapon, the food and the water, or thought he had. All he had to do was stay awake throughout the long cold night and wait for his prey to come to him. As the heat of the coming new day made its relentless approach, LeBrereton was aware Connoly would quickly dehydrate and lapse into unconsciousness if he did not get water. It was just a matter of waiting for him to reveal his position – he had to finish the killings before retrieving the barrels and leaving. There were to be no witnesses, no matter how unlikely the survival for more than a few days in such a remote location.

Connoly was banking on the fact LeBrereton would not know how to hot-wire either vehicle, but if he did, he would still not leave until he had completed his assignment to retrieve the barrels and get rid of the witnesses. And it was only a matter of time before the last witness appeared.

Connoly grinned, as if on premonition LeBrereton suddenly ran over, desperately opened the door of the truck and slammed it shut when he saw the ignition key was missing. He did the same with the digger. It was obvious he had no idea of hot-wiring ignitions. Connoly quickly retreated further into the scrub when he saw LeBrereton commence circling through the stunted mallee trees and undergrowth, looking for his target. Connoly knew he had the advantage for now. The frantic efforts under the emerging relentless heat would soon dehydrate and exhaust his pursuer if he kept up the frantic pace. He would also suffer the same unless he got water which the killer controlled.

Connoly had the advantage of elevation - a gentle slope that rose to the west. He scooped out a hollow in the sandy earth, gently broke branches off surrounding salt bush and constructed them over himself in a crude attempt at shade and cover. He had a clear view of his adversary. He knew he was safe as LeBrereton would quickly realise pursuit and discovery was hopeless in the thousands of kilometres of near-desert surroundings. He was also aware Connoly would have to come to him to survive and he would be waiting.

He watched as LeBrereton pulled Dinny's body out from under the truck and dragged it into the scrub out of sight. He did the same with O'Brien. Next he pulled the cover off the tray and arranged a shade attached to the side of the vehicle. He was out of the sun and propped up against a rear wheel, but he was clearly nervous. His line of sight was to the north-east, whereas Connoly was slightly to the north-west. He could observe his every move. LeBrereton constantly got up and walked around the perimeter of the clearing alert for the danger of a surprise attack. Twice during the course of the morning Connoly noted him drifting off under the shade before jerking to an alert state and quickly getting to his feet and looking around. The pattern was repeated constantly during the afternoon, but Connoly did not move, although he knew he could have quickly approached and attempted to remove the pistol from his inert hand. It was too much of a risk and believed he had the advantage over a nervous assassin by waiting for the opportunity. As night fell he watched him gather wood and prepare a fire, eat a cold meal of a can of tuna on bread and drink two cans of beer. Connoly's throat was parched and his stomach was telling him he hadn't eaten in more than a day. The beer and the heat of the fire had the desired effect as the fire died down and LeBrereton fell asleep propped up against the rear wheel. He watched for a further half hour before slowly circling and approaching from the opposite side. He almost laughed when he heard the loud snoring and abandoning caution, walked around and picked up the pistol from the earth, where the inert hand had released it. He kicked the sleeping form which burst awake in fright. LeBrereton attempted to scramble to his feet. The expression was absolute horror as his mouth opened, the scream trapped in his throat. Connoly squeezed off two shots.

By mid morning he had cleaned up the site and buried the three corpses. He had been surprised to find LeBrereton carrying a large amount of cash in a backpack and a forged passport. He was even more surprised to find Emmett and Dinny both had passports, not in their names, but clearly showing their photo identity. Emmett was also carrying more cash than needed for the brief trip. He felt sorry for Dinny as he covered him over and swore as he dropped an extra heavy load on top of Emmett's lifeless face. He threw the passports into the hole and covered everything over. Three men had just disappeared somewhere in the desert. Who would raise the alarm and come looking for them and when? Within a few days the scene would match the barren surrounds of the landscape with no feature to indicate the burial site. Emmett had used his false identity when he hired the digger and truck.

Connoly drove the digger into a deep depression and covered it with a thick covering of salt bush. He doubted it would be found by either a ground or aerial search, not that a search would be mounted as no one was aware of their destination. The weak link in that thinking was LeBrereton's contacts, but then again they probably only had the area and not exact location. He drove south, passing the abandoned site of the Watson railway siding where he had jumped the train those years before and on south to Ceduna on the transcontinental highway – a now sealed stretch of bitumen spanning from coast to coast. He crossed the highway and drove up to the edge of the sheer cliffs rebuffing the pounding seas of the Great Australian Bight. He removed the licence plates and tossed them over the edge before engaging low gear and sending the truck into the sea two hundred feet below. It would never be seen or recovered. It took him half an hour to walk back towards the small township. It was the last filling point for vehicles travelling in either direction for hundreds of kilometres. The service station was busy as was the diner as he pushed open the fly-screen door and walked in. He bought a coffee along with a hot pie and looked around for a vacant table.

'Mind if I sit here?'

'Help yourself,' the solitary figure indicated with a sweep of his hand. 'I'm just about to leave.'

'Can I ask in which direction you are going?' Connoly thrust out his hand with a beaming smile to disarm any suspicion. 'The name's Jim Collins. I got a lift over from Perth, but the driver wants to hang around here for a few days to do some fishing, so I'm looking for a lift to Adelaide if you're going that way?'

The stranger shook the outstretched hand, but was not entirely convinced. 'Just call me Alex. 'I might be going in that direction. What's the accent? You're English are you?'

'Yes, I got off a ship in Fremantle and thought I'd have a look around this great country for a year or two before heading back.' The smile never left his face.

'Okay, finish the pie and coffee and we'll be off. You're not looking for work are you? I run a sheep station south-east of Melbourne and could do with an extra hand for a few weeks.'

Connoly laughed and shook his head. 'No Alex, I'm on holiday. I don't want to know about work. I may get to Melbourne eventually, but for now Adelaide will be fine.' He had been about to jump at the offer, but restrained the invitation of a lift to Melbourne. He did not want to be in company in the confined space of a car where questions would inevitably be asked about his background during a three day drive. He might inadvertently reveal too much about his identity or intentions. Alex dropped him at the central bus depot in Adelaide late that afternoon. He knew more about Alex's background than he ever divulged about his. An hour later he was on a bus to Melbourne.

# 22

H*e knocked on the door, apprehensive as to who would open it. The youth, was assured and confident. 'If you're selling religion, we don't need it.'*

'No, I'm not selling anything. What's your name lad?'

'Martin Bellamy, what's yours?'

'Who are you talking to Martin?' There was no mistaking the voice although it had been many years. The woman came to the door and looked at the stranger before putting her hand to her mouth in shock. 'Oh my God, is it really you Martin?'

'I told you I'd be back someday. Are you going to invite me in Caroline?'

She grabbed him by the arm and pulled him towards her as she burst into tears. 'Of course, I see my rude son has already introduced himself.'

Connoly smiled and held out his hand. 'You don't know me Martin, but I would like to get to know you.' There was no mistake he was looking at his son as Martin stepped around him.

The boy nodded and smiled, the handshake perfunctory with no real emotion. 'See you later Mum. I'll be home around five.'

'I'm not intruding am I Caroline? I don't expect you to welcome me with open arms after all this time?'

She looked hesitant for a few moments before breaking into a nervous laugh. 'No, no, it's just Martin and I. You're most welcome.'

'In that case I will come in.'

Caroline looked outside the door. 'Is that all you're carrying, or did the airline lose your luggage?'

'No, I'm travelling light as usual.'

She gave him a knowing look. 'On the run, or are you back permanently?'

'It's a long story, but my situation hasn't changed a lot. I'll explain it inside.' He closed the door and followed her into the lounge of the apartment with its sweeping views over the park. He sank back in a chair and let the memories flood back.

'You look tired. Can I get you some breakfast?'

Connoly nodded. 'Yes, I would like that.' He got up and followed her out to the kitchen. 'I caught the bus from Adelaide and only got in half an hour ago.'

'Why didn't you catch a plane? And why didn't you phone?'

'Oh, buses give you time to think and take in the landscape. I'm in no hurry,' he lied. The real reason was he needed time to think. Could he risk flying out of the country under an assumed passport, or should he wait and disappear into the local scene for a few years – he had done it before? It was that unfortunate accident which blew his cover or he would still be living quietly as Martin Bellamy. He was not wanted in Australia, but he certainly would be if he returned to the U.K. or attempted to hide in Europe. There would no doubt be an Interpol red-notice out on him within a few weeks. 'And I didn't know whether you would be still here, or more to the point, whether you would be in a situation where you would welcome me.'

'Martin.' Caroline checked herself as she put bread into the toaster and bacon rashers in a pan. 'Is it Martin, or have you reverted back to Declan?'

'It's neither.'

She was about to crack two eggs into the pan when she slowly turned around. 'Good God man, I can't keep up with you. You're in more trouble aren't you?'

Connoly slowly nodded as he met her gaze. 'Yes, but I can't tell you the whole story without implicating you.'

'C...can they trace you here? You're not endangering Martin or myself are you?' He caught the hesitancy in her voice – she was hiding something.

'You know I would never do that Caroline. Have you told Martin about me?'

'No, but he's smart. I saw the look on his face when you shook his hand. He knows he just met his father.'

'Am I his father?' He realised immediately it was a question he should have avoided. There were more subtle ways of broaching the question.

Her face flared as she put the plate down in front of him. 'I was a few months gone when you went to jail. I was in love with you Martin and still am. I don't know how you feel about me, but my feelings won't change. You provided this lovely unit and...and Tony has always made sure all the bills are paid on time.' Once again there was the hesitation. 'You did not shirk your responsibilities as most men in your situation would have done by now. You have a wonderful son, who excels at school and sport. He's a credit to you.'

'I'm sorry Caroline. I was out of line, but I had to know. I apologise for putting it so bluntly.' He finished the dish and picked up the coffee she had poured. 'That really hit the spot, I was starving.'

'What are you going to do now. Is this just a flying visit before you disappear again? This is your apartment and I would love you to stay, but by the look of you I know you can't.'

'How do you think Martin would react to that if I was able?'

'We're going to tell him the truth for a start and let him make up his own mind. Your name is on his birth certificate as the father. I preferred to leave it as Bellamy rather than Connoly, as that's who I knew you as. It may take some time for him to accept you, but I feel he's looking for an anchor, someone to look up to.'

Connoly shook his head. 'I'm not exactly someone he can take inspiration from with my record. I was on the run when we first got together and I'm still on the bloody run.' He hit the table with the flat of his hand in frustration, knocking over his cup. 'You don't really know me Caroline and I don't want Martin to know anything about my past, or why I've suddenly turned up on your doorstep. I believe it would be best if we kept the past to ourselves. I will stay the night and take off again in the morning. I don't want Martin to suffer from the guilt of association if I should suddenly be arrested or come under the media spotlight. I'm putting you in danger if I stay here.'

She stifled a look of despair as she wiped down the table. 'You have just walked back into our lives and now you want to leave. Where will you go?'

'I won't go far. I'll pick up a place down on the coast, some little burgh between here and Adelaide. I'll stay in touch, but you cannot expose yourself to the danger if I remain here.'

'Whoever is threatening you, wants you dead. Is that right?'

'They want something and they know I'm aware of its location. It's of no monetary value to them and of absolutely no value to me at the moment. It was the result of something stupid I did which caused me to desert from Maralinga in '63. I realise it's very confusing, but to answer your question, I believe they will certainly kill me if they find me. With me dead, the whereabouts of what they're after will die with me and that will be the end of their concerns. Case closed. On the other hand, if they let me live, they run the risk of me selling what I know to some other source. The truth is, I don't know who is after me. Either way, I face a slow death of life behind bars or a quick exit if whoever it is, catches up with me. I don't make any sense do I?'

'Not a lot, but I'm worried about you. I assume you are no longer Martin Bellamy? What name are you using now?'

'Declan Connoly,' he lied. Mark Bonner would have to remain in the background. 'Look Caroline, I can't subject you to my problems. I just wanted to make sure you were okay. I want to clean up and catch up with Tony Basili and then I'll get out of your sight. I believe you should not tell Martin of my predicament. He's never known me and I want to leave it that way.'

'Well, you know where the facilities are. You'll find a clean razor and toothbrush in the cabinet and I'll get you a towel and clean underwear and shirt. You and Martin are the same size and he won't miss them.'

He shaved and stood under the shower for a good five minutes trying to cleanse the dirt and accumulated guilt of the past week. He had wanted to take his shoes off when he arrived, but couldn't. He knew his feet were not exactly a neutral odour. He slowly dressed and picked up his shoes. He would have to ask Caroline for a clean pair of socks as he opened the door and began to pad down the long corridor towards the lounge. He heard a muffled voice and stopped dead.

'Yes, he's here now. I've been trying for the last ten minutes to get you, but your phone has been engaged?'

Connoly's blood ran cold – she was going to turn him in. The tears of welcome were a front – she wanted him out of her life. He quickly walked back to the bathroom, opened and firmly closed the door and broke into a loud tuneless whistle. She could not fail to hear it. She tried to hide her nervousness as he walked into the lounge and sat down. 'Can you stretch Martin's accessories for a clean pair of socks Caroline?'

'Of course.' She returned a minute later with the socks. 'I..I..I'm just going to pop down to the supermarket for a few minutes. I promised Martin his favourite, a spaghetti bolognese tonight and I haven't got enough pasta. I'll only be a few minutes at the most. Now don't you go and disappear on me again, will you?'

Connoly walked over to the window and waited for a car to pull out of the underground garage. He got a clear view of Caroline as the red Mazda hatch drove off. He turned and quickly went back through the four bedrooms opening the built-in wardrobes and scanning the contents, until he finally arrived at the master. One look in the walk-in wardrobe told him immediately what he suspected. He quickly finished dressing and exited down the fire stairwell and over the quiet road into the park. He headed for a sheltered pergola with a flowering creeper covering the sides of the lattice work, providing an excellent view of the front entrance to his building. He had only just sat down when he saw the first of two cars pull up to block the entrance to the apartment driveway. The second pulled up behind and two figures jumped out to join the two in the lead car. He saw the urgent hand signals as they rushed for the front entrance. They had obviously been given the code as he heard the foyer door crash back onto its stop.

He was going to push the buzzer to his apartment when he first arrived, but decided against it when the foyer door code flashed back into his memory. He muttered a prayer to whoever it was looking over him now. If he had announced his arrival in the foyer, Caroline would have had enough time to alert the current visitors to his arrival. It was a narrow escape. A third car slowly pulled to a stop further up the street and the driver lowered the window to get a clear view. There was no mistaking the face of his trusted lawyer. Likewise, there was also no mistaking the owner of the clothes in the walk-in wardrobe of the master bedroom – Tony was a creature of fashion. Caroline had tried to express the pleasure of surprise when she saw him at the doorway, but it was really one of abject shock. She masked it well and she almost had him trapped. The fact he'd walked down the hallway in bare feet and overheard a conversation had saved him, for the moment at least. He was still in grave danger from whoever it was who had just crowded into his apartment. He swore at her treachery, but then again could understand. It had been a long time with no contact and it was entirely of his making. He had allowed her to live in the apartment and could do nothing about it. No doubt she and Basili had looked at ways of gaining the title, but he had taken the precaution of registering it through a blind trust located in HongKong. They could never own it, but then again he could never return. He believed her when she said Martin was his son – they had the same build and features – polar opposites to Basili. It was only natural she would have fallen for Basili. He had control of the money and offered complete protection. For a fleeting moment he wished he'd kept the pistol he'd shot LeBrereton with. It would have been a simple matter to walk up to the car window and pull the trigger. The short sharp crack of a .22 calibre would go unnoticed in this quiet suburb. He got up and using the cover of the park shrubbery started to quickly walk away. He got to the far side and looked back from a position from where he could not be observed. The four figures were standing out front of the building talking in a group. There was no sign of Basili's car. Then he saw the red Mazda slowly drive up the street and pull over beside the group. Caroline got out and started gesticulating like she always did when they got into heavy discussion or a minor argument. Their arguments had always been petty, neither holding a grudge. He could see she was agitated. He had seen enough. He turned and was startled – his son was standing in front of him.

'Hi there Martin, what are you doing here?' He tried to mask his shock.

'Doing what you're doing, watching your supposed arrest, only you managed to avoid it. I can't believe Mum did that - she betrayed you. Don't worry, I'm not about to yell out and attract their attention.'

'You knew I was coming then and you know who I am?'

'Yes, I know you're my father who did a runner before I was born. Mum talked about you often and I know she's still in love with you. And now you're going to abandon us again?'

Connoly patted him on the shoulder. 'I've got no choice Martin. Is there somewhere around here we can sit down and have a coffee.'

'Two streets over there's a little bistro. The flying squad back there won't know in which direction you went.'

# 23

*Martin pointed to a table in the corner with a clear view of the roadway and entrance. He went to the counter and ordered two coffees before returning and sitting down facing his father.*

'Did you know it was me when you answered the door?'

'Dad, I've looked at myself in the mirror often enough in the morning to immediately identify you. I've got your photo in my room. Besides, I knew you were coming.'

'How did you know that?'

'Two of those guys back there came last week around nine at night and frightened Christ out of Mum. They refused to present any identification and just pushed their way in when she opened the door. One of them gave me a biff over the head when I picked up the phone to call the police. They searched the place to make sure you weren't there, but were suspicious when they saw Basili's clothes in the wardrobe. However, Basili walked in on the scene, which was unusual as he normally only fronts on weekends. They reduced the quivering load of crap to a jelly in half a minute flat. He attempted to pull lawyer bullshit and demanded to know what they wanted you for. They would not say, but made it clear you are a dangerous fugitive. By the time they left, they had given Mum and Basili the message they were to be informed immediately if you appeared. They were expecting you, which was a surprise to Mum. She said she had no contact with you in years. In fact she thought you were still in jail in England. Anyway, after they left, Basili insisted she phone him the moment you turned up at the door. He would immediately come around and assist in anyway. I told her to ignore him as he was going to sell you out the first chance he got.'

'But your Mum didn't take your advice?'

'No. I realise now she was trying to protect me. She didn't want us thrown out of the apartment and that's what Basili was threatening, in addition to cutting off the income, He hammered into her that she was to phone him immediately if you turned up. The excuse was, it would be better if you were removed permanently from our lives.'

'Has Tony ever threatened your mother with violence?'

'You've got to be joking. He used to slap her around, but that stopped when I threatened him with a cricket bat when he gave her a black eye last year. I wanted her to go to the police, but she refused. He's a thieving manipulative bully at heart. He makes it very clear who controls the money. I know it's your apartment and we don't pay any rent, but there's no way Mum could pay all the outgoings for such a beautiful setup with an outlook over the park. It must be worth a few million. And I know you left her with an income to live on, only it's controlled by Tony bloody Basili. And he has no hesitation in reminding her of that fact. At first he was very friendly and would just come around for morning tea and a chat, but then his wife was diagnosed with dementia and he decided to climb into Mum's bed. I was forced to turn a blind eye. It was no use threatening him with the bat again, because as Mum said, he controlled the money and our lives. The live-in arrangement has recently become more permanent now his wife has been moved into a private hospital, which I've no doubt you are paying for.'

'You were in the park. Were you watching for that lot to appear and arrest me?'

'I was going to warn you what was about to happen. Mum said if you came to the door and she greeted you by your name, I was to make out I was just leaving. She said to go sit in the pergola for an hour because she would cook you something and then you would want to clean up. She didn't want to turn you in. I was hiding down in the garage as she drove out just now. She was bawling her eyes out. If it wasn't for me, she would have told Basili to go take a jump long ago. I know she loves you. Is there any chance you will come back into our lives?'

Connoly patted his son on the shoulder. 'I don't know. Maybe I'll just pop around to say hello now and again. I reckon I'll be living on the streets from now on,' he remarked dryly. 'I really have stuffed my life up, but at least I've had a shower and am wearing some of your clothing. I hope you don't mind.'

'I must say you didn't look or smell too fresh when I brushed past you this morning,' Martin laughed. 'Anyway she promised under duress, she would phone Basili if you did show your face. I pleaded with her not to, as I didn't trust the bastard. However, she was petrified because of his hold over her. For some strange reason I believe she thought Tony would never betray you. Finally, she agreed to at least take a precaution just in case I was right about Tony. If you showed, she would then drive out with the excuse she had to go shopping. I was to watch from here and when she left it was my cue to warn you what she'd done and make sure you got away if my assumptions were correct. I was just about to sprint up the steps from the garage and tell you to move when I saw you emerge and walk over to the park. It must have pissed Basili off when they came up with nothing. I saw him parked up the road watching. He obviously didn't want you recognising him if he got too close. He's a real sponging coward. If I had the money I would hire a couple of thugs to do that arsehole over – really smash him up. Do you blame Mum for what she's done?'

'No Martin, I don't. You're explanation is correct – she did it to protect you. I've been out of her life for a long time and I don't blame her at all. So you recognised me immediately?'

Martin pulled a face and grinned. 'I would have to be a retard if I didn't. You're my father, Martin Bellamy. Only you're not, you're Declan Connoly an army deserter, thief and murderer. Is that correct?'

Connoly raised his eyebrows and looked across at his son. 'I did desert, I was convicted of theft, but I did not murder anyone. It was an accident. We were both drunk, but I knew I would be charged with murder so I decided to make it look as though the other soldier had deserted along with me. I made good and met your Mum, but then I had an unfortunate accident which brought me undone. I hit a cop standing on the road in pouring rain. I just didn't see him, but you can imagine the result when they finally identified me. I served time here and then was taken back home to serve a term for desertion and following that a life sentence for the killing of the soldier when they turned up his remains in a rotten stroke of luck. I won't go into details, but I'm being hunted for something I know the whereabouts of.'

'What are you going to do now? I'll help you in anyway I can if you will let me.'

Connoly reached over and squeezed his son's shoulder. 'You can't help me Martin. They know I'm here now and will no doubt watch you around the clock. You and your Mum will have a tail on you everyday from this moment, until they catch me. You can't use the phone and neither can I phone you. It's just too dangerous.'

'But, who is after you? Is it the police? I heard Mum demanding some identification when they first burst in, but they refused. They got real aggressive when I picked up the phone to call the cops. I then got roughed up again after one of them clipped me when I stepped into the argument. I thought I could handle myself, but I was no match. One moment I believed I could get in a good solid punch and the next I was on the floor staring at the ceiling. Who are those guys?'

Connoly had been wondering that himself ever since the O'Brien's had picked him up following the car wreck resulting in the death of three people. Now that number had climbed further with the death of the O'Brien's at the hand of LeBrereton and his killing of LeBrereton. 'I wish I knew Martin. I wish I knew.'

'Well you now know Basili's a two timing creep. What are you going to do about him?' Martin suddenly noticed the lad about his age walk in. 'Hey, Idris, how are they hanging?'

The lad walked over laughing at the recognition of his friend, slapped him over the back of his head, and sat down.

'Idris's Mum owns this place. We've been friends since kindergarten, haven't we?'

'Yeah, worse luck, he only comes in here to sweet-talk my Mama. He knows she's good for a free baklava. He's a real free-loader,' Idris said punching his friend on the shoulder.

'I can't help it if women find me irresistible, can I?' Martin replied with a feigned look of offence.

'Martin here is an old family friend of my Mum. He's just called into say hello. Mum was out, so we thought we'd have a coffee and he could tell me where he's been all these years.'

Idris snorted as he looked at his friend, while shaking his head. 'You've never been a very good liar Martin.'

'What the hell do you mean by that crack?'

'You're almost identical – you two would stand out in a crowd. He's not your friend, he's your father isn't he? He's your father you often talked about, but had never met.'

Martin was about to deny it when Connoly stepped in. 'Yes, that's correct Idris, I am Martin's father.' Inwardly he was regretting coming back to Melbourne. He should have observed from a distance and then faded from view for all time. Martin had unwittingly introduced his criminal parent, the parent who had been on the run before his son was born.

'I...I..I'm sorry for being so rude sir. I couldn't help it. The likeness is unmistakable and I couldn't stop myself.'

Connoly shook his head and gave a wry smile. 'There's no need to apologise lad. I suppose Martin was trying to cover up for me, by introducing me as a friend. You don't owe me an apology, I owe Martin one. From what I've noted already, you are open and spontaneous and honest. I'm pleased Martin has such a friend.'

'I will talk for my friend then. I know something of your background because Martin has confided to me over the years and it's a trust I've never broken. And if Mama knows anything, she has never raised the subject. I am astute enough to realise you are in some kind of trouble.'

Connoly was taken aback at the blunt accusation, but tried not to show it. 'How do you arrive at that conclusion?'

'Simple, Martin has always said you were named after him, so you must be Martin Bellamy, or have you changed it? So what is your name?'

'Let's just leave it at Bellamy for the moment please Idris. And to answer your accusation, yes I am in some trouble.' Connoly was looking for a negative reaction, an expression that would reveal a glimpse of what the lad was thinking, but the smile never left his face. 'Would you like to help me?'

'Sure, as long as you're not asking me to do anything way-out and Martin agrees, I don't see any problem.'

'I can't contact Martin and neither can he contact me. Would you act as a go between by passing messages onto Martin and likewise his to me?'

Idris whistled softly while slowly nodding. 'Sure, I don't see the harm in that. I'll put Mama in the picture so she knows the score.' He saw Connoly's look of concern. 'Don't worry about my Mama, she's a Kurd, as tight as a clam.'

'Well, I'd better get going then,' Connoly said as he rose from the table and took out money to pay for the coffees.

'Don't worry about that Mr Bellamy, the coffee's on me. Can I ask where you're headed?'

'I haven't a clue Idris, but I just know I've got to fade into the shadows for God knows how long.'

'Would you like somewhere to hole up? Papa was mad on fishing and bought a shack in a coastal town in Gippsland just after I arrived on the scene. He died last year,' he said as his voice trailed off and then quickly recovered. 'Mama and I have been there a couple of times since, but it's too far to travel and we're both too busy, but she refuses to sell it. No one would ever find you there. There's a store and pub about a mile down the road and the fishing's great.'

'What would your Mama say to that?'

'No problem, I wouldn't have made the offer if I thought she would object. I'll explain it to her and I know she'll agree as she's worried about vandals getting in and trashing the place. Any friend of Martin's is a friend of hers.'

'Well, in that case I'd better find a place to stay tonight and tomorrow I'll have to look at bus timetables.'

'Can you ride a motorbike?'

'Sure, but it's been years since I've been on one,' Connoly laughed. 'Why do you ask?'

'It might be too dangerous catching a bus. It's a long way and someone is sure to remember your face. Take my motorbike – it was Dad's, but I don't have a licence to ride it. And as for somewhere to stay tonight, I live upstairs to look after the place. Mum won't sell the family home a couple of doors down and it's a perfect arrangement as she's a typical Kurdish mother, all over me like a rash. And very inconvenient when Martin and I want to invite a few friends around, particularly girls she does not approve of.' He let out a long sigh. 'And that's a real problem I'll never be able to overcome. She has my matrimonial future all mapped out – it's a Kurdish girl of her approval, or she will disinherit me.'

'Don't take any notice of his bullshit Dad,' Martin said pushing his friend in the arm. 'She's a smasher. I wish she would turn those gorgeous eyes in my direction.'

'I've got a spare bedroom, so you can crash here tonight Mr Bellamy. I'll just go and clear it with Mum and be right back.'

Connoly watched him go and then turned to his son. 'You've got a real friend there lad.'

'He's the best. Say, before he comes back, what are you going to do about Basili? Mum's petrified of him and I won't be held responsible for my actions if he persists in what he's doing. I'll stick a knife into him.'

'Don't give it another thought my boy. I'll phone Tony and give him the message he's to be out of your lives by this time tomorrow, along with all his belongings. He will not contact your mother directly, but will administer my trust accounts as per my original instructions. I will check with you next week to ensure he has complied. If he hasn't, I will come back and deal with him. I'm supposed to be serving a life sentence for murder, so an additional charge won't bother me,' he chuckled in dark humour. 'And besides, I prefer Australian prisons to the stone-age English hell-hole I was supposed to be consigned to. However, before I leave in the morning I want you and I to have a private discussion without Idris present. I want to give you the information and whereabouts of what my killers are looking for. Mind you, I should have handed back what they're seeking long ago, so they could have buried the whole saga. However, I doubt whether they will let me live if I disclose it now. When governments realise they've screwed up big time, they want all evidence and any collateral damage disappear completely and forever.'

'Did you see your father? Where have you been?'

Martin slumped into a chair. 'Yeah Mum, I did. I don't think we'll be seeing him again, at least not for a long time.'

'He did tell you where he's going though, didn't he? Don't lie to me, you've never been good at that.'

Martin nodded. ' Yes I do, but I'm not going to tell you. He won't be calling or phoning, but we will hear from him. And by the way, I believe Tony Basili will be moving out for good and behaving himself as far as money's concerned. No more blackmail. Dad saw his clothes in the wardrobe after you drove out and he also spotted him up the road watching the guys who turned up to grab him. He'd heard you talking to someone on the phone after you cooked him breakfast, so he decided to leg it. He just got out with probably only a minute to spare. I didn't have time to warn him.'

Caroline slumped onto a couch and held her face in her hands. 'Oh God, I hope his threat works. I'll pack Tony's clothes in a couple of boxes and put them down in the garage. You can make the call and tell him where to pick them up. However, I don't believe he's going to disappear out of our lives that easy.'

Martin got up, sat down beside his mother and wrapped his arm around her shoulder. 'Mum, Tony Basili is out of your life, I can promise you that. Now stop worrying.'

'If you say Martin will not write or call, how will we hear from him?'

He was about to say something, but checked himself. 'I don't know how he's going to do that Mum, but he will be in contact, I'm sure of it.'

# 24

'*How the hell did we miss him? It only took us ten minutes to get to the apartment, but he was gone. The woman must have warned him we were coming,*' one of the two sitting at the table commented.

Adrian Holman, the senior figure remained stony-faced as he nodded in agreement. 'It wasn't the lawyer. We really shook him up and I don't believe Connoly would be too happy he moved in on his ex-partner while he's paying all the bills. Basili admitted as much and already told us he would like to see Connoly captured and taken back to serve his time. He's an ally, not our enemy. I think it's more likely the woman, Caroline Burton. With Connoly back in the pen she could continue the status quo.'

'So, Connoly has plenty of money stashed somewhere? It shouldn't be too hard to find his money tree and cut it down, surely?'

'Our man took precautions when he deserted in '63 and set up shop here. He built a fortune from money, jewellery and gold he had stolen when he deserted, but it's all controlled from blind trusts in Hong Kong. Basili can draw down on the funds as required, but otherwise he has absolutely no control. That luxury apartment Burton lives in belongs to Connoly and is also controlled through a trust. I would lay money Basili's days as his lawyer are about to be cancelled.'

'Can I suggest you have a word with the local constabulary to help us track him down? After all, he can't have got far.'

'Lister,' Holman replied to his young associate. 'We're in enough trouble without broadcasting we are carrying on an illegal manhunt in a country where we have absolutely no jurisdiction. No, we've got to find Connoly all by ourselves.'

'And we terminate him with extreme prejudice, to use the American expression?'

Holman grunted. 'No, we give him the chance of telling us where two barrels of some mysterious material are located and secondly what happened to LeBrereton and that IRA character and his son. If he complies we take him back home, if he doesn't we have got to remove a potential terror threat.'

'Chief, why get blood on our hands? I don't like the thought of killing someone just because we think he's a terrorist. I'm not prepared to do that. Why not deliver him back to the authorities and let him rot?'

'Because I have my instructions Lister, but I will seek further advice if we catch him. And that's the most annoying aspect of this whole business. We know Connoly has something a certain agency wishes to recover, but I don't know what it is. My instructions are to locate him and either get him to divulge what he has in his possession, escort him home, or kill him. I believe if he does tell us what we want to know, the next instruction will be to make sure he ceases to breath. We are duty bound to follow orders. We've been following LeBrereton's activities for some time and when that O'Brien character became involved with him, we assumed there had to be some connection between LeBrereton and Connoly and sure enough there was. They were both at Maralinga for the atomic tests. LeBrereton was Connoly's commanding officer. Connoly deserted and although LeBrereton managed to dodge the flack for a number of years, he was eventually court-martialed for gross negligence in not being able to account for two highly classified missing items. He signed a declaration stating he had personally consigned the material back to the U.K. Atomic Energy Commission, but the lie eventually caught up with him when it was discovered he had left Maralinga days before he claims to have put his signature on the consignment note. At first the proverbial hit the fan as the hunt started, but when no explanation could be given and in the light of the serious nature of the consignment, the powers-that-be decided to sweep it under the carpet. All was quiet for a few years until some inquisitive busybody decided to look more thoroughly and discovered the reason for the sudden shutting down of enquiries. The Officials Secrets Act was invoked and the whole business simply removed from further scrutiny – buried for all time. LeBrereton had already been censured – the army is always looking for scapegoats, so he was quietly court martialled. He was permanently stuck as Captain LeBrereton, with no hope of advancement, so at some point, resigned. We know LeBrereton and O'Brien organised the car crash that released Connoly and we know he organised false passports.'

Alan Lister screwed up his face and shook his head in exasperation. 'This is absolutely screw-ball chief. How did they get out of the country on false documents? Who the hell is behind this pulling the strings? Who tipped us off about what's going on and what's happened to LeBrereton and the other two? How did we know Connoly is on the loose and in Melbourne?

Holman had been considering the question ever since his team had caught the flight from Heathrow. He had been given a partial explanation for the sudden assignment to find Connoly. He found it curious some operative locally knew Connoly was in Melbourne and LeBrereton and the O'Brien's had disappeared. He was not being told the whole story and he resented it. Someone was standing in the shadows, watching their every move.

'Although your questions are valid Lister, I can't answer them. I've been given specific orders and we must disregard we are being watched by some of our own. Now, let's look at this clinically. We can't rule out Basili, but I doubt he's playing a double game. As I said, I believe it's Caroline Burton. After all, she owes him certain allegiance.'

'What about the son? Could he have tipped off Connoly?'

'It's certainly a possibility. From what I observed of him, he's very aggressive and protective of his mother. Perhaps, one of you could have a word with him. Maybe he doesn't like Connoly and if his mother's not within earshot, he'll let it slip as to where he's headed.'

'It's Connoly we have to find and not the other three?'

'That's correct. My advice is O'Brien hired a truck and digger in Adelaide and they gave a destination that has proved to be false, although I'm sure this whole case has something to do with the atomic tests at Maralinga. Why something that occurred more than fifty years ago is now of the highest priority, I don't understand. The truck and machinery were never returned so we can assume they're still out there in that wilderness with three dead people. Connoly has killed before and will no doubt kill again, so we've got to be careful. He's got absolutely nothing to lose.'

'What's in those barrels that so important? They've been out there since '63.'

'It would be interesting to know, but that's not my brief. Whatever it is, has got someone in London worried and ours is not to reason why. Our instructions are not to fail in locating Connoly and the barrels.' Holman cursed under his breath. Why couldn't MI6, Scotland Yard's SO15, SIS and the Australian Feds combine forces and track Connoly down? After all, he was a convicted murderer on the run. It was clear he had murdered again – LeBrereton and the O'Brien's had disappeared. Connoly was now in Melbourne, so he had to be the sole survivor. Would he tell Caroline Burton where he had gone? She would eventually break down under pressure and he intended to apply plenty of that. It was out of the question he would have told his lawyer of his intentions. Basili was reduced to a nervous wreck when questioned in front of Burton and soon turned against his client. And Connoly would hardly put his son in danger at such a young age. No, Connoly was the sole guardian of the knowledge and it was him he had to find and find quickly before he disappeared again.

'So, what's our next move sir?'

'It's the son, he's the contact with his father. It's he who we should keep tabs on. The question is, how will he establish and maintain that contact? It has got to be through an intermediary. I want a tail put on him from the moment he leaves home until he returns from school in the afternoon. I want to know who is friends are and more to the point, any particular friend. He's sure to have someone he's knocking around with.'

It was two weeks later when Lister walked into Holman's office. 'I think I've found the link we've been looking for. Martin Bellamy is very close to a certain Idris Barzani, son of Kurdish immigrants who own a small bistro not far from Bellamy's apartment. They spend a lot of time in each other's company and are both in the same football team. I watched them last week and they were certainly the standout players shooting home one goal each.'

Holman nodded. 'Good work Lister, now all we have to do is find out whether that's Burton's link to Connoly and that may prove difficult. My enquiries through some old agency contacts who've migrated down here, has turned up nothing. The phone tap on Burton's home likewise, so I imagine she's been alerted to that danger by Connoly. She only goes out to the shopping centre and a weekly game of tennis, but otherwise leads a very quiet life. Basili has refused to co-operate any further, despite my pleadings to do so. He's been thrown out of her apartment and warned not to return. He admits it was Connoly who issued the warning, so he's aware our man is within striking distance. We know he administers Connoly's finances through an offshore trust arrangement, but I would imagine that will soon be stopped. No doubt he's regretting tipping us off Burton had received a visitor confirming Connoly was alive and well and back in Australia. He thought we would quickly apprehend and transport him back to England and he would be able to continue with his cosy arrangement in Burton's bed.'

Lister shook his head with a dismissive shrug. 'Typical bloody lawyer, pretending to be protective of the client, while shagging the client's mistress and protecting his own income. I..I believe...'

Holman cut him off. 'Have you checked out the Barzani's? How long have they been here? Are they citizens and what property do they own? Try and get a full rundown on Barzani senior's background. Any run-ins with the law? Anything at all that may lead us to Connoly, but keep it discreet. We have absolutely no authority to be here doing what we're doing and if the police start sniffing around, or the media gets interested, we've got to terminate immediately and get out of the country. This matter is high-priority, but extremely sensitive. We've probably got a month at the most to get results or we have to pull out and go home.'

'I'm well aware of that sir, but it's difficult to operate with a hand tied behind our backs. I don't know how I'm going to access police records for anything on Barzani without disclosing some detail. Property records and immigration data is far easier, but police pull the shutters down when unauthorised people start delving into records.'

'Leave that with me Lister. I maybe able to get some information without raising too many eyebrows.' Holman picked up the phone while signalling to Lister the meeting was over. He did not want his partner to overhear any conversations. Fifteen minutes later he called him back into his office.

'We may have struck gold Lister. A Jamal Barzani was picked up on a speed camera at Paynesville last week. He was riding a motorbike registered to him and the address on his driver's licence checks out, it's the bistro young Bellamy frequents.'

Lister nodded. 'Not a strong lead sir. I take it Jamal is Idris Barzani's father and was photographed riding a motorbike over the speed limit. That doesn't tell us where Connoly is hiding, or does it?'

'It may be a very strong lead Lister. You see, Jamal Barzani is no longer with us. He died a year or so ago. The son is too young to hold a licence, so the question is, who was riding the bike? My contact tells me there are no other Barzani's registered at that address, just the son and his mother Ayrana Barzani. She owns the bistro and a house just down the road. It's my bet Connoly was the rider of the bike.'

'And he could be another thousand miles away by now sir. He could be anywhere?'

'We're going for a drive tomorrow, so pack a spare shirt and a toothbrush. I've got a hunch Connoly's luck is about to run out. I've just looked on the map and Paynesville is located on some lakes right on the coast. It's billed as a popular unspoiled low-key holiday destination, just the sort of place our target could disappear into. My bet he's still got a pad he's owned since he became Martin Bellamy and evolved into a very successful property developer, amongst other pastimes.'

'Why not phone the local council and ask if he's a ratepayer, or more to the point, why not drop around and have a chat with Basili. He would surely know what property his client owns?'

'No Lister, I feel like a ride in the country. Connoly may well know someone in the council and the lawyer is equally as dangerous. He may try and redeem himself by tipping Connoly off, we're onto him. We can't afford anymore stuff-ups. Get a hire car, we're off in the morning.'

# 25

*L*ister walked across the road and got into the car. 'No joy there sir, absolutely no record of a Connoly or Bellamy owning any property in the area. This place is God's waiting room. All retirees waiting to shuffle off to the check-out counter.'

'What about Barzani?'

Lister rolled his eyes, opened the door without answering and walked back across the road. Ten minutes later he emerged with a broad smile. 'Bingo,' he said as he got back into the car. 'A mile or so out of town, turn right at the first side road and it's the last house set back in a cul-de-sac.'

Holman nodded, started the car and pulled away. 'Did you ask if the place was occupied?'

'I did, but the lass behind the counter said she didn't know. She said there are a lot of holiday homes in the area only used during the summer months. I didn't want to make myself conspicuous by asking too many questions.'

Holman drove in silence and turned down the road as instructed. The house was barely visible, appearing deserted with an overgrown garden which had not been attended to in years. There was no sign of a motorbike, but he could see a closed garage in the rear. He turned slowly and headed back out to the highway. 'We'll come back tonight and pay a surprise visit. In the meantime, let's go and have lunch and relax down by the lake.'

It was dark when they slowly drove back along the road, the only sound the gravel under the tires. They passed two houses about one hundred metres apart, one in darkness while the other was showing a glimmer of light from a behind a drawn curtain. The Barzani house was in total darkness as they slowly came to a stop.

'Looks as though no one's home sir,' Lister said peering down the driveway at the outline of the house. 'I can't see any lights.'

'Let's go for a walk. You watch the front while I go around the back. Be careful, Connoly is a bloody dangerous individual. We're only going to get one crack at him.'

Holman took a pistol out of his jacket pocket as he walked around the back and took a tentative step onto the rear verandah. He stood to one side as he twisted the the door handle. It was unlocked. He pushed it open, his hand holding a high-power torch as he flashed it around the small interior. He quickly went to the front door and let Lister in, signalling for him to check two bedrooms.

'It's all clear sir. I think we've struck out on this one.'

'Well, someone's been here recently,' Holman replied as he opened the fridge and pointed to a steak lying on a plate, along with a carton of eggs and a packet of bacon. 'If this is a holiday joint used by the Barzani's they would not leave food in the fridge. In fact they would not have left the fridge on. I believe our boy is around here somewhere. Go check that garage for the bike and if it's empty put our car in there. We'll both wait in the house tonight and see if we get lucky.'

'Okay, time to move,' Holman kicked the armchair with the sleeping figure. Lister was delivering a soft melody of snoring, occasionally interrupted by a snort of a change in breathing patterns. They were supposed to be taking it in turns to keep watch, but several times during the night Holman awakened with a start imagining he had heard a sound, before drifting off again. He could see the first light of day streaming in through the voile curtains. Connoly had eluded them. He had obviously seen them earlier and could be anywhere, but it would be miles away from here.

'Do we wait around chief, or do think our man has moved on?'

Without a reply, Holman got up and went out into the yard slowly walking the length of the driveway looking at the sandy ground before pointing to some wheel tracks. 'Those are ours, but look at those single tracks. If I'm not mistaken those belong to a motorbike. He's gone, that's for sure. Either he saw us yesterday or someone tipped him off. So much for the lunch by the lake. I should have taken the chance and barged in yesterday. My only concern was he was armed and I wasn't sure what we'd be walking into.' He kicked the loose sand and swore. 'Okay Lister, get the car out and let's head back.'

They were passing the next house up the road when Holman pulled over and got out. He walked up the driveway towards an old man bending down pulling out weeds in the sparse garden. Suddenly, a terrier leapt off a verandah chair and rushed up barking in its most menacing tone. It stopped within a metre of Holman and bared its teeth with an angry snarl.

'Oh stop it Pudding,' the figure demanded as he turned and straightened.

'That's some watch dog – real savage.'

The old man laughed as he tipped his straw hat back and wiped his forehead with the back of his hand. 'The only thing he can savage is a sausage. His teeth are like mine – down to the gums,' he laughed. 'But he's a great companion and watchdog – no one gets near the house without him giving a warning. Just like my departed wife, he sits on the verandah while I do all the work. What can I do for you?'

Holman pointed to the Barzani house. 'Have you by any chance seen anyone at that house in the last week or so?'

'Yes I have. If I'm not mistaken you were here yesterday, weren't you? I saw your car from the kitchen window. Well anyway, when you drove away he called in and picked up his motorbike and said goodbye. He stored it in my garage because he said the Barzani's was full of junk. Thoroughly nice fellow and great company.'

'Did he say where he was going?'

'Travelling north to Sydney, where he said he lives. I'm also off home this afternoon. I only come down here to check on the place every month, pull a few weeds while Pudding waters the trees and chases birds. Say, why do you ask? You're police are you and he's wanted, is that it?'

'Something like that,' Holman replied as he turned to walk back to the car. 'Thanks for your time.' He got in, slamming the door. 'Jesus effing Christ,' he cursed as he hit the steering wheel in frustration. 'We had him and lost him because of our stupidity. We should have rushed that house yesterday. He was there.'

Lister raised his eyebrows. He had caught the plural – he was also shouldering the blame. Suddenly, he was not the subordinate, but an equal. 'So what now?'

'Let's go eat and then head on out. There's no use hanging around here, because he isn't coming back. This one is not going to look good on our record. We were a hundred metres from our man and we stuffed up.' Lister remained mute.

It was late afternoon when Lister, lost in thought, slowed the car and made to turn.

'What the hell are you doing?' Holman had been dozing with his head against the window pillar and awoke with a start.

'We're going back sir. You can have my resignation if I'm wrong, but I've been thinking about this character, Declan Connoly.' He held up his hand as Holman was about to interrupt. 'Hear me out. This is only a theory, but we're dealing with one very smart individual. Let's start with the motorbike and why he hid it in the old guy's garage using the excuse Barzani's was cluttered, which we know wasn't true. My theory is he did that so he could nip through the woods at the back of the property, retrieve his bike and take off if we suddenly came through the front gate. Secondly, why did he befriend old Fred, to give him a name? I believe he quickly determined Fred was only there for a few days and would head back to his home, wherever that is.'

'I don't get your drift?'

'Hang about sir, I'm coming to that. Connoly takes off, saying he's heading to Sydney, having been told by Fred he was also leaving the following afternoon, which is today. I believe that's what you told me. That means Fred has probably left for home by now. Now consider what Connoly's thinking was in regard to the motorbike. Unless I miss my guess, that's exactly what is happening right now with Fred's house – he's gone home and Connoly's moved in. He knows Fred will be gone for another month, because that's what Fred told you and obviously told Connoly. He's got the perfect lookout if we, or anyone else comes snooping again, which we won't as we have assumed Connoly is headed for Sydney. He will know if this, or any suspicious cars roll slowly down this quiet road looking for signs of life in Barzani's house, but I'll lay money he won't be returning there. He will hole up in Fred's house while he plans his next move. There's no hurry, as Fred won't be returning for a month. Why don't we go back and see if that dog barks tonight? My guess all will be quiet because Fred's gone and Connoly is in residence.'

Holman nodded. 'You may have something there, it's worth a try.'

It was dark when they slowly pulled up a hundred metres away and Lister switched off the motor. 'Let's walk from here sir. We don't want him getting away this time. If Fred's still here, that bloody dog will let us know. If there's no barking and there's a light on, we've got our man. At least that's my theory.'

Holman raised his eyebrows and nodded without comment. He should have thought of it – Lister would soon have his job if he was right. They could see a light showing through the slatted blinds as they drew level, having quietly walked the hundred metres towards the house. Both drew their pistols as they started to walk across the lawn to the front door. They could hear a TV, but there was no sound of the anticipated alarm.

'I'll go around the back. Give me two minutes and then knock on the front, but be careful, don't shoot Fred if you've got this wrong.'

He was standing on the bottom step when he heard a noise from inside and the back door burst open. There was no sound of a dog and the person looking back over his shoulder at the front door wasn't Fred.

'Declan Connoly, move back inside please,' he said pointing the gun into the startled face. With a panicked expression Connoly swung towards the front door.

'No, no, that's well covered. Sit down or I will end it right now.'

Connoly slumped into the lounge chair in resignation. 'Who tipped you off?'

'No one tipped us off. You happened to be booked for riding a motorbike belonging to a dead man. It was pure luck and yours has just run out. Tell me, what happened to LeBrereton and the O'Brien's. Did you kill them all?'

'No, whoever you are.' He had no doubt the gun pointing at him was owned by an Intelligence agent – the accent was a giveaway. The game was up – there was no point in running any longer. His head and thinking was scrambled as he knew he had only minutes to live. He decided to put the history file in the correct sequence. 'I shot LeBrereton after he killed the O'Brien's.'

Holman smiled thinly. 'So, you did locate the barrels he was after?'

'Yes, I did, but I knew immediately I was being double-crossed by LeBrereton. Despite his assurances, I knew I was on the hit list. He should have shot me first instead of the O'Brien's, because it gave me enough time to escape. I'd taken the keys out of the truck so he couldn't leave the scene. Eventually, he went to sleep and I shot him with his own gun in self-defence.'

'I'll make a deal with you. I want you to show me where those barrels are and then you're free to go. You've got a new identity, so you can move back in with Caroline Burton.'

Connoly burst out laughing. 'Don't give me that. I would have no problem in taking you back to Maralinga, but I'm not stupid enough to believe I would ever emerge.'

'So, you won't pinpoint those barrels for us?'

'No, they can stay where they are. They've been responsible for enough deaths and mine is just another to add to the list. And I don't feel like being dragged back to serve out the remainder of my life sentence.'

'Have it your way Connoly, but I'm not going to kill you. Believe me, I would if I could, but too many questions would be asked when the local police discovered your corpse and identity. You are going back to serve the remainder of your sentence in some stinking prison.'

Connoly laughed cynically as he shook his head. 'Kill me now, because you're not taking me back. They won't let you drag someone kicking and screaming onto an international flight for twenty hours. Finish it now.'

Lister was standing behind him as Holman nodded. Connoly tried to fight the stranglehold around his neck as he gradually lapsed into unconsciousness. Holman retrieved a small container from his jacket pocket, removed a retractable syringe and snapping the top off a small vial of liquid, slowly drew it into the syringe.

# 26

**2019**

'*Have you ever heard of anything with the tag line of fox?*'

'No, other than they're dynamite if they get into the hen house. What's the interest?'

Carl Mazarin pushed his chair back and nodded at his computer screen. 'I don't know yet, but I think I've caught the thread of something interesting.'

Ric McCord leaned across to look at what his colleague was indicating. 'How many times have you picked it up?'

'I first noted it in an email coming out of Syria months ago. It was a smiling emoji under the heading *"beware the geese - the fox strikes at night"'*

'And the message?'

Mazarin shook his head. 'That's all it said. And then I saw it again about a week later from another server I traced back to Iran.'

'How many languages do you speak.' McCord chuckled as he swung back to his computer. Mazarin never ceased to amaze him – he never projected his talents – they were only delivered in answer to a question.

'Farsi, which is Persian. Also Arabic, as well as Russian and all the main European languages. I learned Farsi and Arabic as a kid when my father was stationed in Iran as an oil engineer. I've always found languages easy.'

'And that's how you came to be here in the Pentagon trolling through millions of emails every day.'

'It's the only job I could get in my condition - it keeps me off the streets.'

'I'm sorry Carl, that came out the wrong way.'

Mazarin dismissed the apology with a shrug. He cursed the loss of his legs in Syria. He was there in an advisory role ostensibly trying to protect the civilians from the islamic terrorists and the murderous al-Assad regime. He had served two tours in Afghanistan where he saw dozens of American and allied soldiers become the victims of concealed improvised explosive devices - IED's - cut down in ambushes or murdered by trusted advisers turned rogue. His command of languages had seen him posted to Idlib in northern Syria as a non-combatant adviser. It was there, a week before he was due to pull out and head home, he stumbled and was unable to avoid stepping on the child's doll in the dirt. He saw the ground underneath the toy begin to erupt, but felt nothing. He woke up in Landstuhl, the U.S. Army hospital in Germany, minus his legs.

'The emails are only in Arabic then?'

'No, they're translated into Turkish, as well as every European language. I've hooked into dozens of servers worldwide with an algorithm I developed. Except for the one

I've attributed to Iran, the messages derive from untraceable servers to meaningless recipients – none of them register on our data base as being dangerous. At first I thought it was just some bozo playing an aimless game, but I've noticed the responses becoming more prevalent. The recipients merely forward the email back to the sender, by way of acknowledgement they've received it. There are never any additions, comments or attachments. The message is never altered – it just goes around in a continuous loop.'

'The Chinese are not in the loop? It's not them up to something?'

'No, it's not their style. I'm certain this game originated in Syria, but what it means or what message it's meant to convey, I am yet to determine.'

McCord nodded and went back to his screen. Mazarin was a brilliant cryptographer, but distant and totally immersed in his work. It was as though he was trying to contact some alien force, so intense was his telepathic concentration.

Mazarin picked up his phone and punched in an extension. 'Hi Gene, have you or any of your team picked up anything on intercepts regarding the mention of someone by the name of *fox* or any mention of that animal?'

'You're a bit slow off the mark Carl. We've been watching it for some time. It's coming out of northern Syria – it could be the Syrians, the Iranians or even the Kurds. Maybe the Turks are involved for some reason – I really don't know.' Gene Mathias was the head of the Signals division in Homeland Security which tapped into phone and cell connections world-wide. 'We've taped every message if you would like to read them. We can't see anything sinister so far, other than the usual propaganda.'

'And nothing from the recipients of the messages?'

'We've tracked them all. They're all Muslims of course, but all appear to be clean with no apparent terrorist connections. Mind you, that doesn't mean a thing. They'll turn on you in the blink of an eye and slit your throat. We've intercepted a few we suspect may have originated in Iran – they had the bloodied hands of the MIOS, written all over them. However, I wouldn't put too much trust in that source – someone maybe just trying to fit them with the crime to stir trouble. Other than that, without a solid lead, there's nothing I can add.'

'What about Mossad?'

'They're aware of it of course. Nothing gets through their filters, but they are getting concerned.'

Mazarin knew Mathias had no problem in intercepting messages and phone calls from operatives of the Iranian Ministry of Intelligence and Security- MOIS. The organisation was infiltrated by Mossad, the Israeli intelligence agency. That was one of the weaknesses in Iranian intelligence – there was a significant historical population of Jews within Iran. It consisted of a large underground who had run the bazaars for a thousand years and although oppressed over the millennium, had not lost their allegiance, nor their covert willingness to assist their Jewish faith. The notorious Evin prison outside Tehran was the final address of countless numbers of the faithful who had been identified as traitors to the corrupt regime. Once in Evin, death was not a quick process. The torture was prolonged until a *'confession'* was obtained to ensure release from the hell by the hangman or a bullet. As well as being despised by the Jews, the majority of the younger intelligent Iranians, accounting for more than half the population, detested the ruling Ayatollah, the corrupt Mullahs and the

Basiji, one of the five forces of the Revolutionary Guard - the murderous thugs who kept the theocracy in power. Nothing was secret in Iran and Mossad were masters at exploiting that weakness.

'Have you checked with anyone else?'

'The French have confirmed their interest, the Germans wouldn't admit to it, but that's par for the course with them and the Brits just laughed it off with the comment fox hunting is banned in England. Serve them right if it rears up and bites them on the butt. However, I've got an excellent MI6 contact who really knows what's going on. I'll be in London next month for one of our scheduled meetings, so I'll have time to take him aside and get the guts of what he knows, if anything.'

*E*dward Lascelles rose and extended his hand to Gene Mathias, indicating the seat opposite in a quiet London restaurant. 'It's great to see you Gene.' The pleasantries covered small talk and the respective families until their orders had been taken. 'Now what's this all about?'

Mathias could see his lunch companion was nervous. It was the clipped answers and strained expression which gave him away. Lascelles knew exactly the subject Mathias was about to broach. 'Have you heard of the increasing chatter coming out of Syria about an impending threat code-named *fox*?'

'I have heard it mentioned, but we're not taking it seriously. It will have originated in Iran and is just some of the usual crap it distributes. As you're aware, they're always about to deal a death blow to the great American satan.'

'So you think Iran is the source?'

Lascelles shrugged and threw us his hand with a dismissive gesture. 'I simply don't know, but it's from somewhere in that region.'

Hmm.... Ed, why is it I don't believe you? What are you guys hiding we should know about?'

Lascelles sat back in his chair with a startled look of offence. 'I don't like your tone Gene. We've always been an open book with your mob. What I'm telling you is we are no doubt aware of the *fox* threat, but are not giving it much credence at this stage.'

'Yeah, well we are. After ignoring the warning signs about 9/11, we now run down every rat hole to see where it leads. And I can smell a rat. Mossad are aware of *fox*, as is the French DGSE, the German BND, which last week came clean after weeks of denial, and we even got an enquiry from the Italian AISI. And you're telling me this is a joke, put out by a bunch of mad mullahs?'

'I'm not suggesting it's a joke, but even if I was aware, I'm not cleared to discuss it. You would have to take it up with the director and as you know directors only speak to their opposite numbers, not to the hired help.'

Mathias nodded his head as he picked at his Dover sole. He knew it was delicious. J. Sheekey in St Martin's Court was his favourite restaurant when in London, but it wasn't registering as such today. His mind was elsewhere – he couldn't taste a thing. Lascelles had just given him the message - they knew something and it scared the hell out of them.

'Yes, that's probably a good place to leave it Ed. I'll be seeing the chief when I get back. I've briefed him already as to what I know. I think he'll be real interested he's got to take it to the highest level and speak to your boss direct.'

'Don't misconstrue what I just said Gene. I wasn't implying I know anything. I'm merely stating it's probably best to direct any enquiries to the appropriate person and that isn't me.'

Mathias held up his hand. 'Don't worry Ed, this lunch never happened. We've known each other long enough and traded notes to our mutual benefit, but I can sense you're holding out on me and Homeland Security is going to be really pissed if you're not telling me something that will have a direct impact on the lives or security of American citizens. We don't want another 9/11 sneaking up on us because you Brits know something we don't.'

'I've already given you the truth, I don't know anything definitive.'

Mathias leaned over the table, his face flushed with anger as he pointed his fish knife in Lascelles' face. 'There you fucking go again,' he hissed. 'You know something, but it's not definitive. In other words it scares the crap out of you, but you won't call in the cavalry until you determine you can't handle it yourselves. It must be a truckload of Semtex you're juggling?'

Other than attracting the attention of other patrons and the manager to the outburst, Lascelles remained completely impassive.

'Just answer me one thing before I shove this knife into your eye in frustration. Iran has nuclear devices and perhaps the worst of all, biological weapons which could wipe out millions just by releasing something into the air or waterways. They could have buddied up with that little shit in Moscow and got themselves a tanker load of novichok. Is it any of those, because if it is and you don't tell me when it's about to happen I will personally hunt you down and kill you. And that goes for all your family.'

'Calm down Gene, you're getting carried away. I should really report you for making such a threat. How do you expect our co-operation when you carry on like that? However, I will give you an answer to your question and it is no, I don't know anything about a *fox* or a threat with that name and even if I did, it's way above my pay scale to discuss it with you. Sure, Iran is expanding its nuclear threat, but not even the mullahs who profess they can't wait for the day they'll ascend to join Allah in his glorious heaven, are crazy enough to put a missile or chemical weapons into the hands of terrorists. It would be quickly identified who supplied it. They know if anything like that happened, Iran would be nuked and cease to exist within the hour. Not even Russia's mister-muscles Putin would be insane enough to let them have novichok.'

Mathias put the knife down and picked up his beer with a sigh of relief. He nodded and grinned wryly at the agent. 'Thank you for that Ed. That takes a load of my mind. However, perhaps I was being too narrow with my enquiry. I should have.....'

Lascelles anticipated the question and cut him off. 'Let me make it clear, no one we know of is going to launch a nuclear warhead, unleash some hideous organism into waterways, or is intent on throwing a drum of novichok from a great height. Is that clear enough?'

Mathias held out his hand and laughed. 'I apologise, but I had to know and I knew you would give me something. And you have and it's something to do with an elusive threat named *fox*. I saw you flinch when I mentioned it. You never know, I might find some reference if I Google it? We'll get to the bottom of it and I warn you, it better not be at the cost of American lives when the balloon goes up.'

Lascelles shook the extended hand. Mathias had bought the deceit, or had he?

'Lunch is on me.'

'It was always going to be Gene. My expense account doesn't match yours and after all, you invited me. I would like to make it absolutely clear, I've given you nothing you and your colleagues would not know already.'

'So, there's no terrorist organisation going to come out of left field and catch us off base then?'

'The world's full of crazies wanting to kill someone for thrills. Just look at the number of gun-carrying psychopaths running loose on your patch. America is not a safe place. You can be shot dead for just knocking on someone's door without being invited. The second amendment is a licence to kill, but it's too late now to re-write it. The crazies are in charge of the asylum. There's no point in being only worried about left field - you've got a 360 degree threat at home.'

The remark stung, as it was meant to. 'Well, I'll be going Ed. When I'm next over the lunch is on you.'

'Tea and a shared cucumber sandwich in the canteen it is then.'

Lascelles watched as Mathias paid and walked out. He sat finishing his beer aware of two men observing him from a table across the room.

'What did you get?

'Nothing really definite Carl, but I left with the clear impression my contact was in denial. I would call it pre-panic mode. It may have just been a coincidence, but I could have sworn a Mossad agent was in the restaurant we lunched at. I recognised him from a meeting I attended in Paris a few years back. I'm going to recommend to the director he put the heat on his opposite number in London. It's vital we find out what the Brits are so worried about, that they won't tell us.'

'While you were in London I noticed something interesting happen. It could have been intentional or something new to keep us confused. A new email chain letter appeared mentioning the word *vulpes* instead of *fox*. It was from a different server, but I've traced it back to Syria.'

Mathias shrugged. 'I don't know what to make of that. Is that another threat emerging, or more shit from Iran?'

'*Vulpes* is the Kurdish name for a *fox*. The message was headed *vulpes is about to leave its den*. I believe that is a definite warning something is about to happen. I don't care how we do it, but someone is going to have to take a big stick to the Brits. We simply cannot afford another 9/11.'

# 28

*T*hree people entered the spacious room in an old manor house comprising the hospice. Connoly was clearly excited at their arrival. Although he had only seen his son a couple of times over the years, he had never met his grandson.

'Don't get excited Dad, just take it easy,' Martin Bellamy said to his dying father, as the emaciated frame struggled upright in the large reclining hospital chair. His release from prison a few weeks previous had been act of compassion on the part of the parole board. The life sentence had expired years before, but his annual applications for parole had been repeatedly rejected without explanation. The knowledge he possessed and refusal to comply were a risk that could not be tolerated. He was no longer a threat to anyone. He was old and clearly incapacitated, his voice weak, but his mind unaffected. The diagnosis of terminal lung cancer meant he only had weeks at the most, to live.

'This is your grandson Declan and his partner, Zehra.'

Connoly motioned the couple to come closer. He held out his hand to his grandson as he studied him. He was the mirror image of his father in stature and looks, but missing was the expression of invitation and openness. The blue eyes were cold and fixed, the way an assassin would look as he was about to pull the trigger. Connoly knew the expression, he had looked at it every day while shaving.

Zehra took the old man's hand and gently rubbed it with feeling. He felt an immediate attachment of warmth and connection, the eyes drawing him in with their intense magnetism. The olive skin of her face was perfect, matching the aquiline features of her Indo-Persian heritage. Her long black hair draped down over a colourful shawl, pulled around the shoulders of her heavy overcoat to counter the winter chill.

'Zehra is from Syria. Declan has been in the Middle East for a couple of years with Medecins Sans Frontieres working as a medic.'

Connoly nodded and smiled at his son, with the strained effort of someone in pain. He motioned for them to sit down as he lay back and momentarily closed his eyes. They sat quietly for ten minutes as the eyes constantly closed and then opened with a start as the dying man fought to overcome the soporific effect of the morphine feeding into his arm through the attached canula.

Martin Bellamy reached out and took Zehra's arm. 'Let's leave these two alone for awhile. We'll go and have lunch and come back in an hour. '

He had been surprised his son wanted to meet the grandfather he'd never known and never enquired about until he received a reply to an email in which he had mentioned his grandfather's  impending death. Declan had replied the next day saying he and Zehra were booked on a flight to Manchester and asked him to meet them. Martin had picked them up and driven them to the hospice in York where he had admitted his father after his discharge from Britain's most notorious prison, Wakefield, established in 1594.

It was a long flight from Melbourne - he had a well established business and the years just evaporated until the onset of guilt whenever he received the occasional letter which his wife inevitably ghost-wrote a reply to on his behalf. It was the shock of receiving the email from prison authorities saying he could take his father into his care, or he could remain in the prison hospital until the final moment.

He had shuddered and his eyes filled with tears as his father was placed in an ambulance, the mere shadow of the man he had last visited two years previous. Martin had been constantly at his father's bedside since he arrived. They had reminisced, laughed and cried together, particularly when Caroline's name was mentioned - the loyal partner and mother who had died some five years previous.

Declan was looking out the window at the drizzling rain and overcast sky when he felt a feeble hand squeeze his. He had lost track of time, but time was not something he could afford, nor had the patience to endure. He smiled thinly at the living corpse - he had seen too many dead and dying to express any real emotion.

'Hello there stranger, I must have dropped off. Where are the others?'

'They went to lunch granddad.'

'Ah my boy, I'm so pleased to able to put a face to the letters you have been sending over the past few years. I don't understand how you got them through the system?'

Declan grinned broadly and leaned over in a whisper. 'The same way you got your letters out. The governor doesn't know it, but his secretary is married to one of Zehra's countrymen. She was appalled at the way you've been treated and agreed to help, although it took time to organise. It was her job to read and censor all letters to and from high-security prisoners, so our correspondence always got through. She would have wound up in a cell if she had been discovered.'

'Ah..ha.. that explains everything. In that case, I owe her a debt I can never repay. I'm so pleased you came – my time is nearly up.'

'Tell me granddad, you were locked away for life. What did you do to deserve that?'

Connoly groaned as he tried to pull himself up. 'I was convicted for the murder of a fellow soldier. It was an accident, but I knew I would be charged with murder so I bolted. I got away with it for a number of years, but finally they caught up with me. The rest is history.'

'I don't understand? Life for murder is generally only ten years with good behaviour. You were locked up for a lifetime – it was inhuman treatment. You must have been a really violent prisoner to serve that long?' Declan did not wait for an explanation, he had a pressing need, but realised he would have to be careful. 'You were at Maralinga for the atomic tests weren't you? Did your sentence have anything to do with that?'

Connoly slowly nodded and pulled a pained smile. 'Of course it did. That was the sole reason I was sentenced to life with no chance of parole or release. It's the very reason you are here, isn't it? You are going to release the vixen?'

'Yes, they locked you away because they wanted something you're not prepared to give. I'm bitter at what they've done to you and I'm going to make them pay.'

Connoly had a clairvoyant view into his grandson's mind. In the short time they had been together he had been able to read it. It was the natural ability of any long-serving prisoner to quickly assess the weaknesses and strengths of any inmate and particularly those with psychotic and psychopathic traits - Wakefield was full of them. In his early years he'd been subjected to physical violence and more serious attacks from inmates he felt he had befriended. He finally rejected all close company and confined himself to his solitude and the escape the library and gym afforded him – he always kept fit and aware. It was live or die violently in this place for the unwary. Two attacks were almost fatal. In one instance a prisoner had been placed in his cell. A memory came flooding back as it drifted from the presence of his grandson.

'You two can talk about the people you've murdered,' the screw had said as he locked the door and walked away.

Connoly immediately realised what he was dealing with and the danger. 'You've been sent to kill me, haven't you?'

The prisoner had been lying on his bed reading. He propped himself up on an elbow, looked across and smiled. 'That's a nonsense question. I'm in here for a long stretch, just like you. Why do you ask?'

'Because you're in the wrong wing of the prison. This wing is for dangerous psycho's, which you're not. We've all got *"never to be released"* stamped on our files. And the strange thing is I've never heard of you. I'd get your backside out of here before something nasty happens. You're a Judas and you know what happens to them when word gets around?'

The prisoner lay back and continued reading. The smile had disappeared. He knew he would have to move quickly now his cover was blown. It was a dangerous assignment, but he'd been guaranteed early release if he was successful.

You never knew when an attack was going to happen, but you were always on your guard. However, you could not be aware every moment of the day, nor who in this isolated wing would suddenly snap and come at you with some implement of death. Connoly could defend himself, his aggressive attitude earning him a sole-occupant cell although it contained two bunks. That was until this prisoner was suddenly introduced when there were other vacant cells in the wing. The comment of the jailer rang in his ears. He was sure any attack would happen at night within the next few days. This prisoner wanted to get the job done and disappear, but he was an amateur in the world of professionals trying to stay alive.

It happened when least expected. He had just got up and was standing relieving himself into the toilet pan when he sensed a movement behind him and something sharp being pushed into his back.

'That's your last piss Connoly.'

With a swift movement he spun and took hold of the arm wielding the shank, sharpened to a needle point from a small metalworking file. He twisted it down and away from him in one savage movement, a skill he'd been taught as a raw army recruit all those years ago. He jerked the arm back and over his assailants head, bringing it down again with full force in a twisting action that could not be countered. The weapon spun out of the hand and across the cell, followed moments later by a scream of pain as the arm was snapped in two with a compound fracture. The assailant continued to scream and sink to his knees trying to support the useless arm held together by skin and torn ligaments. Connoly kicked him in the side of the head, immediately silencing the noise. He grinned to himself. That was something the army did teach him. The would-be assailant had no time to react if a gun or an object was being pushed into your back – spin in one fluid movement, grab the wrist and complete the action before the assailant could thrust a knife or pull the trigger.

# 29

*Connoly slowly opened his eyes as the incident faded. He would never be able to defend himself again, but where the assailant had failed, time was about to deliver. He looked at his grandson – the cold penetrating gaze confirmed he was looking at a killer.*

He dismissed the thought his grandson was a plant, inserted by whatever authority controlling him, to find out whether the dying man would finally disclose what he knew. He was determined not to give them that satisfaction, but to leave a lingering doubt that would only diminish with the passing of time. 'Tell me who you really are boy? Who sent you here?'

'No one sent me granddad. I came to see you.'

'But will you betray me, or are you really my grandson?'

'I am your grandson, although I didn't arrive here with that name. I used the passport of a dear friend who died in Syria, Aras Barzani. We were both Kurdish resistance fighters. I've been in Iraq and Syria witnessing the slow annihilation of the Kurds by the Turks and Russians, assisted by the Americans and European allies. Now the Americans are pulling out, the Turks will massacre the Kurds as they did the Armenians more than a century ago.

Connoly held up his hand. 'You say Barzani? Your father had a friend with that name, Idris Barzani.'

'Aras was Idris's son, a great friend of mine from school in Melbourne. Soon after we graduated he took me to Turkey for a holiday. However, we were pulled into the Kurdish cause and went to fight in northern Syria. Aras died by my side, his head exploding like a melon, the result of a sniper's bullet. We looked very similar, so I borrowed his passport just in case the authorities here wanted to detain me. So far so good. I intend to go back.'

'And Zehra - is she as committed?'

'Yes granddad, she will fight to the end against the oppressors assisting Syria or Turkey to wipe out the Kurds.'

'And who do you hate the most – the Turks, Assyrians, Americans or the Russians? You can't hope to win against those odds.'

'I hate the British for what they've done to you and I hate the Turks. You can't imagine the unreported massacres they're inflicting in order to make sure the northern Syrian lands don't fall into Kurdish hands. I also hate the Americans and their money which maintains and fans the conflict.'

'You've got a lot of hate in you boy, but I can understand. I would love to hit the British where it hurts most.'

'And which establishment would that be granddad? Just give me the power and I'll do it.'

Connoly laughed as he tried to control a coughing fit. 'How do you know I have any power? God, I wish they'd turn the machine up a notch or two, so I could end all this. If only I could reach it.'

'I know you have the power because Aras heard his father and Dad discussing it occasionally when he was growing up. I tried to bring it up with Dad, but he always got angry and told me to forget about it. Apparently, it concerns barrels of highly dangerous material you stole. I believe Aras really thought he would unite all the Kurds one day and become the supreme leader. We were childhood friends and remained so until the day he died. We started to spread the word that *vulpes* would emerge to wipe out the Turks. *Vulpes* is the Kurdish name for a fox. We had no idea the rumour would spread so quickly - we were put in the position of having to deliver or suffer the consequences and humiliation. We both planned to go back to Maralinga next month in attempt to locate the material you confirmed in your letters does exist. However, for all that, I cannot understand why you didn't you tell the authorities where the barrels were and save yourself from all the trouble?'

'Plain Irish stubbornness boy. I hated being pushed around. I could never accept authority and when I was jailed for accidentally killing a policeman and being brought back here and jailed for murder of a fellow squaddie, I just lost the plot. Finally, they threw away the key when three escorts taking me to Wakefield died in a road smash and another three disappeared when I took them back to Maralinga. I was also subjected to two attempts on my life in Wakefield. Finally, they must have given up trying in the knowledge I would end my days in prison, which will prove to be the case.'

Connoly looked around the dismal room. 'I suppose this is as good as any place to die. At least it's warm and I can order a whisky anytime I push the bell. I'm not going to die of alcoholism in this place.' Blood flecked spittle sprayed as he laughed at his gallows humour.

'So where in England would you suggest as a target?'

Connoly coughed and spat a gob of bloody phlegm into a towel. 'The City of London boy. The very beating heart of European finance and the world's biggest money exchange. But the collateral damage would also take out the whole of London and much of the surrounding countryside. There would be no blast and no damage to buildings or infrastructure, but the population could never return. Britain would be finished as a nation, the panic indescribable.'

Declan's eyes lit up in surprise. 'Good God granddad, if it's not a nuclear bomb, what is it you have hidden and where exactly is it?'

'If I tell you, will you promise to do something for me? You won't like doing it, but you must.'

Declan smiled and slowly nodded. 'I believe I know what you want granddad and I promise I'll do it. I also promise they will pay for what they've put you through.'

'Good, hand me that pad and I'll write down some directions,' he said indicating the bedside table. He scribbled instructions and drew a rough map. 'There's only one road in and you can't miss the old tower. You won't need any heavy equipment, or a metal detector as they're only a few feet from the base of the tower. You'll be able to retrieve them by yourself, but go prepared with plenty of water. It gets very hot out there,' he said tearing out the page and handing it to his grandson. 'I know it looks like a pirate map, but this one does lead to the treasure. That's it boy, now keep your promise and do it. I'm tired.'

The old man closed his eyes as his grandson walked around to the drip and turned the control up to maximum. He watched as the pain killing fluid went from a timed drip to a steady flow. It only took a few minutes until he heard his grandfather's death rattle and the final exhalation of breath. Declan felt no guilt or remorse – death was a natural occurrence. This was what his grandfather had requested and he had simply hastened the inevitable – he had fulfilled his promise. He turned the machine back to its original setting and left the room.

# 30

*They were walking away from the crematorium when Martin turned to his son. 'If I didn't know better, I would have thought you had something to do with his death. One minute he was alive and an hour later he was dead. Did you assist it? Don't worry, it was a brave thing if you did. He had begged me to do it, but I couldn't.'*

'Death can be very sudden Dad. I've witnessed it many times as a medic.'

Declan had evaded his question, but he decided not to pursue it. 'Did your grandfather tell you what you wanted to know?'

'That's a strange question Dad. Why do you think I wanted something from him?'

'Because son, you'd never met him, but you rushed back from Syria to be at his bedside. Although I haven't seen you for a number of years, I can almost predict your motive. You may not be aware, but I know you and Aras Barzani were only briefly attached to Medecins Sans Frontieres – I checked. When Idris told me his son had been killed and you had witnessed it, I knew you were actually engaged in the fighting. For which side, I didn't have a clue. I haven't said anything until now because it's your life, but why don't you leave that scene of death, bring Zehra home and get involved in the business. I have been in control of your grandfather's trusts for a number of years now and he's certainly left you very wealthy.'

'I will come home for a week or two and show Zehra around. If she likes it we'll stay, otherwise we'll head back to Turkey, or rather Kurdistan - an ancient civilisation the Turks want rubbed out completely. And now the Americans are pulling out, they will no doubt achieve their aim. The party-going toss-pots at the United Nations will turn a blind eye and any positive action will be stymied by Russia and China in the Security Council. The Kurds don't have a hope of winning with the Americans walking away.'

'Are you sure you haven't been brain-washed? Their problems are nothing to do with you. Get the hell out of it now.'

Declan put his hand on his father's shoulder. 'Dad, Zehra is my life. We will marry, have children and settle somewhere in the Middle East. I'm sorry, but I won't be joining you in the business.'

Martin stopped and turned to his son. 'I guess I'll have to accept that. Will you answer my questions?' He already knew the answer, but wanted to confirm he was completely lost to his son - there was a barrier which would never be reconciled.

'Yes Dad, granddad told me what I wanted to know and I did assist in his death. He made me promise. If you intend to take it further, I'll just have to accept that, but in defence he was only days away from death and I did what he asked.'

'Would you do it for me?'

'Yes, I would if you were in the same condition. Why prolong the inevitable for a few hours of pain and misery? Palliative care is a nonsense. I made a pact with a dying man. I know you will find it hard to believe and I won't compromise the person who assisted, but granddad and I had been corresponding for the past three years. I knew when he told me he had lung cancer it would be terminal, but I had no idea the end was so close. He knew what I wanted, but wanted to meet me face to face. In return he wanted something and I did it. I suppose he didn't think I would have the moral strength to help him die. Aras Barzani and I had a similar pact, if one of us was badly wounded and about to be taken by the Syrians, Daesh terrorists or the Turks - one of us would pull the pin on the grenade and we'd go together. However, in his case he died, not in a skirmish, but from a sniper's bullet in an area supposed to be clear of any enemy. And I've managed to survive to date - *inshallah*. It was a memory I'll never erase.'

'You really have become hardened and tough. I don't know you anymore. I will always love you as my son, but I feel I've lost you. And no, I don't condemn you for helping your grandfather, but what I'm really afraid of is what he's given you. I pray to God you won't do what I now realise you're capable of. Does Zehra know about this?'

'Yes, she's aware and in complete support. She has already lost her two brothers and father to aerial attacks on their village. Her mother is still alive, but completely deranged. Zehra would have no problem in shooting any Turk, American, Russian or Brit on sight. I've witnessed her slit an Islamic terrorist's throat as he begged for mercy.'

# 31

*iles Hartigan was leafing through an old file when he looked across the desk at a colleague. 'Have you ever come across the name Nicholas LeBrereton?'*

Ashley Spencer looked thoughtful for a moment before shaking his head. 'No, nothing rings a bell. How far are you going back?'

'Way back, before our time. It appears we were running him as an agent. He was originally in the army, but resigned when he realised there was no hope of advancement. It looks as though he was closely connected with an IRA operative by the name of Emmett O'Brien. LeBrereton and O'Brien were sent down to Australia on some secret mission and completely vanished off the radar. O'Brien's son Dinny was with them and he also can't be accounted for.'

'What was LeBrereton doing down there?'

'This file doesn't disclose that, although it refers to another marked "Top Secret." Due to the length of time since this file was consigned to records I've asked for access, a request that's been denied.'

'So, who asked you to open it again?'

Hartigan pointed his finger at the ceiling. 'I got the urgent summons from above yesterday. There was another person accompanying LeBrereton and the O'Brien's, a convicted murderer by the name of Declan Connoly. He was a thief, deserter, murderer and escape artist, until we finally ran him to ground. He was sentenced to life in Wakefield prison, Yorkshire. He must have been a real violent individual to have copped such a long sentence. Anyway, he's just died.'

'So, what's the chief asking you to investigate? Hasn't MI6 got better things to do than dredge up old cases? What the hell if all the players are now deceased? Connoly probably murdered LeBrereton and the O'Brien's, but he's now fallen off his perch, so it should be relegated to history.'

'That's what I assumed. The purpose of the trip down to Australia was for LeBrereton and O'Brien to recover some obscure highly dangerous goods left behind from the Maralinga atomic tests. The concern was the material would fall into the hands of the IRA to be used for a major terrorist attack on London, but O'Brien was not aware LeBrereton was working for us. It would appear we were using O'Brien as a decoy, for what reason I cannot understand. Maybe, Connoly was cosy with O'Brien and was really an IRA sympathiser. There had to be some compelling association or background. Connoly was being escorted to Wakefield prison when he escaped with the help of O'Brien and LeBrereton. It unfortunately, resulted in the deaths of two of our agents plus a prison official. Connoly was given a new identity, an obscene payout and along with the other three was waved off at Heathrow. This file states Connoly murdered his fellow travellers, although he claimed it was self-defence. The strange thing, he was never brought to trial for those deaths when we brought him back, but packed off to Wakefield under the Official Secrets Act – his file marked *never to be released*.'

'Maralinga. That's the cause of all the cancers and related diseases and deaths our veteran's have unsuccessfully sued the government for?'

Hartigan nodded. 'That's correct. Connoly was stationed there during the latter period of those tests. LeBrereton was his commanding officer, but Connoly deserted after murdering a fellow soldier. He was known as a thoroughly unpleasant character suspected of murdering a Dion O'Brien, Emmett's son, in Liverpool a month or so before he was shipped out to Australia with the army.'

'Where's this going? You mean to tell me we organised his release? He's then implicated in the deaths of three more people and when he gets to Australia he knocks off another three. Is that what you're saying? It's no bloody wonder they hauled him back here and threw away the key.'

'Maybe he had good reason Ash. Whatever the mission was to Australia, LeBrereton was given a clear directive Connoly was never to make it back – it was to be a one way ticket. It's right here in this report. My guess is Connoly twigged to that, or LeBrereton got careless and paid the ultimate price. The O'Brien's were just incidental damage.'

'That begs the question of when he was eventually picked up, why he wasn't bumped off then? Why waste money on a return air ticket?'

'That's what I thought, but I suspect this goes much deeper. I suspect the trip back to Australia had nothing to do with IRA guns or explosives. Connoly knew something we were desperately trying to get him to divulge. But there the trail ends. The report hits a brick wall. I know the answer is in that secret file I've been denied access to on national security grounds. When one talks about nuclear explosions, you naturally think of such a device falling into terrorist hands, such as the IRA in those days. But that was in the dark ages before the internet. You can find out how to build a nuclear bomb by Googling it these days. I've checked and nothing exists at Maralinga except a few concrete cairns marking the sites of the explosions we carried out. Nothing has changed since we pulled up stumps and finally took the last man out in 1965.'

'I can't help you with that one Miles, but it does sound curious. Connoly is dead, so what have you been asked to follow up on?'

'It might be the sins of the father being visited on his son, or in this case, the sins of the grandfather being visited on the grandson. When Connoly did a runner from the army, he assumed the name Martin Bellamy. Connoly aka Bellamy accidentally killed a cop and once again tried to abscond. At the time he was living with a woman by the name of Caroline Burton who, while he was in jail for the killing, bore him a son. She named the boy, Martin Bellamy after his father. It was this son who flew in from Australia when they released the old boy from Wakefield. Bellamy had him admitted to a hospice for the final couple of weeks of his life. He had terminal lung cancer. I checked Bellamy out with the Australian Federal Police and he comes up completely clean. And this is where I've been asked to pick up the thread. The grandson, Declan Bellamy arrived to be with his grandfather on his deathbed. He entered via Beirut.'

'Lebanon is a very picturesque country. Maybe he was on holiday?'

'True, but Bellamy wasn't on holiday. He entered Lebanon under the name of Aras Barzani with a valid Turkish passport, or so it would seem. He then arrived at Manchester using that identity. We had an all ports detention notice out for Declan Bellamy, not Aras Barzani, so we missed him. I spoke to a contact of mine in the Turkish Intelligence Organisation half an hour ago, He's going to dredge up what they've got on Barzani and phone back.'

'Why don't we pick up Declan and find out whose passport he's travelling under? He would still have it on him.'

Hartigan was about to answer when his phone rang. He picked it up and acknowledged the caller. 'Ahmet, that was fast, What can you tell me?' In five minutes he had scribbled on a notepad, offered his thanks and hung up. He raised his eyebrows as he turned to his colleague.

'Well, that was interesting. Barzani has a valid Turkish passport, but not for long if they catch up with him. He's in fact a Syrian Kurd who the Turks want to wipe out as they control some large areas of northern Syria now the Syrians have lost control. The Kurds want their own national identity which the Turks have always been hell-bent on denying. The Americans have been protecting the Syrian Kurds up until now, but it's clear what's going to happen if they pull out. Anyway, Barzani comes from a long line of Kurdish terrorists, as Ahmet called them. His grandfather, Jamal Barzani emigrated to Australia years ago and when the heat died down applied for a new Turkish passport as Kurdistan is not a country. However, the old boy never returned to Turkey. His son Idris and grandson Aras managed to regain Turkish identity and passports after getting good report cards from Australian authorities. At that stage the Turks were trying to make peace with the Kurds, hence the relaxation of restrictions on granting citizenship to the relations of former so-called terrorists. However, the attitude has since changed and an arrest warrant is now out for Aras Barzani, so I don't like Declan Bellamy's chances if he's caught carrying Barzani's passport. I shudder to think of what will happen if he falls into their hands and slung into Diyarbakir prison. Those military psychopaths running that place are the masters of torture. Somehow, they're aware of Bellamy's connection to Barzani and are looking for him. They have labelled him as a terrorist because of his connection to the Kurd's, and want us to arrest and deport him if he's still here.'

'No chance of that. We would refuse extradition on the grounds he's likely to be executed. We don't have him marked as a terrorist, or do we?'

'Too late for that. Bellamy slipped through our surveillance and departed for Rome the day after his grandfather's funeral. We don't want an argument with Turkey now he's out of our hair. He's an Australian citizen so he can go to them for help, which I doubt he would get. It's interesting, he departed Manchester with a woman by the name of Zehra Kermandi who was holding an Iranian passport. It was strange – at the mention of her name Ahmet hesitated, but then said she was of no interest to them. I could tell by the hesitation he was looking at a computer screen and what he saw, he wasn't prepared to share with me.'

'So, all this doesn't really answer the question as to why Connoly was taken back to Australia under an assumed identity. And it doesn't really explain what LeBrereton was up to. Someone within this building must know something, although it was years ago. It had to be to do with the atomic program. I would say you've got to get access to that secret file and the only person who can authorise that is the man upstairs.'

'That's the problem Ash, he asked me to background the Connoly file, but he won't authorise me to dig deeper. I have a strong suspicion Connoly was mixed up in something MI6 wants to keep off-limits. All I can assume is whatever it is, must be tied up with Connoly's presence during the Maralinga tests. It must be one hot issue if we pursued him for more than fifty years and now we're interested in his grandson.'

'Have you had a word with SIS or SI05?'

'No, and Crowther warned me off. He's aware I have a close contact in SIS and nearly had apoplexy when I mentioned the SI05 anti terrorist squad at Scotland Yard. He indicated this was an MI6 problem from years ago and he wanted it to remain strictly in-house at this time.'

'Sounds as though the chief upstairs has got you running around in circles just to occupy yourself – giving you the message you should retire and take up lawn bowls.'

Hartigan ignored the facetious comment. 'Ahmet did ask me whether I'd heard the name *vulpes* mentioned in regard to a terror threat. Have you by any chance?'

'Nope,' Spencer replied as he returned to his computer screen. I don't even have a clue as to its provenance.'

'*Vulpes* is the name for a red fox in Kurdish. He seemed very concerned about it and it's one of the reasons they would like to get hold of Barzani or Bellamy, as their names have been mentioned in connection. I didn't think it necessary to tell him Declan Bellamy appeared to be travelling on Barzani's passport. They can work that out when and if they get hold of him.' He twirled the pen between his fingers before finally tossing it on his desk and rising to get himself a coffee.

artigan dropped the file onto his superior's desk as he sat down. 'We'll, I'm up to date on Declan Connoly sir, but as we both know something is missing?'

Linton Crowther gave Miles Hartigan a jaundiced look. 'And what is that?'

'Why did we chase Connoly for nearly fifty years and incarcerate him until a few weeks before his death?'

'He was convicted of murder and was implicated in many others. He got what he deserved.'

'I don't accept that sir. I've heard it on the grapevine, one of our agents was dispatched to York and Wakefield prison when we discovered Connoly had an inoperable cancer. However, we were too late in whatever was supposed to happen – he died before we could talk to him. We were wrong-footed in that we had no idea, until weeks later, that Wakefield released him into the care of a hospice for the dying. It would appear we got word his grandson could be intending to visit the old man. Again, we stuffed up in that the grandson was supposed to be detained on arrival. No one thought he maybe travelling on another passport. I maybe drawing a long bow, but I believe the agent was dispatched to speed up Connoly's demise and make sure whatever secret he held went with him. He wouldn't tell us after more than fifty years, so we wanted to make sure he did not impart his knowledge to his grandson. If the grandson had managed to talk to his grandfather before the agent arrived, he was also to be given a quick exit by whatever means the agent considered viable, without drawing too much attention. And I can only read into that, the intention was to make sure Connoly died before his grandson arrived. Connoly was going to tell the grandson something of vital importance, so important, it was imperative it never happened. And if we hadn't been so lax in not detaining Bellamy, we would now have been able to charge him with murder. We have really screwed up on this one.'

'Murder?' Crowther replied raising an eyebrow. 'Who did he murder?'

'I believe you know sir - he murdered his grandfather. Declan Bellamy was with his grandfather alone for over an hour. He turned the old man's morphine drip to maximum, witnessed his death and then switched it back to the correct level. However, this was quickly noticed by the medical staff and reported. It filtered quickly back through the system to your desk and that's where it will remain buried. I am on the right track, aren't I sir?'

Crowther straightened in his chair. 'Pure speculation Hartigan? You shouldn't be listening to rumours – we deal with facts in this agency,'

'Sir, MI6 exists on rumours that turn into suspicions which are either proven groundless, or investigated further. It is clear Connoly has hidden something from the Maralinga tests. The question is what was he hiding we are still trying to recover after more than half a century?'

Crowther nodded as he considered his best agent. 'You're too bloody smart Hartigan. You are correct. We are still trying to recover some lost material contained in two small barrels, but I cannot tell you what it is. However, this much I will tell you – the contents are diabolical. Connoly would never tell us where he had hidden them, but in my opinion they must be still at Maralinga. Yes it's true, I did send someone to assist in Connoly's death before his grandson arrived and your assumptions are valid. It came as a shock when I found out young Bellamy had assisted his grandfather's departure.'

'Interesting, but how did the doctor establish that? It was a pure guess on my part.'

'The doctor who signed the death certificate got suspicious and started looking at the morphine dose being applied for the pain of the cancer. Connoly was on a controlled drip automatically administered through a pump. Sometime during Bellamy's visit, when it's been established he was alone with his grandfather, the pump volume was accelerated to deliver a sudden burst of an additional twenty five milligrams of morphine before being turned back to the normal.'

'The old boy must have really gone out on a high,' Hartigan commented dryly. 'But how did the doctor know the lad did it?'

'Simple maths Hartigan. He knew exactly what should have been in the morphine bottle when it was attached and noted the contents on Connoly's death – there was twenty five mills unaccounted for - but it could only be in the one place and it hadn't been spilled on the floor.'

'So, Bellamy is looking at a murder charge, but the problem is he's now out of the country. Surely, we're not interested in pursuing him?'

'No, we're not and the doctor was advised to sign the certificate as death due to natural causes, the result of terminal lung cancer. We have no further interest in Declan Connoly, but we do have a real interest in his grandson, Declan Bellamy. I'm as certain as I can be that Connoly told young Bellamy exactly where he buried those barrels.'

'Do SIS or SI05 know anything about this sir?'

'No, not at present, but you know how hard it is to keep the genie in the bottle. However, I wouldn't count on it, because as you know we don't meet and share notes.'

Hartigan gave an imperceptible shake of his head. The two major agencies in conjunction with Scotland Yard were supposed to be acting in the national interest, but in this instance they were out of the picture for a reason he could only speculate – MI6 had stuffed up - they wanted to fix it without the other agencies knowing.

'In reference to Bellamy and his connections in Turkey and Syria, have you ever heard the name *vulpes* mentioned?'

'Where did you hear that?'

'From a contact in Turkish Intelligence when I was making enquiries about Declan Bellamy who appears to have assumed the name Aras Barzani – at least that's whose passport he's travelling on. Both Aras Barzani and Declan Bellamy were born in Australia in the same town and I assume, must have known one another. The only conclusion I can come to is Barzani is dead or Bellamy is using his passport. They were born weeks apart and it would be very easy to substitute a photo. Anyway, Barzani is a Kurd and someone the Turks are very keen to talk to. It was at the end of the talk with the Turkish operative, he asked me if I knew anything about *vulpes*. I've since Googled it and it appears to be the Kurdish botanical name for the common red fox.'

Crowther was suddenly paying attention. 'That's correct. I suspect it's the acronym for some terror group or threat. I wouldn't be too concerned about it as it's way out of our sphere of interest. Barzani doesn't interest us either, he's Australia's problem. Keep in touch with your Turkish friend.'

Hartigan returned to his desk and looked blankly at the computer screen lost in thought.

'You look dejected Miles. Did the old boy bawl you out?'

Hartigan shook his head. 'No, nothing like that, but I'm sure he's not giving me the complete picture. He knows something, which he feels is too sensitive to relay to the likes of me. After all, he's been around since Adam was in short trousers, so there can't be too many things he doesn't know about. And I've got the distinct feeling he knows something about a terror threat calling itself *vulpes*. It was his reaction when I mentioned the name. One moment he was glued to something he had started to read and the next he'd snapped to attention. I'm convinced he's aware of the red fox and what it represents.'

'My advice is to stop spinning your wheels Miles. You've found nothing of real interest and Crowther's signed off on it, so bury it.'

Hartigan had no intention of burying it. Crowther's reaction had raised his alert antenna to maximum. He picked up his mobile and jacket. 'I'm going out for an hour Ash.' He walked out onto the street to be clear of Spencer and make a phone call. The little pub two blocks away was empty except for a few early drinkers. He ordered a coffee and went to sit in a quiet corner where he could not be overheard as he dialled a number.

'Terry, it's Miles Hartigan. How are you?'

The greeting was met with a chuckle. 'Hello Miles, what can I do for you?'

'I thought we might get together for lunch and chew over what we did last summer.' Hartigan and Terence Maynard knew their phone conversation would be recorded or overheard by someone in MI6, SIS or SI05 or some clandestine foreign intelligence service. London was a bristling hot-bed of intelligence operatives from every major economy vitally interested in the the world's leading currency centre. Money attracted the whole spectrum of international intrigue from legitimate to illegitimate of governments and business with their varying degrees of influence and levels of associated crime, from the oligarchs of Russia, to the despots of the Arabian peninsula and Asia, to the vast scale of Chinese money with its insatiable demand for influence and advantage.

They had both served in the army, both opting out and both joining the intelligence service within weeks of one another. They were firm friends, but not that firm they could discuss what was going on within the respective organisations. It was simply too dangerous if they wished to prolong their careers and retire on a full pension.

'Where?'

'The usual. I'll see you here in half an hour.'

Hartigan dialled another number and identified himself with a code. 'I would like to put a trace on a couple of people please. One is an Aras Barzani and the other is a female, Zehra Kermandi. They flew out of Manchester for Rome two days ago. I want to know their final destinations. I believe it could be Beirut. This is urgent.'

Hartigan often amused himself when waiting for someone by observing his surroundings and in particular anyone who appeared to be out of place. Not that it mattered in this case because it was already well known to their superiors both he and Maynard were friends and associates from their days in Afghanistan. Both had served two tours before deciding the campaign to get rid of the Taliban was a lost cause, a scourge that could never be overcome. The allies would fail as the Russians had done thirty years earlier. They had each resigned their commissions.

Maynard walked in right on time. He did not acknowledge Hartigan as he ordered two pints, walked over and put one down in front of his friend.

'You look thirsty.'

Hartigan grunted. 'I've got a thirst for information Terry. What do you know about an organisation or threat going by the name of *vulpes*?'

'Steady on - I thought this was a quiet lunch to discuss leisure pursuits. We could have at least chewed the fat for a few minutes until I worked out what you were after. I didn't know it would immediately launch into a full official enquiry.'

'Ah, stop screwing around Terry. You know bloody well I don't shout lunch unless I'm after something. Now tell me, what do you know about *vulpes*?'

Maynard was about to answer when Hartigan's mobile rang. 'Oh, excuse me Terry, this is a call I've been waiting for.'

Maynard sipped his beer as Hartigan got up and walked out of earshot. 'Melbourne, and he had a woman with him?' Hartigan had raised his voice in a momentary lull in the voices in the rapidly filling lunchtime trade restaurant.

Maynard clearly heard the remark, but pretended to be distracted as he strained his ears. He heard a name which he immediately recognised, as Hartigan closed his phone and returned to the table.

'What are you grinning at?'

'I thought MI6 and SIS operated within strict Chinese walls? Liaison is only to be authorised at the highest level. Do you have that clearance?

Hartigan looked at his friend sharply. 'What do you mean by that crack. I was just enquiring about some friends who are holidaying in Australia – nothing to do with the job.'

Maynard nodded as he took a sip of his beer. 'What are you buying me for lunch?'

'Sausages and mash if I get what I want?'

Maynard leaned over the table. 'You know all too well I can't talk to you about any ongoing investigations, Miles.'

'This is not anything new Terry, it's something from way back which was thrown at me. It's to do with a character by the name of Connoly, or a threat by the name of *vulpes*. You must....'

Maynard held up his hand and cut him off. 'I can't discuss anything like that with you Miles, even under the most secret of Masonic oaths and assurances you may offer me. I'd advise you just to forget it. I can tell you now, it will cost me my job if you pursue it further.'

'Then you know I've been working on it?'

Maynard nodded. 'I do, but that's as far as I'll go.'

'You've already informed your superior of this meeting, haven't you?'

Maynard met Hartigan's glare of accusation. 'You know I cannot break wind without reporting it. Yes, it's on record this meeting is taking place. Now, why don't we forget about what SIS may or may not be interested in and just enjoy lunch. Just drop the line of questioning, otherwise I will get up and walk out.'

Hartigan could see his friend was not bluffing. Maynard had been given strict directions, which if he transgressed, would immediately cost him his future.

Hartigan picked up his knife and pushed his fork into one of the thick sausages covered in his favourite gravy which had just been put down in front of him. He would have to admit defeat – his friend was not going to be of any assistance.

'I feel as if I've been assigned to put my hand into a badger sett and expect to be immune from the consequences. *Vulpes* is similar - I know it's dangerous, but I don't know it's size or the threat it poses. It is something I'm sure SIS must be aware of.'

Maynard did not look up as he cut into a sausage. 'You've got it in one Miles, then again you have always been very astute. You should move across to SIS.' He held up his fork and pointed it across the table. 'That remark was not to be meant as facetious and I apologise if you considered it so. You're wasted at MI6.'

Hartigan was disappointed - they had been friends for a long time and had faced dangers together. Both were hardened professionals and knew how to play the game. Anything said in confidence would never be repeated. They finished lunch by discussing general topics, but they both realised they were uncomfortable. The meeting and its purpose was over. Hartigan followed Maynard out of the pub where his friend hailed a cab. As they waited for it to pull up, Maynard whispered in an almost inaudible tone while pretending to look straight ahead. 'You're good Miles. You are one jump ahead of us with Aras Barzani and Zehra Kermandi. Like you, we missed them here because we were also looking for Declan Bellamy and had no idea he had assumed Barzani's identity. The surprise is, they're in Melbourne – you're ahead of us with that one. What's Bellamy doing down there, is the question?'

Hartigan swung around in surprise, but Maynard was already inside and pulling the door closed. He waved as the cab turned and headed in the opposite direction. Hartigan smiled to himself as he walked slowly back to his office. The meeting had not been a complete loss, but he was unsure what he could do with the information. It looked as though MI6 was playing bridesmaid to SIS. What was the reason? Why couldn't the two agencies work together?

It was the following morning when he got the summons - he knew immediately what it was about. Linton Crowther was not in an accommodating mood when he walked in, the expression on is face, clear.

'Yes sir, you called me?'

'Sit down Hartigan. You and agent Maynard from SIS had a meeting yesterday. What was its purpose?'

'He's a long time friend of mine from army days sir.'

Crowther shook his head in frustration. 'You know damned well what I'm getting at Hartigan. What was the purpose of the meeting?'

He could see it was pointless lying. Maynard would have also been called in to give an explanation. And he knew his friend could not afford to implicate himself in a lie when their explanations were cross-referenced.

'I wanted to know whether SIS is also on the case. In short, I want to know what is the material we are trying to recover and what is the threat it poses? You won't tell me, so I thought I would call in a favour from a friend. Terry

Maynard refused to tell me a thing and warned me to go no further, otherwise our lunch meeting was over.'

'And by inference, you believe I'm not being truthful with you. You should be entitled to the whole story?'

Hartigan looked at his superior trying to think of a diplomatic answer, but it was pointless. Crowther could read him and was expecting a straight answer – he detested sycophants.

'Yes sir, I believe you aren't telling me the full story and I believe I am entitled to be put in the picture.'

Crowther glared at the agent and then smiled thinly. 'Have you ever killed anyone Hartigan? And I don't mean in the line of duty as a soldier.'

'No, I haven't, but I often felt inclined when I was young and angry with the world. I got into my fair share of pub and football fights, but that was about the sum total until I served in Iraq and Afghanistan.'

'Would you kill someone if I authorised you to do so?'

Hartigan sat back in the chair and drew in his breath. He was stunned at the question. 'I....I don't know sir. It would depend what the assignment was and my moral attitude to carrying it out. I would consider it, if it meant saving lives or avoiding an impending major threat, like an act of terrorism.'

'It's both. MI6 bungled a major operation years ago early in my career. An agent had been assigned to locate certain items. The agent, Nicholas LeBrereton was to terminate Declan Connoly, along with a key IRA man and his son once the items had been located. Instead they all disappeared with the exception of Connoly.'

'I read about LeBrereton in the files you gave me and I must say I wasn't impressed with his background. Resigned from the army after some unexplained blot on his copy-book and then we engaged him.. I can only assume he was somehow mixed up with the IRA and Connoly sir.'

'Connoly and LeBrereton go a long way back. The introduction of Emmett O'Brien and the IRA was a stroke of luck at the time, but a disaster in hindsight. Connoly was in the military prison at Colchester and was due for transfer to Wakefield in Yorkshire from which he would never be released. We knew that once in there we would lose him for all time. He would become more hardened and we were desperate to retrieve what we knew he alone knew the whereabouts of. It so happened we were tapping phone calls from the prison and we discovered the Commandant, Colonel James Nesbitt was an IRA sympathiser and well known to O'Brien. O'Brien had some sort of long-standing vendetta against Connoly and Nesbitt had agreed to tell O'Brien when Connoly was to be released so an old score could be settled. That plan was short-circuited when we planned to step  in while he was being transported to Wakefield. We didn't count on Connoly causing an accident resulting in the deaths of three people. We had no idea LeBrereton, who had only been with the agency a short time, also knew O'Brien and knew exactly where Connoly was hiding. LeBrereton put forward a proposal he would approach Connoly and in exchange for a new identity and a substantial payment, he would get Connoly to lead him to the location of the missing goods. He was banking on the fact Connoly would agree otherwise he would be going to Wakefield, or he would be dealt with by O'Brien. It was a drawn out death in the first instance or a quick demise in the second. The man didn't have much choice. LeBrereton's brief was to kill Connoly and O'Brien if the goods were found, but something went badly wrong.

'If I'm following your drift, you now want me to locate and dispense with his grandson? What about the woman he's travelling with?'

'She's just as dangerous if my guess is correct. You see, I believe Connoly has told his grandson where the items are buried. That's why Bellamy has gone back to Australia. But there is a confusing note to all this. Bellamy may have known already, because the rumours of a major terrorist threat to London, or possibly New York have been rampant in Syria for some months now.'

'So that's where *vulpes* comes into the picture. What is it about that name, that's got the Turks and Kurds so excited?'

'It's not only them – the Americans are having a fit. For fifty years we have managed to keep a lid on it, while coping with Connoly. Death was a permanent shadow of that man. However, about six months ago we got intelligence from a Kurdish contact that Istanbul and London and possibly New York would be wiped out unless the Kurds were granted statehood and all that part of northern Syria and parts of their ancestral lands in Turkey were folded into the State of Kurdistan. You can image the Turk's reaction to that if they found out. Huge areas the Kurds have captured in northern Syria would disappear into the new State.'

Hartigan laughed. 'Surely, no one has taken the threat seriously? It's absolutely preposterous.'

'No, it's a serious threat. And it was we Brits who caused the present problem. At this point in time we believe neither the Americans nor Turks know what the threat is, other than its name is *vulpes*. If the truth gets out, the whole world will become aware of what we're trying to hide and that's not a legacy I want to be saddled with.'

'In short, you want me to fix what LeBrereton stuffed up all those years ago. You want me to kill Declan Bellamy in the hope the problem will be buried for good? But what guarantee he hasn't told someone else and you are dealing with a mythical Hydra – chop one head off and another immediately replaces it?'

'Precisely the problem, but I've no option but to start chopping in the hope the beast will finally die.'

'Then if I'm to accept, and I don't mind telling you I will have no concerns about dealing with Bellamy or his partner, if they pose that much of a threat. But I would like to be put fully in the picture. What is *vulpes*? What is the threat?'

Crowther slowly shook his head. 'I'm sorry Hartigan, I can't and won't divulge that. It's just too sensitive. If you fail to catch Bellamy or he catches you, I'll have to assign someone else and then when he fails, someone else and so on. It's then likely the real threat will become common knowledge.'

'Is SIS also assigning someone to coat-tail me? I don't want to be looking over my shoulder.'

'Richard Hamilton at SIS says it's our stuff-up from way back and they don't want to know anything about it. LeBrereton was our man. We've got to clean up the mess.'

Hartigan knew that would not be the case. Obviously they had assumed Bellamy and Kermandi would head back to Beirut. But now his raised voice of surprise in the pub with Maynard had tipped SIS off, Bellamy and Kermandi were in Australia. 'Where do you want me to start and when?'

'You're already booked on Emirates to Dubai and then direct to Melbourne. I have alerted an agent in Melbourne – he's been assigned to track their movements. I've no doubt Bellamy will be head for Maralinga. What we want to locate has still got to be there. I can't stress on you enough, how important this mission is.'

'Am I to ascertain whether Bellamy has located the hazardous material in question, because that's what it obviously is, or do I literally shoot him and Kermandi on sight? And what are the repercussions in regard to myself? I don't want to be charged with murder.'

'You have absolute authority and complete immunity as far as we are concerned. You make the hits and then fly out immediately. The authorities down there won't have any idea as to the reason for the killings, or who carried them out. They will be kept totally in the dark and it has to remain that way. However, if you are caught with the smoking gun in your hand you're on your own, so don't fail.'

Hartigan screwed up his face. 'Why don't we hand it over to the Australians? If these two are so dangerous, why not spread the net and responsibility? It just doesn't make sense. Why not bring them in under the tent?"

'That's just the thing, they don't know what we are trying to locate. They don't know two extremely dangerous terrorists are on their patch. If we did inform them and they managed to apprehend them, it would take years to get them before the courts. The civil rights movement down there is very strong and it will take powerful evidence to get a conviction for terrorism in view of the fact Declan Bellamy is a citizen and has a clean record. And we have absolutely no proof he's involved in possible terrorism. Australian Signals, our equivalent number for the control of espionage will not take it seriously unless we confide in them and then the shit will really hit the turbine. I can assure you it would quickly rise to the political level with government intervention. We can't afford that publicity.'

Hartigan exploded in exasperation. 'Sir, are you telling me neither Signals nor the government of Australia have any idea what *vulpes* is, or represents? That's just unbelievable?'

'And that's the way it's going to stay Hartigan. They don't know and neither do you. I've given you the assignment - it's up to you whether you accept. But I reiterate, if *vulpes* ends up in London, Istanbul or New York, those cities will cease to exist as habitable entities. There now, I've given you a clue as to what you're dealing with.'

# 33

*Three weeks later Miles Hartigan was sitting opposite his superior once again. 'I'm afraid we've drawn a blank sir.'*

'But, I don't understand? Didn't our agent keep tabs on them?'

'Yes, he tracked them to a private house in the suburbs of Melbourne. But, there the trail ended. Despite around the clock surveillance, they simply disappeared. The house was owned by a Kurd who had emigrated to Australia some years ago, but he denied any knowledge of what happened to them after they left his place. I found there is a very strong presence of Kurds and disaffected Turks living in Melbourne who wouldn't lift a finger to assist the Turkish government. They've all suffered some form of oppression, or their family or relatives have. Anyway, I've just checked with my contact in Interpol and have been informed Bellamy and the Kermandi caught a flight from Jakarta to Beirut two days ago. There's no record of them leaving Australia for Indonesia. My guess is they chartered a plane out of Darwin to any of dozens of small airports in Indonesia – it's only a couple of hours flying time. Corruption is rife and it would be just a matter of slinging a few bucks to gain transit visas from Jakarta on-wards. In addition, Zehra Kermandi is no doubt a Muslim and in a country of near three hundred million Muslims, there would be any number willing to assist. I did try sir, but there's nothing more I could do. I do believe the Kurd community in Melbourne was their ace-in-the-hole. Bellamy knew exactly what he was doing. This was no spur of the moment adventure down under. It was all set up - they got complete co-operation and they got away. However, I don't believe they had the time to go anywhere near Maralinga. I think it was a dry run to arrange everything.'

Crowther had to agree. 'It would appear the case, so it becomes absolutely imperative we don't let them slip through the net again.'

'Don't you think it's time we let the American's and Turks help us track them down? This is getting to the critical stage sir. By pulling their intelligence services into the frame, along with Interpol, Bellany and Kermandi would be the two most hunted targets in the world of terrorism. I'm certain we would quickly run them to ground.'

Crowther swivelled around in his chair, his eyes fixed on St Paul's as he gazed vacantly at the view outside. The Turks knew of the threat, but as yet didn't fully understand it. However, the Turks treated any rumour or threat with utmost concern. Suspects were quickly arrested and subjected to days of questioning and torture. Depending on the result they were released, or simply disappeared. The Americans had started asking questions and becoming more persistent as captured Kurds and Jihadi terrorists when interrogated, made growing reference to *vulpes*. He, on the other hand was fully aware of the problem and it didn't go by the name of *vulpes*. It was an unimaginable threat his government's scientists had perpetrated more than fifty years previous. They had full knowledge of the crime and danger they were unleashing. They deemed it an experiment – an experiment that went horribly wrong – a crazy scientific idea that should never been allowed to happen if it were not for the vast isolated wilderness of Maralinga. It was a shocking indictment of the probity and ethics of the scientists involved. The nomadic native inhabitants who had roamed free and lived off the land for millennia were given no consideration whatsoever. They were of no consequence as was neither the wildlife nor environment. How things had changed since the dark aftermath of the war that shattered Europe and Pacific. The sins of nuclear warfare and the ignorance and crime of its consequences were now an abhorrent threat fully understood by mankind.

Hartigan could see his superior was lost in thought. He waited for a few seconds before interrupting. 'What now sir – are you going to declare this an open shooting season and pull in the Americans and Turks?'

'No, certainly not,' Crowther replied as he snapped out of his revere and swung back. 'Not yet anyway – we have too much to lose. You'll start in Beruit and see if you can find whether Bellamy is operating from there, or just uses it as a staging post into northern Syria. Who knows, the Turks, the Assad Syrians, or some Daesh terrorist groups, may get hold of him first and solve the problem. On the other hand, the old saying is hide where they don't suspect you to be and that's right in the midst of them. If he's threatening the Turks, what better place to be than in Istanbul.'

'In that case it's probably a good time to blow his cover and give the Turks a heads -up we would like their assistance to detain him.'

'No, we can't do that. Although born in Australia, Bellamy by birthright via his grandfather, is entitled to British citizenship, a right he will take advantage of if arrested. And as you are well aware, you cannot expose a Brit to a jurisdiction where the death penalty exists. Okay, the legal premise is rather tenuous in this case, but the Turks would have no compunction in torturing and executing him. They don't give a toss about what we may think. Similarly, the Americans would throw him into Guantanamo and stone-wall us. And if the press got hold of the story and their superficial investigations suggested we had crucified someone on flimsy evidence the government could not sustain, then the axe would fall within this department.'

'But....but the man's a bloody terrorist. Don't you understand that?'

'He may be a terrorist in our eyes, but we have absolutely no clear evidence he's engaged in any such activities. We now know his claim to be working with Medecins Sans Frontieres is false, but he could be working for another charity, or he could be perfectly harmless bleeding-heart out to save the disadvantaged. All we have at this stage is suspicion, but no evidence. And are we looking for Aras Barzani or Declan Bellamy, or are they one and the same?'

Crowther stroked his chin while silently cursing under his breath. He didn't give a damn if the Turks or Americans got Bellamy or Kermandi and finished them off. His main concern was the political risk to his friend, Alexander Stoyan. The political storm would not be survivable. He swore under his breath – he only had a year to go before he retired. If the truth came out, he would not be retiring with full recognition of a long career as a protector of the nation's security, but rather as a liability who wilfully hid the truth. He would be socially ruined, all thoughts of a peerage gone.

'I hear what you're saying Hartigan, but before we sound the general alarm, I want you to start in Beirut and see what you can come up with!'

# 34

*Hartigan turned and dry-retched into the corner of the fetid stone-walled room already stinking from the evacuations of various bodily functions – an aroma that hit him with stifling force. The Turkish Colonel smiled at the weakness of the English – he would retch many more times during the course of the hour. He turned to the two naked individuals spreadeagled and bent across a long table, their legs tied to steel loops in the floor, their arms likewise tied into identical loops on the opposite edge.*

Hartigan judged the two to be no more than youths from the form of their lithe bodies, their faces turned sideways towards him, with fear-crazed eyes aware, but beyond hope.

'My God, you're not going to torture them are you? I cannot be party to this.' He turned to leave, but the doorway was blocked by two uniformed guards.

'Come, come Mr Hartigan, they are PKK – members of the Kurdistan Workers Party. They know their fate and have committed themselves to Allah if they are Muslims, or into the arms of God if they are Christians, or Jews, or whatever. It makes no difference to me - my only job is to find out what they know about *vulpes*.' He stepped forward with a thin cane and whipped it across their bare buttocks, resulting in cries of suppressed pain. He repeated the action until the cries gave away to screams as the blood began to flow from the cuts the cane had inflicted. 'They would kill you in an instant Mr Hartigan, so don't feel any compassion for them.'

He was relieved as the beatings stopped and the Colonel turned to him. 'I don't want to mess them up too much at this stage. I want the executioner to have his pleasure first.' He shouted as a hulking individual came into the room and casting aside his robe, made his intent clear. Priapus had nothing on this one, Hartigan mused sickly to himself. He wondered if this was what Lawrence of Arabia was supposed to have experienced when captured and raped by Hajim Bey's guards in 1917? In the present case the rape was swift and clinical, interposed with more screams and grunts of pleasure. The rape of the second youth was perfunctory, the pleasure already satiated by the first. Blood was running down the insides of both pairs of legs from the torn orifices as the hulk disappeared. The Colonel moved closer and started to shout in Turkish at the first of the youths, the cane lashing down on the bleeding cuts from the first lashings. A gob of blood was aimed in his direction, but fell well short. The cane started to work up from the buttocks to the back of the victim, leaving long cuts which immediately opened and oozed blood. A shout went up and the hulk returned dressed in a loose shirt over his baggy salvar trousers. He quickly undid the knots and turned the victim onto his back. The arms were momentarily freed and with a sudden movement of retaliation the victim tried to stand up, but was beaten with a crushing blow to the face. The youth fell back unconscious and was quickly tied to the loops again.

'Let us retire to the next room and have coffee Mr Hartigan. It is more pleasant with no smell. It will be a few minutes before Ali can resume.' They were only just seated when two servants with trays walked in and set them down. One prepared the thick brown Turkish coffee while the other set out two dishes, with assorted pastries and sweets on each. Hartigan relished the coffee only the Turks knew how to prepare and was about to reach out for a pastry when he checked himself. The stench of the torture room came flooding back, as he withdrew his hand in a poorly concealed movement.

The Colonel smiled. 'You don't like Turkish pastries Mr Hartigan?'

'Colonel, I'll make it very clear, I don't like anything about what's going on. I don't know how you can stand it? I simply cannot eat anything in these surrounds.'

'Mr Hartigan, I know you served in Iraq and Afghanistan. You have seen plenty of people die, both at your hands and at the hands of the Saddam Hussein's butcher's and Taliban Mujahideen. I've no doubt the British soldiers and your MI6 have been involved in atrocities in those countries. The Americans have, as has been widely disclosed in the press. I don't know why you are so....what do you say...so squeamish, about seeing a little distress and blood now.'

'The difference now Colonel is, I've never inflicted torture and have never seen it until now. It repulses me that you stoop to these tactics. I really would like to get out of here now if I may. I really have seen enough of your methods.'

'Finish your coffee Mr Hartigan, you are not going anywhere until I say so. And do try a pastry, they really are excellent.' He waited a few seconds for a reply, but seeing the conversation had ended, he got up and motioned for Hartigan to follow him.

The Colonel approached the form lying on its back. The cane pushed into the side of the face until it was looking directly up at him, the eyes now open in absolute hatred and defiance. The contorted face was about to spit another mouthful of blood when the cane whipped savagely across the genitals. The blood choked the screams as the action was repeated time and again. Hartigan shook his head in revulsion – at the least the Americans got somewhere with waterboarding, a practice surreptitiously adopted by the British on occasion, until it became too dangerous after the U.S. exposure of the practice.

Finally the youth broke and started to babble in an inaudible stream in answer to the Colonel's questions. Another stroke of the cane incited an immediate response if the Colonel thought the answers were not satisfactory. Finally he shouted for the rapist who appeared and began to untie the knots. The victim was beyond resistance, resigned to be the subject of another attack. He was pulled to his feet, taken by an arm and the neck and shoved from the room.

'That's the end of him, is it Colonel? Did he tell you what you wanted to know?'

'What he told me Mr Hartigan is that *vulpes* is real. It will wipe out the whole of Istanbul for what we have done to the Kurds. He also said *vulpes* would mean the end of London and New York. What I can't understand Mr Hartigan, is why he refers only to specific cities? Nothing short of a nuclear explosion could achieve that and the Kurds don't have access to such technology, or the ability to construct such a device. The only rogue nations are Pakistan and North Korea and I don't even think they would be crazy enough to make such a weapon available. Maybe this one can add more to what I've just been told,' he said turning to the second youth. 'I can read the fear in this one's eyes, he will break easily now his companion has gone. Stupid peasant thinks he's going to live.'

The torture was swift and effective. The Colonel lit a cigarette and then held the flame of the Zippo lighter under the youth's testicles. There was a sudden whoosh of burning hair and smoke. The scream was endless as the Colonel stood back and waited for it to subside, before re-igniting the flame and moving in again. The threat was enough as the victim started to answer the rapid fire questions in the language Hartigan could not understand. Finally, the Colonel grunted with a look of delight and stood back as the youth fainted. He shouted at the two guards on the door and the youth was dragged out of the room.

'You had some success I see Colonel?'

'I may have. I don't have a name, but I've ascertained *vulpes* is not Kurdish. It is of course the Kurd's name for a fox, but in this case it is not a Kurdish fox, it's a foreign fox. I think that will do for today. I'll bring him back tomorrow and see if I can't extract a nationality or name. I'll make sure he's well treated, his injuries dressed, drugged and allowed to sleep in a comfortable bed. He will be assured he's done well and will be released.'

Hartigan could read the Colonel's warped mind. 'Only that's not going to happen?'

'Of course not Mr Hartigan. He will break completely when he's stripped and shown back into this room. I will get what I want and then he will be executed. There's no point in letting him go as his tribesmen would know he's talked and would kill him. They'd know we'd broken him.'

'And the other one?'

The Colonel looked puzzled for a moment. 'Oh, he's already dead.'

'I don't think I'll attend tomorrow Colonel, I've seen enough and you seem to be well in control.'

'Oh, but you will Mr Hartigan, I insist. You are my guest, after all.'

# 35

*artigan cringed at the thought of just how far MI6 had lowered its defences and security. It was twenty four hours previous when he had cleared Customs and was walking through the foyer of Ataturk airport. He was suddenly confronted by two army uniforms, one with the tabs of a Colonel and the other of lower rank, obviously his minder. 'Good morning Mr Hartigan. I'm Colonel Yusuf Aksoy of National Intelligence. And welcome to Istanbul.'*

Hartigan could not hide his look of surprise. He had just flown in from Lebanon where he had been for the past week. Beirut offered nothing in the way of intelligence about *vulpes* other than confirming Bellamy had flown in under the name of Barzani accompanied by Zehra Kermandi. That was all the Beirut MI6 operative could confirm. They had not booked into any hotels, but simply melted into the general populace.

Aksoy grinned at Hartigan's discomfort. 'I can see you are surprised Mr Hartigan, but you have been under surveillance since the time you landed in Lebanon. I take pride in maintaining a strong network. I'm always interested in why foreign agents should be visiting Turkey without prior notification. It's as you British would say...very rude or simply not cricket.'

'Yes, you have surprised me Colonel, but I can assure you this is a private visit - just a holiday to see the sights of Istanbul.'

'How interesting Mr Hartigan. In that case, I'll give you a short tour before I take you to prison. I know what you're here for - you are following up on the *vulpes* threat. Did you find anything in Lebanon?'

Hartigan stopped in his tracks so quick the escort ran into him. 'Prison? Are you charging me with some crime?'

'Oh, I could easily do that if I was so inclined. A few days in detention to give London notice you can't fool around with Turkish Intelligence, would be a suitable warning not to persist. Of course, I would release you and ensure you caught the next flight back to Heathrow. But no, I'm not going to detain you, I just want to sit down and compare notes. We recently captured two young Kurdish terrorists. Normally, we would have shot them on the spot, but one uttered a threat about a fox and its threat to the existence of Istanbul. I believe you will find the interrogation most interesting. Shall we go? I have a car waiting.'

The black Mercedes was in the no-parking zone, guarded by a soldier who opened the back door for Hartigan to get in. The driver opened the passenger door for the Colonel and then got in behind the wheel. The guard climbed in beside Hartigan. They drove in silence through the traffic of the vast city of fifteen million people until they pulled up at the gates of what was clearly a prison. The gates opened and they drove in. 'Welcome to Pasakapisi prison Mr Hartigan. I've had the prisoners transported here from Diyarbakir military prison overnight so that you would not have to endure a long car journey.'

He did not sleep at what he had witnessed that day - the horror of the scene of torture inflicted with sadistic ritual was beyond belief. It was sick and beyond all norms of civil treatment of prisoners and he had voiced those opinions. However Aksoy had brushed them aside. 'We are dealing with terrorists Mr Hartigan, they have no rights whatsoever. It's we kill them, or they kill us and I will use any means to extract information. I would suggest you keep any further opinions to yourself.'

He had opened his door after midnight to go for a walk, but the guard outside shook his head. In the morning the car was blocking the foyer entrance to the small hotel - the driver taking no notice of the protestations of the concierge to move forward a few metres to let other cars pick up passengers and drive through. Hartigan got in and contemplated with foreboding about what he was about to witness again. He could not get the inhumanity out of his mind. Maybe he was getting too old and soft and should hand in his resignation. He was shown into the same stinking room. Aksoy was seated at the table talking softly to the youth crouched naked on the floor a few metres in front of him. He was sitting in a pool of blood, his eyes completely unfocused and uncomprehending.

'Mr Hartigan, I started early as Ali convinced him to talk.' The giant of a man was standing right behind the cowering figure in case he should lunge at Aksoy. 'Ali has just given him a strong hit of morphine to overcome the pain, so I don't need to talk to him further. Allah will take care of him now.'

He motioned his head and the youth was dragged to his feet by the massive arms and taken away.

'I think the boy told us everything. He would not have known the full story, but he had been told to incite the rumour of *vulpes* if he was apprehended. It turns out he is the son of a Kurdish insurgent leader we have been after for a number of years. The boy who died yesterday was his cousin, so between them, I was convinced they must know something more. He told Ali the person behind *vulpes* is an Austrian, or that's what he understood from overhearing his father's conversations. Can you accept that, because I don't have any record of an Austrian terrorist in this part of the world? It's way out of character. Anyway, the boy insisted the Austrian is in that part of northern Syria now controlled by the Kurdish rebels. We could easily move in and wipe them out, but they're protected by the Americans, so our hands are tied. Mind you, the Americans will cut and run soon, so we can get rid of the Kurdish problem and take over the Syrian lands they control. To hell with Bashar al Assad of Syria, he's merely a Russian puppet. Putin is now an ally of ours, so we don't have anything to fear in that direction. It really is a crazy situation Mr Hartigan. You were going to say something?'

'No...no Colonel. I was just about to agree the Austrian involvement does seem a bit weird.' In fact, he was just about to correct him, but refrained - Aksoy would have noticed the look on his face if he had not appeared distracted by the prisoner being dragged away.

'The lad said the Austrian was now in Syria, he confirmed that did he?'

Aksoy nodded. 'Yes, there was a lot of excitement when he arrived at his father's camp. The Austrian confirmed *vulpes* the fox, would arrive in Istanbul within the next couple of months. How it is coming, or in what form, the boy was unable to say.'

'Can I get into northern Syria? Will you allow me to go there?'

'For what purpose? You take a risk in trying to contact the Austrian. The terrorists will kill you the moment you open your mouth. They don't trust anyone, even their own. They are not one representative body Mr Hartigan, but many groups fighting for control of their tribal and ancestral area.'

'Maybe so Colonel, but I would like to give it a try.'

Aksoy raised his eyebrows and shrugged. 'I really don't have any objections, it's your neck. I'll give you a driver and car to take you to the Syrian border, but that's the extent of my help.'

Aksoy got to his feet and held out his hand. 'Next time Mr Hartigan, if you should survive, please let me know you're coming. It would be more courteous – it is a trait of we Turks. I don't want to accost you at the airport again. My driver will take you back to your hotel and I'll arrange for an escort to pick you up in the morning.'

He followed Hartigan across the room and opened the door for him. He paused with the look of death in his expression. 'I gave you the chance Mr Hartigan, but you failed didn't you? We both know we're not looking for an Austrian, but someone from the other side of the world. What has an Australian terrorist got to do with Turkey? And why a terrorist threat from that source has got the Kurds so excited, is beyond me. I understand there are any number of Turks and Kurds in Australia and they are treated well, but how could they mount any kind of threat?' Hartigan was about to make some lame excuse when the door was closed in his face.

Aksoy turned and walked back across the room and sat down. He could not believe Hartigan had treated him as an ignorant fool. He had openly invited the man to correct his assumption about the nationality. He had seen Hartigan's momentary reaction, but the agent had declined to co-operate. He had felt like terminating the meeting and escorting him back to the airport to catch the first flight out, but decided against it. Aksoy had other plans. Hartigan would be escorted to the border and then taken across into the Kurdish terrorist region of northern Syria. From there he should be able to contact the Americans supporting those groups and find out more about *vulpes*. Hartigan had been sent by MI6, so they were particularly worried about some threat. It had to be as much of a threat to England as it was to the Turks. He was well aware the Americans were also concerned as the National Security Agency (NSA) had been making enquiries at the direction of U.S. Home Security. The Americans were quite happy to co-operate, but obviously not the English. They were hiding something.

# 36

He sat in the front with the driver who indicated he did not speak or understand English. Hartigan thought otherwise, as they drove over the Bosphorous bridge connecting Europe to Asia. He felt for the Kurds, a population of thirty million denied their ancient birthright of Kurdistan. However, their downfall was they were not a single entity but a community spread over the vast areas of Iran, Syria, Iraq and Turkey, all having a multitude of factions and internal rivalries. The Kurdish aspirations for a State had been brushed aside by world powers, including his own country. The Turks were too powerful a linchpin in Asia for the Americans to ignore or anger. But on the other hand, the Kurdish rebels, with the help of limited American boots on the ground combined with airstrikes, had been instrumental in defeating the Islamic terrorists in northern Syria and capturing strategic ground which they had no intention of relinquishing. Now the Turks wanted the American support and involvement *to finish so they could deal with the Kurds. America had made it clear they wanted out of other people's problems and if that involved the continued oppression of a few million Kurds, the world would have to accept the price. Britain would stand helplessly by and raise a voice of concern, but take no action. It also had vital interests and alliances to protect. But why was it getting involved with an isolated terror threat, unless it was also a threat to Downing Street? And who in that establishment knew about it? He could not understand why Crowther had not taken him into his confidence. He shook his head in frustration as the countryside disappeared in a blur of fields and small villages – a scene of peace only disturbed by the appearance of armoured vehicles and heavy loaders transporting army tanks parked at various intervals, waiting to move forward in the same direction he was now travelling. The Turks were intent on crushing the Kurds the moment the opportunity arose. The world could do and would do nothing.*

The driver had been under instructions where to deliver him as they pulled up at a Turkish command centre near Manbij on the Euphrates River, the natural border separating Turkey and Syria. He was immediately ushered into the commander's presence, a heavy-set man with bushy moustache and thick eyebrows that almost hid the tired brown eyes. The muscles in his forearms strained the short sleeves of the khaki uniform. He did not rise as he motioned for Hartigan to sit while he finished a phone conversation. Finally, he put it down and glared across the table before rising slightly and offering his hand. 'Major Mustafa Ozdemir, Mr Hartigan and what is MI6 doing in this part of the world?'

'I'm looking for someone and you maybe able to help me.'

'Colonel Aksoy has informed me you're looking for an Australian? A terrorist posing as *vulpes*, the fox?'

'That's correct Major, are you aware of him?'

'I'm aware of *vulpes* of course, but have no knowledge of any Australian being in this area now. Any that may have been, were fighting with the Islamists and are probably dead, been captured, or have deserted when the fighting got too tough. It's no quarter given over the border Mr Hartigan, you are liable to die from our artillery fire, the Russian bombings or Assad's forces and gas attacks. Any Kurdish rebel falling into Assad's hands is summarily executed. Similarly, we are not very lenient. Are you telling me you really want to cross over the river into Manbij province? How do you know the Australian is there?'

'I don't Major, but I have a belief that's where I'll find him. Can you arrange it?'

'And what are you going to do when you find him and what if he finds you first? The moment you step over that border and start asking questions about someone they are protecting, the Kurds will turn on you. It might be best if you just take my pistol and go out in the desert and shoot yourself, because they most certainly will.'

'If and when I find him, I should be able to ascertain very quickly whether *vulpes* is a real threat or just a rumour. However, it has got MI6, American Home Security and your National Intelligence concerned, so it must have some substance rather than being a rumour. If he won't co-operate I will turn him over to the Americans.'

Ozmedir leaned back in his chair and roared with laughter which reverberated around the room. He had a coughing fit as he shook a cigarette from a pack and lit it. The sweet aromatic smell of the strong tobacco wafted across as he exhaled. Hartigan declined as the Major, as an afterthought, offered him the pack.

'You are a fool Mr Hartigan. You don't negotiate with rebels. They'll recognise your intentions immediately and shoot you on sight. These people are not stupid.'

'I'll take that risk Major. Now, will you help me? I also want to make contact with the Americans in that zone. They may know something, or they may have apprehended him without knowing his true identity.'

Ozmedir nodded and slowly shook his head. 'I don't think our allies know what they're doing. One day they're supporting us and the next they're protecting the rebels and on top of that they're training an army of tens of thousands of Kurds who will oppose us. They believe they can keep a foot in both camps, but they're sadly mistaken. We won't tolerate them training and organising an army of Kurds. At the moment they are the meat in the sandwich with the Syrians, aided by Iran and Russia, pushing from the south and Turkey from the north. The American people are not going to tolerate huge casualties when the sandwich is squeezed and American blood begins to flow. They've already lost thousands of troops in Iraq and Afghanistan, for what gain? Absolutely nothing and they're about to repeat the mistake here if they train the rebels. We will annihilate the rebels and we won't be giving any of our gains back to Syria. Yes, I will help you Mr Hartigan. I will give you a guide to take you across to the Americans, but there any assistance will end.'

'As you know Major, *vulpes* has made a direct threat to attack Istanbul. Colonel Aksoy is well aware of the threat. What would his reaction be if Istanbul was hit because you had ignored any intelligence I was able to gather and you refused to assist?'

'You've made your point Mr Hartigan. I suggest you rest tomorrow and I'll have a guide take you across in the evening. He may, or may not wish to accompany you on what I term is a suicide mission. He could be with you one moment and gone the next, so don't expect any allegiance. I'll get you a change of clothes - you can't go across dressed like that and you'll need a sidearm.'

'I don't want a gun Major, I don't plan on shooting anyone.'

'Mr Hartigan, the pistol is not for your defence. It's so you can shoot yourself if you run into any Islamic terrorists. There are still plenty of them out there along with the Kurdish rebels. The Kurds may show you some mercy, but the Islamist's will slice off your head for the fun of it and anything else they can take hold of. And that would be quick death. If they're in a more playful mood they will strip you, tie you to a pole and then gut you so that your intestines drop onto the ground in front of you. It's a slow and lingering death while they sit around laughing. Finally, just as all pain has faded they will slit your throat and leave your head at your feet. You can imagine what they do to the Kurdish women fighters. I still maintain you are a fool, but a brave one. '

# 37

*It was dark as the battered punt slowly crossed the Eurphrates. As it nudged the opposite bank, the guide jumped out, followed quickly by Hartigan. Within seconds the craft had drifted back into the stillness of the river and disappeared. Not a word had been spoken on the way across. They quickly climbed the bank and were about to step onto a track when the guide pulled him back and down. Hartigan could see nothing except the rubble strewn remains of dwellings in either direction. The interposed fields were studded with shell holes from artillery fire. It was a scene of utter devastation. The guide suddenly pointed into the gloom - it was some moments before Hartigan caught glimpses of two forms slowly walking through the fog towards their position.*

'Daesh, and they've spotted us,' the guide hissed, as he pushed Hartigan's shoulder into the ground. At least this one spoke English. The two figures stopped and sat down on a pile of rubble less than one hundred metres away. Neither group had a clear view of the other through the mists of distance.

Hartigan had played this game before in Afghanistan while on patrol. They were about to enter a reported deserted village when their Afghan guide suddenly disappeared. One moment he was talking softly to the trusted native, then when he looked around he'd gone. He quickly cut his patrol in two with three men on each side withdrawing in opposite directions at least twenty metres apart. They had only just gained cover when the ground they had been huddled in moments before was raked by gun fire. The machine gun position identified, his patrol wiped it out with a triangulated bursts which also took out the Taliban rushing forward to finish off any survivors.

Hartigan tugged the guide's sleeve and indicated for him to move off to his left behind a pile of broken trees, while he looked for a safe position to the right. He could feel the adrenaline surging and his heart-rate increasing – he was in mortal danger, but it wasn't the Taliban he was now facing, but AK47 carrying Islamists. All he was carrying in defence was a pistol he had never fired nor familiar with – it was no contest. He ducked instinctively as the stillness was broken by a burst of automatic fire, as one of the figures raced forward regardless of the danger. He saw the other one peel off and circle towards where his guide had vanished. The occasional burst of fire bounced off the mud brick rubble as the gunman approached. Hartigan stood slightly to one side of a narrow slit that had once been a window in a partially demolished dwelling and waited with his weapon poised. Ozmedir was right, he quietly thanked him for insisting he needed some protection, seemingly useless as it was. This was the exact situation the Major had referred to – an

Islamist terrorist with no purpose in mind other than to kill. The bursts became more frequent as the gunman got closer. It was as though his intent was to frighten his quarry into the open in a plea for mercy. Hartigan held the pistol up to the side of his face as he broke into a sweat. The gunfire stopped and he could hear footsteps carefully treading through the rubble, before pausing briefly and then recommencing. The terrorist knew he was within metres of his target - he was being careful or so he thought. But his prey had previous experience and just waited, barely breathing. The sideways profile of the gunman's face passed the window slit and if by instinct whirled around to level his weapon when he realised he had become the target. He got the first word *'Allah,'* out before the single shot tore open his head. Hartigan did not move. There was still another one out there and the gunfire could have attracted more. He sensed the movement behind him, spun and crouched in a single movement, the pistol pointed at the sound. The guide held up his hand clutching the bloodied knife. 'Quick, we've got to get away from here.'

Hartigan needed no encouragement as he quickly followed. Gone were the days when he could handle the pace – he'd become used to the sedentary life of fighting from behind a desk. He trotted after the guide until the point of exhaustion forced him to stop. The gasps came in deep lung-fulls as his companion flopped down beside him.

'We're okay for five minutes. But we've got to be clear of this area before daylight. If they catch up with us.....' The guide made the hand movement with a single finger slicing across his throat.

It was early morning - he was trying to maintain his positive posture and bearing without appearing exhausted, when they rounded a huddle of stone structures and walked straight into dozen armed men sitting around a fire. He looked around hopelessly for an escape route, as his guide greeted them as brothers. He was not introduced, but quickly accepted the invitation to sit and eat the onion, tomato and cucumber with slices of goat piled onto a wrap of flat bread. He knew he was the centre of attention of questions and purpose. He heard *'Australie'* mentioned several times by his guide as he listened and sipped the sweet tea through a sugar cube placed in the mouth. They all acknowledged the name and babbled in reply. He made to ask the guide what he'd been told, but a hand was held up to silence him. It was an hour later when the group broke up.

'Two of them are going with us. They will get us all the way to the American base without problems. We are in their tribal area, so you are safe. This is Kurdish territory the Turks want to take off us.'

They started to walk, the two Kurds leading the way when Hartigan turned to the guide. 'I thought you were a Turk and yet you are friends with these people – can you explain?'

The guide laughed. 'I'm both a Turk and a Kurd and a Syrian and an Iranian. The Kurds are widespread throughout. We are all brothers although we do have our differences and individual conflicts. In this case, we are threatened by the Turks who want to totally dispossess us and grind us under their boots. That's their mistake - by doing what they're doing, they are uniting the Kurds into one ethnic group, something the Kurds have been unable to achieve in a thousand years.'

'I don't understand? Does Major Ozdemir know you're the enemy?'

'Of course he does, but I'm a Turk while he pays me and he knows that. He knows he cannot buy my loyalty, so he must work with it. I had my early schooling in England when my father was a clerical assistant to the Turkish ambassador. I could never understand the English weakness, if I can call it that, of total allegiance. On the other hand we Kurds have a weakness in that we will never unite, unless we have a common cause and it is that we don't have. Certainly, as an ethnic identity we despise the Turks, the Syrians and the Iranian's for their oppression, but the opposition is singular and not united. Until that happens, the Kurds will never achieve a nation of their own. So, at the moment I'm working for the Turks because they pay well. I worked for the Americans at one stage, but they are just too suspicious of our intent and don't pay well - they don't trust us. However, we do tell them what they want to hear and we do try and keep them out of danger. Now enough of the small talk, we are in danger and must remain alert. The Islamists will know we've crossed the Euphrates when they find those two bodies back there, so we've got to keep moving.'

It was the following day when they cautiously approached the American compound and a forward patrol mounted in an armoured vehicle. Hartigan recognised it as a Stryker, complete with a 105mm cannon, an M2 0.50mm heavy machine gun and the lighter 7.72mm rapid fire weapon. It was the heavy machine gun pointing directly at them now. The guide put down his weapon and raised his hands, indicating Hartigan to follow as he went forward slowly while the two other Kurds stayed back.

'Halt. Stop exactly where you are,' was the command when they were about fifty metres distance. 'What do you want?'

It was Hartigan's turn to take the lead. 'I'm Miles Hartigan, a British citizen on official business.' It sounded a rather ludicrous declaration – a British official in the middle of hostile surrounds, without bowler hat, leather briefcase and furled umbrella, facing the threat of a weapon that could rip him to shreds with one burst.

'Okay buddy, just drop any weapons you're carrying and come forward slowly. Your companion is to leave now and I mean now.'

Hartigan turned to the guide and held out his hand. 'Thank you. Tell me, what is you name?'

The guide shook his hand firmly as Hartigan handed him his pistol. 'You don't need to know my name, other than I am a proud Kurd.' With that he turned and walked away following his already retreating companions. Hartigan walked slowly towards the vehicle with his hands raised as a precaution. A light vehicle emerged from the compound and drove around the armoured vehicle before stopping beside him.

'What's you're name sir?' was the polite demand of the Lieutenant in the front seat. 'We have no record of a British tourist.'

'Miles Hartigan is the name and I'm not a tourist. I'm here on business, although I admit it is rather unusual just walking up to your front gate without prior warning.'

'You're right there fella. You almost got turned into dog tucker – we wouldn't have known whether to scrape you off or paint you over if he'd pulled the trigger. We were attacked yesterday, so we're a bit gun-shy at the moment. I'll take you to see Colonel Pitbull.'

'Is that his name, or nom de plume?'

The Lieutenant looked at him, for a moment not understanding. 'No sir, that's his name and Colonel Cyrus Pitbull bights real hard if he don't like you. I'll give you a warning sir, I don't think you're welcome.'

'Oh, no coffee and doughnuts then?' His attempt at humour was ignored as he got in. They drove through a heavily armed outer guard post and into an empty village of scattered mud-brick buildings. It was easy to spot the command post with the Stars and Stripes flying high.

Minutes later he was shown into a building where he became face to face with Pitbull. The name fitted the canine equivalent – the closely shaved head and neck folds of flesh almost concealed the two sunken eyes and small ears, matched by a row of barely retracted teeth. He introduced himself, but there was no reciprocal greeting or extended hand of friendship – just a nod as he was indicated a chair. He sat as the Colonel retreated behind a campaign desk and sat down. 'I lost five men yesterday and I've got letters to write to their folks. What the hell are you doing out here and who are you?'

'Colonel I'm here trying to track down an Australian terrorist. I am an MI6 agent of the British Government.'

Pitbull snorted. 'One of those desk-jockeys who never get their hands dirty eh? Do you know anything about combat Hartigan?'

'I served two terms in Iraq and Afghanistan as a Major in the Royal Marines. We worked in close contact with your forces.'

Pitbull's demeanour changed immediately. 'Sit down Major and tell me what you're really after?'

Hartigan gave a brief and heavily redacted background of his purpose. 'As I've said Colonel, I'm here trying to track down a terrorist who goes by the name *vulpes* or is part of a terror group by that name.'

'I'm aware of the name Major and we're hearing it more frequently. You say the guy you want to make contact with is an Australian? What do you want to do when you find him?'

'I'm going to kill him. It's as simple as that.'

Pitbull raised his eyebrows and slowly shook his head dismissively. 'You say this guy has bonded with the Kurds? If that's so, you're the one who's going to die. They'll not give up one of their own. They must have been Kurds who brought you here. Did you tell them the reasons for your visit?'

'No, but I did tell the Turkish officer who organised the guide. The other two, we just picked up on the way here.'

'I must say you're one lucky man. You wouldn't have made it if you'd mentioned you were after *vulpes*. You must have the balls of an elephant to attempt what you're doing. I really can't help you at this stage. Do you have a description or photo of this guy? I mean, among thirty million Kurds, who am I looking for? And we're here to protect the Kurds against our allies the Turks. It's a crazy situation Hartigan – you're wasting your time and chancing your life coming out here.'

'Colonel, it would be in your government's interest and that of mine and the Turks, if you do come across someone with an English accent, who doesn't ring true as a Kurd, you will immediately detain him.'

Pitbull was not going to disclose he had already let the Australian slip through his hands. He had even talked to him the previous week when he met a group of Kurdish tribal leaders. He had heard him talking in English to a woman accompanying the group. It was the following day he had received the order to be on the lookout for an English speaking foreigner, possibly referred to by the Kurds as the fox – *vulpes*. It was a name he was becoming increasingly aware of as it reverberated through the Kurdish rebels they were sheltering, like a wave of subliminal sound.

The rebel commander had laughed when Pitbull asked him about *vulpes*. 'It is the fox that will wipe out the whole of Istanbul, Colonel. It is coming. The Turks will be forced to abandon the city and retreat to the Asian side of the Bosphorous. It is then, we Kurds will rise up against them.'

He had dismissed it as rumour and fiction, but now he wasn't so sure. The Brits must be worried if they sent this crazy man out here walking around by himself. But he wasn't crazy, he was a former ranking army officer who was well aware of the danger. To do so in Afghanistan or Iraq would have met with a very quick end.

'By your expression Colonel, I sense you've met *vulpes* the Australian haven't you? And it must have been very recent?'

The accusation was ignored, but he could see it hit home. Pitbull was not going to admit he had a prime terrorist in his sights and failed.

'You're welcome to stay for a day or two Major, I was also in Iraq and Afghanistan so we can compare notes and reminisce. I can arrange for a patrol to take you back part way to the Euphrates, but from there you're on your own. Islamic terrorists still control pockets and it's a no-go area for us. Neither are the Russian fighter bombers or the Syrian helicopters too friendly and wouldn't express much remorse if they hit one of our Stryker's by mistake.'

It was three days later when he departed Camp Pitbull, as he had named it. It was followed by hours in the Stryker before it stopped and the rear door dropped down. The commanding Lieutenant was standing there looking around nervously. Hartigan recognised the village where he and the guide had met the group of Kurds. He could see the remains of the fire and the bones of the roasted goat.

'This is as far as I go sir. I can't hang around as this rig is a prime target for RPG's.'

Hartigan sat down with his back to a wall and watched the Stryker depart, belching diesel fumes from its turbo-charged engine. No wonder the Lieutenant was worried - the sound of the vehicle could be heard for miles. Stationary, it was an irresistible target for any terrorist armed with rocket propelled grenades.

It was too hot to keep going, so he sought shelter in one of the empty rooms of a partly destroyed house. Pitbull had given him a **GPS** with pre-loaded co-ordinates, a Heckler & Koch **MP5**, a commando's knife, water and food. He would wait until nightfall, before heading towards the river crossing point. How to cross the river was a problem he would address when he arrived.

# 38

*He awoke with a start. There was a group sitting on the other side of the room in the semi-darkness watching him, their scarves covering their heads and obscuring their faces. He started to breathe again when he recognised his guide, the only one with his face visible. 'You gave me a real scare.'*

'Your head would have been lying on the floor if we were Daesh Islamists, Mr Hartigan. You would not have had time to be scared as the knife was pulled across your throat.'

Hartigan could still feel his heart beating in a frenzied rhythm. It had been a close call – he should have known better and found a more concealed hiding place. 'I didn't expect to see you again.'

'Colonel Ozdemir asked me to look after you, and that's what I'm doing. I knew the American's would bring you back here, so it was just a matter of waiting. We'll take you to the river and get you across safely. I'm sure you will have an important message to deliver to the Colonel.'

'I don't think I've got much to tell him other than to say the American's were very hospitable and you are an excellent guide.'

'You're not safe yet Mr Hartigan, I still have to get you back to the river and across. However, with my friends here, I'm sure we'll be able to achieve that if we don't run into too many Islamist's. And once across, you will deliver an important message on behalf of the Kurdish people, but don't ask me what it is now.'

It was pre-dawn when they set off, the guide taking the lead, his fellow tribesmen following on behind. No one spoke, all well aware of the danger. The light of the new day was just beginning to show through the heavy morning mist when they cautiously approached the ruins where he had shot the terrorist. Hartigan could sense the tension within the group. Suddenly, the guide grabbed at his sleeve and pulled him to the ground while the others silently disappeared into the surrounding rubble. He then smelt the smoke and the low murmur of voices from behind the wall of a crumbling building.

'Daesh,' hissed the guide. 'We will have to deal with them before we can get you across the river.' They slowly inched forward. Hartigan was about to take the safety off the MP5 when the guide stayed his hand. 'No, Mr Hartigan, this is not the time to make a noise. There could be other groups around and we cannot afford to alert them. They know we crossed the river here and will assume we will return this way. We are in real danger as I can't signal until tonight for anyone to come and get us.'

They cautiously looked over and down into a space outlined by what remained of the walls of a large dwelling. There were three of them leaning over a dish and scooping

the food between folded flat-bread into their mouths –
they talked quietly in between sipping small glasses of tea.
Their weapons were within easy reach. Hartigan could see
there was no hope of taking them by surprise. The slightest
noise would result in three AK47's tearing them to shreds.
He glanced across at the guide who was grinning with a
malicious smile as he looked back at the rising sun.

'Just wait and don't make a sound Mr Hartigan. They will
be taken care of.'

The terrorists suddenly finished eating and unfolding
small mats, knelt down almost in a uniform line, facing
directly north-east towards Mecca as they began to chant
prayers. It all came flashing back as Hartigan remembered
his first time in Afghanistan – he was leading a patrol when
he looked behind only to see the Afghani soldiers assigned
to him all on their knees, bent over in prayer and oblivious
to danger. The scare of sudden abandonment and exposure
had shaken him. He had been warned, but had forgotten –
from then on the timing of the five-time-a-day ritual was
permanently imprinted in his memory.

And then it happened. Three figures appeared out of
the rubble and quickly walked up behind the praying
group. He watched in total shock as the knives appeared
almost in unison as each praying head was jerked
back and the bursts of blood erupted from the severed
throats. None of the victims had time to react. There
was no sound except for the gurgle of gasping air trying
to displace the choking blood of the severed wind-pipe.
The horror of what he was witnessing did not stop there
as the heads were completely severed, the butchering
carried out clinically without a word being spoken. Two
heads lay on the ground beside the twitching corpses.

The third head was held up as the killer spat into the dead expression and propped it on a prominent block of masonry.

'Christ, did they have to do that?'

'We dare not stop the women Mr Hartigan. It is revenge for what those Islamist animals do to our Kurdish women when they capture them. And it's not only their heads they cut off when they finish with them. In return, the Islamists and Turks are in fear of being taken by our women fighters – they show no mercy.'

It was then Hartigan realised the scarfed killers were women. He had not taken any real notice when he first saw the group in that room earlier. He had noticed a clean-shaven young male when he lowered his scarf to eat something, otherwise he kept his face averted. That was until Hartigan caught him staring at him with the shadow of a smile when he thought he was not looking. An older Kurd with a thick black beard and gimlet eye slits disappeared occasionally during the night. Hartigan noticed he was not present when they set off that morning. And yet here he was like a silent shadow standing at the guide's side.

'Okay, let's go Mr Hartigan. Yuseff here, has been down by the river all night. The boat is waiting for you now, but will leave without you if we don't hurry.'

They reached the river and he was about to step aboard when the guide held out his hand. 'Give me your weapon Mr Hartigan. The Turks will only take it off you so I may as well have it.'

He had noticed the startled expression on the guide's face when one of the Kurds started to shout and point his weapon, indicating for him to step aside. The guide broke into a torrent of exchange, throwing his arms wide and moving in front of Hartigan as though to shelter him. 'Quick, give it to me.'

Hartigan handed it over without thinking. 'You're not coming with me?'

'No, I cannot to go back, due to a threat I've just received. They will kill both of us if I step on that boat. I've got to go with them and forget about any further contact with the Turks. They don't entirely trust me. Please give Colonel Ozdemir my regards.'

Hartigan looked up to see the AK47's pointing directly at him He felt sick, but resigned – he had handed over his only defence and was about to pay the price for his stupidity.

'And you can give the Colonel a message. Tell him you met *vulpes*, the fox,' came from a voice up the bank.

Hartigan looked up towards the young Kurd who had removed the scarf and was now smiling mockingly down at him. 'The female fox is a *vixen*. There is no equivalent in Kurdish so its referred to by the male gender, *vulpes*. You can tell the Colonel and the world, you met the *vixen*, or rather the person who is going to unleash the power of *vixen* on Istanbul, London and maybe New York.'

There was no mistaking the accent, having mixed with Australian personnel in Afghanistan. He now realised why the guide had asked for his gun as he would have surely carried out his assignment, despite the AK47's pointed in his direction. The rapid fire spray of the MP5 machine pistol had the advantage, but it was no longer in his hands.

'I've just saved your life Mr Hartigan,' the guide remarked quietly. 'They wanted to kill you, but I convinced them there was no point because you could not stop *vixen*.'

'And which one are you, Aras Barzani or Declan Bellamy?' He directed his question at the Australian.

'Either will do,' the young man replied with a backward laugh as he turned to walk away. 'You can tell Ozdemir, the Turks are about to suffer for the oppression of the Kurds.'

# 39

*Two weeks later he was back in London. He had been delayed by Colonel Aksoy who insisted on a full debriefing and then in what amounted to a cross examination of the recorded interview, it was repeated the following day. Hartigan felt like an accused in the witness box as Aksoy went over and over his statement, looking for flaws or points of unrecognised significance. It was on the way to the airport that the Colonel turned to him from the front seat. 'I've been thinking Mr Hartigan, why the subtle difference? Why did the terrorist make specific reference to vixen? Why did he do that when he could have let you assume the threat was vulpes? I can't help thinking he was trying to tell you something.'*

Aksoy was no fool. It was something that had exercised Hartigan's mind. Was it just an offhand comment to identify the threat as being feline and more dangerous, or was it just a meaningless correction?

'Yes, that occurred to me Colonel. Although the Kurds apparently don't have a name for a female fox, I'm sure they will be able to pronounce *vixen*. Unless I miss my guess I believe you will be hearing the new name whispered in place of the old.'

'So, you don't know what *vixen* refers to, or could refer to? The more I think about it, I believe it's not something just picked out of the air. It is something specific to do with you English.'

Linton Crowther was waiting for him along with someone he did not recognise. 'This is Sir Richard Hamilton of the SIS. Please take a seat and let's have your report.'

Hartigan nodded in deference to Hamilton as he sat down. 'I'm still working on a full written report sir. I would like to delay this meeting until I've made further enquiries and ........'

'We want a verbal report now Hartigan,' Crowther snapped. 'Did you apprehend this *vulpes* fellow and did you kill him?'

'I did neither sir, but I did meet him. Unfortunately, I was not in the position to kill him. In fact the roles were reversed – he could have easily killed me.'

'What do you mean by that convoluted jargon?" Crowther was trying to control his look of frustration. 'You met him, but you didn't kill him, but he let you go. Is that what you're saying?'

'Precisely sir. I was not in a position to do otherwise. It was at the last moment when I was due to cross back into Turkey from northern Syria that he revealed who he was. There were some women with him, but I don't know if one of them was Zehra Kermandi. However, he would not confirm whether he was Aras Barzani or Declan Bellamy. I was at a distinct disadvantage as he held the gun and I was unarmed. By the way sir, he corrected me, the name is not *vulpes,* but *vixen.* And I believe you know exactly what he was referring to.'

Crowther shot a quick look at the head of the counterpart agency. 'Yes I do, but first, you had better tell us how much you know?'

'What baffled me at first was how someone from the antipodes could have MI6, Homeland Security, SIS and the Turks so worried about an obscure threat. Now I see the SIS is involved with the presence of Sir Richard and I've no doubt the American's are going to be pressing very soon as to what you know about a threat called *vixen.*'

'We don't need the lecture Hartigan. Get on with it.'

'Google is a wonderful invention sir. I recalled Declan Connoly had been a member of the forces sent down to Australia during the atomic tests. Those tests were carried out on the Monte Bello Island group in Western Australia and finally at Maralinga in South Australia. A particular series of tests were assigned the name *vixen,* and in particular a series code named *vixen B* which Connoly would probably have witnessed as he was on site, or in the vicinity when they occurred. I can't positively connect Connoly to a terrorist threat code named *vixen,* but I believe it's too much of a co-incidence. Given a bit more time I may be able to put forward a better explanation. Going back through Connoly's records I see he was also known as Martin Bellamy after he deserted in 1963 and lived in Melbourne for a number of years. He had a son named Martin Bellamy and a grandson, Declan Bellamy. It's either Declan or Aras Barzani I met in Syria. Both young Barzani and Bellamy went to school together and both their father's were friends. But that's as far as I've got to date. I don't believe *vixen* was a name just chosen at random. There has to be some connection with those tests.'

Crowther nodded. 'There is Hartigan, but whatever I tell you is never to be repeated, even to your closest associate. I want to make that absolutely clear.'

'Not even the Turks or the American's?'

'No, definitely not, at least not unless we can short-circuit the present threat. You'll have to leave that one in our court.'

'Understood sir.'

'Okay, well it's obvious you've done a bit of research on the main blasts at Maralinga, the legacy of which has been a long-running thorn in our side. However, there were, as your research has uncovered, a series of highly classified tests code-named *vixen*. They weren't nuclear bombs as such, but a series of tests using TNT to blow up simulated nuclear warheads containing a deadly form of nuclear material – plutonium 239, which has a half-life in excess of 24,000 years. Once released, it cannot be eliminated or contained. The persistence of radiation and the threat of any number of cancers posed by inhaling the smallest of wind-blown particles gives you an idea of the magnitude of the threat to all forms of life. At first the contamination was being estimated at four hundred square miles, termed Section 400, but that was a joke. Later studies have indicated it has spread over thousands of square miles by wind and dust. It can never be eradicated.'

'Who was the idiot who proposed such tests. Surely, the Australian government must have known about it?'

Crowther shook his head and pulled a pained expression. 'They had no idea. They were kept totally in the dark. The

Australians readily agreed to Britain carrying out nuclear tests when the Americans locked us out of their nuclear program in 1952. Being strong supporters and at that time comprising a resolved British heritage, they were only too happy to concur without knowing the facts. A total of twelve *"Mushroom Cloud"* bombs were exploded – three at Monte Bello, two at Emu Field and seven at Maralinga. These were known as the major trials – all authorised. Then there were the top secret *vixen* trials. which were designed to investigate the behaviour of the components of a nuclear device by the simulation of the type of conditions that might cause a nuclear weapon to detonate by accident, such as a plane carrying a nuclear device crashing. Little did the Australians know the disaster we were creating and little did they know of the legacy we left behind. In hindsight, the nuclear scientists involved, William Penney, Ernest Titteron and Mark Oliphant were a cosy club of criminals indulging in genocide. However, for their efforts Titterton and Oliphant were knighted while Penney was made a Baron. Oliphant was an Australian and well knew the effects of plutonium 239, but chose to withhold it from his government. You can imagine the scream for blood that will go up if we don't neutralise this whole problem by locating those two barrels. Eventually the *vixen* trials and 239 filtered through to the Australian government, but by that stage they had bought the lie there was nothing to worry about. Penney, Titterton and Oliphant were in the clear. It remains Britain's dirtiest secret of that period, and one we should be eternally ashamed of.'

'But I read we paid compensation and cleaned up the sites. And then we did a final cleanup around 1990 which cost more than $100 million. The Australian government was happy - I can't see the problem?'

'The problem is Hartigan you haven't been listening, plutonium 239 has a half life of 24,000 years plus. At the end of that period it will have lost half it's strength and then it will be another 24,000 years before it loses another half. It can never be cleaned up. An independent Australian scientist who witnessed our last cleanup in the 1990's, wrote a report criticising the work as a cover up and of absolutely no value whatsoever in removing the threat. He noted the dozers and scrapers were throwing up clouds of dust as they scraped off the topsoil, which of course just rolled across the landscape causing more contamination. He noted we did create burial pits for contaminated structures used in the tests, but when he took readings at surface he noted the level of plutonium 239 had not diminished from the material buried. The whole program was a farce and we knew it. By then the Australian government had woken up – they also knew it. However, rather than cause a national outcry and panic at the danger, they decided to do what we did – they concealed it. By that I mean they buried the facts, along with the material. They classified any records under National Security, so no suspicious academic or nosy journalist could get at the truth. The danger was way out in desert country, inhabited by tribes of aboriginal natives wandering around, oblivious to the danger. Who would notice, or investigate the cause of deaths from thyroid or lung cancer, or the incidence of other cancers in such remote communities? The Australian pollies, like politicians the world over, simply pushed it under the too-hard carpet. The public is unaware Maralinga remains one of the world's most contaminated and deadliest sites. And will remain that way for millennia to come. However, the truth has a habit of climbing out of the darkest corners.'

'So who authorised the *vixen* tests? It sounds as though the lunatics were in charge of the asylum?'

'It was under the complete control and direction of our most eminent nuclear physicist, William Penney, the chief scientist of Armament Research, along with his partners in crime, Oliphant and Titterton. '

'They must have been aware of the consequences of fooling around with plutonium?'

'No doubt about it. Plutonium 239 is an unstable isotope of plutonium, and the primary fissile isotope used for the production of nuclear weapons. Penney knew what he was playing with. But, in his opinion, he was the ultimate authority and could do what he liked. In those days the Cold War and the Soviet's were foremost on everyone's mind. Every hideous avenue of resisting and annihilating the enemy was being pursued. Maybe there were thoughts of contaminating large areas of enemy territory by unleashing 239 as the silent killer, rather than a nuclear explosion. In hindsight, Penney was a certifiable lunatic for doing what he did. He simply constructed crude platforms on which a barrel of plutonium was detonated by putting a case of TNT beside it. He knew full well the plutonium would oxidise under the heat of the explosion and immediately disperse, but he wanted to make sure it would not have the same effect as a full-blown chain reaction resulting in a nuclear blast. The difference between a controlled nuclear explosion is that the plutonium is the critical mass which causes the chain reaction – hence the mushroom clouds we've all seen on tele. With Penney's *vixen* experiments there was no nuclear reaction or explosion – the barrels just burst open and erupted the deadly plutonium into the atmosphere where it was spread by the winds and be ever present in the soil. I would liken it to throwing a bag of flour into a fan. Ingestion of the dust does not cause any outward signs of harm, but once drawn into the lungs, becomes the silent killer. Exposure to asbestos has the same effect – it can take up to forty years before mesothelioma manifests itself and kills. There's no doubt Maralinga was a crime against humanity. When we were given the go-ahead by the Australian government for the main mushroom detonations, the then Prime Minister Robert Menzies, condoned the tests by stating there was nothing in the area worth considering, as it was desert country populated by a couple of aboriginal tribal groups. And at that time the natives were non-citizens and therefore by inference, of no consequence. How times have changed.'

'I can't believe it sir. He actually said that?' Hartigan was startled by the comments, but Richard Hamilton showed no reaction. He knew it to be true.

'He did, but years later claimed he had been misquoted. But the denial of aboriginal existence and rights persisted long after that. Only in recent times, has it been acknowledged as one of the oldest geographically isolated humanoid groups tracing its direct ancestry back more than forty thousand years. The tribes were rounded up and transported from their homelands by train to Western Australia, while others were herded into what only can be described as a concentration camp at Yatala, some one hundred and fifty miles away. Others were made to walk out, dying of thirst or starvation during the journey. Some nomadic groups could not be located and simply wandered into the danger zones resulting in sickness and death. There were tragic accounts of aboriginal families living in the bomb craters, oblivious to the danger. As well as the natives, thousands of servicemen, both English and allies were used as guinea pigs following the main and secret experiments. They were directed to walk through the blast areas following the detonations, to monitor the effects. It is now known that more than forty percent of the twenty or so thousand personnel present during the tests, died as the result of, or suffered some form of cancer in the following years. Hundreds of children and grandchildren of veterans exposed to the radiation were born with shocking illnesses including tumours, Down Syndrome, cleft palate, cerebral palsy, autism, missing bones and heart disease. And as for the poor natives – no one considered their plight. They were simply too insignificant to be considered. The name Maralinga derives from the aboriginal translation meaning *Field of Thunder.* For them it resulted in the *Field of Death* and will continue to be the case, for that is their ancestral homeland, their dreaming lands and the land of their very existence. Spiritually, they can never be removed from it, at least not until the last of them dies. Penney and his scientists, were indulging in genocide – it's as clear as that.'

'That gives me an explanation of the rather vague connection with Connoly, but what was his direct involvement? He didn't just go out and fill a jar with 239, or pick up a bit of contaminated material. I still can't see the threat *vixen* poses to us or the Turks or the Americans now? I realise it's out there for all time and the natives and tourists are ignorant of the risks of walking around in it, but how does that threaten three of the world's biggest cities?'

'I believe that's explained by Penney's actions following the tests. He knew the risks of sticking around the scene, so headed home to these green shores. Connoly explained in one of his interviews that fully suited-up people were running around with clicking instruments, while he and all the other personnel on site were totally unprotected.

That caused somewhat of a panic and the order was given to pack up and pull out. The area was to be declared out of bounds. Connoly was given orders to bury everything he was in control of, vehicles, machinery, structures, stores – you name it, he and a fellow squaddie buried it. Just over twenty kilos of plutonium 239 was used in the *vixen* tests. Some years later, Armament Research discovered a further twenty kilos was unaccounted for. It had been signed off by a Lieutenant Nicholas LeBrereton as being consigned back to Armament Research here in the U.K. He signed it off because he had instructed Connoly and a private Darrel Casson to make sure it was picked up for dispatch back here. In the meantime, satisfied his orders would be complied with, LeBrereton decided he didn't like the risk of being subjected to contamination and followed Penney home. Smart lad. The problem was Connoly hid the plutonium, murdered Casson and deserted. I believe in his warped mind he thought it could be something of value he could trade at a later date. God only knows what he was thinking.'

'And you believe that's what Declan Bellamy wants to recover? That's the *vixen* threat?'

'Correct. The unused plutonium 239 was contained in two small heavy lead-lined barrels. The plutonium pellets were manufactured, packed inside heavy lead shielding and welded into the stainless steel containers by the Atomic Energy Commission. Plutonium metal oxidises when exposed to the air, hence the packaging. However, it has a low melting point of around 600 celcius. The upshot is, if you tied half a dozen sticks of gelignite around the drum or surrounded it with the common terrorist explosive of ammonium nitrate, you would empty London, Istanbul or New York within hours of the alarm being raised. Can you imagine the panic traffic jams as people gather what they can and get out. This is a silent killer with no threat of a nuclear explosion – William Penney proved that - there is no mushroom cloud. It just disperses with the wind and lays around until the end of time. It's one of the most deadly killers ever devised by man.'

'You mentioned only two barrels sir. Could this material be split into three or more?'

'No, my advice is once those barrels, or whatever you want to call them, are opened, they cannot be re-sealed. However, I know what you're driving at Hartigan – three cities are rumoured to be the targets, so which one is going to miss out?'

'Precisely. During my meeting with *vixen*, as I term Bellamy, he made specific reference to London, Istanbul or New York being the targets. He's only got two barrels, so there can only be two targets. I would suggest he wants to punish us for his father's treatment, so London is on the list and if Barzani is in on the act, he's a Kurd, so I would guess Istanbul is close second. However, if America pulls out of northern Syria and allows the Turks to overrun the Kurds, as indications suggest they will do, the target may change. After all, where would the biggest impact be felt? How many crazies would like to see America suffer another 9/11 disaster, only this time on an unbelievable scale?'

Crowther leaned back and looked up at the ceiling and then across at his colleague. 'Do you have any idea how to proceed Richard?'

'I believe we should inform the Prime Minister for a start. This is a national crisis we simply cannot continue to ignore.'

Crowther shook his head in derision. 'That would really cause panic – the smell of shit would be covering the walls of Downing Street within thirty seconds as the PM's bowel's voided and within five minutes, the whole of Westminster would be smelling of the same as the pollies exited. There would be absolute bedlam with all decorum disappearing in an instant. No, this is not to go further than this room. We have to solve the problem.'

Hamilton rose to his feet and leaned over Crowther's desk in a burst of anger. 'You cannot do that Linton. If you don't inform the Prime Minister, I will.'

Hartigan was debating whether it was Crowther's earthy description, or the smell of excrement that caused Hamilton's reaction. Crowther had no pretence of social standing, whereas his SIS counterpart had the air of an elite unused to, but certainly aware of such repugnant statements.

'Oh, sit down Richard before you blow a valve. It's a case of we're damned if we do and damned if we don't. If we inform the PM, it's going to leak out almost immediately. We'll both be called in to explain how this happened. The military top-brass will be called in for advice. The responsible parliamentary minister and his advisers will be called in followed by senior public servants. Within five minutes one of them would have told his wife in sworn secrecy and then the phones would melt when she confided in her closest friends. But the danger is still there – it's panic time. On the other hand if we remain stumm, we either neutralise Bellamy and recover the barrels, or the balloon goes up just the same. Can't you see we're in a no-win situation?'

Hamilton slumped back into his chair. 'Good God Linton, I had not idea it was this critical. How the hell do we proceed? Or more to the point, how long do you think we've got before *vixen* is let loose? Have you any idea Hartigan?'

'It will take them some time to organise sir. He can't just simply dig up the plutonium and ship it out. He will need help to achieve that. My guess is he won't consign it on some freighter which could come to the attention of Customs in any port the vessel called into. How would he explain two barrels of some unspecified goods concealed in a container. It's simply too risky. No, he's got to come up with a more clever solution. We can rule out airfreight – the contents would have to be explained and the likely demand the barrels be opened, puts paid to that idea. My belief is he will have to charter a small freighter with a considerable range of at least six thousand miles which is the approximate distance between say Darwin and Kuwait in the Persian Gulf, the closest point to southern Turkey, or likewise if the target is London. Impossible to contemplate. Too many questions would be asked. Just think about it gentlemen – if you were the charter company, or even the owner of small ship, what would your reaction be if I asked you to transport two small barrels as sole cargo, half way around the world? No, what we are looking for is a long-range vessel, such as a trawler, with the capacity to stay at sea for months. However, the problem with that is two-fold. It will be immediately stopped and searched if it tries to enter the Persian Gulf without a valid reason. Neither the United Arab Emirates, nor Iran is going to allow a foreign fishing vessel into their waters. There is no way any vessel can get through the Straits of Hormuz without being identified. And similarly, any trawler attempting to get through to the Mediterranean via the Suez canal, would simply be denied entry. The Med is a no-go area for any commercial fishing and an excuse the vessel was being delivered to a buyer in England would be laughed at. As you are aware, we're cancelling fishing licences, not issuing them. We're being choked to death by those EU bureaucrats in Brussels.'

Crowther had been listening intently. 'So, how do you think they're going to do it?'

'I don't know, but he's got a big hurdle to jump if he's to pull this one off. We know it was Bellamy or Barzani accompanied by Zehra Kermandi who was in Australia recently. We know they somehow got to Indonesia and from there to Beirut, where the trail ends. However, I did meet Bellamy or Barzani in Syria, and one of the women with him could have been Zehra Kermandi? I believe it was Bellamy I met, which begs the question, where is Aras Barzani and is he still alive? Bellamy and Kermandi could have also returned to Australia by now. He could not have recovered the barrels and shipped them out in the time he was down there. He was probably just making contacts and determining how he was going to successfully move them. I'm convinced the barrels are still exactly where Declan Connoly buried them more than fifty years ago. And, assuming Bellamy has already returned, we have to move quickly.'

'And we can't ask for assistance from the Australian authorities to keep an eye out for any of these people if they attempt to go near Maralinga?'

'Precisely Sir Richard and you well understand the reason why, I trust?'

Richard Hamilton nodded. He knew the reason – he would face severe repercussions if he was forced to admit he was concealing something he had been well aware of for some considerable time. It would most certainly be the end of his career and his pension for concealing it. He cursed Linton Crowther for drawing him into this mess. He should have immediately excused himself and driven to see the Prime Minister, but it was now too late. 'Go on, go on,' he said, waving his hand impatiently.

Hartigan continued. 'There are three possible ports they could ship this stuff from. The first is Adelaide, only a few hundred miles from Maralinga, but the difficulty with that is no large sea-going trawler, or vessel of that type would have the range to travel across the Australian Bight and then on up to the Arabian sea without refueling somewhere. The second, and more likely would be to truck it across the Nullabor to Perth and knock two thousand miles off any sea voyage, but my pick is Darwin. It's alive with small vessels, all trading up through the East. Such a vessel could hook-up with one of those large Arab dhows which trade all the way from Malaysia, around the Bay of Bengal and up to Dubai. As opposed to a large trawler which will attract attention, the dhows are so numerous, they're totally inconspicuous. They've been doing it for a thousand or more years, transporting every illicit and legal cargo under the sun. Darwin is my choice and that's where I would start any investigation.'

'I can follow your reasoning Hartigan, but from my understanding, Dubai is the choke point to the Persian Gulf for anything intended for Iraq, Iran, the United Arab Emirates, Kuwait or Saudi Arabia. I think the only entry point, if by some miracle the cargo is not discovered in Dubai, is Iraq. Iran is out of the question as they would be sure to intercept anything their high-speed patrol boats viewed as suspicious. Then like a cloud hanging over the whole scene are the U.S. and allied naval vessels which let nothing suspicious pass, without being searched for weapons and armaments. The Persian Gulf route is simply out of the question for hiding such a shipment and then landing it in Iraq and hoping to send it by road through to Turkey and on to Istanbul.'

Hartigan stroked his chin and pulled a wry expression. 'I would have to agree with that sir, which leaves only two possible alternatives. The first is across the Indian Ocean, around the Cape and then up the African Coast to England if that's the initial target and then on to Turkey via Gibraltar and the Mediterranean. I would completely discount that route. The most probable is the more direct route through the Suez Canal, dropping off one barrel somewhere in the Med and taking the other through to the U.K. The problem with that, as I've already explained, would require a transshipment from the trawler to another vessel with no restrictions of entry to the Canal or Med and no suspicions about what it would be carrying.'

'We may get lucky and find Bellamy or the woman, if they have returned to Australia. We should really try and coerce the authorities down there to assist us. They could be arrested on sight and questioned.'

'We would have a problem with that,' Crowther replied turning to Hamilton. 'Unlike here, you can't arrest someone in Australia without charging them. You can pull them in for questioning, but if they're aware of their rights, they can simply tell the police to go take a jump.'

'But, this is terrorism on a grand scale. Surely, that overrides any petty concerns about someone's rites?'

Linton Crowther raised his eyelids to the heavens as he counterpart glanced across at Hartigan. 'Without doubt, that would have an immediate effect Richard. The mention of terrorism would dispense with any legal formalities. In that event, what happened at Maralinga would have no comparison to the immediate explosion in relations between Australia and here when the press and television media found out what we've been hiding. However, why don't I accept your suggestion and hand this problem over to you and your SIS team, so that Hartigan and our SI05 Counter Intelligence chaps, can get on with more pressing work.'

'Don't be so bloody sarcastic and impertinent Crowther. This is your problem and you're obliged to handle it. I should never have attended this meeting. You've compromised me and I've no doubt you did it deliberately.'

'Well you did attend and yes, you are compromised, but I deny it was deliberate Richard. We have a potential monumental problem of terrorism and I wanted your ideas. If you don't agree to assist and I'm only asking for your singular assurance, I will say no more, but you must realise if the balloon goes up and this story leaks, we can both look forward to immediate retirement and worse. We will be funding our own defence and with the prohibitive cost of London barristers, we would be bankrupt before any trial commenced. And I don't see how we would hit it off together in a a cell.'

Richard Hamilton straightened in his chair as though hit by an electric charge. 'Okay Linton, but we are going after these three now and I mean now. We both have operatives in Australia, but I'm going to assign another two and I want you to do the same.'

'And what do you propose these people should do?' Crowther already knew the answer, but wanted confirmation.

'They are to find all three and eliminate them immediately. With them dead, hopefully the plutonium will stay buried and no one will be the wiser, except for us in this room. The operatives will not be given a reason for the hit.'

'But what if they've already dug it up and it's on the move?'

Crowther could see his colleague was feeling the strain as he realised his implication in the enormity of the problem.

He was looking at one very rattled individual - rattled both by his personal status liability and what was being proposed. He was sanctioning murder and he was well aware every word was likely being recorded. It would certainly be the case if the meeting had taken place in his office. He could not retreat or show reticence.

'The operatives will be under firm instructions their primary object is to locate the material in question. There are to be no limits as to the methods they use to extract the information. One of the three is going to crack and I imagine it will be the woman when the interrogation gets rough, as it certainly will if she doesn't cooperate. In any event, they are all dead. There will be no survivors,' Crowther countered.

Richard Hamilton rose from his chair and turned for the doorway. 'I don't like your methods Linton, but now you've pulled me into it, you've got my full attention. I'll assign two people immediately, so let's get on with it.'

Linton Crowther's expression was blank as the door closed and he looked across at Hartigan. 'That's one of my problems taken care of. I was afraid if I didn't get SIS on board, a leak was sure to occur and I wasn't going to countenance that. Now let's get back to the three. Do you think they're acting alone? By that I mean, do they have backing from the Melbourne Kurds, or could it be some other terrorist group? Who else was this Connoly character connected to? After all, when you think about it, there must be connections. This operation will take a bit of co-ordination and planning.'

'Sir, if it's Bellamy, he has an axe to grind with us because of what we put his grandfather through, whereas Barzani will be siding with the Kurds to take out Istanbul. I believe this whole program is being funded by the Kurds, because they have been, or will be the most affected, depending what

America does in Syria. I believe I should start in Darwin and get a schedule of shipping movements.'

'I agree with that, but I'm wondering whether we shouldn't alert the Turks. After all, we do have an undeniable responsibility? I don't want to be the person targeted for what amounts to culpable homicide on a mass scale. We're talking about millions being displaced and subjected to a complete spectrum of cancers in regard to Istanbul.'

'I would counsel you resist from that course sir. They would immediately start dragging in every Kurd, man woman or child and commence interrogating them. I've witnessed their methods of interrogation first hand and I can tell you, it's not pleasant to watch. There will come a time when we will have to take the Americans into our confidence. There are thousands of American tourists in Turkey during summer and if they were exposed to the risk, we would most certainly be looking for a safe place on earth in which to hide. The Americans would never forgive us. Give me a month and then let's have this conversation again.'

# 40

The stifling humidity hit him as he stepped out of the aircraft. It reminded him of Singapore. He found an hotel and checked his emails just in case Crowther had instructions. Following the meeting, he had been given a month to come up with something solid. He knew there were agents from both MI6 and SIS in the country, but he had no contact or names. Each had their assigned tasks. It was typical – no co-ordination.

The air-conditioning in harbour master's office was a welcome relief as he introduced himself to the cheerful receptionist. 'Is it the weather, or does everyone look so happy in this part of the world?'

'That's correct sir, no gloom around here. The only things to fear are snakes and crocodiles. The locals are all friendly. Mr Jeffries is expecting you.' She knocked and pushed open a door marked with the title and name of the person he had come to see.

'Bill Jeffries, Mr Hartigan. I've been expecting you.'

'It's Miles, Bill. I would like to get straight down to business as this is a very pressing matter.'

'Yeah, take a seat and tell me what you're after and why it's so urgent?'

'I'm particularly interested in any cargo vessels or large trawlers which have departed in the past week or are leaving in the next two.' He was banking on the fact he had seen Bellamy in Syria only weeks before. If one of them, along the Kermandi, was now back in Australia, he had a rough idea of when they could have shipped out the plutonium. 'I can't tell you why it's so urgent, but I would like to know the movements of any vessels headed for the Persian Gulf or the west coast of America in particular.'

Jeffries raised his eyebrows at the expanse of the question. 'All of the shipping from here is destined for Asia, namely Indonesia, the Philippines, Malaysia, Singapore and right through to Dubai on the Persian Gulf. As for America, I could count on one hand how many sailings a month leave here including company-chartered oil rig supplies and equipment to and from the States - we don't do a lot of trade with the west coast. Can you give me an idea of what size vessel you're looking at? Is it a large container vessel for general cargo, a livestock transport, or a smaller trading ship able to get into the shallow-draft ports. There are any number of smaller freighters carrying a few hundred to a few thousand tons, but they're only short regular sailings throughout Indonesia, Thailand and the Philippines. Take your pick.'

'Just give me a list of the smaller ships and their ultimate destinations. I have to wing it a bit as I simply don't have the time.'

Jeffries pulled up the sailing dates on his screen and searched through the entries. 'Six vessels have sailed in the past two weeks, four destined for Port Moresby and Rabaul in New Guinea with the other two headed for Timor Este. Just regular runs, straight there and back. As for sailings in the next two weeks, one is bound for Singapore with a cargo of mangoes, a regular at this time of the year. The others are general cargo, one headed for Colombo in Sri Lanka, the other for Mangalore and Mumbai, India, while another is bound for Chittagong in Bangladesh, then onto Goa and Dubai.'

'That's the one that interests me,' Hartigan replied. 'Can you tell me where it's registered and the name?'

Jeffries peered closer at the screen. 'Arabian Venture, 4000 tons, registered in United Arab Emirates.'

'How long would it take to get to Dubai?'

'I would guess anything up to a month. It could be longer as although these vessels note their final destination, they often get sidetracked to pick up cargo in other ports along the way. The smaller vessels can get into provincial ports and are more flexible - they are a vital cog in the vast wheel of Asian trade.'

'Anything headed across the Pacific?'

'One, it brought in a load of oil and gas-line pipes and heavy equipment and is due out in three days.'

'Can you give me description?'

'Nova Centrus, 25,000 tons, registered in Liberia and headed for San Diego and then through the Panama to Houston. It's a regular visitor mostly carrying oil drilling equipment and machinery.'

'Would you run off the details of all those vessels please, Bill. The Nova Centrus doesn't appear to fit the profile I'm looking for, but the one headed for Dubai could be of interest.'

Jeffries hit a key on his computer and turned to take the sheet of paper as it emerged from his printer. 'All yours, Miles. Can I ask what you are looking for? Obviously, it's something that's been shipped out of here. Maybe I can help if you could be more specific?'

'What about large ocean-going trawlers?'

'Any number of those, but they mostly operate in the Gulf of Carpentaria to the east, although there are some that go west into the Indian Ocean. In addition, we see foreign trawlers pulling in for repairs and fuel. This is a very busy place.'

Hartigan took three photos out of his satchel. 'Would you have seen any of these people around the port or in town?'

Jeffries studied the head and shoulders shots and shook his head. 'No, can't say I have. It would be a good idea to check with the local police. This place is full of blow-ins and misfits trying to avoid the law, their wives, defactos, or the bailiffs. Darwin is also a good jumping off place if you want to be dropped off in Indonesia without clearing Customs here. Although this place looks dead and deserted because of the heat, there's a very active underworld intent on some criminal activity. Drugs are the main curse – you name it and you can buy it. The pushers are just like cockroaches, they infest the scene after dark. Tell me, what are you really after? Is it the three in the photos, or something else?'

Hartigan extended his hand as he ignored the question. 'Many thanks Bill, I appreciate your help. Say, is it possible to stroll around the docks?'

Jeffries shook his head. 'Not possible, Miles. Security is very tight for health and safety reasons. Also this port is owned by the Chinese and they don't like anyone just strolling around. In fact, it would take a week just to get clearance and if granted you would be escorted by security. You would not be aware at the time, but they would then file a report as to their observations of your purpose, the nature of your questions and who you talked to. And from what I can deduce, I don't think you want that attention, do you?'

Hartigan smiled at the accusation. 'Thanks once again Bill. I appreciate you help.'

# 41

*The hotel was the closest to the port, drowned out by the noise of workers talking and drinking, playing pool and either watching some replay of a football game or the rising voice of a race-caller as horses crossed the finishing line on another similarly large screen at the opposite end of the bar. The place was all noise and activity, a working-man's hotel where the revenue was generated by the common camaraderie of associated maritime occupations. He would have to be careful. Was it like similar dockside pubs in England where it was not wise for a stranger to start asking questions in a very close community, or was there a different atmosphere here?*

'What'll it be love?'

'A beer thank you Maxine,' he replied, reading the tag on her shirt. Having no idea of the brews available, he pointed to a tap.

She smiled as she poured the cold beer. 'What part of England are you from? Are you lost, because you're not a tourist if you're in this part of town?'

'That obvious is it?' he replied pushing over the ten dollar note. 'You're a Geordie, aren't you?'

'Yes, Newcastle United born and bred. Six months more here and then I'm off home.'

'Can I ask you a question or two?'

'If you're going to ask me out, the answer is no. For one, you're too bloody old and two, my Mum told me never to talk to strangers, particularly cops.'

Hartigan laughed at her candour. 'I'm not a cop and I don't want to ask you out, but if I was younger, I wouldn't hesitate.' He took the photos out of his jacket and pushed them across to her. 'I would just like to know if you've seen any of these people?'

She was about to pick one up when an older man, stepped beside her and pushed the photos back across the bar. 'We don't like private investigators in here and you ain't a cop. I know all the local cops mate and you ain't one of them, so fuck off. Don't ever make the mistake of coming in here again asking questions. I never forget a face and I certainly have yours marked.' It was said loud enough for part of the bar to go quiet as faces turned. 'Maxine, don't serve this guy again. And mate, finish your beer and get out before someone takes exception and helps you through the door with his boot.'

Hartigan was not to be intimidated. He had seen her glow of recognition of one photo. He had to talk to her, but she ignored him as she attended to demands along the crowded bar. He was also being closely watched by the bar manager as he slowly sipped his beer. Suddenly, she was in front of him pouring a particular beer a patron had called for. 'You recognised one of them, didn't you?'

The reply was near inaudible through barely moving lips. She had not diverted her attention from the beer she was pouring. 'One of them is in here now, with that group at the end of the bar to your right.'

'Can I meet you somewhere after work?'

'No you can't. You've most likely cost me my job already. That was another thing my mother said - my big mouth would get me into trouble.'

In his peripheral vision, Hartigan saw the bar manager begin to move in his direction. He got up from the stool and slowly walked the length of the bar studying the faces, but could not recognise the one he was looking for. The group was all laughing and talking at once, but not a face to match the photo. Then he noticed a single empty bar stool nearest the entrance. Maxine had alerted him too late. The target had obviously heard the manager's comments and fled. Hartigan stopped as he was about to follow. 'Any of you chaps know the fellow who just left in a hurry?'

'Yeah, that's Flash, as in Flash Gordon, the comic book character from your era grandpa,' one of the group answered in a mocking Scottish accent. 'He flashes around everywhere. He's too bloody fast for you to catch. Anything else you want to know?'

Hartigan laughed at the challenge. He wasn't going to get anything further out of this lot – obviously a bunch of young tourists on working visas. 'No, you've given me all the information I need,' he replied as he walked past and out onto the street. There were any number of people about, but none matched the photo of Declan Bellamy, or was it Aras Barzani? It was hard to tell them apart in the passport photos. Both had strikingly similar features. They could easily be mistaken as brothers despite their differing ethnic heritage.

He was sitting on a bench under a poinciana tree with its flowering canopy shading him from the late afternoon sun when he saw her walk out of the pub about an hour later. He walked quickly across the street as she drew level. He expected her to retaliate, but she smiled.

'Oh, it's you again. Still after a date are you?'

'No, no, you've already given me your opinion on that score,' he chuckled. 'I just want to know if you can give me any more information on that fellow you identified. Who was the group he was with?'

'They're just a bunch of Irish, Scottish and local lads who get together every day for a beer. The one you want to know about is an Australian. No mistaking that accent anywhere in the world,' she said, not checking her pace. 'What do you want him for? Are you after him for some crime, or does he owe you money?'

'No, he's in the clear on that score. He hasn't done anything wrong. I would just like to talk to him. Do you know where he lives, or how long he's been around?'

'I don't know his name, I don't know where he lives and don't want to and he's only been coming into the pub for a week or so. Any more questions?'

'Maxine, I know you think I'm a cop, but I'm not,' he said in his most convincing tone. 'I now live in Australia after serving in the navy back home. My job is to repossess boats on behalf of finance companies and sell them. Anyone who walks into our offices in Sydney is caught on a CCTV camera and those photos I showed you were of a group from up here who did just that. The long and short of it is, I'm about to repossess a large trawler which I think this group may be interested in buying. The problem is I can't find any of them and someone else has moved into the address they gave. That bar was so crowded I wasn't in there long enough to have a good look. That's why I decided to short circuit things by showing you the photos. I hope I didn't get you into too much trouble with the manager?'

She waved her hand in dismissal. 'Nah, that's just bloody Warren the Weasel, as we call him. He's always trying to hit on us casual girls. He's why they don't stay long. He thought you were moving onto his patch and wanted to bare his teeth. Only problem he's got no real teeth,' she laughed. 'I'm sorry, I can't help you, but come to think of it, that chap I identified was looking for a trawler to buy. In fact, if he didn't join a group, he would pop in every day to just chat with the trawler skippers who are regulars in the place. They all gave him the cold-shoulder because they have no intention of selling their livelihood. However, this morning I heard him telling a group of regulars he was finished in Darwin. He had given up trying to buy a trawler as he had found an alternative and was leaving the country next week.'

'You're not having me on are you? Just telling me what I want to hear?'

She looked offended. 'No, I'm bloody not. Look, I've told you all I know, so if you don't mind, I'm off. However, would you do something in return for me?'

'If I can.'

'Please don't come into the pub again. It's hard enough putting up with that slimy bastard, but if you show up it will get even tougher as he tries to frighten you off. I've only got a few months to go, so I don't want to be fired and have to find another job in the meantime.'

'Agreed. And thanks very much, you've been a great help.'

She swung around as she started to walk away. 'And one final thing, whatever your name is. You're full of crap. You're an agent alright, but it has nothing to do with shipping.'

# 42

*L*inton Crowther told him to phone at anytime. *'Sir, it's Miles Hartigan. I know what time it is there, but I may have a strong lead.'*

'Just a moment, while I turn on the light and put on my glasses. Don't worry about the time my boy, this is more important than sleep. Now fire away.'

'It's either Barzani or Bellamy here in Darwin. Whoever it is, gave me the slip and although I've been here a week, I haven't laid eyes on either again. However, the harbour master gave me a tip-off today. A small coaster named the Crescent Castle, which regularly sails up through the east to Dubai has just departed. It's first port of call is Colombo, Sri Lanka.'

'Is that all the evidence you have? It appears somewhat skinny?'

'Bill Jeffries, the harbour master said it was unusual that it would arrive and depart on the same day. It was unusual because it is generally in port for up to a week waiting for cargo. In addition, Jeffries said it took on a crewman at the last moment. He checked out as a Cypriot marine engineer working his way home.'

'So what's the suspicion?'

'Sir, as you are aware, Cyprus is a divided island. Greeks on one side and Turks on the other. You can't tell a Turk from a Kurd and depending on the convenience of the situation, they can claim either. I've a feeling the Cypriot is in fact Barzani, as he spoke both Greek and Turkish according to Customs fellows who inspected his papers and questioned him. There was no record of him boarding with anything other than his bags, but that doesn't discount there was a pay-off and the barrels were already on board. I'll give you his name so you can check him out in Cyprus.'

'What do you intend to do now? I can easily get someone to Colombo to meet the ship on arrival. I'll check out the Cypriot connection in the meantime. If he's a phoney or carrying false papers, we'll soon determine his real identity. I know some people high up in the government there. I just pray your hunch is correct - Richard Hamilton is becoming more panicky everyday. He wants to dump the problem on the Prime Minister in a desperate effort to lay-off some of the responsibility and pressure. This whole affair is really playing on his nerves and I'm afraid he's going to snap. He doesn't realise it's going to bury us all if we fail. As I was saying, what's your next move?'

'I'm going to hang around here for awhile as they must be hiding somewhere in this vast country, if in fact they are here. I don't believe they've retrieved what they came for and departed. Have the other agents come up with anything?'

'No, not as yet. They appear to have drawn a complete blank, but they're good and won't stop. Tell me, why have you changed your focus to this particular ship? I thought you were of the opinion they would try to ship the barrels onto something the size of a large ocean going trawler?'

'Sir, I'm desperate and it's the strongest lead I've come up with to date. However, there are dozens of large trawlers operating out of here and in other ports around the coast. The Cypriot may be a decoy while the others buy or charter a trawler from somewhere close to Darwin. I'm also looking at New Guinea. It has to be somewhere local, as no trawler would have the range to get up near the Persian Gulf or anywhere close from any of the ports in southern Australia. I'm convinced the action is here, but I'll still check out some of the ports in Western Australia. I'll stick around until I hear from you.'

'Good, I'll phone you when that vessel gets to Colombo. If the result is negative and he checks out, you won't have wasted your time by flying up there. By the way, what about anything sailing for the U.S?'

'I believe we're drawing a long-bow on that one, but it's worth a try I suppose.' He gave Crowther the name of the vessel and departure date.


'Catch the next flight out for Dubai. That vessel didn't call in at Colombo, but headed straight for Dubai. I believe I can use my influence to have it detained and searched. I don't know about the one to San Diego. Without alerting their Homeland Security, I would not be prepared to request a search of a vessel in an American port. Leave that with me to think about.'

Three days later Hartigan was standing in the Harbour Master's office in Jebel Ali, Dubai's commercial port. Muhamed Sharif was dressed in immaculate white, the gold bars on his shoulders signifying that of a master mariner.

'Good afternoon Mr Hartigan, I've been expecting you. The vessel we got the request to search has already sailed for Khorramshahr, Iraq. However we conducted a thorough search and I mean thorough, but there was nothing of interest.'

'Did you possibly test for.....' Hartigan was hesitant about asking the question, but Sharif was anticipating it.

'Yes, we also tested for any trace of radioactive material. Once again, that proved negative. The vessel was absolutely clean, if you can call any vessel that trades in these waters clean, from the sanitary point of view. Nothing was found to match the description our security forces had been told to look for. We are extremely careful about cargo going up the Red Sea to ports in Iraq and Iran. We recently apprehended some sort of seismic device containing a radioactive material used in the exploration for uranium. It was bound for Bandar Abbas, just across the strait in Iran. It was on the American banned list of exports to Iran and was eventually found inside a container packed with other goods. It emitted a very low level of radiation, but we did find it. If a similar article had been on the vessel in question, we would have detected it.'

Hartigan smiled as he realised the ruse used by Crowther to have the ship searched. Obviously, he had heard of the arrest of an item of radioactive equipment by the Dubai authorities and decided to make the same case. There was no need to describe in detail what was been looked for – just search for a radioactive reading and that would probably be the plutonium. 'So, there was no trace of any radioactive material or equipment?'

'I can give you my assurance in that regard. We had been tipped-off to look for a very low signature count of radiation, but none was found. It was completely clean, so we let it sail. Believe me Mr Hartigan, we're just as keen as you and the Americans not to let anything sinister get into Iranian hands.'

Another dead end. Hartigan went back to his hotel, sat down in the bar and ordered a beer. He took out his mobile and dialled Crowther's direct line.

'I've drawn a blank here sir. Not a trace of radiation on the vessel that came in from Australia. I was late getting here, but I was assured it was thoroughly searched and cleared to go. I thought I had it nailed as it was the only vessel out of Darwin bound for this part of the world. It had to be on that ship, but where?'

'Don't waste time Hartigan. If anything on that ship was radioactive, it would have been found. Come on home and plan out next move.'

# 43

*It was a grey London day when Hartigan slumped into a chair in Crowther's spacious office and gave him a look of despair. 'Did you manage to get anywhere with the Americans sir.'*

'No, I drew a blank on that one. The vessel went straight through to Houston and did not call in at San Diego. I made some enquiries, but Homeland Security was soon on the phone asking why I was particularly interested in that ship. I didn't want to push it further because those oil drilling and supply companies are security conscious. I don't believe anything not strictly on the manifest could have been loaded in Darwin. I think we can discount that avenue of enquiry.'

'Have you checked that Cypriot engineer lead?'

'Still ongoing, but we can't wait on that enquiry. Let's assume it amounts to nothing, we still have to focus on Darwin. The barmaid identified either Bellamy or Barzani, but there's been no trace of them since. What if either of them did find a small trawler rather than a large deep sea vessel and simply island hopped across to Indonesia and so-on from there by a series of small boats. Have you thought of that?'

Crowther was giving him a mild, but direct rebuke. He had thought of it, but the conclusion was if that occurred there was no hope of ever tracking or recovering the plutonium.

'It's possible sir and I had thought of it, but where to start is the problem. There are dozens of small vessels such as large motor yachts and fishing vessels that could easily drop them and their cargo off in Bali or some other close port in that archipelago. Because security is so lax and bribery the name of the game, it would be a simple matter to charter any of the thousands of small trawlers and dhows to island-hop around the Bay of Bengal and up to the Red Sea. Pay enough money for a couple of innocuous looking barrels to be taken on and there would be no questions asked. The more I think about it, I do believe the goods and one of our suspects have departed from Darwin, or will leave from that port. I don't know what to suggest now sir.'

Crowther swung his chair around to look at the low cloud-base outside with its view of St Paul's. 'As I see it, trying to locate the exact boat we think we should be looking for is an impossibility. We've got to locate any of that trio. Find one and we stand a chance of finding the two missing barrels.'

'I agree sir, but I believe the situation is becoming critical. Let's look at the facts – we know the *vixen* threat is real and we can safely assume Connoly gave his grandson the location of the barrels and what they represent. That material has left, or is on its way to Istanbul and London. To date, we cannot locate any one of the offenders in Australia, so we must widen the net and that means alerting the Turks and the Americans. I don't believe there is a risk to New York, but there's certainly a major threat to holidaying or expat U.S. citizens who may be in Turkey or London when the contents of the barrels are released. We have to reveal the identity of who we're looking for and the threat. The more people aware and looking the better. I mightn't agree with the Turkish methods of interrogation, but in this case the risk is too great. Likewise, I don't think the Americans would be too tolerant either, particularly if they were aware of the scale of the potential disaster. And with all due respect sir, aren't you forgetting London? I don't want to see it turned into an uninhabitable pile of derelict buildings for the next twenty thousand years.'

Crowther turned back to face Hartigan. 'I'll have to bring Richard Hamilton up to date on this. He's likely to have a nervous breakdown, but I don't want the poor dear rushing off to the PM just yet. I don't want the Turks to know exactly what the problem is. The whole world would then know within five minutes. You're to go back to Istanbul and brief their security there is a real danger headed their way. No need to explain the full story. And also brief them to be on the lookout for Bellamy and the woman. I will call in American Homeland Security and give them a full rundown and that's one meeting I won't enjoy. I don't believe the language will be exactly diplomatic and I don't blame them. However, one thing does puzzle me. Why can't we at least locate one of these people? I want all stops pulled out and by that I mean all stops. I also believe we may have to bring the Australians into this and forget about continuing to cover up the threat. They're well aware of some of the aftermath of the *vixen* trials, but they don't know the full story - the dirty laundry is about to get an airing. It will give them a real jolt when told the truth. If they try and fob us off by pretending the *vixen* problem has been fixed, then maybe it's time the Australian public was told the truth. If we don't get full co-operation, we'll leak it to the media. That is sure to get the politicians attention. Also, I didn't want to, but I'll have an Interpol notice issued. We know there are two males, Aras Barzani and Declan Bellamy along with the woman, Zehra Kermandi. Either Barzani or Bellamy could be dead, but we still should be looking for all three. Find any one of them and we stand a chance of locating the plutonium.'

# 44



'You've got something serious on your minds for you two gentlemen to have summoned me here.'

'Indeed we have Emile. Would you like a tea or coffee before we start?'

'No thanks, why don't we stop shooting the breeze and get on with it?' He had noted Crowther was trying to maintain the air of control, but it wasn't working. The formalities had been dispensed with. The man was nervous and Hamilton was going to let Crowther do the talking and take the flak.

'Emile, we are concerned certain radioactive material might have fallen into the hands of terrorists.'

'We wondered when you were going to tell us about it?'

Neither Crowther nor Hamilton could hide their shock.

'It's the *vixen* problem, isn't it? Now, how about coming clean and telling us what this is all about and why we should be concerned? Our guys in Syria, Iraq and Turkey have been getting a bombardment of rumours about a supposed terrorist threat that's going to wipe out certain cities for all time. Nearly every PKK terrorist they pick up keeps taunting the interrogator's that the wrath of Allah is about to fall upon them. What the hell is it?'

'What we are looking for are three terrorists who have got their hands on two barrels containing about twenty kilos of plutonium 239.'

Subritzky whistled through his teeth. 'Where the hell did it come from and how the hell did they get hold of it?'

'It originated in Australia.'

'You've got to be joking. Who in Australia would have the capacity to manufacture that stuff? It's absolute Armageddon. Don't tell me they're developing nuclear weapons down there?'

'Nothing of the sort Emile. Sit back and I'll put you in the picture and then we can work out how we're going to counter it.' Subritzky sat in silence until Crowther finished relating the background.

'You say there are two barrels of this stuff, overlooked following the completion of the Maralinga tests and the possible targets are New York, London and Istanbul? In my opinion this bunch of crazies will go after the target with the most hate factor attached and that would have to be New York, followed by either London or Istanbul. You say you guys have been sitting on this information for more than fifty years, without warning us of the potential problem?

Who was the crazy mother who originally blew twenty kilos of plutonium into the surrounding countryside without considering the consequences? The guy should have been taken back out there and put in a cage so he could observe the effects at first hand.'

'That wasn't the aim of the *vixen* tests Emile. The aim was to test the effect of blowing up plutonium 239 with TNT to see if it would cause a nuclear reaction, as opposed to detonating it in the normal manner through fission. Combined with that, William Penney, one of three nuclear scientists involved, wanted to test the fall-out effects on humans and those humans were the army personnel who witnessed the explosions.'

Subritzky shook his head slowly. 'I just can't believe the jerk thought he could do that without explanation. Surely, someone must have been in charge of the asylum to check these lunatics were up to, but obviously not. Jesus, imagine if he'd attempted that anywhere in England? They'd have nailed his balls to the wall for even suggesting it. But because Australia is on the other side of the world, out of sight and out of mind, the military guinea pigs were totally ignorant of the consequences.'

Crowther could see Subritzky was getting angrier by the moment as he absorbed what he had just heard.

'You say plutonium 239 has a half-life in excess of twenty thousand years. If I recall my high school physics, that means it takes a similar length of time to lose another half of its effect and so on. My understanding then is there must be an extreme danger of radiation from it floating around in the dust and debris. Anyone inhaling it during that time is a prime case for some form of cancer. And you say you assholes have been sitting on the threat for how long?'

Crowther held up his hand in an attempt to calm the situation. 'Th.... there's no need to get personal Mr Subritzky. I think you should take the more rational approach and work with us to solve it.'

'Rational approach,' Subritzky replied, raising his voice to a shout. 'Fucking rational approach you suggest? I suggest you stand in Leicester Square in London, Times Square in New York or Taksim Square in Istanbul and tell the masses how you fucked up. But tell them not to panic, because you want them to consider a rational approach. You can tell them the good news is there are only two barrels of this stuff, but the terrorists want to hit three cities, therefore one of the cities is going to win the lottery and miss out. That should really calm them down. Not. You would only have seconds to pray before they tore you to pieces. You disgust me. It's no wonder we tossed you out of our nuclear program in 1952 when we found your man Klaus Fuchs was feeding all our research directly to the Russians.'

Crowther said nothing, while Hamilton was studying the plaster-work of the ceiling cornices. Subritzky let out a explosion of breath as he sank back into his chair. They all remained silent waiting for someone to take the lead. Subritzky's anger began to subside as the the colour returned to his face and his breathing returned to normal.

'Okay, okay, you've told me. Have you already briefed your government or the Turks?'

'Neither as yet, although one of my operative's is on his way to Istanbul and following this meeting I will tell the Prime Minister.'

'Well, call the Turk messenger off now and don't tell your PM until we've had time to think this through. As I see it Crowther, we'll only cause a general panic of monumental proportions if this gets out. We've got to pool our resources and intelligence and put this into high gear. You say *vixen* is being perpetrated by an Aras Barzani and Declan Bellamy, both renegade Australian's? Also in their company is a Kurdish national by the name of Zehra Kermandi? They must be located and interrogated as to the whereabouts of this stuff. And I mean interrogated. Waterboarding won't be good enough for these three. These people are terrorists of the highest degree and must be treated as such. Meanwhile, I'll be heading back to Washington tomorrow to talk to my director of Homeland Security and the National Security Agency. It's really going to make their day, so duck for cover when the shit begins to fly. In the meantime, you two rev up your hunt for the three operatives by alerting the Turks they are possible terrorists. However, at this stage, don't mention what *vixen* actually represents. Refer to it as a chemical scare, or a plan to detonate some high explosives in the vicinity of the Blue Mosque. That should get their attention to start searching every vehicle in the vicinity.'

Crowther did not interject and correct Subritzky's comment – it was too late, the Turks were already aware of *vixen,* but not the magnitude of the problem.

# 45

‘*That's a nice looking vessel. Where's it bound for?' The Fremantle harbour-master peered through his binoculars at the departing vessel. 'Nice lines, the way it just slices through without leaving a wake. It doesn't really look like a trawler.'*

The assistant glanced out to identify what the harbour-master was looking at and shrugged. 'That isn't a trawler any longer boss. It's been converted to one hundred and fifty feet of pure pleasure, including a chopper pad and a couple of high speed tenders. It has a range in excess of twelve thousand miles. A classic case of one man's failure, being another man's fortune.'

'Tell me more.'

'It was constructed locally for some east-coast insurance agent who wanted to get into prawn trawling up in the Gulf of Carpentaria. He made the mistake of not keeping his eye on his investment and took the attitude all he had to do was sit back and watch the money flow in. It took him the entire season to wake up the money was only flowing in one direction and that was out. The excuse by the skipper was it was the luck of a poor prawn season. When in reality, from what I've heard, the ship was catching tons of prawns, but they were being offloaded for cash to Korean and Chinese mother-ships out at sea. A week or two before the end of the season, the skipper tied the vessel up in Darwin and disappeared along with his bonanza bonus. Result, the insurance agent was into the banks for around three mill. They pulled the plug and the vessel was sold at auction for just under a million. When it arrived here it was immediately refurbished as a pleasure yacht.'

'So who owns it now?'

The assistant tapped into his computer keyboard. 'Some crowd going by the name of Erbil Technology registered in Melbourne. Probably some high-tech guy who's made a fortune inventing some new computer application. Anyway it's trawling days are over.'

'Where is it headed?'

'Calling at Port Hedland and then cruising off up to Malaysia, Indonesia and Thailand, from what I can see.'

'Mmm...interesting,' the harbour master murmured to himself before turning to his assistant. 'Drop Coast Watch a memo and alert them the *Kuro V* has just departed.' He put the binoculars down as he watched it clear the harbour and slowly pick up speed.

'Are you suspicious about something?'

'Nothing in particular, but doesn't it strike you as odd a gin-palace on an apparent pleasure cruise, would be venturing into that part of the world at this time of the year? You're slap-bang into the monsoon and cyclone season and not the place anyone expecting a balmy climate and smooth seas would want to be. Even our aerial and navy patrol boats don't like being out in that weather. Also, I noted there was only a skipper and two deckhands, which is too few for a vessel of that size. And not a single female. Whoever it is, is not on a pleasure cruise. Something just doesn't smell right.'

# 46

*he sales agent eyed the swarthy looking individual accompanied by a woman with soft almond-brown eyes and perfect features. This was one lucky guy, he reflected as he tried to keep his thoughts to selling boats. 'Joe Enright,' he said holding out his hand. He had seen the pair looking in the window of his brokerage. 'I take it you're in the market for a trawler? And your name is?'*

Costas Kyriakou ignored the question. 'Yes, I'm interested in that ninety footer you've got in the window. Can you give me a rundown on it's present condition?'

Enright took a few moments to recover. He had held his hand out to the woman, but she smiled and ignored it. 'It's a sound boat, with good engines and electronics. But it doesn't have a licence to fish for tuna, if that's what you're thinking of doing with it?'

'Licences hard to get, are they?'

Enright gave a long belly laugh. 'Impossible. Strictly controlled and traded only within the local Port Lincoln club of tuna boat millionaires. If you're not from here, you're wasting your time.'

'No, I don't want it for tuna. I want to take it up to Indonesia and refit it for shark fishing.'

'Well, you'll have no problems getting it up there. It has the usual large fuel capacity because these tuna boats fish thousands of kilometres into the southern ocean. Just top-up the fuel and off you go. Half a million dollars and you can drive it away. It's in sound condition, but it could do with some cosmetic maintenance. You won't buy better.'

'Can I inspect it now?'

'Sure. It's moored in the boat harbour five minutes away. I'll drive you down. Say, I didn't catch your name.'

'Costas Kyriakou.'

'Aha, a man from a real fishing background. You must be Greek with a name like that?'

Kyriakou nodded. 'Yeah, something like that.'

Enright realised he was potentially dealing with a tough client. From his experience the Greeks did not give anything away by showing emotion. He doubted this guy was serious, but he was bored-stiff sitting around in the office and this would be half an hour of relief. He tried to start a conversation, but was ignored. He decided this Greek and his girlfriend were wasting his time, but at least he could report to the owner there had been an inspection. Kyriakou barely glanced at the hull and deck fittings as they walked onboard. The deck and engine room inspection was brief - far too brief for a genuine buyer.

'How long has this boat been parked up?'

'A couple of months now.' They were standing in the wheelhouse. He had noticed the Greek's casual glances at the instruments and electronic panels. Long experience told him here was another dreamer with no money. He was not about to waste any more time giving him a sales pitch – he'd rather sit in his office and watch a re-run of last night's game.

'Show me the log books.'

'They...they're, not here onboard. I don't have them in the office either. I would have to contact the owner.'

'Well, start the engines and let's fire up some of this electronics panel. I want to see what's working and what isn't.'

'I just hope the batteries aren't flat,' Enright replied as he went through the starting procedure. One of the engines cranked slowly into life, before belching a cloud of black diesel smoke and settling down to a steady rhythm. The second engine fired more readily, having received a direct charge from the re-energising batteries. He switched on the navigation, radar and breathed an audible sigh of relief when everything lit up. 'You've still got full fuel in the starboard tank and more than half in the port,' he said as he turned with a grin of relief. 'That's a real bonus, you've got twenty thousand bucks of fuel which should be added to the price.'

'When was it last slipped and cleaned?'

'Just before it was tied up and offered for sale. You're getting a real bargain at the price.'

Kyriakou made no reply. He had already determined the vessel was in good sea-worthy condition, although he was sure it had been tied up for well over the time given. It was more like six months, judging by the surface rust apparent on the winches and the chipped steel railings. However, it must have been started in that time, otherwise the batteries would have been dead. 'Okay, I've seen enough.'

Enright was not encouraged as he drove them back to his office - his potential client could not be drawn into conversation. He should have been more honest. It was clear Kyriakou had not bought his explanation of the vessel being tied up for a couple of months. Even blind Freddy would have noticed the algae trailing from the hull suggested it had been there longer. 'I..I may have been wrong about when it was decommissioned,' he stumbled. 'Time goes so fast, doesn't it? If the vessel doesn't suit, I've got a couple of others, but they're smaller and do need work. I've got some photos in the office.'

Kyriakou shook his head as he got out of the car. 'No, I like that one. I'll pay four hundred thousand for it. That's the final offer.'

Enright laughed and shook his head. 'The client wouldn't even consider a cent under five. These tuna guys don't need the money and this owner is not desperate. He can wait.'

'By the looks of the weed on the hull, he's been doing a bit of waiting already. It's depreciating and costing him money just sitting there. You've got the offer, so put it to him. I'll call around in the morning.'

'Where can I reach you?' Enright was desperate to maintain the contact. 'I...I'll have to discuss it with the owner. He may consider accepting a counter-offer, but I'll have to work on him. He's one tough customer.'

'He's got the offer and it's final. It's up to you to convince him to sell now, while I'm in town and ready to buy. If it's no, I'll start looking elsewhere.'

It was after midday when they pulled up in front of Enright's office the following day. He had hardly turned the motor off when the agent burst out of his office with a broad smile.

'You're in luck Mr Kyriakou, your offer has been accepted. But it really took some hard talking on my part to convince him. If you come inside we'll complete the paperwork and organise settlement.'

Half an hour later Kyriakou shook hands and walked out of the office with his companion.

'You're a tough negotiator Costas? I didn't think your bid would be accepted. All we need now is to retrieve and load the cargo, fuel-up, buy provisions and we can depart?'

'Not quite Zehra. There's something we have to do and we'll do it tomorrow night when there's no moon.'

# 47

They slowly passed the road construction site looking for any activity. It was lit up, but there were no dogs, nor any signs of human security. The steel wire gates were chained and locked. He drove on for several hundred metres and pulled in behind a large pile of gravel, stockpiled for re-construction of the road. The Toyota 4WD wagon was well-concealed.

'What are we doing here Costas?'

'They'll have an explosives magazine here and we're going to borrow some gelignite. Now keep your eyes open and don't make any noise or talk. It looks deserted, but there could be security cameras and alarms.'

Zehra followed closely behind as they walked up to the main gate. Within minutes he had picked the large lock and they were in. They kept to the shadows as much as they could as Kyriakou headed for two shipping containers at the back of the compound. He glanced at the first and ignored it as he could see it was not locked. He turned his attention to the second and gave a smile of success. The heavy padlock was soon lying on the ground as he swung a door open and shone a torch inside. He handed the light to Zehra as he ripped the top off one of the flat boxes stacked in the rear of the container, confirming its contents, before hefting it onto his shoulder. He picked up a small box of detonator caps and a large roll of fuse wire from a bench, before nodding in the direction of the door. 'Okay, mission accomplished. Let's get out of here.' She moved ahead, not noticing him sweep a loose item off a desk as he passed. They were quickly out of the yard and back at the vehicle when a high power torch was trained on them.

'What do you think you two are doing? Turn around and put your hands on top of the bonnet, otherwise I'll let this dog go.' As if on cue the Alsatian began to snarl and pull at the lead. 'I watched you come out of the yard and I can see you've stolen explosives. You are both in deep shit.' The torch dipped, as distracted, he reached for the UHF radio on his breast, while striving to restrain the dog.

The lapse in concentration was all Kyriakou needed to drop the box and whip the pistol out of his jacket. The two shots found their mark. He took the torch out of Zehra's hand and walked over to the fallen figure. The bullet had caught him in the left side of his chest – the result, final. The dog was hit in the stomach, but would die soon enough. He had no intention of making more noise with a compassionate bullet to finish it off. Zehra showed no emotion at what she had just witnessed as they drove back towards the town and the trawler. Kyriakou stored the gelignite in a cupboard at the back of the wheelhouse.

'Isn't it dangerous putting that stuff in here where we're going to be? I'd be hiding it in one of the fridges down below.'

Kyriakou laughed. 'No Zehra, that's the worst place for it. Too cold. Gelignite has to be kept warm, otherwise it's liable to explode if jolted or dropped when cold. I took a chance back there when I dropped it, but I had no alternative – I had to get my gun. This wheelhouse is the warmest place at the moment, so that's why I've put it here. It will be safe, but if it does go off, we won't be around to relate the tale. Now, let's lock up and get on our way. It's a long drive over some very rough roads from what I understand.'

'Why don't I stay here? I can keep watch on the boat?'

'No, I prefer to have you with me to help with the driving as we won't be stopping anywhere. Besides, Declan said I wasn't to let you out of my sight in case anything happened to you. He's the boss. I'm only following instructions.'

'Okay, that's fine with me. I'm hungry. I noticed a Macca's on the way in so let's stop there so I can get something to eat. I'm starving.'

They found a seat in a corner. 'Call,' Kyriakou said as he flipped the coin, caught it and covered it with his right hand.

'Heads.'

He lifted his hand. 'Tails. You've got to go and order. I'll have an Angus burger, large fries and a coke.'

Zehra smiled and shook her head as she got up. She was looking up at the menu board with her back to him when he reached across and retrieved her phone from where she had placed it on the table. He quickly looked through her call list and scribbled a number onto a napkin. He retrieved the paperclip he had taken from the desk at the roadworks yard and quickly popped the sim card, putting several small barely perceptible scratches through the printed circuit before pushing it back in. As he placed it back on her side, he noticed someone looking across at him from another table. His destructive actions had been observed. The youth quickly turned away as Kyriakou glared at him and shook his head, an action noticed by Zehra as she returned and put the tray on the table.

'Someone about to make trouble?'

'No, no. Just a local lad noticing a stranger in town, so I though I'd give him the *mind your own business* expression. He's trying to work out whether I'm your father or some dirty old man attempting to seduce a good looking chick like you. I was going to walk over and put him straight.'

Zehra choked on the mouthful of burger as she tried to laugh. 'I don't want anyone fighting over me,' she replied as she glanced around and smiled at the youth. 'You should be ashamed of yourself Costas. You could knock that kid over with one swipe of your hand.'

'Yeah, but I can't stand the competition,' he replied giving a mock growl. 'I had to put the frighteners into him. Now, let's eat and go. We've got a lot of ground to cover.'

'Meet you back at the wagon,' she said as she finally rose and picked up her phone. 'I'm going to the ladies and I want to wash the smell of burger off my hands.'

Kyriakou sat in the vehicle. He could clearly see the inside of the restaurant and the door into the washrooms. It was minutes before she finally emerged in obvious irritation as she tried to activate her phone.

'Something wrong with it?' he asked as she got in.

'I was trying to get Declan, but it doesn't appear to be working.'

'You can use mine if you like.'

'No, there's no hurry. He's not expecting me to call.'

# 48

*It was late the following day when Kyriakou pointed to the structure in the distance. 'That's got to be it.' He turned off and followed a dirt track winding up to the base of the derelict tower. They got out and walked up to the slight rise as Kyriakou looked around at the desolate landscape.*

'So this is where *vixen* is buried?'

'Yes Zehra, if old Connoly was telling Declan the truth, the barrels are buried right there against that northern leg. We'll soon know whether we have the power to wipe out entire cities. I can't wait to give those Turks some of their own medicine, not only for the Kurds, but for the atrocities they committed in Greece and Cyprus. You make a fire and cook some of those sausages while I dig.'

It took only ten minutes before his shovel gave the first metallic ring. Another ten and he had both barrels exposed. He slowly dug them out and grunted at the weight as he lifted each into the back of the Toyota.

'They look new. How long have they been buried?'

'More than fifty years. They look new because they're stainless steel which is practically indestructible in these arid surroundings. They could remain there for another fifty and would still look the same. To think what's in them, is deadly for another twenty thousand plus years.'

'Aras told me hundreds of miles in every direction is contaminated and yet the natives still live in this wilderness. I think he would have given anything to have been here with us.' She spat on the ground. 'Bloody sniper.'

'Yes, but the natives don't know the threat they're living under. And the government is not about to tell them. What do the lives of a few natives matter? They'll gradually die out from cancers and the problem will disappear and fade from memory. Only the effect will never fade from Turkey's memory when I open one of these in the centre of Istanbul.'

'So, where's the other one destined for?'

'Declan's emphatic the target is London. I really don't care what happens to the second barrel, that's up to him. One barrel is all I'll need to send fifteen million people stampeding back across the Bosphorus to Asia or north into Europe. I will die happily doing it.'

'Costas, I will be with you to do that. Declan wants me to go with him to London because that's his target. I haven't told him yet, but I want to be in Istanbul with you. And don't get me wrong, my attraction is business and not romance.'

'You realise what you're getting yourself into, don't you? We may achieve our objective, but we'll probably never survive the international manhunt.'

'I'm well aware of that Costas, I've been living with death staring at me for the past five years.'

The drive back to Port Lincoln was a mind-numbing experience of distance and the boredom. They had run out of conversation as they pulled into a truck-stop for fuel and something to eat.

He was filling the tank when he noticed Zehra disappear around the side of a building with her phone, only to return minutes later mouthing some expletive. He turned back to his task and smiled to himself. His sabotage had been effective. He knew she would not ask to use his phone as the call would be recorded and even if she did delete it, she couldn't take the risk of it being retrieved. But who was she calling? It could only be Declan, or one of her Kurdish contacts?

'I'll see you in the restaurant – order me something large,' he said as he watched her enter and disappear. He quickly pulled out his phone.

They arrived in the dark. Zehra was getting out of the cabin as Kyriakou opened the back door of the wagon. He was about to take hold of one of the barrels when he felt a hand on his shoulder. He froze momentarily before realising the hand was not one of arrest, but friendship. He slowly turned and let out a sigh of relief as he recognised the beaming face. 'Alipio, you could get yourself killed doing that,' he said as they threw their arms around each other.

'You told me to be here, so I'm here.' The young man grinned and laughed quietly. 'I don't know about me getting killed, but you nearly died when I touched you.'

'Yes, that's true. My heart stopped. You got my SMS then?'

'Sure,' he replied turning to Zehra. 'Are you going to introduce us?'

'Zehra, this is my cousin Alipio. His family comes from Cyprus, but he was born in this country.'

She smiled and shook his outstretched hand. 'Pleased to meet you Alipio. What a surprise. Costas has never mentioned your name.'

'Oh, I've been in Port Lincoln for two years now working on the tuna boats. I would like to buy one with a licence, but they cost millions, so I guess I'll be a deckhand for a long time unless I win Lotto?'

Zehra turned and walked away. Costas had never mentioned taking on another crew member, so why now? It had been accepted they could easily handle the trawler on its long voyage. She was suspicious and uneasy and cursed her phone being out of order. Why hadn't Declan mentioned it when he introduced her to Costas? Surely, he would have if he'd been aware? And who was Costas Kyriakou? She had to get to a phone.

'Now cousin, help me with these barrels and let's get on our way.'

'We're not going now are we Costas?' Zehra turned with a surprised expression. 'I'm dead on my feet and you look the same. Besides, I want to go shopping for a few things before we leave. Can't we rest until the morning?'

'I thought you got all the stores while I fueled up the other day? That was a delivery van I saw, wasn't it?'

'Yes, it was, but I've forgotten a few women's things,' she snapped. 'Do I need to go into specifics?'

Costas waved his hand in dismissal. 'Okay, but hurry. It's too dangerous now that we've achieved what we set out to do. I don't want any police making a casual call that suddenly turns into a full investigation. I've been worried for days the tire tracks at the road camp would be recognised as belonging to this type of vehicle. And we left footprints in the mud. It won't take long for them to work out a male and female were involved. I had no choice but to shoot that guard and his dog. The cops may be slow, but I've no doubt they'll come knocking sometime and I don't want to be around when that happens. Here Alipio, grab that other drum and follow me.'

They stowed the barrels in one of the insulated freezer rooms below and returned to the deck. As he entered the dark wheelhouse, he hesitated as he was about to switch on the lights. He had caught a movement near the vehicle on the waterfront.

'Alipio, I've just got to get rid of the wagon. It will only take a minute.'

He walked along the jetty watching for any further movement, but could see nothing, although he was sure it had been no illusion. He climbed into the Toyota and slowly drove it down the long launching ramp, stepping out just as the front wheels entered the water. There would be no evidence of fingerprints. He quickly jogged back up the ramp, turning away from the trawler, towards the shadow of the old building facing the harbour. Cautiously, he padded around one side towards the rear and came in behind a car with the driver's door open. The occupant was distracted, texting on his phone. At the last moment he realised he was not alone as he turned towards the threat with a startled expression. But he was a fraction too slow as Kyriakou reached in and grabbing a handful of hair, smashed the head down into the steering column before whipping it sideways into the door frame. The unconscious figure slumped sideways as he pulled him out and tossed him over his shoulder in a fireman's lift. He quickly leaned down and retrieved the phone from the floor of the car. This was no casual civilian – this was someone on serious business. Minutes later, he was deposited in one of the freezer units onboard. Kyriakou quickly searched through his clothing. The contents of his wallet and his passport quickly determined his identity. The lethal Ruger .38 pistol was no surprise – it was fully loaded with a spare clip. He drew in his breath as he noted the contents of the unsent text message. He scrolled through and found another and a phone number he did not recognise. Here was one agent who would not be reporting in again as he closed and locked the freezer door. A glance at the control panel showed it was set to minus ten degrees.

He ran back to the car and searched it. Along with an overnight bag there was a small box containing an instrument he did not recognise and another, he did. He shoved the box into the bag and took it back on board, stowing it in the wheelhouse. It took him another fifteen minutes to find the transmitting part of the instrument he had recognised. It had been attached magnetically to the base of the radar sweep. He twisted it off and tossed it over the side into the harbour.

Zehra was hurrying on board as he started the engines. Alipio had already let go the forward mooring line and was running along the jetty to cast off the stern. The vessel started to drift quickly away from the pier, forcing him to leap the quickly expanding distance between the pier and the boat. His foot slipped on the edge of the deck as he grabbed for the railing. He hung five metres above the ice-cold water, the pain shooting through his tortured arms, before slowly pulling himself up over the railing and staggering into the wheelhouse. 'That was close. I'm not as fit as I used to be.'

Kyriakou grinned and nodded as he applied power and slowly moved out of the harbour.

# 49

artigan put down the phone. 'Yes, yes,' he yelled to himself as he ran out and up the stairs. The news was more urgent than waiting for the lift.

'I must see the chief now. Is he in?'

The secretary looked flustered by the sudden intrusion. 'He is, but he's too busy and not to be disturbed. Is it urgent?'

'He'll want to hear this,' he replied as he swept past her, knocked on the door and pushed it open. His superior's desk was empty, but he noticed the top of a head begin to stir from a large comfortable chair turned towards a shelf of books and away from the doorway.

'What the hell?' Crowther said as he got to his feet trying to collect his composure and shake off the remnants of sleep.

'Great news sir. I'm positive we have located one of the *vixen* group.'

Crowther nodded as he ambled over to his desk. 'Highly irregular, just bursting in like that Hartigan. But, now you're here, give me a full account.' He glanced at his confused secretary who was standing in the doorway, dismissing her with a wave of his hand.

'One of our agents is in Port Lincoln, South Australia and he believes he has identified Zehra Kermandi. She was with an unidentified male when photographed by the agent. I've confirmed it's definitely Kermandi and instructed him to take extreme measures. The agent was apparently down at the dockside when he saw a Toyota cruiser pull up and Kermandi and a male companion get out. They were then joined by a third person. It was dark, but he saw two small heavy items taken aboard a trawler tied up at the dock. I believe what was carried aboard was what we're trying to locate.'

'But how do you know it was the 239?'

'While they were busy taking the barrels aboard, the agent swept their vehicle with a handheld XRF device. He could not identify whether it was a reading for plutonium, but he said it did register the vehicle had been in contact with radioactive material. They had obviously just got back from Maralinga, as that area is still highly radioactive. The agent first thought he recognised Kermandi a week or more previously, but could not get a photo. She disappeared, but then suddenly reappeared. It was then he managed to get a snap of her when she was in a shop – she was in a hurry. However, after the first sighting he was smart enough to make some enquiries and discovered Kermandi and her companion had purchased a large ocean-going trawler, fueling and provisioning it for a prolonged stay at sea.'

'When did you last talk to our agent?'

'I haven't sir. The reception keeps dropping in and out so we've been texting.' Hartigan looked at his phone. 'He said he would report progress every hour, but it's been several hours since he last made contact.'

'So, we can assume he has solved our problem, or paid the price for being careless. The last thing I want is having to explain what a dead MI6 agent was doing in South Australia. In addition, we could have a major problem if he has found the missing plutonium. How the hell do we get it out of the country and what do we do with it?'

'I've thought about that sir and believe it would be a simple matter to take it out to sea and dump it, along with Kermandi and her accomplice. Those are wild seas and deep waters off that coast. The problem would be solved for all time.'

Crowther let out a breath of exasperation. 'I've got a feeling of dread about this. Why didn't you ask for backup when he first reported he'd seen Kermandi?'

'That's just it sir. He didn't report it because he wanted to confirm it was actually her. And he wasn't able to do that until he took the photo which I confirmed. We lost more than a week. I've got two other agents on the way to assist him, but they won't arrive until tomorrow morning at the earliest.'

'He could be dead and Kermandi and companions at sea by then. Talk about a bloody stuff up Hartigan. I'll have that agent's head if Kermandi has given us the slip. Let's assume the worst and she's got away. Where would they be heading?'

'Into the southern ocean to get well offshore.'

Crowther shook his head with a look of despair. 'Hartigan, you frustrate me at times when you state the obvious. Off course they would be heading offshore, but where?'

'It has two routes. It can either cross to South Africa, refuel in Cape Town and head up the west coast of Africa, or across the Atlantic to the Caribbean if one of the targets is New York. However, I firmly believe it will head up into the Indian Ocean and Arabian Sea, or attempt to get through the Suez Canal. As I've explained previously, if it gets through the Suez it can drop those barrels off anywhere in the Med and haul them by road to either London or Istanbul.'

'But we can easily apprehend it if it goes anywhere near Dubai or Suez. We have navy patrols in that area around the clock. But, how are you going to keep track of the bloody thing? There's a lot of ocean out there and we cannot mount aerial patrols. And it would be an impossible task for our navy lads to find a lone trawler in such a vast area?'

'It will be extremely difficult logistically. However, it will need to refuel at some stage. Our people in South Africa will be alerted so that fueling points would be well covered by the time it reaches there. If it moves up into the Indian Ocean it will be difficult, but one of our aerial patrols or navy frigates out of Diego Garcia should be able to intercept it.'

He noticed the look of doubt on Crowther's face and the anticipated question. 'Oh, I meant to add sir, the agent was able to plant a locator beacon on board. As of two hours ago the vessel was still tied up in Port Lincoln. The moment it moves, we'll know about it.'

'Yes, well let's pray he has secured and hidden it well and the trawler is headed for the Indian Ocean where it can be intercepted by the navy. I would emphasise the plutonium is never to be brought back here. If it's intercepted in the middle of the Indian Ocean, that's where I want it buried. I was near buckling to Richard Hamilton's demands we alert the PM and start the panic reaction. At least, now that we think it's on its way, we won't have to tell the Australian's we screwed up and have been lying and hiding something all these years. We can now bury the problem forever when we get hold of that trawler. And when we do, I don't want anyone alive to write a memoir from a prison cell. Understood?'

'Yes sir. That won't present a problem.'

'How did you do it? One day we were wandering around in total darkness, then the next you burst in here saying problem solved – we have located *vixen* and we know where it is precisely at this moment. Where did the tip-off come from? It's obvious you know more than you're letting on?'

'No sir, I've not withheld anything from you. It was simply a matter of getting on the phone and contacting every ship broker in Australia enquiring about ocean-going trawlers for sale, or had recently been sold. It appeared to be a dead end until I found a broker in Melbourne who suggested I try Port Lincoln as that's the centre of the tuna fishing industry. Any trawler based there is a long-range deep-sea vessel able to travel thousands of miles into the worst seas in the world. He even gave me the name of a broker. It was search over when I contacted him.'

Crowther gave him a withering look. 'Why didn't you think of that months ago? Didn't you learn the basics while training for this department? But then again you're army, so that would account for it I suppose? The army doesn't train you to think for yourself.'

He caught the smirk of irony on Hartigan's face at the deprecating remark. He had only just thought of it himself and yet he was the head of MI6 – it was clear he had also failed basic training. He tried to recover with an outburst of bluster.

'In future I want to be fully informed of every line of enquiry you are making. Now get out of here while I call Hamilton and give him something to control his heartburn,' he chuckled as he leaned over to pick up his phone. 'The nervous wreck has been apoplectic for days'

Hartigan attempted to keep the smile of satisfaction from his face as he got up and walked out. He knew exactly what his superior was about to do. MI6 had redeemed itself and SIS could call off the search, only it would be spread on liberally with a trowel of thinly concealed sarcasm. Hamilton would get the message.

# 50

'*That's the Kuro V, the one we got a heads-up on.*' *the Coastal Patrol officer indicated with his binoculars. 'Let's keep an eye on it. I don't know what the Fremantle harbour-master is so concerned about, but something must have caught his attention. It might be a good idea if you wandered around and introduced yourself. Nothing official, just a welcome to Port Hedland and how long does it intend staying?'*

The staffer nodded. 'Will do chief. Anything in particular you want to know?'

'The usual – how many on board and where are they headed and when. Have a look at the crew papers and note their names. It looks like a pleasure yacht to me, probably just going to take a tour of the Kimberley coastline. A bit late in the year for it, but there's nothing to stop them, except for the threat of a cyclone.'

It was an hour later when the staffer reported back. 'Nothing of interest on that boat chief. It's chartered by someone who's flying in here and then it's headed for Langkawi, Malaysia, before travelling down through the Indonesian islands and back to Darwin. It's skippered by a Milos Niarchos from Fremantle. There was a Customs guy already on board when I got there. He didn't look too hard, but reckoned there was nothing suspicious. Everything checked out. You can discount the Fremantle harbour-master's concerns. The *Kuro V* has the all-clear to throw off the mooring lines when the guy who chartered it shows up.'

It was late night when the truck pulled up alongside and two figures started unloading extra provisions, including several flat boxes which were quickly moved up the gangway and taken below. A car pulled up silently behind and a solitary figure got out and came up the gangway.

Niarchos recognised him despite being wrapped in a jacket with a beanie pulled over his head to disguise his appearance. He greeted Niarchos and slapped him on the shoulder. 'Thank you Milos and here's what I owe you,' he said handing over a thick envelope. Niarchos ripped open one corner and ran his finger through the notes.

'I've also included a bonus of five grand for your help. I take it you will remain discrete about this?'

Niarchos gave a broad smile. 'Declan, any friend of a Cypriot, is a friend of mine. I've seen nothing and heard nothing. My only problem is, how do I and my two crew get back to Fremantle at this time of night?'

Declan pointed to the truck on the dock. 'Take it and dump it somewhere, but make sure you wipe it for prints.'

'A word of warning, we both know what's in those boxes just loaded – they are unregistered and therefore, illegal. If you look like getting stopped by patrols before you clear the coast here, make sure you toss them overboard first. If you don't, this fine vessel will be confiscated and both you and I will be doing time. I'm still listed as skipper of this vessel and will be held liable.'

Bellamy shook his hand and slapped him on the shoulder. 'No fear of that Milos, I'm well aware of the risk.'

'And the crew you brought with you – can they be trusted?'

'The big fellow Davut, is the cook and a better chef you won't find this side of Istanbul, I've been told. The other one is Cemal. He holds a first-mate's ticket and is an experienced engineer. The three of us will be able to handle it.'

'Yes, but do they know where you're heading and have you thoroughly checked them out?'

'They know they're going for a cruise to Malaysia and Indonesia, but I'm sure they've guessed it's something more than that. I will fill them in when I get into international waters. As for checking their backgrounds, they've both been guaranteed by our friends in Melbourne. Although they both hold Turkish and Australian passports, Davut is a Syrian Kurd while Cemal's forebears are Iranian, I can only accept the assurances I've been given.'

'Well, it's your ship now. I trust you know how to drive it?'

Declan watched as the lines were thrown off and hauled in by the crew fore and aft. He waved to Milos as the vessel pulled away. They were well offshore when he looked up from the chart he was plotting.

Davut put down a cup of coffee and plate of thick sandwiches. 'Thought you might like something to eat. What do I call you now we're at sea, Declan or skipper?'

'Declan,' he said thrusting out his hand with a broad smile before returning to twist a pair of dividers along the chart.

'As well as being a cook, I've got my seagoing mate's ticket and can relieve you anytime you want to take a rest.' He took papers out of his jacket pocket, and carefully unfolded them.

Declan studied them before handing them back. 'Why did you sign on as a cook? You're just the man I can do with.'

'No one could tell me the purpose of this trip, other than it is highly classified. What are we supposed to carrying or doing?'

'You're right, it is highly classified and we are carrying something I'm in a hurry to deliver, but you don't need to know anything further at this stage.' Although he was confident of Davut's credentials, he would have been carefully checked out in Melbourne to gauge his loyalties and background, he remained wary. He was not prepared to disclose anything further until he became more comfortable with the man.

'If you like, you can relieve me for a couple of hours, I could certainly do with a rest. The course heading is set on autopilot so you can just sit in my chair and keep watch on the radar for other shipping, particularly trawlers running without lights. Anything you're not sure of, don't hesitate to wake me.'

Declan turned to the rear of the wheelhouse and opened the door to his cabin. It was small with a single bunk and desk. He lay down and went through the intended plan of the weeks ahead. So far, so good, but it could all come unstuck if anything happened to Kyriakou and he failed to make the rendezvous. They could not contact direct by radio other than in prearranged code which would simply give present position and heading and any indications of delays or mechanical troubles.

# 51

*'What the hell does this fellow want?' Declan murmured to himself as he watched the approaching naval vessel through his binoculars. It was not an Australian patrol boat - it was too far to the south-west and well away from its zone of jurisdiction. As it got closer there was no mistaking the White Ensign, the flag of a Royal Navy frigate, a long way from its base in Diego Garcia, a thousand miles to the north of their present position.*

The radio sprang to life with a demand to stop from the swiftly closing vessel. Declan reached over and picked up the microphone before putting it down again. He was in international waters, well within his rights to ignore the command, but there was no point in protesting. He would remain calm and ride out the inquisition and search he knew was about to take place. How the hell did the navy know he was here? There had been no aerial patrols and they had not seen another vessel since leaving Port Hedland a week previous. The frigate slowed and came around in the half circle to come onto his heading and matching speed. Declan pulled his engines back to idle and watched as a RIB was lowered and detach itself from the frigate. The high-power rigid-inflatable quickly closed the distance between them. The officer clambered up onto the rear deck, followed by four heavily armed marines and a civilian.

He left the wheelhouse and went down to greet a stony-faced Lieutenant. He smiled but his extended hand was not reciprocated. 'What can I do for you officer?'

'This vessel is to be inspected for contraband we suspect it maybe carrying. I also want to see your papers and list of personnel on board. Do you have any objections?'

'You have no authority for what you ask, but I'm happy to oblige. Your chaps can search and if you accompany me to the wheelhouse, I'll show you the documents.' As the Lieutenant started to follow him he saw the civilian take an instrument out of a knapsack and switch it on.

The officer studied the log and crew papers, but it was obvious this was only a distraction to his real purpose. He hesitated as he studied Declan's papers and photo. He was about to say something when he suddenly handed the documents back. 'Thank you for your co-operation Captain Niarchos.'

Declan was uneasy. It was obvious the Lieutenant had seen through the lie, but that wasn't the reason they had been stopped. Unless he had a photographic memory, there was no way the officer could have remembered the names and personal data of the people onboard. They had been boarded for one purpose only and that purpose was the instrument in the hand of the civilian.

'I note you're supposed to be heading for Malaysia? You're a long way off course. How do you explain that?' Declan was startled by the change of tone as the voice went up an octave to a demand, rather than a polite enquiry. The Lieutenant suddenly stepped to one side as if to shift Declan's attention.

'This is a pleasure cruise. We've been debating whether to keep the present heading for Sri Lanka or bear west for Mauritius. We could even head for the Suez Canal and spend some time in the Mediterranean. We're not in a hurry.'

By the time they got back to the rear deck, the marines were already climbing back down onto the RIB. The civilian gave an imperceptible shake of his head as they approached, but the negative gesture had been noted. The Lieutenant turned as he made to follow him over the side and held out his hand. 'Thank you for your co-operation , I apologise for the inconvenience.'

'Nothing of interest Lieutenant?

'No sir, all clear on that one. Skipper's name is Milos Niarchos, but he didn't look Greek to me. We have no jurisdiction out here, but Niarchos raised no objections. However, I found it a bit strange he really didn't know where they were headed. What are we supposed to be looking for sir?'

The navy Commander shook his head. 'I don't know and if Command doesn't want to tell us, then it's none of our business. Carry on Lieutenant.'

'Shall I transmit a short note to the Australians? They may want to know that vessel is not headed for Malaysia as indicated on their log?'

The reply was emphatic. 'No Lieutenant. It's none of our business. Did we manage to attach a locator beacon?'

'Yes sir. One of the lad's attached it securely to the underside of a forward hatch cover. It won't be seen unless someone gets suspicious and really starts to look for it.'

'Well, that's our job done. We'll be able to keep track of it anywhere on earth. You can take us back to Diego Garcia.'

'Can I ask you a question sir?'

'What is it?'

'How did we know exactly where that vessel was? How did we intercept it with such pinpoint accuracy? There are tens of thousands of square miles of empty sea out here and yet we had no problem at all with the intercept? The information didn't come via satellite communication, nor did the radio personnel receive any communication since we left Diego. I checked. And yet when you walked onto the bridge early this morning you gave a precise heading and location point. How did you do that sir? What is it I don't know?'

The Commander's face hardened as he turned away. 'You have the makings of a good officer, Lieutenant, but you must learn to accept things as they are and not ask too many questions. Carry on.'

'Oh, sir, I've worked it out,' the Lieutenant said as he smirked at the realisation.

'Well, in that case you and I are the only one's in the know. And I'm warning you, if I hear any rumours floating around in the officer's mess, your career will be very short. Do you understand? Nothing you have seen or heard or assume, is to be repeated or discussed with anyone.'

The Lieutenant had come close to stepping over the mark and here was one person not known for being too familiar with anyone under his command. His rare lighthearted comments were to be acknowledged, but never rebutted or expanded on with a quick riposte.

'Aye, aye sir,' he replied as he turned to his bridge duties. He had worked out how they had been so accurate. The answer had to be in the Commander's cabin, but any incursion into that space without invitation would certainly result in a court martial and dishonourable discharge.

The Commander turned to the civilian who had entered the bridge. 'I take it you didn't find what you were looking for?'

'No Commander, the vessel was clean so I'll be leaving as soon as we dock.'

*Declan set the engines to fifteen knots as he watched the frigate gather speed and leave a long stream of turbulent wake. Within an hour it was out of sight. His gamble had paid off, but had it? The Lieutenant had glanced at his Master's Certificate papers without looking at them closely. He would have only had to ask him the name of his last command and he would have been sunk – a question he would not have been able to answer, although all Niarchos' commands were clearly listed. It was a close call, but it was part of the deal. Niarchos had given up the sea and was happy to share his identity in return for a healthy payment.*

'Were you expecting that?' It was Davut with a plate of spaghetti meatballs and a glass of chardonnay on a carefully arranged tray. 'I think he knew exactly where to find us.'

'I agree with you on that score. That was no chance encounter. Thanks for lunch, this looks really good,' he said as he began to twirl a fork into the pasta. 'Just before you go, would you ask Cemal to check if they left anything on board. I think you know what I mean?'

'We've done that already. One of us just followed that civvy guy around with the instrument he was waving. We didn't take our eyes off him and he didn't try to divert our attention. He didn't find what he was looking for and he didn't leave anything. He was in and out of the engine room very quickly, it was too hot for him.'

'Good for you Davut. However, I don't think we've seen the last of that ship, or others like it.'

'Take a rest skipper, I'll relieve you for a few hours if you like.' Davut looked at the course setting and down at the map with a ring drawn around a point a thousand miles from land. 'What's the significance of 75 east 15 south, I see you've got marked. Are we meeting someone there?'

'No, they're just plot points,' he lied. 'But, I want to know when we reach them.' Declan realised his answer was very unconvincing, but Davut said nothing. It was several hours later when he emerged from his cabin. The sea had the appearance of a slowly undulating mass of liquid glass, the surface reflecting the glare of the sun. Davut was leaning back in the skipper's chair, his bare feet propped up on the console. He heard the movement behind him and looked around.

'Hi skipper, nothing to report.'

Declan glanced at the instruments and at the active radar screen. 'You don't need that on out here,' he said as he switched it off.

'Just checking to see if there's anything within range.' Davut pushed himself out of the chair. 'I'm just going to make myself a coffee. Would you like one?'

'Yes, thanks Davut. Black and sweet and run me up a sandwich if you would please?'

'On the way skipper. Oh, before I forget, I did notice something odd about that radar. You probably know what it is, but with every sweep of the screen it's recording a very strange return signal. It took me a while to distinguish it from the background noise of the engines, but then I noticed a faint spot of light in the top right corner of the screen each time it sounded. Probably nothing, but it could be the set is going on the blink.' He turned and opened the door. 'I'll be back in fifteen with coffee and snack.'

Declan dismissed the comment as he sat back in his chair and glanced around, his brain atrophied by the boredom and endless horizon. Suddenly, he reached over and turned on the radar and watched. It was as Davut stated, the faint sound and light appeared with every rotation of the scanner on top of the wheelhouse. It was a new unit with a wide scan, sensitive to picking up small craft such as sailboats through to supertankers. Was the repeating sound and minute flash of light some new feature he was unaware of, or was it about to fail and leave him in a critical situation? It could be some sort of interference caused by solar activity or some unexplained anomaly. The answer was most likely in the manufacturer's manual in his cabin. His mind wandered until he heard the door behind him opening.

'Have you worked out the problem skipper?'

'No, I haven't, but I'll go through the manual later and see if I can isolate it. There's got to be an explanation.'

Davut set down the tray and turned to leave. 'I'll be back in half an hour skipper. I've got to whip up some lunch for Cemal. He's quiet, that one. Just sits in a chair under the shade of the rear deck and reads when he's not down with his engines. Can't even get him to talk except for grunts. What's with him?'

'He's here to do a job and he's doing precisely that. It would be wise to leave him to himself. Maybe he just likes solitude – I don't have a problem with that.'

'I feel I've become involved in something I know nothing about. I was lead to believe it was something to do with my Kurd heritage?'

'It is Davut, but just be patient and all will be explained. All I can say is, we are on a mission and both you and Cemal are vital to its success.' He held up his hand to block a question he knew was about to follow. 'Would you mind taking over for half an hour? I want to have a walk around. The only thing to look out for is shipping containers. There are thousands of them washed overboard every year and the thought of running into one, or one floating just below the surface would tear this hull right open. I don't relish the thought of getting into a life raft out here. On second thoughts, it might be wise to leave the radar on permanently, just in case one is sticking up out of the water.'

What was it about Davut that made him nervous and Cemal was certainly an odd character? He never spoke and only answered when spoken to. He was an Iranian claiming to be a Kurd, but had the checks been thorough enough? From his experience fighting in Syria he was aware allegiances could switch in a moment. Watching your back was just as important as watching for the enemy in front. Trust could only be built up of long association with who was at your side constantly, facing the same peril. Would he be there when the first shot whistled past your head, or would he suddenly disappear, having led you into a trap?

'Those navy guys obviously didn't find what they were looking for? Although those crates we loaded are well hidden, they would have been found if the search was thorough.' Davut had already assumed the captain's chair.

Declan ignored the comment as he turned and murmured to himself. 'But did the navy leave anything?'

'What did you say?'

'Just an idle thought. I want to walk around the deck for some sea air.' He closed the wheelhouse door behind him, descended the central stairway and out onto the deck surrounding the cabins and main salon. He glanced over the railing in both directions and up at the ceilings - anything foreign or out of place, would be obvious. He slowly walked aft to where the RIB had tied up. There was nothing attached to the stern or to the structure, either inboard or over the side. He was about to dismiss his suspicions, when something triggered his attention to the fore-deck. He remembered the Lieutenant and he had been facing each other when the officer stepped sideways as if to distract attention from something happening on the foredeck. He had thought nothing about it at the time, but now the Lieutenant's voice raised in distraction and sudden movement had a possible explanation.

He leaned over the extreme front of the bow, looking down as though attracted by the vessel cleaving the sea, throwing up two perfectly shaped waves which folded in unison before disappearing beneath the hull. He turned and looked up at the slowly revolving radar and then down again at the hatch directly in front of him. The large hatch cover was raised about half a metre above the deck with a thick, rolled-combing lid. His eye caught a slight shadow about a metre in from one corner. He stood, walked over and sat down on the cover with his back to the bridge. Davut would have to lean forward in the skipper's chair to observe what he was doing. He sat down and ran his fingers along the underside of the lid until he felt the obstruction. Leaning down as though to pick something up from the deck, he glanced sideways and up at the object almost entirely concealed by the overhang of the combing. The tiny flash of a blue beam told him exactly what it was, who had put it there and why. He swore as he gripped it. His first instinct was to rip it from its magnetic hold and toss it overboard, but he restrained and straightened back up. Why disclose he had found it? The navy would be able to track his course and note any diversions into other ports or anchorages. They knew his exact position 24/7. Why make it hard for them and invite another search when he could use it to his advantage? He was clean as far as the navy was concerned and as long as he didn't stop anywhere, they would not pester him again, or at least that's what he was banking on. His only concern now was the beacon had been placed there by either Davut or Cemal. That would explain the navy intercept and continued tracking. But which one was acting as the lone wolf, or were they acting in concert? The finger of suspicion pointed directly at the person who liked to be in the wheelhouse offering his services. He was engaged as a cook, not as a qualified first-mate. Had Davut really been checked out and by whom? It was too late now - he would have to watch his back.

# 53

'I expect that's our contact skipper,' Davut said handing over the binoculars and pointing at a ship's running lights in the encroaching darkness. 'It's precisely on the way-point you've set in the GPS and roughly corresponds to your chart.'

Declan took the binoculars. Davut had to be the weak link. He had been in and out of the wheelhouse all day with excuses, cups of coffee and plates of sandwiches. He was plainly aware there was to be a rendezvous with an unknown vessel.

Neither said anything as the two boats slowed as they closed and started to run alongside. Minutes later they were secured fore and aft while still maintaining a positive heading. He sent Davut down to assist with the transfer of two small, but heavy barrels, along with four empty forty-four gallon fuel drums. Kyriakou followed carrying the gelignite and bundle of fuse wire, while Zehra and Alipio cast off the mooring lines, watching the trawler as it slowly drifted away. Declan heard the running footsteps coming up the stairway and the wheelhouse door being thrust open.

'Full ahead. Clear that boat as fast as you can.' They were no more than three hundred metres away when the dull explosion reverberated across the water. Within minutes the flames from the burning trawler were slowly swamped as it disappeared, the only trace some debris and an oil slick. 'That was a fine seaworthy boat. It's a shame it had to be scuttled.' Kyriakou made no mention of the corpse it carried in the freezer – it was a murder he would never be sent to trial for – there was no evidence.

The two men shook hands, as Declan turned to Zehra. 'Hi there darling, has this fellow been looking after you?'

She beamed as they embraced and kissed. The affection was obvious. 'A perfect gentleman at all times Declan.'

Declan had his back to the doorway when Davut entered the wheelhouse. Kyriakou raised his eyes and pitched his head slightly back in a signal to get rid of the intruder.

Declan saw the movement. 'Davut, would you go and rustle up something hot for us.'

'It's a good thing you turned up when you did,' Kyriakou remarked when the door closed. 'My fuel burn was twice what I anticipated due to the weed fouling the hull and I really had to push it to make it here on time. Another day and I would have been idle in the water. Where to now?'

'We were intercepted by the Royal Navy and they've tagged us with a locator beacon.'

'What the hell?' Kyriakou exclaimed. 'Does this mean the whole project is just like my trawler – blown out of the water? All this for nothing?'

'Calm down Costas, I believe it's to our advantage. We have been searched once and as long as we keep going, I believe we're in the clear. It wasn't a chance encounter – they had been tipped off, but whoever it was didn't know about our planned rendezvous. Their problem was they didn't know about your boat, which has now disappeared. Another day and they would have apprehended you and found what they were looking for. This vessel has now been confirmed as clean, so as long as we don't divert to a port or mess around in some strange anchorage, we're in the clear, or that's the way I'm reading it. I could be wrong. However, we do have a problem and that is someone on our side tipped the navy off, because they knew exactly where to find us. Whether it was someone on this boat or someone on shore, I don't know, but someone is in touch with the enemy.'

Kyriakou shook his head. 'What next then?'

'We head directly for the Red Sea and on up to the Suez Canal. We will have to call in at Djibouti to refuel and that's our most significant point of danger. If we're boarded and searched, the game could be up.'

'But, surely Customs will want to know what's in two small barrels. I suppose we can account for four empty fuel drums, but those two small one's will attract immediate attention.'

'They will, but that's why I asked you to load four empty fuel drums. The two small barrels will be concealed in the two of the larger drums, which by then will be resealed, repainted to hide the welding and full of fuel. It's the perfect excuse of carrying extra fuel for such a long trip. We won't attempt to conceal them, but leave them on the aft deck in full view. The navy will have already reported they did not find what they were looking for. However, we will have a problem if they board us again and ask me to explain the appearance of extra crew. That's when they'll want to make a thorough search and look into those fuel drums – that's when we'll have a problem. I've got a suspicion the navy hasn't finished with us just yet. My guess is we will see that frigate in Djibouti and if we do, you can bet the navy has figured out there's been a switch and we must be carrying a certain cargo. It's there we will run the greatest risk as they would probably love to do another search before we cast off for Suez, but that will be up to the local authorities. It is way outside the Royal Navy's jurisdiction and they certainly wouldn't want to divulge what they were looking for.'

'Good thinking. I just hope you're correct. But what are you going to do about our danger man on board. Won't he be inclined to open his mouth?'

'That is the only communication we have on board,' Declan replied pointing to the radios. 'And no one is allowed up here unless one of us is present. I believe we should make a point of quietly telling Davut his place is in the galley and not in here. The only other place someone could communicate is when we dock in Djibouti, but I doubt we'll be allowed ashore without visas. We'll just fuel up and clear out as soon as we can. Anyway, we may have another problem the closer we get to the Horn of Africa and Djibouti and that's pirates. Those waters are invested with them. Although the various navies have been mounting strong patrols to counter the problem, a pleasure vessel such as this will attract immediate attention. The thought of wealthy individuals and big ransom demands is an opportunity too good to miss. We'll have to have to keep our eyes open and I would suggest we start rotating four hourly shifts to keep watch.'

'That's all very well, but how do we resist them? Kyriakou countered. 'They will undoubtedly be well armed?'

Declan grinned, shaking his head. 'I took the precaution of obtaining four pump-action shotguns with plenty of shells.

They're not what I was really after, but the best I could do. Luckily the navy did not find them as they were not really interested in searching. They were only interested in what the civilian wandering around with the instrument would come up with and that proved to be nothing. However, they did leave a little souvenir so they could keep track of us. But I won't risk taking the guns through the Suez. I don't want to wind up in a Djibouti jail charged with transporting illegal weapons. One can only guess at the conditions would be like inside.'

'I've also got most of the jelly. I figured I only needed six sticks to blow a hole in the trawler and something told me not to waste what remained.' Kyriakou replied.

# 54

*It was a week later when Kyriakou entered the wheelhouse for his shift and pointed to the fast disappearing sun on the port side. 'Have you noticed them? I'll bet they're not fishermen.'*

'Yes, I've been watching them for the last fifteen minutes. They've kept their distance, but they're on our heading and keeping apace with us. With their powerful outboards we have no hope of outrunning them at our top speed of twenty-five knots.'

'I read that as meaning they're going to close in and attack as soon as that sun disappears below the horizon in a few minutes.'

'And they're sure to be packing the weapon of choice with plenty of automatic firepower, the AK47. How the hell are we going to counter that?'

'With total surprise Costas. An AK47 is no match for a shotgun at close quarters and with a couple of sticks of your gelignite, it should be an interesting diversion.'

There was no moon and they were running without lights - the vessel was soon in total darkness. But all eyes were strained and stress levels high as they listened for any signs of danger - the tension eased when it looked as though they had avoided the threat. Then it happened. Bellamy, Davut and Alipio were propped up against opposite sides of the after-deck out of sight, when they heard something grind against he hull. Declan could feel his heart pounding as he indicated for Davut to keep low and join him. With a slight swell running, the grinding became more constant as the helmsman pushed the nose of the boat into the side of the *Kuro V.* The invaders had less than two metres to reach the top of the railing and swing over onto the after-deck.

'They're coming,' Declan whispered as they rose into a crouch position waiting for a head to appear. It was a pair of hands gripping the railing, followed by a grunt as the intruder heaved himself up and one leg appeared over the side to straddle the railing. His eyes opened wide as he made to shout a warning when the shotgun stock smashed into his skull. He fell back without a sound, crashing onto the deck of the sleek craft below. It was quickly followed by a burst of automatic fire which thudded into the deck above his head.

'Declan, we know exactly where their boat is so let's move at least twenty feet apart. When I stand I'll start firing to get their attention and then you catch them in a cross fire. Just keep pumping it into them.'

As he rose and peered over the railing he could see shadowy faces staring upwards at the position their fellow bandit had fallen from. It was carnage within seconds as his first shot containing an expanding arc of a thousand tiny lead pellets tore into the exposed flesh below. Davut simultaneously, had jumped to his feet and repeated the action from the opposite direction. They did not stop until they had unleashed the full five shots each of their limited magazines. Declan started to reload as the craft commenced to drift away with its lifeless forms. Davut was looking over the side casually reloading his weapon.

'I think we're finished with that threat skipper.' They were the last words he spoke as the burst of fire ripped open his back and reduced him to a bloodied form as he toppled over the side. Alipio was too slow to react as the next burst caught him as he began to turn. He had been carrying two sticks of gelignite which rolled harmlessly across the deck, the still burning Zippo lighter dropping from his lifeless hand, momentarily distracting his killer. It was the second Declan needed as he crouched, pumping two rounds across the fifty foot beam of the deck. The shot turned the head of the assailant into a pulp as blood, brains and bone exploded all over the deck and roof of the deck above.

He cursed himself for not realising there would likely be more than a single boat and the attack would come from both sides – the initial boarding party had been a diversion. But where were Cemal and Kyriakou? One of them should have been watching the port side. He moved forward slowly, waiting for another figure to come over the railing on that side, but was forced to take shelter when the darkness was shattered by successive blasts of automatic fire, the bullets ricocheting off every metal surface. It was a random spray as the gunman quickly withdrew to hide behind the opposite side of the deck cabin.

Declan turned and moved towards the stern to give himself a hazy view and line of fire when the gunman showed himself. It was too late when he sensed the movement behind him. The burst had been another diversion so another killer could silently move into position in his rear. The barrel of the AK47 and the grin on the face waited a fraction too long as the shotgun blast caught him in the back. Zehra showed no emotion as she glanced down at the bloodied corpse before nodding to Declan and running silently back along the companionway before disappearing around the corner between the two lower-deck cabins. The killer on the far side of the deck was now caught between a crossfire. Declan was not visible from where he was crouching as the gunman peered around the corner and saw his dead companion. Any further thought of fight disappeared in an instant as he made for the railing and the waiting vessel below. Two of his companions were dead. He shouted instructions as he jumped down into the boat. The high power outboard was thrust to full power. It slowly began to gather speed and swing in a circle as Zehra and Declan opened fire. The motor screamed as the dead helmsman fell over the controls, while his companion toppled sideways into the sea.

'There's another one on board,' Kyriakou said as he stepped out of the shadows with a stick of gelignite in his hand. 'I'll finish this one off.' He lit a short fuse and tossed the explosive into the drifting hull. They all turned and ran to the other side of the vessel just as the double explosion occurred, first the gelignite followed by the exposed fuel tanks of the pirate craft.

They heard a series of shotgun blasts followed by AK47 fire when seconds later Cemal staggered around the corner, his bloodied arm holding a shotgun. 'I'm okay,' he said wiping blood from his head, noticing Kyriakou's look of concern. 'I ran into the stairway. There's another boat forward. I got two of them but, there could be others.'

Kyriakou ran forward to see the craft beginning to pull away. It was manned by an older turbaned figure and a boy of about fifteen who was looking up in terror. He hesitated as he was about to the light the fuse of a stick of gelignite. Zehra quickly picked up an AK47 from beside a corpse and discharged two short bursts into the old man and the boy.

'Now you can finish it off. I'm going to make a thorough search because I thought I saw one of them go below.'

Kyriakou shook his head as he watched her run forward along the deck. 'She's one tough bitch, that one,' he muttered to himself as he lit the fuse and tossed the charge into the drifting boat. He had hesitated because the boy was about the same age as his son.

Declan and Zehra quickly circled the decks, but they were all clear. 'He's got to be down below,' Declan said as he slowly opened the door to the engine room and shouted into the dim light.

'Down here,' Cemal shouted back. 'It's okay, he's out cold.'

They cautiously descended the stairs to where Cemal was standing over the inert form lying on its side. 'He didn't see me standing behind the stairs,' he said holding up a heavy wrench.

Declan leaned down, noticing too late as an arm moved and the body began to roll over. He was powerless as the knife thrust upwards towards his exposed stomach. Zehra was an instant quicker as she crashed the butt of the AK47 into the side of the exposed skull. She had saved his life twice in the last half hour. Neither said anything as they looked at one another.

'Take his feet Cemal. We'll toss him over the side along with the others on deck. Then we've got to clean this ship up.' An hour later they had cleaned every trace of blood, body flesh and parts from the deck with a high pressure hose. Cemal had just finished winding up the hose when he picked up a discarded AK47 he had propped against the cabin. He turned towards Declan, the weapon dangling in his hand as he tried to balance it. Zehra screamed a warning as she levelled a shotgun.

'What the hell are you doing Zehra?' Declan shouted when he saw the threat. 'No, no. Have you gone mad. Put that bloody gun down.'

Cemal opened his mouth, his confused brain attempting to counter what he knew was about to happen. *'Jash,jash,'* he screamed, pointing at her with an outstretched arm in a vain attempt to stop the discharge. The blast tore open his chest as he fell backwards and crumpled over the railing. Zehra walked forward and grabbing the legs, flipped the body over into the wake of the moving vessel. Declan was horrified by what had occurred, too shocked to move. She turned slowly and lifting the weapon, pointed it at him.

'Bang, you're dead Declan Bellamy,' she laughed as she lowered it. 'I just saved your life again. If I hadn't done that, you would have been next.'

'What the hell are you talking about?' He was not only shattered by the cold-blooded killing he'd just witnessed - he was shattered by what he didn't know or understand. He had seen her kill many times, but there had always been a clear and real reason - she had been facing a kill, or be killed situation, or worse still, the bodily violation before her death. He had just witnessed her kill an innocent person without explanation or reason.

She sat down beside him on the hatch cover. 'Who picked Davut and Cemal to crew with you?'

'The Melbourne contacts in the Kurd community. I know most of them. What's the problem?'

'Because Davut and Cemal were working for the Turks. They may be Kurds, but they'd obviously been bought off by a higher bid.'

Declan shook his head in disbelief. 'I don't buy that one. Impossible, but obviously you know something?'

'You have always been puzzled how the navy found you in the middle of the Indian Ocean, haven't you?' She stood before he could answer. 'Well, come and I'll show you.'

He followed her into Cemal's cabin where she pulled a carry-bag from under his bunk and tipped its contents out. 'A satellite phone and a GPS,' she said pointing. 'That's how the navy knew where to find you. Cemal had given them your exact co-ordinates. And once they'd planted the locator beacon, the phone was of no further use. On the other hand if you had discovered the beacon and tossed it overboard, Cemal was still here as a backup.'

Declan picked up the phone and slid the back off. 'The sim card's gone. Do you have it?'

'No I don't. That was the first thing I checked when I found it.'

'But how did you know Cemal was in fact, the mole?'

'I didn't, but I suspected it was either him or Davut. I could not get access to their cabins until the firefight just now. That's why you probably wondered where I was when the bandits boarded, but it was the only chance I had. I first searched Davut's cabin, but it was clean. I hit the jackpot when I found this bag under Cemal's bunk. The priority of this mission is absolute. I was not going to let him jeopardise it.'

'What was he screaming at you when you shot him? By the look of it, he was accusing you of something?'

'Oh, he was just screaming some abuse in defiance. Just terrified babble. He was well aware of the price he would pay if found out and I just made sure he paid it.'

'What about Davut? Did you also suspect him?'

'Yes, but I didn't find anything incriminating, so his reputation is clear. Davut was a loyal Kurd, above suspicion of collaborating with the Turks. It's unfortunate he died.'

Declan was unnerved. Of the two, he picked Davut as the weak link, always asking too many questions and being continually in the wheelhouse. Cemal stuck to his cabin and his engines, rarely asking questions and seldom joining in conversation. However, he had to accept Zehra was right - Cemal had been the informant. But a doubt lingered at the back of his mind. If it was Cemal, why had he not reported it immediately to the navy following the transfer of the barrels from the trawler to the *Kuro V*? He already knew the answer and now it had been confirmed. He did not believe he had been mistaken in what Cemal had shouted, but it was screamed and barely intelligible. He dismissed it as he turned to Zehra.

'Okay, let's forget about it and get underway. We're only a day or so out of Djibouti, so we'll have to toss all the weapons over the side when we get the port in sight as Customs is sure to sweep this vessel clean looking for contraband and the discovery of weapons would get them very excited.'

# 55

Declan was standing in the wheelhouse with Kyriakou watching the Customs launch as it guided them in.

'You threw all the guns over the side. Was that wise? It's a long way up the Red Sea to Suez and it's a bloody dangerous stretch of water?'

'We had no choice Costas. My feeling is these boys have been tipped off to look for something. Just look at that launch. I can count six people - two are obviously the pilot and the skipper, while the other four are uniformed and all carrying artillery. They would have found the guns very quickly and we would have been marched off for interrogation while they tore this vessel apart. The very presence of the uniforms tells me we are expected. And look over there,' he said as he picked up the binoculars. 'That's the Royal Navy frigate that intercepted us, if I'm not mistaken. I wonder if he's going to escort us up to the Suez. Mind you, it would be a bonus if he did, as we wouldn't be bothered by pirates again.'

They were guided to an isolated section of a wharf, well apart from the dozens of ocean going wooden dhows and frenetic activity of hundreds of natives hurrying up and down narrow gangplanks loading and unloading cargo of all descriptions.

'Sturdy looking vessels,' Declan remarked. 'Some of them must run into hundreds of tons dead-weight.'

'And more. All built from pit-sawn, hand-adzed timber and put together without nails. The Arabs have been building them for a thousand years and trading right around the rim of the Indian Ocean from Indonesia to southern Africa. They move the bulk of all trade, including anything illegal,' Kyriakou said as he pulled the engines back to idle. 'Hey, you'd better get down there and help Zehra toss those mooring lines ashore and run out the gangplank. If they perceive any disrespect or lack of co-operation, they'll make it hard for us.'

As soon as they were secured, four uniforms quickly came aboard. One remained guarding the gangplank, two peeled off in either direction along the decks, while the obvious commander with excess silver braiding on his uniform and cap, gave Declan an officious look and then a curt demand in excellent English. 'You are the captain?'

'No sir, he 's in the wheelhouse, if you would follow me please I will introduce you.'

'No need for that. I'm sure I can find my way.' Declan made to follow him. 'Just stay here with this officer. You are not to leave this vessel.' The command was final and not to be questioned. 'Where's the woman I saw?' He did not wait for an answer as he stepped into the cabin and began to mount the short flight of stairs to the bridge where Kyriakou was waiting for him along with Zehra.

'Your papers please and passports. And I want to look at your log and I want to know the reason for your visit.'

Kyriakou handed over all the relevant documents and passports which the officer studied before handing them back. 'You appear to have three passengers missing ? Where are they?'

Kyriakou cursed for not disposing of Davut, Cemal's and Alipio's passports, having tossed all their other possessions overboard. He had forgotten their papers were in the wheelhouse. 'We were attacked by pirates and they died during the conflict.'

'How did you defend yourself against what would have been armed pirates? And what happened to those weapons?'

'We threw them overboard along with the pirates and their guns. I can assure you sir, you will not find any weapons aboard this vessel,' Kyriakou replied with just the right tone of subservience. 'Unfortunately, the missing crew were shot dead before they could take cover. We buried them at sea. If you care to have a look at the lower aft deck you will see evidence of the gun fire.'

The commander nodded. He was not interested in pursuing deaths that had occurred in international waters. He turned and walked over to the chart table and leaned over to study the clearly marked course. 'You have not called in at any port since you departed Port Hedland?'

'No sir, as soon as we re-fuel here, it's on up through the Suez Canal and into the Mediterranean.'

'Very good, but you don't have visas, so you are all confined to this vessel until you leave and that will be immediately you finish refuelling. In the meantime, if anyone steps off this vessel, they will be arrested.'

Kyriakou glanced at Zehra with a look of relief as the officer stepped out of the wheelhouse and down the stairs to the main deck. As he reached the gangplank and barked an order, one of the officers hurried back along the deck and muttered something to him.

'What's in the drums on the rear deck?'

'Diesel fuel sir. Just a contingency.' Declan replied. 'Would you like to check them to satisfy yourself?'

The commander shook his head as he turned and walked down the gangway with his three officers following. They climbed into their open Jeep and drove off.

Declan let his breath out with an audible explosion. 'My God, that was close Costas. I thought for a moment there he was going to take me up on the offer. We would have all been marching off in handcuffs if he had.'

'Too close for my liking,' Costas replied. 'Why did you do it?'

'Reverse psychology. I saw one of them paying particular attention to the drums so I went back to see what he was doing. When he told me to take the caps off all the drums so they could be dipped, I was playing for time. I had put the two important drums in the front when we loaded them. I thought anyone looking for something we were attempting to hide would focus on the rear drums first and that's exactly what happened. He was about to dip the two in front when he heard the boss calling. He just dropped everything and trotted off. In another thirty seconds, or if the boss had shown any interest, we would have been cactus. It was that close.'

'You were lucky this time, but I wouldn't have attempted it.' Kyriakou replied with a smirk of sarcasm. 'Meanwhile, let's fuel up and get the hell out of here while our luck holds.'

# 56

'*What's that blip that comes up on the radar screen?*'

'That Costas, is the result of that tracking beam the navy placed onboard when they intercepted us,' Declan replied laughing. 'It's just under the rim of that forward hatch cover.'

'I'd forgotten about that,' Kyriakou replied slapping his forehead in mock ignorance. 'I'll go down and get rid of it. We don't want them tailing us any longer, do we?'

'No, let's leave it there for now. They know exactly where we are and if we deactivate the thing, it will only raise their suspicions. I've got no doubt they're going to try and stop us again. If it's not this side of the Suez they may have someone waiting once we get into the Med. Let's just wait.'

The shipping traffic was heavy in both directions as they motored north up the Red Sea - streams of container ships and smaller freighters along with the indeterminate vessels of all tonnages flying foreign flags of registration.

Late one afternoon Kyriakou entered the wheelhouse rubbing his eyes and clutching two mugs of coffee. 'Any sign of the navy?'

'Yes, they're about ten miles astern hiding behind a large container ship. There are two more ships in between.' He pointed to the constant radar returns on the screen. 'See, there he is, that smaller pattern return nearly up that larger ship's backside.'

'How do you know it's him?'

'Pure luck. I've been looking through the binoculars every hour or so and I just caught a glimpse of him. He must have pulled out to confirm he was following the right vessel and then he ducked for cover.'

'What do you think he will do?'

'I expect him to overtake and board us tonight if we stay where we are. It's his last chance before we reach the canal. So, what I want you to do is go down at sunset and throw that bloody device overboard. Then I'm going to advance both engines to maximum speed and lose ourselves within a few of these smaller vessels ahead. There's so much traffic he won't be able to positively identify us. In addition, without a definite signal he won't dare step up to full speed in order to catch up. That would be far too dangerous. And in morning we should be in the queue to get into the canal if I can get permission. If we can enter with a few of these smaller cargo boats, we'll get into the Med a day ahead of him. Mind, you, if there's another navy vessel waiting for us, we'll be in trouble.'

'But why is he specifically following us, if he's already cleared us of carrying anything suspicious?'

'Costas, I think they've worked it out. They've realised there had to be another vessel involved, but how did they confirm that? Let's assume that Cemal, if it was him, tipped certain authorities off I was onboard *Kuro V,* so it was reasonable to assume it would be carrying the goods. When intercepted and the initial search found no trace of radioactivity, they knew another vessel had to be involved. Satellite imagery was of no use because we made the transfer in the evening. However, there could be imagery of two small vessels in a vast ocean seemingly closing on one another in previous days, but that would take days to gain access to through the proper channels. The only thing I can think of is the fact the tracking beacon would have noted the exact speed we were maintaining, but was it sensitive enough to note a sudden slowdown for half an hour? And another thing which you may not have noticed while we were in Djibouti, was one of those Customs officers took a snap of us on his phone. It was the one on the gangplank.'

'No, I didn't see him do that. I saw him fiddling with his phone, but thought he was playing some game or texting his girlfriend. I didn't see him point it at me.'

'Well I did. The British navy would never have got permission to conduct a search, but that wouldn't prevent them from paying off some local official to take a few happy snaps. And what do you think the navy commander's reaction was going to be when he saw those photos? Two of the original crew are missing and suddenly a bearded Greek and a women turn up on board. How did they get there? The only conclusion would be we made contact with another boat. Sure, the two crewmen could be accounted for because we got into a fight with pirates and I reported they'd both been killed, but how did you and Zehra get on board? This would confirm there had to be another vessel involved. I'll bet the coded messages have been literally flying between him and the Admiralty and MI6, or whatever agency is involved. The skipper of that frigate is getting desperate. He knows we're just ahead, but he can't possibly stop us and make a search in these crowded waters. I believe he will follow us into the Med and board us there.'

Kyriakou looked worried as he shook his head. 'But surely, the Egyptians will stop us on entering or leaving the canal?'

'I'm banking on the fact they won't because they won't be aware of what we're carrying. The navy is not going to tell them the true nature of what we have, because they're probably unaware themselves. I believe they'll just be following orders from higher up. And how do the Brits explain they have allowed a vessel carrying a deadly cargo, venture into Egyptian waters. It would be a gross violation and breach of protocol. All hell would break loose. I'm gambling on the fact we'll get through okay, but there could be someone on the other side waiting to pounce. But that's a risk we've got to take.'

'There's something I should tell you. It's about....'

Declan held up his hand to stop him as he reached for the radio transmitter. 'This is our call sign from the canal authorities. I've been haggling with them for a few hours trying to get a slot in behind the vessel in front. It's only a five thousand tonner, so we should be able to follow it.' He gave a whoop of joy as he listened to the confirmation. 'With a bulk container ship behind us, it was logical they would go along with my proposal.'

'Where does that place the navy?'

Declan laughed as he thumped Costas on the shoulder. 'They tried to pull rank, but were promptly told to fall in behind two container ships, so that means they are three ships behind us. I think we could be a good day ahead of them, which means there's probably no one on the other side to intercept us. They've been assigned to complete the intercept, retrieve the cargo and allow the whole matter to be quietly buried. But in reality, if that happens we're all as good as dead. They're not going to let any witnesses live to write a book about what might have happened.'

'So, after you drop me off with one of the barrels, you won't be taking this vessel through the Med to England as planned?'

'No, I've given it some thought - we're going to drop our cargo off on your side of Cyprus. It will be a simple matter for a fishing boat to land us in Turkey undetected. From there it's a straight run for you to Istanbul and I can take the other barrel through Europe and into England.'

# 57

*L*inton Crowther was in no mood for excuses. He was furious with the frustration. 'What do you mean, the navy failed to apprehend them?'

'Sir, the navy was not exactly co-operative in regard to this operation,' Miles Hartigan replied. 'They were particularly nervous about boarding a vessel on the high seas without some explanation of what they were supposed to be looking for. And they weren't very happy about planting a tracking device on it without due cause. It was very delicate having to explain to the navy high-command we could not tell them the purpose of our operation. They initially refused point-blank to have anything to do with it until they got the green light from the Admiralty. If you and Sir Richard hadn't stepped in with a joint appeal, it's highly likely our request for assistance would have fallen on deaf ears. It was the joint approach of MI6 and **SIS** that finally convinced them to agree. I also think there was a degree of adventure in that they'd been asked by the country's two intelligence agencies to fall into line.'

'But for all that, Her Majesty's Senior Service has stuffed up. They've lost track of a bloody boat they'd put a tracking beacon on. They lost the unlosable – how incompetent is that?'

'Not quite correct sir. The navy had been tracking them from the day they planted the device when they boarded in the Indian Ocean. The target then made directly for Djibouti at the mouth of the Red Sea to refuel, where the navy frigate was also docked. The frigate had arrived two days earlier, but a request to apprehend and search the suspect vessel when it arrived, was denied by port authorities. And of course we could not resort to making an approach through our attache, as that would have raised eyebrows and questions. However, we did manage to get photos and details of the crew, courtesy of a Customs officer and a small payment. The photos confirmed Declan Bellamy was on board, but the real surprise was that Zehra Kermandi, along with a fellow by the name of Costas Kyriakou was present. Two original crew who had boarded in Port Hedland were missing, alleged by Bellamy to have been killed when they repelled a pirate attack.'

Crowther screwed up his face trying to absorb what he was being told. 'So, how did Kermandi and Kyriakou suddenly appear on the scene? And why are you convinced the vessel we are trying to apprehend is carrying the plutonium?'

'A pure failure of communication sir. Let me explain - one of our agents was able to confirm a large tuna trawler had been purchased in Port Lincoln, South Australia following my tip-off. The names given by the selling agent didn't mean a thing to him so he flew down there from Melbourne. When shown photos, the boat broker confirmed the woman was Kermandi and Kyriakou had negotiated the purchase of the boat. Although they had bought the boat, they disappeared the following day before re-appearing a week later. The agent was refused an inspection of the boat by the broker and the offer of an inducement was rejected. And that, I'm sorry to say is the last we heard from him. I can only assume he's been murdered. His hire car was found abandoned and likewise a vehicle rented by Kyriakou was found submerged in the harbour.'

'And the trawler had disappeared?'

'Precisely. But we had no way of restraining it and no way of tracking it. We can assume Kyriakou and Kermandi retrieved the barrels from where they were buried at Maralinga and simply sailed away. Meanwhile, we then found out what Bellamy was doing. He had acquired a very large trawler, which had been converted to a pleasure craft. It was registered to a company by the name of Erbil Technology. The name of the vessel was *Kuro V.* It didn't ring any bells with me at the time, but of course Erbil is a Kurdish area in northern Syria and Kuro is Kurdish currency.'

'I can see we need to book you into a bell ringing class,' Crowther replied facetiously. 'When did you wake up? And I suppose that's another case of where we lost the unlosable?'

'No sir, we didn't lose it. In fact we knew exactly its location from when it departed Fremantle, to when it arrived in Port Hedland and the exact location where the navy intercepted it in the Indian Ocean.'

'How did we track it for a couple of thousand miles without the help of the local authorities? It could have gone in any direction.'

'We had an agent on board. Not one of our regulars, but someone who was interested in a considerable financial incentive. He was taking a real risk, as if he'd been discovered would not have survived for long. He confirmed the *Kuro V* was not carrying anything of the description he'd been told to look for. However, I became suspicious when he reported the vessel was not heading for Malaysia as originally stated to Customs in Port Hedland, but was heading directly west into the Indian Ocean. When intercepted by the navy, the vessel was clean, but they tagged it with a beacon and let it go on its way. The navy commander was heading back to base in Diego Garcia when I persuaded Command to have it track for Djibouti and wait there until the *Kuro V* turned up, as Bellamy had told the navy he could be headed for the Suez Canal and the Med. And the navy eventually confirmed that appeared to be the case from the returns they were getting off the beacon they planted. I figured if he was going through to the Med, he would have the plutonium on board as there was no other way he could achieve his eventual aim of threatening London or Istanbul. The choke point would have to be Djibouti if he was to take delivery from another vessel such as one of the large sea-going dhows prolific in the area. I had agents on every vantage point just looking for a contact and transfer. I thought I had all bases covered. You can imagine my concern when our agent aboard Bellamy's boat suddenly stopped reporting. I immediately contacted the navy to see whether the beacon was still operating. It was – the boat had maintained a steady fifteen knots and had not stopped from its original interception point. And it was still maintaining that speed as it closed on Djibouti. The barrels could not have been transferred to it while underway. The risk of losing them from a sling or manually handling them was too great. They were just too valuable. So the exchange would have to happen in Djibouti.'

'So, when did you find out your assumptions were wrong? Did the bells start to ring?'

Hartigan ignored the sarcasm. He was used to the bureaucratic chain of command where a scapegoat was the mandatory requirement for any successful public servant. Any successes would be claimed by the senior bureaucrat, while the failures would be assigned to the scapegoat - someone junior enough to take the fall. And Hartigan knew exactly where the axe would fall unless he solved the problem. Not that a demotion worried him – if he failed, no one in London would be around to censure him. And the thought of the potential disaster kept him awake at night.

'No sir, it wasn't the bells that started to ring. It was some photos from an Iphone transmitted to me by one of our agents in Djibouti. He had obtained them along with an SMS text of the identity of the crew from one of the Customs agents who boarded the *Kuro V*. I was stunned to see Zehra Kermandi's face along with that of Costas Kyriakou. Bellamy was also there, but two crew were missing, one being our agent. Apparently, they had a skirmish with pirates, which accounted for the two absent faces. It became very apparent Bellamy had met up with Kermandi and Kyriakou somewhere following the encounter with the navy patrol. I had the agent contact the navy commander again and ask him to run a trace of the *Kuro V* from the time they boarded it. Sure enough, on close inspection it was noted it slowed to less than five knots for about an hour the day following the navy encounter. And there's only one explanation for that – that's when they met Kyriakou's trawler and made the transfer. And after that, I assume they scuttled the trawler and ended up in Djibouti.

'There's one flaw in that assumption Hartigan. If you had an agent on board, why didn't he report the contact and the fact a transfer had been made? And it puzzles me how he made contact.'

'He had been supplied with a satellite phone and a GPS, both of which he was told to toss overboard when the navy made contact. He was under no illusions as to what would happen if Bellamy found out what he was up to. Bellamy reported he was one of the crew killed during the pirate raid, but you can draw your own conclusions. We are not dealing with ethical people – we are dealing with killers.'

'Where is this *Kuro V* now?'

'It is due to clear the Egyptian port of Alexandria this morning. From there it's into the Med and bound for where, I don't know. The navy is nearly two days behind and in the hopeless position of trying to track it.'

'And we can't call in the airforce or satellites for assistance without sounding a general alert. It's hard enough to keep the navy command quiet, without involving other services. Have you got any suggestions?'

Hartigan walked over to a large map of the world and pointed at Turkey and the myriad of small Greek islands close to the Turkish coast. 'That's where I believe it's headed, direct for Turkey or one of the Greek islands from where the material could be easily moved to Turkey.'

Crowther shook his head in despair. 'If they land those barrels in Turkey we've lost the race. We will have to alert the Turkish Intelligence and from there the news will spread like wildfire to London, alerting every country in between. Maybe, Richard Hamilton was right. I should have informed the Prime Minister?'

Crowther was wondering for how long he could keep his silence before having to reveal Stoyan was already aware and was being kept informed. By maintaining control of Hamilton he knew the SIS head would not leak any information which could be sourced back to him and threaten his position. However, if Hamilton weakened and ran to Stoyan, he would have gained some clear air – the Prime Minister would be carrying the ball and the person taking all the heat. He would have no option but to confess he had been aware of the threat, but had concealed it. The reaction would not be survivable. Crowther knew he would then be deserted by his lifelong friend Alex Stoyan – his head would be the first to roll. So far he had played the game with finesse, but in politics there are no friends – altruism and loyalty didn't exist. It looked as though he was about to become a casualty of that friendship.

'Look at it this way sir, in the literal sense you're dead if you do and dead if you don't. And I'm quite aware I'll be following you to the block in the Tower courtyard.'

Crowther snorted. 'Thank you for that advice Hartigan, but I don't appreciate it. Hamilton is going to dump this one right in my lap and I feel he's going to crack when I give him the latest news. He will leak it to the PM to save his skin and more importantly, his pension.'

'Something has just occurred to me sir. Costas Kyriakou is a Cypriot. Cyprus would be the perfect landing and jumping off point for Turkey. It would also be the the ideal place to put the plutonium on board a fishing boat and move it the short distance to Greece, or even Italy. If it gets into either of those countries, it will present very little problem in being moved into England. And that would be the end of London for all time.'

The phone on Crowther's desk rang – it was his secretary. As he reached over to the pick it up there was a loud knock and his door burst open. Sir Richard Hamilton of SIS was standing there visibly shaking.

'For God's sake Richard, sit down before you collapse. What's the problem?' Linton Crowther demanded as he rose from his desk. Hartigan was already on his feet steadying the shaken man to a chair.

'I warned you Linton, to alert the prime minister to this threat, but no, you decided to play to your big ego and now it's about to blow up in our faces. You have ruined my career.'

'Calm down Richard and tell me what's happened?'

'I got a call from the Honourable Jonathon Farquhar-Henderson the Minster for Home Affairs.....he.'

Crowther cut him off. 'I can guess what he wanted, but did you tip him off or was it one of your minions in SIS?'

Hamilton exploded. 'Don't be so bloody impertinent Linton. This is getting out of hand and I want no part of it. This secrecy has got to end now.'

Crowther held up his hand. 'Okay Richard, I apologise. What did the hyphenated one want?'

'His son is serving as a signals officer aboard a navy frigate now transiting the Suez Canal in pursuit of a motor cruiser entering the Med. And apparently the ship is abuzz it has something to do with national security. The son has told him it's got nothing to do with apprehending a boat-load of drugs, arms or munitions. It's something far more serious to do with the security of England. How he would know that, I cannot guess. The Minister has demanded a meeting for an explanation. The navy command fobbed him off by saying it was an intelligence exercise and referred him to me as head of SIS. Have you been contacted?'

'No I haven't. So when are you meeting him?'

'Tomorrow morning at ten. I have no option Linton, I'm not prepared to crash and burn with you by lying. The game is up.'

Crowther slowly nodded as he scrunched up his mouth. 'You are right of course Richard. I would not ask you to lie. You have no option, but I think you maybe getting a little ahead of yourself. Farquhar-Henderson has received some scuttlebutt from his son which the son believes is of vital importance. That son doesn't realise how much trouble he's now in. However, you have enough experience to convince the Minister it has nothing to do with security, but is purely an intelligence operation. You're in this up to your neck Richard. I want more time to solve this problem and I believe we are getting closer to achieving that.'

Hartigan's expression remained dead-pan as he listened to his superior's lie. It was being described as an intelligence operation, rather than a matter of security? Crowther's explanation was patently misleading, but who was he to intercede?

'I'm not prepared to grant you that indulgence Linton. I'm putting you on notice I will be revealing everything I know to the Minister in the morning. You're on your own from here on.'

'I appreciate your candour and honesty Richard. All I ask is another week. Surely, you can stall him for that length of time?'

'Not possible I'm afraid Linton. Good day to you.' He did not acknowledge Hartigan as he stood abruptly and walked out.

Crowther sat and pushed himself back in his chair while letting out a burst of exhaled air. 'All hell's going to break loose by this time tomorrow Hartigan. What are you going to do about it?'

The scapegoat was being set up, but Hartigan realised he was being setup by someone with a vain hope he would also retain his position and escape liability.

'How can we delay a meeting? What would you do if you were still in the army and wanted to make sure a traitor did not meet the enemy. What would the CIA or NSA do if they had prior warning an individual was about to dump another load of highly classified intelligence onto the open market? Or in this more extreme case, a bunch of terrorists opening a drum of plutonium in the City - the very nerve centre of world financial transactions? That's how I would classify this mess. Look at the damage Julian Assange, Chelsea Manning and Edward Snowden have caused. If the NSA or CIA had been given prior warning, I've no doubt all three would have quietly disappeared, never to be seen again.'

'That's going a bit far sir. There's such a thing as due process.'

'Dammit Hartigan, can't you see there's no such thing as due process in this case. I'm not talking about a mass of restricted files being leaked, I'm talking about a city that will be wiped out as habitable with nine million people rushing for the exits, never to return. The pain and suffering will endure long after a few dated files are thrown onto Wikileaks. That bloody gutless Richard Hamilton will spill the beans to Farquhar-Henderson, if he hasn't done so already. Instead of fobbing him off with some story about a possible security breach of no real consequence, he'll reveal what we're trying to contain in order to save his own position. Little does he realise, he will have released a fire-storm which won't save him, or any of us. And as for Farquhar-Henderson, he'll immediately go to jelly and panic. His shoe leather will be smoking in his rush to get to Downing Street.'

Hartigan could feel the subliminal pressure being applied. 'What are you suggesting sir? I don't see how I can stop Sir Richard. You've tried to reason with him.' He knew exactly what his superior was suggesting.

'I'm not suggesting you do anything Hartigan. I'm merely making an observation.' He scribbled on a notepad and shoved it over in front of his agent, before pulling it back and thrusting it into a shredder beside his desk. Hartigan glanced at his superior while controlling his expression of shock. He would take the fall if anything went wrong, with what the implications of the note contained. Inwardly, he was boiling with resentment at what he was being instructed to do. He'd done far worse in Afghanistan, but in this case the individual was a Minister of the Crown and not the enemy.

Crowther looked at him. 'There is no other solution. We are playing for time and it's imperative no rumours start to circulate.'

Hartigan sat back in his chair with a defeated expression. The assignment was simple enough and easy to complete – he was just trying to justify why he should carry it out on a benign target, offering no physical threat. But, there was no denying there was a threat with irreversible implications – he could justify it on those grounds. 'Okay sir, I will look into that for you,' he said as he stood and made to leave the room.

'Excellent – I would like to read about it in the morning.'

# 58

*J*onathon Farquhar-Henderson paid off the taxi at the entrance to his Chelsea home. He was unsteady on his feet as he fumbled for his front door key. There was no light on upstairs – Elizabeth would have been in bed hours ago. She would accept his explanation in the morning, without comment. He was an extremely busy man and their devotion had never wavered over the past thirty years. However, sex was confined to procreation, not pleasure. Farquhar-Henderson had felt like relief after his tiring day in parliament, followed by dinner and a bottle of fine wine at his club. It only cost fifty pounds and he didn't have to take his trousers off. He was too tired for the full two hundred quid service.

He was looking down, trying to remove some of the fog of one glass too many, as he brushed past a camellia bush intruding on the pathway. The blow from a length of plastic-coated cable smashed around the back of his head. He was already unconscious when the next blow curled around his mouth, breaking his teeth and jaw. The assailant quickly ripped off his expensive Breguet wrist watch, removed his wallet and bundled him out of his heavy overcoat. He picked up his brief case and tipped the contents out on the path. Within a minute he had let himself out the front gate and was casually walking down the street. It was clearly the work of an opportunistic thief looking for just such a drink-affected victim? On the next corner were a row of rubbish bins waiting for early collection. He tossed the coat into the first one, along with the piece of cable and the empty wallet into the second. The cash, he could use, the watch was worth at least ten thousand pounds, but it had to go. It could never be put in for servicing as it was easily identified by its registration number and was certain to be insured. He was about to toss it down through the grill of a storm water drain when he flipped it over and read the two engraved sets of initials – it was obviously a gift. That was a crime in itself, engraving a Breguet masterpiece. He walked up the steps of a grand terrace house and shoved it through the letter slot, certain it would be returned to its owner or treasured by the unsuspecting recipient. The assailant thrust his gloved hands into his pockets and continued to walk until he could hail a cab.

'Absolutely disgusting. A member of parliament mugged in his own front yard, savagely beaten and hospitalised with a broken jaw and depressed cheekbone. Police believe it was a random attack because Farquhar-Henderson lost a sum of money, an expensive watch his wife had given him as a wedding present, as well as a Saville Row tailored Vicuna overcoat. Whoever it was, wasn't after any parliamentary secrets as the contents of his briefcase were scattered over the pathway. And no one saw or heard a thing. It was an early morning jogger who discovered him and called an ambulance. It's a wonder he lived because he was suffering from a severe concussion, along with hypothermia and pneumonia, having been out in the cold all night.' Linton Crowther tossed the newspaper across the desk to Hartigan while trying to repress a smile. 'Looks like the poor chap is out of action for a couple of weeks. He probably won't even recall the rumours and the planned meeting with Hamilton.'

Hartigan was at the point of correcting Crowther's assumptions – he had absolutely nothing to do with the mugging. He had not reacted to his superior's implied, but clear directions of the previous day. In fact he had walked in this morning to tender his resignation. However, there was now no point in denying he had been involved – he would not be believed. But the mugging had been no coincidence, of that he was sure, but who was responsible? Was Crowther playing a double game, or was it Hamilton?

'I want you on the next plane to Cyprus. We've got to find that boat, eliminate any onboard and secure what we're after. I reiterate, no one is to be left alive. I'm going to call off the navy as they will attract too much attention, so you're on your own except for an agent I'll assign to you. There's a massive amount resting on your shoulders Hartigan, so don't let me down.'

'What about Sir Richard and SIS?'

'We've already discussed it this morning. He's agreed to give us two weeks unless Farquhar-Henderson recovers enough to demand an explanation to the rumours, in which case he will tell all he knows. However, Jonathon is in a bad way and may not survive and even if he does, he'll likely be convalescing for months. Whoever mugged him, used too much force.'

'Look sir, there's something I want to make absolutely clear. Whatever you may assume, I am not responsible for Farquhar-Henderson's injuries and if......'

Crowther raised his hand to cut him off with a confected look of surprise. 'I never for a moment thought you were. Whatever gave you that idea? Now let's get down to business. Hamilton is adamant he will give us two weeks to wrap this case up, or he's going to the PM. He doesn't care if Farquhar-Henderson lives or dies, the deadline is two weeks. However, he wasn't so confident of himself this morning. He sounded a bit worried. Although his address is a secret, he's still got to walk through his front gate at night and London is full of thugs. And as you know Hartigan, secrets are hard to keep in this city.'

# 59

*D*eclan *was standing beside Kyriakou as he studied the sweep on the radar screen. 'No sign of anyone following us, Costas. That frigate should have caught up with us by now.'*

'No, it either got delayed in the Canal or has been called off the chase I would say. We'll be approaching Cyprus in a few hours with plenty of small coves and islands to shelter in and behind. But, I don't think it would be wise to keep the barrels on board. Those waters are constantly patrolled by Greek Customs and although we may have got away with it once, I think you'll find the Greeks are more vigilant. They will most certainly take a closer look at those drums and when they find two of them contain more than diesel fuel, all our efforts to date will be for nothing. What are your suggestions?'

'I want you to arrange a fast boat to take Zehra across to Turkey so she can make contact with her Kurd group. Once she's done that she'll return and pick up one of the barrels. We'll then head for Greece or Italy, where I'll offload the other and head for London. Within weeks, two of the world's major cities will be vacant,' Declan laughed out loud as he smashed a fist into his open hand. 'And vacant for all time. That will teach the bloody English they've kicked the Irish in the teeth once too often. I'll repay them for hundreds of years of oppression and the jailing of my grandfather, in multiples.'

'I think the place to head for is Pomos on the northern side of the island. It's where I come from and it will be easy to get one of my relatives to take Zehra across to Turkey at night.' However, he won't be able to wait for her as the Turks will quickly confiscate his boat if they catch him in their waters. He will just drop her off and pick her up the following night.

It was early the following morning when they entered Pomos harbour and pulled into a pier behind the breakwater. 'You two stay here while I clear the way with the harbour master. He's one of my many uncles so we won't have any problems, but I want to be sure there are no Turks around. Pomos is only a couple of kilometres from the international buffer zone separating the Greeks from the Turks and there are sure to be sympathetic Turkish ears around. If it's too dangerous my uncle will tell me and we'll have to move quickly, so don't leave the boat.'

Kyriakou stepped ashore and was quickly greeted by loud calls from fishermen tending to the nets of their small fishing boats. Declan and Zehra watched as he made his way up the quay and into the township that clung to the shores of the curvature of the small harbour. It was an hour later when he re-appeared in the company of an older man with a wrinkled face like tanned leather and a beaming smile breaking through the pure white teeth.

'This is my uncle Stavros. Everything's arranged. Zehra can go across tomorrow night as there's no moon and in the meantime we are all invited to his taverna to dine and listen to some genuine Cypriot music tonight. It will do us good to get off the boat, so pack a toothbrush and be prepared to stay the night as Stavros won't take no for an answer. You are going to experience some Cypriot hospitality.' Stavros had shaken their hands and spoke in broken English. The continual waving of his hand towards the village was all the communication required.

'Who's going to look after the boat?' Zehra asked.

'All taken care of. Stavros has arranged for three of our relatives to stay onboard. It will be perfectly safe, I can assure you.'

# 60

*The small fishing boat gently nudged the stern of the larger vessel. The two men, aided by those on deck above, were silent as they worked. Two empty fuel drums were lifted up onto the deck along with a hand pump. The two drums containing the smaller deadly cargo were quickly identified, pumped dry and loaded onto the fishing boat.*

Kyriakou and Bellamy were walking down the stone pier in the morning, both suffering from excess when they passed the three who had been guarding the *Kuro V*. Declan raised his hand in acknowledgement as the greetings were loudly exchanged. It was all he could do to walk straight, let alone notice the nodded exchange as Kyriakou passed the last of his relatives. It was late in the afternoon when Declan finally surfaced and stumbled out of his bunk and made his way to the galley.

'Hi there Declan, would you like a coffee?' Kyriakou was slowly stirring a small cup of thick brown liquid.

'Costas, you Cypriot's know how to turn it on. Yes, I will have a coffee thanks, thick and strong. I thought it was just going to be a quiet meal, a couple of drinks and a bit of music. I didn't know the whole village would turn out. Are they really all related to you?'

Kyriakou placed the coffee in front of Declan. 'They certainly are. We have a saying here, that if you marry a Greek, you marry the whole family. Don't ever expect any privacy, as your door is never locked. Relatives and kids just wander in and out at will and are never rejected. That would be insulting.'

Declan laughed as he sipped the thick liquid. 'No offence Costas, but I'm glad I'm not a Greek or a Cypriot. Say, that reminds me – what happened to Zehra? She didn't seem to be enjoying the scene?'

'No, she made an excuse and went to bed early. I stayed with my sister last night and Zehra was having breakfast when I walked into the taverna this morning. She appeared very nervous about making the run over to the Turkish coast tonight. I told her not to worry if she didn't make contact with her group, as the boat would return every night at the same time. She's one very smart lady and I've no fears she can look after herself.'

'Yes, she's very capable and determined. She'll make the connection and then return to collect the barrel and I can head for Greece or Italy and hire a vehicle to take me through to England. Are you going to stick with Zehra or come with me?'

'It would be dangerous for me to set foot in Turkey. My father was branded a terrorist when the Turks invaded Cyprus. He was very outspoken and actively opposed the division of my country. However, he paid the ultimate price.

If the United Nations hadn't stepped in, Cyprus would be under total Turkish control instead of the divided country it is today. The Turks eventually murdered my father. I was very young at the time, but I've no doubt similar treatment would apply to me if I was caught. However, I will think about it. The Turkish secret police have complete family records of every Cypriot who opposed them. They are not a tolerant race as witnessed by their actions in Armenia. They once overran and controlled Greece and they've never forgotten it. For all their so-called secular tolerance they are first and foremost Moslems and Islam is the biggest political movement on earth. Criticise or oppose Islam and you will immediately feel the baying pack of rabid hounds at your heels wanting revenge for your insult. The Moslem's brain-wash children to instil hatred of the infidel, which is anyone not a true-believer. Turkey was on the road to secular freedom and tolerance - that was until President Recept Erdogen decided to turn the clock back and embrace conservatism and Islam. The west accepts this bullshit without real comment or retaliation. I have no love for the Turks and am right behind what you intend to do. It's a pity London is going to suffer the same fate, but I can understand the motive. As with the Turks oppression of the Kurds, the English have long exploited the Irish. Can I ask you whether you intend to actually carry through with your intentions in London, or are you looking at blackmail for a ransom?'

'Make no mistake Costas, this is not a demand for ransom – London will cease to exist as a habitable city. The economy will come to a standstill within a couple of hours. Then we'll deal with those Orange-men and their bloody Lambeg drums and apprentice- boy marches in northern Ireland.

We'll tip them right out of Ireland and make the whole of the country a republic instead of the divided nation it is today. Anybody who thinks the troubles are over needs to think again – they're about to start.'

# 61

*Hartigan had only a brief description of the Kuro V provided by the navy while it was docked in Djibouti. And no, they hadn't taken a photo of it – it hadn't occurred to them? The days of Britannia ruling the waves were long gone? His problem was there were literally hundreds of pleasure craft matching the size he was looking for, roaming around in the Mediterranean, anchored in isolated island locations or tied up side by side in the main harbours where the look-at-me money from every shade of legitimacy broadcast the fuck-you attitude. The onboard helicopter and crew in their immaculate whites a must, permanently on guard for intruders or the owner making an unexpected visit with his family, or more likely a group of buddies with a mixture of highly attractive escorts flown in from the Ukraine or Bulgaria for a week of business discussions. However, in the world of changing standards and preferences, not an eyebrow was raised when the accompaniment turned out to be a cavorting group of handsome young males of varying physiques and colouring.*

Hartigan was at a loss where to start. He had picked Cyprus as the most likely destination. If his guess was correct, at least he had only the Greek half of Cyprus to look at – the *Kuro V* would not be heading for any port in the Turkish controlled eastern part of the island.

He was jolted back to the present as the British Airways 737 landed heavily at Larnaca on the southern side of the island. The two agents followed the tourists all laughing and talking loudly as they jostled and retrieved their carry-on bags from the overhead lockers.

'What's the plan chief?'

'We're going to hire two cars. You, Ronson will head directly for Limassol in the south and start calling into every fishing port, big or small, on the southern side before moving around to the north of the island. I'm going to go directly north-east from here and through the British Sovereign Base Area to Deryneia, which is dissected by the UN border. I will then retrace my steps to Limassol and follow your route. Don't be in a hurry, but don't waste time sightseeing and be discrete when asking questions. This Costas Kyriakou is a Cypriot and the Cypriot's are all related in some way. We don't want to alert any relative or friend we are looking for him, or to be more precise, a certain boat he maybe skippering. And make sure your phone is fully charged at all times.'

Hartigan spent an hour walking around the waterfront of Larnaca. From what he could see, no boats matched the description he was looking for. There were a few mediocre-length low-wealth floating gin-palaces, but the majority were smaller craft and local fishing trawlers. A few casual questions confirmed nothing had entered the port of the size he was interested in. The following day he drove north-east to Deryneia, but quickly decided Kyriakou would have ruled it out – too many Turkish ears and eyes watching over the departures and arrivals. He back-tracked to the resort town of Ayia Napa, but it was too open for a large vessel the size of *Kuro V.* He was heading back to Larnaca when his phone rang. He was fully expecting it to be Linton Crowther demanding to know progress - it was an almost hourly occurrence. The old-boy was losing sleep and it was clear in his voice.

'Miles, I maybe onto something.' It was Ronson.

'Where are you exactly?'

'In a small port not far from the town of Paphos in the far south-west. One of the local fishermen said he saw a vessel fitting the description of the *Kuro V* a couple of days ago. He said it had the outline of a trawler, but had none of the gear or winches. What attracted him was the aluminium hull for such a large boat, very rare in this part of the world and the chopper pad above the stern deck. It passed him about a mile to seaward and appeared to be heading directly for Turkey. It looks as though we're too late and would have needed the navy's help in any event to apprehend it. I would say you can drop this in Crowther's lap and we can head for home. I'll turn around and meet you back at Larnaca.'

Hartigan wasn't so sure. Ronson had no idea of the cargo it was carrying. The only instruction he'd been given was it had to be stopped at all costs before it reached Turkey. 'Just hang about a minute. I'm going to pull over and look at the tourist map of Cyprus, if this car has one.'

He found what he was looking for and quickly opened it across the steering wheel. His eyes followed the coastline north from Paphos and up and around Cape Arnauti, into the broad sweep of the Bay of Khrysokhou. He had a hunch. The *Kuro V* was clearing the shallow waters off the Cape when spotted by the fisherman and wasn't headed directly for Turkey – it was headed up and around the Cape for a Greek Cypriot port directly facing Turkey.

'Ronson, I want you to continue north and wait for me in Paphos. I don't want you to make any enquiries. You are a tourist just wandering around the island. Is that clear? Find a quiet little taverna and take a rest until I arrive. And don't, I repeat don't, start to talk about boats and the particular boat in question.'

'But what if I see it? Obviously you think it's in that area?'

'Ronson, if you see it, call me, but not when anyone around can hear you. And yes, I do think there's a chance our target is somewhere in that Bay area. And if by any chance Linton Crowther should contact you in the meantime, you are to tell him you know nothing and have seen nothing. And above all, play the tourist and not the bloody agent.' He did not wait for a reply as he cancelled the connection and pulled back onto the highway.

# 62

*Hartigan approached the outskirts of Paphos with its history dating back millenia to when it represented one of the ten kingdoms of Cyprus. He drove slowly along the main street looking for Ronson's car, or any sign of him in many of the quiet tavernas. It was a town as yet undiscovered by tourists. He stopped under a large olive tree on the outskirts and dialled his subordinate's number. It was answered on the second ring.*

'Where are you?'

'I'm just approaching Pomos further around the Bay.'

Hartigan was annoyed and he showed it. Ronson had been given clear instructions, but they had been ignored. 'I told you to wait in Paphos. What do you think you're doing?'

'My apologies sir. I should have phoned you, but I got a tip-off from a fisherman a large trawler had been seen heading in the direction of Pomos. That gels with what a local further south told me. I'm only about ten miles away at the moment, so I'll phone you immediately if it's there.'

'If it is, don't go near it. I don't want you wandering around the waterfront making out you're a tourist. And make sure you don't start asking questions of the locals. Understood?'

'Yes sir, but what's so special about this boat? Isn't it time you told me? Why the hell are we so interested in it?'

'You just follow my instructions Ronson. And this time, do as you're bloody well told.' A subordinate not following directions was something he would not tolerate. Ronson would be assigned to a desk rather than field work when this mission was completed. It was half an hour later when he got the call.

'Our search is over sir. The name is clearly visible on the hull. There are a few people wandering around the decks, but there doesn't seem to be a lot of activity. I've checked into the Oleanas taverna, right on the waterfront.'

'I'll find another hotel and you don't know me and don't come near me. If you see me, just keep walking and I'll phone you.'

Hartigan was still sitting in one of the numerous tavernas facing the corso around midnight, but there was no sign of Ronson. He had observed the occasional straggling groups of tourists and locals, all walking past in the hours he had been sitting there. The effects of three whiskies had long since dispersed into his system and he declined the constant offer of more coffee. The crab cakes and Greek salad were an excellent choice, but the epicurean enjoyment had since faded. He did not smoke, so he ordered a carafe of the local white wine – it was rough, but at least he had a glass to occupy his attention as he twirled it in his hand. He had tried Ronson's number constantly, but it always diverted to message bank. He was worried. Something had happened. Finally, he paid and slowly walked down the corso and back around through narrow lanes until he was behind the Oleanas. He saw Ronson's car, but he did not approach it. His phone still went to message bank. He walked back to his hotel and climbed the stairs to his room, cursing the incompetence of his associate. It was a warm evening as he lay back in a well-padded divan looking out over the harbour from his balcony. He could clearly see his target vessel with a solitary light revealing the deserted stern. Then he saw someone walk down the seawall jetty and a form stand up from where he had been sitting in the stern. They met on the gangway and talked for a few minutes. Hartigan could see it was a change of shift. The boat was being guarded around the clock.

He awoke to the warmth of the rising sun and smell of the sea. Within minutes he had showered and shaved and retraced his steps as casually as he could to the rear of the Ronson's taverna – his car was no longer there. His phone no longer went to message bank – it was disconnected. It was obvious his fellow agent was in trouble and he had the feeling it was fatal. He would not have left the town without leaving a message of some kind and the only place that would be was at hotel reception. But, he had no intention of following up on that enquiry. That would immediately put him in danger.

The taverna owner recognised and greeted him warmly as he sat down and ordered breakfast and coffee. He had phoned Linton Crowther twice since noting the disappearance of Ronson's car and left messages for him to phone back. He needed back-up and he needed it now. He needed two highly trained agents on the next flight, with no doubts about their intent or mission. They would require weapons once they landed and that would have to be arranged through one of the U.K. Sovereign Base Areas (SBA) on the island. The agents could not carry weapons through Heathrow without a special clearance. But such a request would raise eyebrows of concern and take too long to gain approval. The thought of a Brit wandering around a barely-dormant powder-keg like Cyprus with a gun, let alone three with guns, would raise the alarm at the highest level. Crowther would have to pull every lever and call in every favour if he was to meet the request for muscle and firepower, because that's what it would take to gain control of the *Kuro V* and its cargo of death. He was walking out of the village and through a grove of olive trees when his phone rang. It was Crowther.

'I wasn't able to take your call Hartigan. I was with Richard Hamilton trying to calm him down. How the hell he ever made it to be head of **SIS** is beyond me. He just can't handle pressure. However, I've managed to buy us some time. What have you got for me?'

'I'm afraid it's a first-rate emergency sir. I can confirm the *Kuro V* is tied up here in Pomos. The bad news is it appears to be well guarded and the worst news is Ronson has disappeared.'

'What do you mean disappeared?' Crowther' exasperation was evident. 'How did that happen?'

'To cut a long story short sir, I ordered him to wait for me in a town further down the coast, but he ignored me. He then phoned later saying he had followed up on a tip-off and driven here to Pomos where he had observed the *Kuro V* tied-up. He gave me the name of his hotel and I was to phone him to arrange a meeting. His phone would not answer, so I eventually went looking for his car. I found it, but when I checked again this morning, it was gone. I can only draw one conclusion from that.' There was a silence on the other end of the phone. He could not hear Crowther's usual belaboured breathing.'Are you still there sir?'

'Yes, yes,' was the snapped reply. 'It looks like you've screwed up on this one.' Crowther heard the sharp intake of breath and sensed the suppression of a strong verbal rebuttal. Hartigan was his best agent who had rejected Ronson being seconded to him, but he over-rode the objection. Hartigan had a reason. Ronson had overstepped the mark once before and it looked as though he would repeat it? 'So, there you are with no backup, the target right before your eyes and nothing to work with except your charm and wits? Tell me what you want?'

'Two agents with no doubts, nor scruples and armed. This is a dire emergency sir and I don't want anyone who's not prepared to pull a trigger or break a neck. And I want them now, because I've no doubt one of those barrels is bound for Turkey. If it gets there, the consequences of our involvement will be impossible to hide.'

'What makes you think it hasn't already?'

'The boat is being guarded which suggests the barrels are still on board. I'm working on the theory one drum is for Istanbul and the other is bound for London. The *Kuro V* is still tied up here, so I'm assuming the Turkish transfer hasn't taken place. If it had, the boat would have already departed for Greece or Italy, assuming they would land the second barrel there and move it by car across Europe to England. I believe it would be too much of a risk to take both barrels to Turkey. I'm also assuming one of the three on board, Kyriakou, Bellamy or Kermandi has already crossed over to Turkey to make contact with a Kurd rebel group. They would surely do that in advance before risking running into the Turks. How long one of them has been gone would only be a day at the most, so I believe we've only got a couple of days to rescue the situation. I maybe too late already. It could happen tonight. Can you give me what I want?' The urgency in Hartigan's voice was evident.

'Slow down Hartigan. You will have your men and arms by this time tomorrow. I anticipated there would be problems and have been working on it for the past twenty four hours. I had to go right to the top to explain............' Crowther had tried to stop himself, but it was too late - Hartigan was too astute not to have picked up on it. 'Oh, to hell with it Hartigan, this whole affair is driving me crazy. You know who I'm referring to. I won't relate the reaction, nor the language and the demand for my immediate resignation if this hits the fan. It will bring down the government, so I won't be alone. Purely by chance, a destroyer carrying a helicopter is within fifty miles of Cyprus right now. The chopper will land in the SBA zone of Akrotiri within an hour with your requirements. The two men are ex Afghan vets used to tough work. Just tell them what you want done and they'll do it. Now get off the phone, so I can set the ball rolling.'

# 63



*The vine covered verandah of the bistro provided an excellent observation point as he sipped a coffee and watched the Kuro V. It was being guarded in rotation by locals, but there was no sign of the people he wanted to identify – Bellamy, Kyriakou, or the woman.*

'Do you mind if I sit here?' The tourist sat down in front of him, partially blocking his view of the quay and the boat. 'Jeremy Bowman,' he said holding out his hand.

'Cedric Ward,' Hartigan replied as he shook the hand he could not avoid - the lie seamless and without hesitation.

'First time in Pomos, is it? I'm a travel writer, sent by my editor to look for attractions tourists haven't yet discovered. It's a beautiful location, but I doubt whether tourists are going to rush to discover it's isolated charm just yet, but it will happen. It starts with a trickle before friends talk to friends, the tourist agencies get involved and then the complete charm of isolation and attraction is destroyed. And what do you do for a living?'

Hartigan studied the person opposite – the sudden approach staged and not spontaneous. 'Oh, I'm just a public servant at home. This is my first time in Cyprus. I just hired a car in Larnaca and decided to check out the coastline. I don't like crowds and I'm enjoying it so far.'

'How interesting.' Bowman pulled out a notepad and began to scribble a few lines. 'What a wonderful quote. I will use it as a heading for an article. I'll title it - *I'm enjoying it so far.* I'm sure to get emails saying they were here years ago and it still sounds boring. As a journalist and just about having seen everything there is to see in the world courtesy of free junkets on airlines and tourism companies, I'm always looking for something new. I believe my column will double tourism to this quiet little village in the next two years. I'm going to quote you. Do you mind?'

Hartigan laughed, but it was not sincere. As long as Bowman didn't insist on taking a photo to go with his column, Cedric Ward would remain anonymous. 'Not at all, but no photo.' He had been distracted, but he caught sight of two people walking past the front of the taverna deep in conversation. He was looking at Bellamy and Kyriakou in profile.

Bowman glanced around. 'Am I intruding? Are you waiting for someone?'

'No, no, just passing the time.'

'Okay, well it's been pleasant talking to you.' Bowman stood up and as he did, leaned forward. 'It's no use looking for your friend. If you hang around any longer you're likely to suffer the same fate. The moment you drove in you were a marked man.'

Hartigan reached over and grabbed Bowman's arm. 'Who the hell are you?'

'I'm a friend giving you a warning, so let's leave it at that. As for your associate, I don't know what happened to him, but I can assure you it wouldn't have been pleasant. He went too close to that boat on the pier and asked too many questions. I believe the only reason they didn't take you out last night was because they are not quite sure if you are enemy. However, don't push your luck.' Bowman pulled his arm free and walked off.

Hartigan sat stunned. Who was he and why was he delivering a message and from whom? He looked around, but Bellamy and Kyriakou had disappeared into one of the small lane-ways. His gaze turned towards the quay. He was utterly helpless, Until his backup arrived tomorrow at the earliest, he could do nothing but sit and wait. But who was Bowman and who was he working for? And why had he warned him of the danger?

It was the sudden gust of wind that awoke him, combined with a light drifting shower of rain. He had been sitting out under the shade of his balcony and had not noticed the weather front moving in as he dozed off aided by a bottle of wine. He quickly gathered up the empty bottle and glass and turned to open the door, as he glanced back down the quay. The solitary stern light was moving with the force of the swells against the boat, but it wasn't that which attracted his attention. It was the nose of a high-speed patrol vessel as it moved slowly towards the *Kuro V*. He ignored the rain and wind as he strained his eyes to follow its progress. The red pennant with white star and crescent trailing from its stern, clearly identified its nationality. This was no secret mission, but a blatant show of strength and purpose. Within minutes it had pulled up alongside and he saw three figures dressed entirely in black, with black head coverings leap aboard. They were armed, which was confirmed when he heard a brief burst of a weapon, the sound almost completely muffled by the wind. Was it Bellamy or Kyriakou on the receiving end of that sound? The patrol vessel was quickly lashed to the side and four more figures leapt aboard. Hartigan sat down in despair as he saw four large fuel drums being quickly rolled from the Kuro V and onto the patrol vessel. Within a minute it had begun to pull away as silently as it had arrived. With it's turn complete and the bow pointing out to sea, there was a sudden burst of power as the engines were thrust to maximum, throwing up clouds of spray as it headed directly out into the increasing squalls. He watched until it was out of sight. It appeared to be heading directly towards Turkey. He had lost – he was too late. The Turks must have known about the cargo and the threat the Kuro V was carrying and knew exactly when to strike. MI6 had been out-manoeuvred and caught flatfooted. The Turks had obviously been tipped off, but by whom, was the question? Maybe Crowther had decided to dump it all in their lap, being too embarrassed to admit MI6 had failed. And here he was sitting on a rain drenched balcony in Cyprus waiting for two gun-carrying associates to arrive and take the Kuro V and its deadly cargo by force. Depressed at his failure, but somewhat relieved, he rose and pulled the balcony door behind him as he went back into the room. He picked us his phone to call Crowther, but tossed it onto the bed. He wasn't in any hurry to report a disaster. He pulled a chair up to the glass door to keep watch. Maybe he would learn more in the next hour or so when the police turned up to investigate the shooting, as surely they must. He kept looking at his watch trying to hasten the time, but nothing happened. The rear deck was still lit *by a dim light, but there was no movement on board. It was as though nothing had happened – there had been no gunfire, no one had been killed and there had never been a patrol boat. It was totally inexplicable. However, in the early dawn he saw the bow and stern line of the Kuro V being cast off as the vessel made to leave. There was no hurry – everything appeared normal as it pulled away and motored out of the harbour. It was also time for him to leave. There was no point in sticking around. He packed his few belongings and went downstairs for breakfast and a strong coffee.*

'Well, I may as well get it over with,' he muttered to himself as he got up and walked outside to phone Crowther, while bracing himself for a blast of criticism.

'Don't worry Hartigan. If it was in fact the Turks who did take the plutonium, we can forget about it. They're not going to say anything to us directly, other than a subtle hint at some high-level soiree, that they solved a problem we couldn't handle. Looking on a positive note, they have removed a major headache for us. We can now relax - I can hand Richard Hamilton back his gonads and the prime minister can cut back his valium to three times a day. Come on home.'

'What about Ronson sir? Surely, I should stay for awhile and try to find out what happened to him. I was told he'd probably been murdered. I also heard gun fire last night, so someone must have been shot, yet there has been no police presence and no bodies taken off that vessel.'

'Hartigan, just forget it. It's a pity about Ronson, but he was aware risks go with the job. Anyway, he was under a cloud, so it's probably better it happened there and not in London.'

Hartigan screwed his face up at the comment – it was uncaring and brutal. What did Crowther mean by that remark?He was about to protest when an order was barked.

'Get out of there – the game's over. I'll contact the people I sent over and call them back.'

The line went dead. What the hell was going on? How many people were playing in this game he wasn't aware of? Crowther was making him look a bloody fool. He noticed a car pull out into the corso and drive slowly towards him before stopping. Bowman smiled and beckoned him over as the passenger door was pushed open.

'Good morning Cedric. Get in and let's compare the experience. I want to see if you agree with the article I'm going to write.'

Hartigan got in and looked across at Bowman. 'You're not Jeremy Bowman and you're not a journalist, are you?'

Bowman pulled a wry grin as he looked across. 'No, I'm no more a journalist than you are a public servant on holiday. It is Miles Hartigan of MI6, isn't it?'

'And you?' Hartigan was trying to suppress his look of shock. 'Are you attached to SIS or SI05?'

'Neither Miles. You don't need to know my name, but we were both assigned here on the same mission. However, my job is now complete as the Turks appear to taken care of the problem. The plutonium 239 is in their possession and no longer a threat to them or London. I can see you are somewhat shocked?'

'I am, but tell me who are you working for and why? How did you know that vessel would be carrying the plutonium?'

Bowman laughed. 'We have been aware of the problem for years. We just could not believe how inept your agency has been in not eliminating Declan Connoly and the threat he controlled, when you had the opportunity. And then you let it slip through your fingers and the grandfather handed the secret to his grandson. You should have killed him before he got to Wakefield. You had the chance in Australia, but you drugged him and flew him home on a charter flight. I'll admit we tried to do it while he was in Wakefield, but failed. The grandson did what we both screwed up, but it was too late – the old boy had given him the exact location of the plutonium. It took us a while to track him down in Australia and like you, were wondering how he would get the material in those barrels to Turkey and England. We had not discounted another major city could be on their radar, but I think that danger has been averted.'

'And the other city?'

'I'll come to that Miles. The *Kuro V* was first identified in Fremantle and was then followed to Port Hedland. The skipper Milos Niarchos, had an unfortunate accident when his truck overturned while driving back to Fremantle, but not before he had confirmed Declan Bellamy had paid him off in Port Hedland. It was then a simple matter to satellite track him right to this port. We had no idea if he had the plutonium on board, but that question was answered when we saw the *Kuro V* closing in on a large trawler in the middle of the Indian Ocean. Unfortunately, it was getting dark so satellite photos were not conclusive as to whether they actually met. However, there was no trace of the trawler the following day, the conclusion being it was scuttled that night following the transfer. Previously, we became aware Zehra Kermandi and Costas Kyriakou had purchased a long-range trawler in Port Lincoln. That agent confirmed it to MI6 and my people, but as you know he disappeared. I have no doubt he was murdered somewhere at sea or went down with that trawler.'

Hartigan could not hide his surprise – Bowman had just confirmed the MI6 victim was a double-agent, but who was he working for? It had to be Homeland Security or the NSA.

'And there you have it Mr Hartigan – game set and match to the Turks, or so it would seem. Problem solved and a hideous threat gone. The Turks have the plutonium, but they will hand it over. I can see you don't understand?'

'No, I don't. You're not making sense. Who the hell are you and who are you working for?' he demanded in a tone of irritation. He resented Bowman's mind games. 'Is it the NSA or Homeland Security. But I don't think you're American by your accent, so who is it?'

'You're almost there, but not quite. We do have major business and political investments, as well as a considerable personal presence in New York, which we have a vital interest in protecting. We have all been watching your agency trying to solve the Connoly problem for some time and were not prepared to endure an attack by terrorists. I'll give you credit though, in the end you have delivered the solution without our direct involvement. However, if the Turks had failed we were prepared to move quickly. That's why I'm here. But now that everything is under control I'm on my way home and suggest you do the same.'

Hartigan stepped out and leaned back through the window. 'At least give me your name and who you represent?'

'Both are irrelevant Miles. Oh, I almost forgot. It was the agent you've just lost who went a bit overboard with that politician who was threatening to run to your Prime Minister. It had to be done, but he did make a mess of the fellow's face. However, from what I hear he will make a full recovery following some plastic surgery and a set of dentures. Your conscience is clear.'

Hartigan stepped back as the car began to move. He watched it as it followed the corso and disappeared around a bend to the south. It was clear who Bowman was working for - *mossad* – the name of the Israeli intelligence service - *mossad* – the world's deadliest and most effective intelligence agency – *mossad* – fall within their radar and there was no escape. But the real shock was Bowman had confirmed there was a mole in MI6. There had to be, otherwise Bowman would not have known about Farquhar-Henderson's injuries? And he now knew his identity, but it was too late.

Bowman, or whatever his name was, had confirmed the Turks had got the plutonium and for a *mossad* agent to say that, it was a certainty. The chase was over - Pomos was a pleasant place in which to spend a few days to relax and he intended to enjoy it. He strolled along the quay nodding and acknowledging the fishermen mending nets and tending to their small wooden *caiques* – the fishing boats common to Greece. He could feel their eyes watching him. It was some hours later while sitting in a quiet corner of the taverna nursing a glass of wine, he saw the *Kuro V* slowly motor back into port and tie up. Soon after Bellamy and Kyriakou were walking back along the quay towards the village, deep in conversation, their expressions strained. It then occurred to him he had not seen the woman – Zehra Kermandi. Was she the casualty of the gunfire he'd heard and was she the reason the vessel disappeared out to sea for most of the day? A Kurd killed on Cypriot soil would have immediately attracted the attention of the police. He had the feeling Bowman had told him Ronson's fate – they had dumped both bodies at sea. Kyriakou's relations and all the village would know what happened, but the silence would never be penetrated.

He finished his drink and was idly watching the *Kuro V* when he noticed something strange occur. At first it did not register – a couple of locals walked down the pier and boarded the vessel. He saw two people rise from where they were sitting in the stern, acknowledge the two arrivals with loud greetings and walk off. Nothing really strange about that, but the shotgun handed to one of the arrivals was the item that caught his attention. He had not noticed it before. Why the gun if the Turks had got hold of the plutonium? What was the point of the guards? Hartigan realised he would not be leaving Pomos just yet.

# 65

'*Are you Miles Hartigan?*'

Hartigan looked up at the person with dark glasses and shoulder-length hair. He was solidly built, dressed in battered jeans and T-shirt which looked as though it had never seen a laundry. He was carrying a small hold-all bag.

'And you are?'

'James Thorburn. I believe we represent the same company,' he said as he sat down opposite. Thorburn's expression was one of open invitation with an expansive smile. Hartigan eyed him with suspicion. Was this *mossad* again? Where had this guy trained and under whom? Was he getting old or were they getting younger these days? However, Hartigan realised this was no kid sitting before him – Crowther would have only assigned the best. 'Where's your companion? I thought there were supposed to be two of you?'

'No, at the last moment Crowther said I would be travelling alone. My instructions were to pick up a weapon at the

SBA zone in Akrotiri and then find you. Incidentally, the people in Akrotiri knew nothing about a gun and weren't very impressed with my explanation of what I was doing in Cyprus.'

'Why didn't you answer your phone? I've been trying to call you. Didn't Crowther phone and give you the news, you're to turn around and go home?'

Thorburn pulled a face. 'A comedy of errors. I was pissed off with Crowther at being pulled in just when I'd earned a couple of weeks off, then the stuff up regarding the gun and then some woman knocked the phone out of my hand and smashed it when I was running for a taxi in Larnaca. Not to worry – I can work without either. What news was Crowther supposed to give me?'

Hartigan ignored the question. He was not impressed with James Thorburn and intended to express his opinion to Crowther. 'And you call yourself an agent? How long have you been with the company?'

'A little more than a year. I was in Greece and then Turkey for three years with a U.S. tech company before I joined up.'

And who are you really working for was Hartigan's immediate thought? Was this another double agent? 'And before that?'

'I was in the royal navy for five years before joining the merchant marine where I gained my master's ticket. You name it and I'm authorised to drive it.'

'You see that boat on the pier. Could you handle that?'

Thorburn turned around and grinned. 'No problem, that's a toy. What do you want me to do?'

'I want you to get aboard that boat and see if they need a deckhand. Make out you're looking for work. Don't rush it.'

'How will I contact you?'

'You can't. It is probably for the best you don't have a phone or a weapon. It would be too dangerous to be carrying either. Don't worry about Crowther, I'll clear it with him and the reason you're off the air.'

'What's this gig all about? I was told nothing, except to report to you.'

'You don't need to know at this stage and I'm not at liberty to tell you. Your brief is to try and get aboard that boat. There are two characters by the name of Declan Bellamy and Costas Kyriakou on board, along with a female by the name of Zehra Kermandi, although she may no longer be present. I'll give you a warning to be ultra careful, as these people are dangerous to the highest degree. Already, someone who was supposed to be accompanying me has disappeared and I believe they are responsible. Now, this is what I want you to do.'

Thorburn listened, shrugged as picked up his battered bag and prepared to walk off. 'I've got the message. Are you sticking around?'

'No, I'm leaving in the morning, but you can contact me,' he said scribbling out his phone number on a coaster. 'If you do get accepted, phone me to confirm, but otherwise you're on your own.'

# 66

*I*t was first light when the high-powered RIB pulled in astern of the Kuro V and Zehra Kermandi quickly climbed aboard. Bellamy and Kyriakou were waiting for her.

'Did you make contact?'

She tried to smile through an exhausted expression as she ran her hand through her hair. 'Yes Declan, I did and it's all set for tomorrow night. We'll be picked up in a covered truck full of vegetables bound for the markets in Istanbul. You can stay with me and watch it happen, or take the other drum through to London by road in a car I've arranged. I can't believe it,' she laughed. 'By this time next week the entire population of Istanbul will be in a blind panic to get away from the threat. I want those damned Turks to suffer.' She threw her arms around Declan's neck and kissed him before spinning around and dancing across the deck in excitement.

'That's not going to happen Zehra. The Turks arrived with an armed contingent last night and removed the barrels.'

A look of shock crossed her face as she stopped in mid-stride and spun around to face Bellamy. 'What are you talking about? That's not possible. The Turks don't know we are here.'

'Well, someone must have told them and it wasn't one of us. We caught someone on board while you were away. He had taken a small boat from the shore, rowed it out and tied it to the offside railing. One of Costas' cousins was guarding the gangway and quay approach and we just didn't think about someone trying to board from the starboard side. Unfortunately for the intruder, the sound of it bumping up against the hull woke me. We were waiting for him and didn't ask any questions. He was carrying no identity, but he was armed, so he wasn't a tourist. We searched his hotel room, but found nothing of interest so we got rid of his car.'

'So where is he now? Surely, someone is going to come looking for him?'

'We dumped him out at sea and yes, we did suspect he was in Pomos with someone, but that person has since checked out of his hotel and gone. We had him under surveillance, but it would appear he was a tourist. If he had not left Pomos, we intended to take care of him tonight. There was also another suspicious character posing as a travel writer, but he drove out this morning.'

Zehra slumped into a seat in the large cabin. 'So, what do we do now? A year of planning and thousands of miles in a boat constantly watching for danger, only to find ourselves outsmarted by the Turks at the last moment.' She smashed her hand into the arm of the chair as she stood with a furious expression. 'How did you two let this happen? You were supposed to be guarding the ship. And Costas, you had a constant stream of your trusted friends and relations supposed to be watching. You knew the danger. We are only a stones throw from the Turkish side of Cyprus. There would be a thousand Turkish eyes across the demarcation line, not a mile from here watching this port and yet you let down your guard. Our dream of giving these cursed people something to remember the Kurds by, has gone and all because of you.' She lashed out and slapped him across the face before falling back in her chair, in despair.

Kyriakou did not react, as Bellamy came to his defence. 'I'm also to blame, but we had no warning and there was nothing we could have done. They were armed commandos who meant business – we only had our bare hands. Costas did make a move, but he wisely stopped when one of them let off a warning burst from an automatic weapon. One more step and he would have been dead. Go and have a look at the side of the cabin outside and you'll see the evidence. Those people were not worried about making a noise or hiding their identity – they were on mission with specific instructions and they knew exactly what they were looking for. Fifteen minutes and it was all over.'

Zehra was rocking her head side to side as she grasped it between her hands. 'What am I going to tell my people? The Turks have always crushed us and they will continue to do so. We will never beat them and attain our own homeland and national identity while those people in Ankara control us. Allah curse them,' she swore as she spat onto the deck.

'What are you going to do now then Zehra?'

'Declan, I'm going to do what I've always done and that's fight, fight, fight. We will never break free unless we continue to fight, but we must fight as a unified force rather than the fractured groups scattered across many countries and recognised by none. Until the Kurds unify as a single force we will always remain subservient to any oppressor. I will be ridiculed and cursed for having failed, but I will return to my people and start again, however pointless that may be. One thing's for sure, I will never be presented again with such an opportunity and neither will the Kurds, but I will die trying.'    She stood and wiped her eyes with the palm of her hand. 'Costas, I apologise for hitting you, but it was more in frustration I failed, rather than blaming you personally. Anyway, I'm going to get some sleep. I'm exhausted.'

They remained silent as they watched her walk out and take the steps down to her cabin below. 'What are you going to do Costas and more to the point, what are we going to do with this boat?'

'Don't worry about the boat Declan. I'll put it up for sale and send you the proceeds now it appears we have lost the game. I suppose you'll be going back to Syria with Zehra, after all you two are an item aren't you?'

Bellamy shook his head with a mirthless snigger. 'No, I would like it to be so and I do love her, but Zehra is like a falcon always intent on circling for prey. She really only has one thing in mind and that's revenge against the Turks. She says she loves me, but I don't really know. She and my lifelong friend Aras Barzani were married, but he died in Syria. It was strange how he died. I've thought about it many times, but always put it out of my mind. We made a pact, no matter what happened to either of us, the other would carry on fighting for the Kurds. But, after this I've had enough of bloodshed and war – I'm going home to Australia.'

'How did Aras die?'

'He was shot in the head – a sniper's bullet from an unbelievable distance took him out. We were in the middle of nowhere, miles from any fighting at the time. Really Costas, why don't we leave it there. I've seen many people die when fighting with the Kurds, but when it's a friend from your earliest days and memory, it's impossible to comprehend or forget.'

Kyriakou got to his feet and patted Bellamy on the shoulder. 'I'm going to get some sleep. Who knows what will happen tomorrow.'

# 67

eclan was sitting in the stern looking at the lights of the village when she quietly appeared and sat down beside him.

'Where is Costas? I've just looked in his cabin and it's empty.'

'Oh, he couldn't sleep and got tired of talking to me so he wandered off into the village to catch up with some of his relations and have a drink. I think we ran out of things to say,' Declan replied with a subdued laugh. 'He did want me to go with him, but I decided I'd had enough for one day.'

'What are you going to do now?'

'Zehra, I've decided to go home. I'm finished with the fighting after what's just occurred. I've have nothing more to contribute now we've lost the plutonium. And let's be truthful with one another, although my feelings for you have never diminished, I realise you're not in love with me. You still can't get Aras out of your mind and I realise I can never replace him. That's why I've decided to leave. Be truthful with me, that's true isn't it?'

She let out a sigh and took his hand. 'Yes, that's true Declan. No one can replace Aras.'

He did not look at her as he squeezed her hand. 'Thank you for that. I can leave with a clear conscience.'

'You'll find someone else Declan. You are a fine person and should not be mixed up in this. You're not a Kurd and this is no place for you. So you believe the Turks did get the plutonium?'

He turned to her with a look of surprise. The mood had suddenly changed from resignation and acceptance, to one of doubt. What had brought that on? 'Of course they go it. I was here with Costas when they boarded and took the four fuel drums. They didn't ask any questions and didn't check inside the drums to confirm their contents. They knew exactly what they were after.'

'Do you really trust Costas? What do you know about him?'

Declan turned and slowly shook his head. 'You are paddling up the wrong creek with that one Zehra. As with you, I would stake my life on him. Without him, we wouldn't have got this far. You spent weeks with him on the trawler and must have formed some impressions. Why the doubt now it's all over, or do you know something I don't?'

She took her hand away and fixed her gaze on the lights of Pomos. 'Nothing really, other than intuition. How did the Turks know two small barrels were inside those drums? They did not search the boat looking for them as they knew exactly where they were. Think about it Declan, the information must have been provided by one of us. We've both been inseparable in the thick of the fighting. I lost a husband and you lost a dear friend, so that only leaves one person.'

'I don't believe it Zehra. It couldn't be, I just don't believe it. No, no, no, he's with us, not against us. he hates the Turks for what they did when they overran Cyprus. The Turks have the plutonium, so what's the point of accusing him.'

She smiled as she stood and began to walk off. 'Because I want to know. I will ask him in the morning. I will know whether he's lying.'

Declan was seated at the table while Costas brewed coffee when Zehra appeared. She glanced at Declan who shook his head in the vain hope she had come to her senses, silently praying the confrontation would not occur. Surely, she would have thought about it overnight and realised the futility. There was no point in conducting a post-mortem – they had lost the game without any chance of a rematch.

Costas put a coffee down in front of her and took a seat opposite. They waited for someone to break the silence.

She could no longer restrain herself. 'You told the Turks we had the plutonium on board, didn't you Costas?'

He calmly picked up his cup and sipped the thick brew. A smile crossed his lips as he shook his head. 'No, Zehra you are wrong. The Turks got the oil drums, but they didn't contain what they were looking for. I had them moved the night we arrived and we all went ashore to my uncle's taverna. I decided to move them because we only a few kilometres from the Turkish NATO demarcation line. I was concerned the Turks could mount a raid and that's exactly what happened. I don't know how they knew, but I can assure you it wasn't me who tipped them off.'

'They couldn't have known,' she hissed. 'Unless you had told them.'

Costas did not react. 'Zehra, have you ever thought this boat may have been tracked all the way from Australia. The heavens are riddled with satellites. How do you know the English, Americans and the Turks haven't been quietly observing, just waiting for us to dock at a very accessible port? I moved the drums at night so we could not be observed from the air.'

There were moments of silence as both Zehra and Declan filtered what they had just heard. She picked up her coffee cup with both hands and leaned on the table.

Declan could sense underneath she was boiling with rage at the deception – many times he had seen her remain calm as she tried to suppress an emotion before it finally erupted. He could not understand the reason for Costas' action - he had played a cruel trick and she would be justified in venting her anger.

Declan shook his head. In some ways he had to agree with Costas' reasoning, but he had doubts. 'Well, it's game on again, but where did you hide the goods?'

'While we were all partying, some of my cousins dropped them into the sea along the coast. They're marked with co-ordinates and easily recovered.'

Zehra could not contain her anger any longer, as boiling with fury, pushed her chair back and flung her coffee across the table into his chest. 'You crazy fucking Greek. Why didn't you tell us this last night. Why did you put us through this?'

Costas looked at her with a blank expression. 'There is a Greek proverb which translated means - *he who becomes a sheep gets eaten by the wolf.* In other words, if you follow blindly without keeping your eyes open, you will get eaten. My father drummed that into me, but he still fell victim to it. However, I can assure you, I have not been collaborating with the enemy.'

'That doesn't explain what you did. Why did you wait until this morning to tell us?'

'Quite simple Zehra. If the Turks had returned last night the secret of the location of the drums would have died with me. I wasn't going to expose you two to the danger. As you are well aware, the Turks don't treat terrorists with any compassion. I know you are both very angry, but I have the barrels and am ready to proceed with our plan. If I was really the enemy you suspect me of being, you and Declan would have  been shot and I would have disappeared and received a handsome payout for my treachery.'

# 68

*eclan glanced at Zehra. He could see she was not totally convinced with the explanation, but her mood changed quickly.*

'Okay, we have the plutonium so the plan hasn't altered. I've made the connection with my group in Turkey, so let's retrieve the plutonium and proceed.'

'First, I must apologise for deceiving you both.'

Zehra got up and started pacing around. 'Forget it Costas. I don't appreciate someone messing with my head, but let's get on with it. How long would it take to retrieve those drums?'

Kyriakou screwed up his mouth as he considered the question. 'Only a few hours, but it would be foolish to take them across tonight.'

'But I've set it up,' Zehra countered in surprise. 'It's all arranged and I can't just change plans because you have doubts. What is it? Are you beginning to distrust me?'

'No, it's not a matter of trust. We have come this far and we are considering handing over what we have to be trucked across Turkey to Istanbul. I'm just being cautious. I believe it would be foolish to take both barrels at once. I think we should make two trips. I've come a long way to kick the Turks in the *haya*, and I want to make sure of landing the kick where it hurts most, right in the nuts.'

Zehra was about to say something when Bellamy chipped in. 'He's correct Zehra, we've too much to lose by hurrying this operation. If one drum gets to Istanbul without problems, we can then proceed with the second and take it through to London by road. If on the other hand we strike problems, I'll be able to take it by sea and drop it off in Greece or Italy. That way we have some insurance that one drum will get through. Costas is right, taking both barrels is too much of a risk?'

She was about to protest, when Kyriakou cut her off.

'Zehra, you and I will go across tonight and make contact. If we're certain of who we're dealing with, we'll come back tomorrow night and retrieve the first drum and get on with the job. That's the only way I will have it. Understood?'

They were both shocked by his firm tone. Declan held up his hand in resignation. 'Okay Costas, let's go with that.' He reached over and took Zehra's hand and squeezed it. 'Don't worry, I've decided nothing is going to break us up. I'm staying and once I've done with London, I'll come and find you.'

# 69

*The RIB nudged into the beach of the sandy cove. They quickly stepped ashore and began to walk towards a pathway leading up to a small village. 'This is where I made the contact and arranged to meet them.'*

Kyriakou nodded, but was nervous and on guard. Something was missing. He glanced around to see the RIB, their only means of escape, disappearing back towards Pomos. Zehra signalled to stop as they entered the shelter of a small grove of olive trees and sat down.

'Where are they? Why is something signalling danger in my brain?'

She could see Costas was clearly nervous glancing around into the dark. 'I said I'd return tonight or tomorrow night. They will have been on the lookout for us and know we're here. Just stop worrying. They will wait to make sure we haven't set them up for the Turks. They know I'm a Kurd, but are still very wary.'

It was a good half hour before they heard a low whistle which Zehra replied to. Minutes later two figures appeared from among the trees behind them. No greetings were exchanged as one of them beckoned for them to follow, the other falling in behind as they walked slowly towards a group of village buildings. Kyriakou was twitchy – he could feel unseen eyes following them. It was just too quiet and deserted. They were guided along a series of small cobbled tracks to one of three large houses isolated from the rest of the village. It obviously belonged to someone of importance by the look of its more substantial construction. Kyriakou's instincts told him to cut and run now, but where would he run to was no longer an option. The door to the largest house opened as they approached. The greeting was quiet, but effusive as Zehra and the host exchanged pleasantries as they were shown in. The scene changed abruptly as Kyriakou heard the door slam behind them. He turned, but it was too late to ward off the blow from the baton which caught him across the temple and sent him crashing onto the stone floor. Zehra screamed an obscenity as she saw the uniformed Turk officer step into the room. The curse was cut short with a backhander which sprawled her beside her companion, blood pouring from the corner of her mouth. Costas attempted to rise, but was kicked in the side by a solid boot. He cried out in pain as he felt a rib crack.

'So who do we have here? Illegal visitors or terrorists?' The officer, lit a cigarette and motioned for two uniformed figures to pick them up and throw them onto a low couch. Kyriakou moaned in pain as he clutched his side and focused on his aggressor.

'We are not terrorists,' he hissed through his clenched teeth. 'I don't know what you're talking about.'

The officer laughed as he sat down opposite. 'If you are not terrorists, why did you illegally enter Turkey from Cyprus? Tell me now, what is the purpose of your intrusion? What is your name and who is this woman?'

'My name is Costas Kyriakou, I'm a Cypriot and I'm assisting my friend to get back to her village in Syria.' He realised it was a transparent lie, but it was the only one he could think of in the moment.

His explanation was greeted with a burst of laughter. 'You're nothing but a filthy lying Greek, most probably wanted by the police. Otherwise you would not be entering Turkey at this time of night. However, these two men here will soon extract the truth. And it will cause you more pain than a broken rib.' He turned his gaze on Zehra.

'And what of you? What's your name?'

'Zehra Kermandi,' Zehra replied while trying to stem the flow of blood from her mouth with the back of her hand.

'You're a Kurd and you expect me to believe your friend's explanation? You're also a terrorist, aren't you?'

'I'm not a terrorist. Costas was merely helping me to get through Turkey and into northern Syria, which is my home. I am a Kurd and a very proud one, but I offer no threat to Turkey.'

'It would be better if you both told me the truth now as to what your true purpose is. We have been alerted to the possible entry of terrorists for some weeks now. You will be held until I have checked with security in Ankara and then you will be dealt with. However, if you are terrorists your lives will be very short.' His eyes never left Zehra as he considered the weaker of the two. He was determined to crack them before handing them over to security. It would mean promotion. He got up and walked over to

Zehra and reaching down, started to pull aside the top of her kaftan.

She slapped has hand away. 'Keep your hands off me, you peasant.'

The officer laughed quietly as he gently patted her cheek. 'In ten minutes you will be telling me everything I want to know.' He turned to the two subordinates. 'Take her into the next room and show her what you have to offer that this Greek cannot hope to match. Take it in turns and I don't care which orifice you prefer. When she's had enough, she will then tell us the truth.'

Zehra screamed as the two approached and dragged her to her feet. Costas was on his feet in an instant, but the move was anticipated as the largest of the guards turned and smashed a fist into his face, sending him back onto the couch as he began to drift into the unconscious.

'You can't do this to me. Call these animals off now.'

The officer grinned. 'And deny my men the pleasure of your body? Can't you see how excited they are? Tell me the truth and it will save you the pain and experience.'

Zehra glanced across at Costas, but she could see he was past being her protector. 'You son of a whore.' she screamed in desperation as she was pulled to her feet. She fought, lashing out with clawed fingers at the exposed face of one of her violators, leaving furrows of bloodied flesh. 'Listen to me and do it before it's too late.' She was losing her mind as as the pleas came out in incoherent disjointed bursts.

The Turk gave a mocking laugh. 'No one is going to be concerned about a Kurd being raped. You can save yourself the pain by telling me who you really are, but in the meantime, enjoy the experience. And I think you're really going to suffer from the look of pleasure on this soldier's bloodied face.'

Costas had heard snatches of the exchange as he drifted in and out of waves of nausea. He heard a piercing scream and tried to get to his feet. He had promised Declan nothing would happen to her and he had failed. He was halfway up when the officer walked over and crashed a baton into the side of his head – everything went black.

When he came to, he was lying on the floor, the first light from the new day playing on his face. He pushed himself up on elbow and looked around groggily. Zehra appeared to be asleep on the couch, dishevelled and in a mess with her face heavily bruised from the treatment she had received. He tried to put her ordeal out of his mind, but the horror would not subside – it would never go away. Someone knelt down beside him and lifted him under the arm.

'Come on, get up.' It was not the officer or one of his men, but someone he did not recognise. 'Sit at the table and I'll get you a strong coffee and something to eat.'

'Who are you? Where are the Turks that were here?'

'My name is Alaz. Don't worry about the Turks - we took care of them. They will never molest another Kurdish woman. We were delayed getting here to meet you because of police checkpoints. The Turk patrols are everywhere along the Turquoise Coast looking for illegal entrants. We'll move you to a safe house as soon as Zehra is up to it and then to the boat so you can return to Cyprus.'

Costas nodded as he sat and looked around the room at four seated figures. None of them looked particularly friendly, although they appeared relaxed. An hour later they were on the move through an olive grove and up a winding path to a house perched on a headland overlooking the ocean. It was not in the style of the village house they had left, but had the trappings of wealth with fine carpets and furniture. He made an effort to assist Zehra, but she rejected his offers of support. His attempts at conversation and sympathy were greeted with incoherent grunts as they walked towards the house. He felt the danger closing around him as he was ushered into a large marble-floored room covered with scattered rugs and low couches. He hesitated as he looked around.

'Don't be concerned Costas, you are safe here. This house is owned by a trusted Kurd the Turks would not intrude on. You can rest until we take you down to the boat tonight.' He looked at the man who had addressed him, the expression in the eyes lifeless.

His head was still aching as he lay down on one of the couches, resigned to the fact he was too exhausted to resist if a Turk patrol did walk in. He looked around, but Zehra had disappeared into another room. Within minutes he drifted into a fitful sleep, his subconscious constantly awakening him to some imagined danger. It was late afternoon when he heard the sound of laughter, coming from somewhere within the house. A door opened and a plate of food and pot of coffee was put on the table beside him. He nodded his thanks as the servant retreated. It was while the door was being closed again he heard the faint laughter – it was a laugh that sounded familiar, but he dismissed it. He poured himself a coffee and got up to walk around the room. A large bookshelf covered one wall as he scanned the titles without interest. Out of curiosity he idly pulled out one of the drawers in the cabinet beneath. The .25 calibre Browning was amongst several other handguns, one of which was a striking example of a trophy weapon. He picked up the small Browning and pulled the clip from the butt – it was loaded. It was a small useless weapon for serious intent, but at close range, deadly. It was really an assassin's weapon – the quietest of the handguns. He was about to put it back and close the drawer when he heard footsteps approaching. It was an instinctive thought of survival that overcame the guilt, as he thrust the weapon into his jacket pocket and closed the drawer. He felt stupid, he was in no danger, so why had he stolen the weapon? By the time the door opened he had pulled a book down and was turning the pages. It was the servant enquiring whether he wanted fresh coffee or something more to eat. Costas declined and as the servant departed, Alaz came back into the room.

'We'll leave in an hour to get down to the beach. We have a place to hide down there and we'll be able to spot any patrols.'

'How is Zehra? I promised her partner I would look after her.'

Alaz shook his head. 'Not good, but she'll recover. Kurdish women are used to being mauled by the filthy Turks. It is in her head that will take longer.'

Although he appeared open and friendly, there was something about Alaz that disturbed him. It was two hours later when Costas' cousin nudged the powerful boat into the beach and he and Zehra climbed aboard, that the danger signal exploded in his brain. It was an unconscious comment muttered by Alaz as he pushed the boat off – a comment not meant to be heard over the sound of the idling motors – a comment made for his subconscious humour only.

# 70

*eclan had seen the RIB coming and was waiting in the stern as it pulled alongside. Costas took Zehra's arm to steady her as he helped her aboard.*

'What happened? You look dreadful Zehra,' Declan said as he reached for her outstretched hand.

'Nothing those Turks won't pay dearly for,' she replied with a pained expression. 'We were caught by a Turk patrol soon after we landed, but were then rescued by members of my group. We recover the plutonium and head back tomorrow night. However, the way I feel at the moment, I need to get some sleep.'

Declan turned to Costas as Zehra descended the stairwell to her cabin. 'What happened over there? She looks exhausted and those bruises on her face – how did she get those?'

'The same way I got mine, along with a broken rib. However, she says the Turks raped her when she wouldn't tell them why we were there. I was knocked out and was unaware of what actually happened.'

'Oh my God, you say she was raped?' he shouted, grabbing Costas by his jacket lapels and shoving him back against the wall. 'You were supposed to look after her and you let that happen?'

Costas pushed his arms away. 'There was nothing I could do. We got ashore and were shown to a house where we were ambushed by a Turk patrol. I was very uneasy when we landed because there was no one there to help with a barrel, if we'd been carrying it, and no sign of a truck. Luckily, at some point Zehra's people appeared, apparently took care of the Turks and got us away. Look, don't worry about me – it's Zehra who needs medical attention. There were two Turks involved and as you can imagine, they would have made a mess of her. I'm amazed she can even walk. She's a brave girl, but in no condition to go back tomorrow night. You've got to stop her. If you can't, I will not be recovering those barrels until I'm sure she can handle it. It could all go horribly wrong – she's aggressive with vengeance uppermost in her mind and I don't intend to get involved while she's in that condition. Her brain is presently scrambled.'

Is there a local doctor who can look at her without attracting the police?'

'Yes, I have a cousin. She's the only doctor I trust who won't ask any questions or spread any gossip. I will go and see her later and get her here first thing in the morning.'

'Who isn't your cousin in this town? I would hate to get on the wrong side of anyone here. Tell me, do you hate the Turks that much?'

Costas nodded. 'You don't understand how much we Greeks despise them. I lost my father to them and one man in particular was responsible for that loss.'

# 71

The sun was up and three of them were sitting in the salon when Zehra appeared wearing a long shift she had obviously been sleeping in, from its crumpled appearance. Unaware for a moment before suddenly becoming conscious, she realised she did not recognise one of them. 'Who are you?' It was not a polite request, but a demand denoting suspicion and instant rejection.

'I'm a doctor Zehra, my name is Maria Anastas. I understand you've been through an ordeal and I'm here to attend to your injuries. Can we go to your cabin?'

'I don't need a Greek examining me. I was raped, but I'll get over it. It's not the first time I've been assaulted by a Turk.' The emphasis of the insult stunned Maria and Declan, but Costas remained impassive. 'I don't need your help,' she said turning on the two men. 'And what right have you two got to call a doctor without consulting me?'

'But Zehra, if you were violated by two men, you are highly likely to suffer an infection. I need to take samples to test for AIDS, which is highly prevalent in Turkey, or you could have any number of venereal diseases. I will take a blood sample and give you a check-over,' Maria pleaded calmly in a quiet voice. 'I'm here to help you. Don't you understand?'

'And then broadcast my condition to these two I suppose?'

'No, of course not. Can't you see, Declan and Costas are concerned for you and that's why they asked for my help. I will not be discussing anything with them, I can promise you that.' Maria stood and put out her hand. 'Zehra, please let me help you. Why don't we go to your cabin and discuss this in private?'

'No, I'm not going anywhere with you. I don't want you examining me or taking samples of any description. Get that into your head and leave now.' The reply was venomous.

'For God's sake Zehra, see sense,' Declan burst out. 'You've been raped by two Turks who could have been carrying any disease. And you've obviously suffered injury. You're at grave risk. No matter what has happened, I'll still love you. Why don't you want Maria's help?'

'Because she wasn't raped.'

It took several seconds for the comment to sink in. Zehra stood stock still in shock while Declan swung on the accuser. 'What the hell are you talking about Costas. You told me she had been raped and she has confirmed it – what game are you playing at?'

Kyriakou remained calm, although he was expecting a more violent reaction. 'Just as I told you Declan – she hasn't been raped. Your dear Zehra may claim to be a Kurd, but in fact she's a Turk. She's got no intention of letting Maria examine her, because she'll find no sign of rape or any injury.

I saw the Turk officer hit her in the face, the evidence clearly visible. The Turk did not know her true identity at that stage. That is her only injury to support her claim of being raped in the hope we'll believe her, but I know it didn't happen. If she had been subjected to the violence she claims, she will no doubt have severe bruising and injury to her thighs and genitals. That would be the case, wouldn't it Maria?'

'Yes, it would be. But look, this is getting out of hand. I cannot be involved in this discussion any further. I'm a doctor and Zehra has declined my help, so I cannot proceed any further.'

As she stood to leave, Costas jumped to his feet and before Zehra could react, had stripped her night shirt down to her ankles. She screamed as he held her arms firmly behind her back, revealing her complete nakedness.

'You filthy Greek. How dare you? I will kill you for this.' She used all her strength as she fought his grip, but he was too strong.

'As I said Zehra – not a bruise in sight, other than your face, nor any sign of injury where it should be evident. There's no need for Maria's medical help, because you weren't raped – pleasured yes, with your consent maybe, but not raped.'

'I was raped. It might not show physically, but I submitted rather than suffer injury.'

Costas laughed and shook his head. 'You were on the point of being raped, but you mentioned a name that saved you. You thought I was unconscious, but I clearly heard you mention the name Yusuf Aksoy and your demand he be phoned immediately to rescue you. The name is imprinted in my memory - in fact his name is burned into my brain. That was Colonel Yusuf Aksoy you were referring to and even if I did hear you call his name, you were banking on the fact

I wouldn't have any idea of his identity. Aksoy is the head of NIO, the National Intelligence Organisation. You told the officer who arrested us to phone him to check, which he obviously did. I know who Aksoy is – he was a junior officer with NIO Cyprus when it was overrun by the Turks in 1974. He apprehended my father, tortured him and then had him murdered.'

Zehra shook her head defiantly. 'I don't know any Aksoy. I don't know what you're talking about. I'm a loyal Kurd – not a traitor. If that's the only accusation you can make, it won't stand scrutiny.'

Kyriakou swung her onto a couch and picking up her torn clothing, threw it at her. 'You lied about being raped and now you're lying about not knowing Aksoy. And there was something that always worried me and that was why you shot Cemal. It now becomes clear he knew your true identity. And finally just yesterday when we were being pushed off the beach to return here, I distinctly heard Alaz, the leader of your so-called Kurd group mumble something to himself. And that was - *and when you return make sure the barrels have something in them.* When you went over on the first visit by yourself, it wasn't to make contact with your fellow Kurds, but to make contact with the Turks. You told them exactly where the barrels were and that's why we got raided the following night, only there was nothing in the barrels, because I had replaced them. You realised you had to cover your tracks by putting on that wonderful, but contrived act of rage making out you were unaware of the raid. It was so good, you would have won an Academy Award if this was a movie. The upshot was, I walked into a trap you were aware of, but the Turk officer who caught us, wasn't. No doubt you would have been raped if you had not shouted out Aksoy's name. That's what saved you and I overheard. Then came the pretence of being rescued by Kurds we could trust. You obviously told Aksoy I would have to escape as I was the only one who knows where the barrels are hidden. You were aware my uncle knows, but he would never disclose their location. You thought you had me convinced we could safely take a barrels across tomorrow night. Only, I can assure you Zehra, no delivery is about to happen. You are a Turkish agent. In addition, you planned to betray Declan. You murdered Aras, so you would have no regard for the person who blindly loves you.'

Zehra sneered as she laughed. 'That is not proof – that's mere speculation. You will have to try harder than that.'

'Let me try then, so Declan can clearly understand your true identity. Davut was working with you and it was he who was carrying the satellite phone, not Cemal. It was Davut who alerted the navy. After he was shot, I saw you taking his bag into Cemal's cabin. However, I was already suspicious of Davut and had earlier searched his cabin. I found the phone and removed the sim card so that it was inoperable. Moments before you shot Cemal he pointed and shouted *jash, jash,* which translates as *collaborator* in Kurdish. You weren't aware I already knew why you murdered him. Cemal must have known of Davut's real allegiances and could also point the finger at you. He had to go.'

'So, you're saying she shot Cemal because he somehow knew she was a Turkish agent?' Declan demanded. 'Have you gone mad Costas? Zehra and I have killed Turks and will continue to kill them if they threaten the Kurds.'

Kyriakou ignored the outburst. 'Declan I can prove she is a Turkish agent and the most damaging indictment of your treachery Zehra, was the phone call you made after we bought the trawler in Port Lincoln. It was the prefix 90 that caught my attention – it was Turkey. I spiked your phone so there would be no more contact – I didn't want you talking to anyone in the interests of security. At that point I had no idea who you were trying to call, but I thought it odd you refused the use of my phone.'

Declan sprang to her defence once again – he was boiling with rage. 'That's no proof she's a Turk agent. She could have been phoning anyone in her Kurd group.'

Kyriakou reached in and flipped the paper napkin out of his pocket, handing it to Declan. 'I've been carrying this since we left Port Lincoln. I think you will find that's Aksoy's direct line. In fact I know it is. I tried it last night when I got back and sure enough I was told Colonel Aksoy was not available. Why don't you give him a call now? He's sure to be in his office. Oh, I nearly forgot, here's some further proof,' he said as he took the sim card out of his pocket. 'If you put that into a satphone I've no doubt you will find it also has Aksoy's number on it.'

'Why didn't you tell me before this?' Declan demanded.

'Because you wouldn't have believed me, but now you can confirm for yourself – we're dealing with a traitor. Our whole operation was compromised from the very beginning – the English obviously knew about it and so did the Turks. Neither side was concerned about who got to the plutonium first, as long as one of them did to remove the threat. And the key to that success was your trusted lover and loving husband of Aras Barzani, the husband she undoubtedly shot. She suckered you both.'

Zehra jumped up from the couch shouting a string of abuse as she fled below to her cabin, not bothering to cover herself. Maria was already on the dock and hurrying back up the quay.

Declan was stunned by the accusations he'd just witnessed. He looked at the number and then at Zehra's departing figure, as he waved away Costas' offer of his phone.

'But I love you Zehra. Wh..wh...why, have you done this?' he shouted after her. 'I've always loved you and always will. Tell me it isn't true?'

He was met with a snarl of defiant laughter as she disappeared. Declan turned to Kyriakou with a look of hate – the messenger was about to suffer the consequences.

The attack happened, but not from the expected direction. Zehra suddenly appeared with a Sig Sauer 226 pistol pointed directly at her accuser. Kyriakou immediately recognised the weapon – it could only have come from one source. It was the trophy weapon he had seen in the cabinet drawer along with his Browning.

'No, no, no,' Declan yelled as he jumped to his feet and held out his hand to stop her. The momentary distraction was all it took for Costas to whip the tiny Browning out of his jacket and fire. He hardly felt the kick of the weapon, but saw the round patch appear in her throat and the flow of blood as she collapsed gasping for air. They both moved in one fluid movement, but Costas was quicker as he kicked the deadly Sig over the side into the water. He pointed the Browning at Declan. 'Just calm down and I'll explain it all to you. Make no mistake, if you come at me, I will kill you.'

'But what about Zehra? You need to call Maria back.'

'She's as good as dead Declan. That shot has taken out an artery – just look at how the blood is flowing. I didn't take deliberate aim – it was just an impulse reaction when I saw the gun. I really owe you my life, as if you hadn't tried to intervene, I would be the one lying on the deck.'

He kept the pistol aimed as Declan knelt and tried to clamp the bleeding, but it was futile as the carotid arterial flow subsided and Zehra's eyes opened wide in acceptance of the final moment. Declan closed her eyes and leaning down kissed her cheek before rocking back on his heels, the tears streaming down his face.

'Why, did it have to end this way,' he sobbed into his hands. 'I loved her, but I don't believe she was a traitor. I just can't believe it – we've been together for so long. We knew each other's innermost feelings and thoughts.'

'And one further thing that really alarmed me. It was just after I disclosed I had hidden the barrels and the Turks had been unsuccessful, she went into the town with the excuse she wanted to get some things. Unfortunately, she was seen talking with a known Turkish sympathiser. That was enough for me.'

'I just can't believe it.'

'Declan, there is one other thing you might consider. You said your best friend Aras was killed by a sniper. Where was Zehra when that happened?'

Declan looked thoughtful for a few seconds. 'She had left our camp. She was gone for about half an hour. I just thought it was a call of nature.'

'And the shot just came out of nowhere from an area you knew was clear of Turks or ISIS terrorists. In fact, you knew you were well within Kurdish lines – you were safe. Have you really thought about who shot Aras? I'll bet Zehra was a first-class sniper with plenty of practice and I would suggest there was friction between her and Aras. In fact, I would say Aras already suspected which side she was fighting for.'

'I..I..I had never given that much thought until you've just raised it. They were starting to get on each other's nerves and the morning Aras was shot, he did tell me he wanted to discuss something with me. I brushed him off. He must have made the mistake of accusing Zehra of something, or at least raising some doubts about her loyalty.'

He straightened and threw his head back while exhaling in shock at the realisation of the truth. 'Aras and I grew up together. We were lifelong friends and would have taken a bullet for one another, we were that close. Only it was he who took the bullet.'

'Let me guess what happened and why Zehra shot him. He was raising doubts about carrying through with *vixen*, while you and Zehra were in total support. You weren't aware Zehra was a Turkish agent and she would betray the locality of the plutonium if it came into your hands. The Turks wanted to get hold of the material and remove the threat for all time, but you believed Zehra's intent was to unleash it on Istanbul and you were in complete support?'

Costas could see Declan was sifting the accusations for evidence as he lapsed into silence. 'You are correct. What a bloody fool I've been, but that doesn't change my intention to teach the fucking English a lesson. I'm more determined than ever to carry it out. Are you with me?'

'I'm not going back to Turkey if that's what you mean. I have no contacts there and would be a dead man the minute I set foot in the place. It won't take Aksoy long to wake up his Kurdish accomplice has gone missing, or more likely dead. He will double the patrols along the coast. Any Kurd found in that area is going to be in for a hard time. No, the fire has gone out of me – I will not go back to avenge my father or other Cypriots who have suffered. There is an ancient Greek saying – *a sweet thing tasted too often is no longer sweet.* Revenge was all I thought about, until now. I don't want to think about it again.'

'Does that also apply to me? You won't help me any further?'

'I will help you Declan. You can take both barrels and continue on your way. I can understand your cause and support it. At least you have a chance of carrying it out, whereas mine has disappeared with the person I just killed.'

Declan let out a sigh of relief. 'You must come with me then? You're the only person I can trust?'

'No, I've had enough. I'm washing my hands of it. I will retrieve the barrels and you can be on your way, but you'd better make it quick, as I believe the Turks will be motoring back into this port very soon. And they'll start asking questions you won't fail to answer after a few hours of interrogation. This is terrorism they're chasing, so don't expect any mercy.'

'Okay, let's retrieve the plutonium at daylight and I'll take off for Greece. My only problem, is I don't have someone to accompany me, but I may have that base covered.'

'No one from Pomos will go with you Declan. You're on your own.'

'I'm not expecting that. There's been a young guy hanging around now for a couple of days looking for a boat going anywhere. He's got no money and just wants to island hop. And he's been around boats and has some skipper's qualifications. They looked genuine when he showed them to me, so I'll take the chance. I'll just bid him farewell when I get to Greece.'

Costas raised an eyebrow. 'Do you trust him? He could be an agent.'

'He's Irish and an IRA sympathiser. He's been roughed up by the English numerous times, so he went to sea to escape the violence. I'm not sure I can trust him entirely, but I've got no choice. I have to get the hell out of here now. If I suspect he is an agent, I'll kill him if you give me that pistol.'

# 72

'Jimmy Thorburn's the name,' he said holding out his hand. 'And you are?'

Costas ignored the gesture. There was no mistaking the Irish accent. 'I'm just a local fisherman assisting in retrieving some goods.' He was wary of this Irishman although he fitted the mould of an itinerant, just island hopping around the Mediterranean. The long hair, well worn clothes and scruffy appearance, with a small bag of belongings, only lacked the guitar to complete the image. He looked to be around forty, well muscled and alert and not the usual laid-back, good-time drifter he had seen plenty of over the years. He put it out of his mind – it was Declan's problem now. The sun was just rising as they retrieved the two drums with their deadly contents and Costas cast off and waved the *Kuro V* goodbye.

'Will they make it?'

Costas turned to his uncle while shaking his head. 'I wish him luck, because he's going to need it.'

'What's so important about those drums? Is it drugs?'

'No, it's not drugs. You don't want to know what it is. It's a curse the English are entirely responsible for and it came close to touching our part of the world.'

Stavros shrugged as he pushed the throttle forward and the small diesel began to belch smoke as it gained a steady rhythm. His was a simple life and simple existence devoid of complications. He refrained from asking further questions.

'Where are we heading for Declan? I'll set the course on autopilot if you give me a destination.'

'We're heading for Greece, although I don't want to be anywhere near the tourist hordes. I just want to be able to tie this boat up for a few weeks and chill out. I'll most probably hire a car and tour around.'

'In that case, we should head for Pylos in the Peloponnese. It's very popular, but it has a great harbour and is a beautiful historic part of the world. I spent a year there and didn't see it all. You can hire a car and drive north to Bulgaria, Albania or Macedonia. Greece is always busy with tourists, but Pylos would be my choice if you wanted to drop anchor, lie on a deck chair with a beer and watch the activity.'

'You're the skipper Jimmy. Set the course and let's go.'

'What did your friends load back there? What's in those drums? If it's drugs or contraband of any sort, I don't want to know about it? In fact, I'd prefer to go back now and look for another way of seeing more of the Med.'

Declan shook his head and laughed. 'No, it's nothing you can smoke, snort or ingest. It's just something I would like to return to its rightful owner.'

'I hope it's not some antiquity, because that's worse than drugs as far as the Greeks are concerned? They really come down hard on anyone trying to take it out of the country.'

'It's an antiquity of sorts, but nothing to do with the Greeks or their mythology. Now why don't you just concentrate on conning the boat. I've got something to attend to aft.'

'Fair enough. I'm just along for the ride. I can't thank you enough for taking me on for the trip, but I must tell you, Pylos is where I want to get off.'

'Pylos it is Jimmy, you came along at the right moment. I've got something to do aft and then I'm going to take a nap,' Declan replied slapping him on the shoulder and stepping out of the wheelhouse, closing the door behind him.

Thorburn knew exactly what task Bellamy had to attend to. If he left it any longer the smell of a decaying corpse in this heat would permeate the whole vessel. He knew the Greek was not accompanying them, so it had to be the woman about to be tossed over the side. He had been watching closely from a concealed position in one of the small fishing *caigue's* close to the *Kuro V* when the Greek and the woman, returned the previous morning. And he had seen a woman with a medical bag go aboard. He had seen the medico quickly disembark and walk away, followed by a muffled shot. There had been no sign of the woman since, so she had to be the task Bellamy was attending to. He was relieved - he did not want to be involved in an investigation if they were stopped by a Greek patrol vessel on the lookout for refugees fleeing across the Mediterranean. If it did look like they were to be apprehended, he would also ensure the drums were tossed over the side to avoid discovery. It had to be more than drugs if MI6 was involved. And he was quite sure Bellamy would assist in doing it, as the discovery of the contents, whatever it was, would undoubtedly result in a long prison term.

He could expect to spend some years in a Greek jail before the diplomacy was worked out between 85 Vauxhall Cross, the headquarters of MI6 and Athens. He could imagine the sentence if they were stopped and boarded on their way to Pylos. He may as well tie himself to one of the drums and go overboard with it. It would be a quick and easy alternative to being incarcerated by the Greeks. He was well aware James Thorburn would become a statistic, totally abandoned and existence denied by English authorities. He himself, could expect no support if he failed in this assignment. As for the Bellamy, he would simply disappear without trace. At least he was taking care of part of the problem this minute in disposing of the corpse. If boarded, they may get away with explaining they were just cruising. But they would not be able to explain a body with a gunshot wound, as he was sure it was the gunshot he heard.

They took it in turns, four hours on and four hours off, as they passed Crete to the south and through the Sea of Crete, before turning north-west for Pylos. It was three incident-free days later, when Bellamy appeared from below to begin his shift. Dawn was about an hour away, but there was the faint light on their starboard side as they headed up the coast of the Peloponesse.

Bellamy looked at the moving chart of their progress. 'Aren't we too far out to sea if we're heading for Pylos?'

'Better to stand well off and then make a turn directly for Pylos. If we hug the coast we are likely to come under the attention of Greek patrols.'

Bellamy nodded as he continued to watch the screen. 'What's this?' he said suddenly putting his finger on an isolated static panel of the screen. 'What's the significance of 36°34′N 21°8′E. What does that mean?'

Thorburn did not hesitate – he had been rehearsing the lie. 'That's just a way-point as we call them – a navigation point we've been heading towards. That's where I will make the turn which is only minutes away. I will continue to take us in as I know all the radio procedures when the port authorities start asking our intentions. You don't understand the standard maritime protocol as I do. With a vessel of this size, it's mandatory to have a qualified skipper. The Greeks are very touchy about large pleasure boats wandering around in their waters and dropping anchor where they think fit. Too many archaeological artefacts have been pillaged by scuba divers and sold into private collections. And, I don't blame them for being cautious. You'd better prepare your story as to why you're here and what you intend to do. I can tell you now, these fellows are no slouches. They'll give us a good going over.'

He was aware Bellamy had pulled open a large drawer with flat-lying maps. 'What are you looking for?'

'I don't like the sound of what you're telling me. I think we'd be better to head for Italy. We've got plenty of fuel and it's only a short hop from there.'

'I don't think so Declan,' he said as he pulled the motors back to idle. 'This is the end of the road for both of us.'

'What the hell are you talking about? Put those engines back on now.' Thorburn could feel the muzzle of the pistol being shoved into the side of his head.

'I would do so if I could, but we have reached the way-point and we have company. Look to your left.'

As he turned, Thorburn spun around and smashed the pistol out of his hand. The small Browning skittled across the floor as they both went after it. Bellamy got to it first and held it within an inch of Thorburn's head. 'This is as far as I'm taking you, whoever you are.'

'I'm a British agent. The game's over Declan. That's a British navy frigate bearing down on our port side and it has just launched a high-speed RIB. We are about to be boarded. You're facing a string of charges already without pulling that trigger and adding another twenty years for murder.'

Thorburn was waiting for the end – it was only seconds away when he realised Bellamy's hand had dropped to the floor with the gun still in his hand. He was staring vacantly out through the open cabin door at the approaching craft, distracted, his mind racing back through his life to the present.

Thorburn could see he had a slim chance of taking the gun or taking advantage of the apparent mental breakdown happening before his eyes. He slowly got to his feet expecting at any second for the weapon to be levelled and his life to end. He quickly turned and walked out of the cabin fully expecting a bullet in the back. He was just about to descend the stairs to the lower deck when he heard a shot. He continued without looking back – there was no point.

Half an hour later the RIB was winched up the side of the frigate and he stepped out onto the deck.

'Well done Thorburn. You've just saved us from an embarrassing situation.'

'Mr Hartigan, I would say saved from a major international incident is more accurate. But it was a team effort. It's a pity it cost the life of Chris Ronson.'

'Yes, it certainly is,' he said turning away and murmuring to himself. 'But moles are expendable.'

Thorburn looked at him sharply. 'Why do I think you're not telling me the whole story?'

Hartigan ignored him as he pointed towards the *Kuro V*. 'Let's watch the show.'

They heard two explosions which broke the vessel's back. It quickly settled in the water.

'Why here? That's a beautiful craft worth a few million. Why didn't we just take it back to England? And we didn't retrieve Bellamy's remains?'

Hartigan shrugged. 'I don't know the answer to that Thorburn. I just follow orders and as for Bellamy, we just gave him a decent burial.'

'I still don't understand? The Mediterranean is very shallow. Why didn't we take it out into the Atlantic?'

'Simple. The way-point you were given and arrived at, is the dead centre of the *Calypso Deep*, the deepest part of the Mediterranean at more than seventeen thousand feet.'

'The Greeks are going to be very unhappy about that – blowing up and sinking a vessel so close to their maritime border?'

'Oh, I don't know about that Thorburn. We had nothing to do with the explosion. It was a terrorist who planted the charges as we were about to board and arrest him. No doubt the Greeks will thank us when they learn Bellamy was intent on ramming and sinking one of their patrol vessels.'

'Hmm...' Thorburn screwed up his face and gave an approving nod. 'Yes, I suppose that's an excuse the Greeks could not refute now the evidence has disappeared. However, the explanation is a bit transparent, don't you think? And, it still doesn't account for the contents of those drums and why we didn't sink them with the *Kuro V*? I can only assume they contain something extremely dangerous and very radioactive. That vessel had to be contaminated and could not be left floating. I can only assume I am correct sir?'

'You assume too much,' Hartigan replied with a wry smile as he turned and walked off.

9 781922 618894